SKY SHIELDER

AN EPIC FANTASY ROMANCE

FIRE AND FANG
BOOK 1

LINDSAY BUROKER

ACKNOWLEDGMENTS

Thank you for picking up the first novel in my new fantasy romance series, Fire and Fang. *Sky Shielder* is a complete adventure (no cliffhanger ending), but I hope you'll enjoy the story and these characters and want to continue on for more!

Before you jump in, please let me thank those who helped the novel come to fruition. I'm grateful for my beta readers, Sarah Engelke, Cindy Wilkinson, and Rue Silver for their early input, as well as my editor Shelley Holloway for helping polish it. Thank you, also, to my narrator, Vivienne Leheny, for the audio version of the tale, and to Deranged Doctor Design for the cover art.

1

"I'VE A NEW FIND THAT YOU'LL BE DYING TO ADD TO YOUR collection, Your Highness." The antiques store clerk drew out a small velvet cube, opened it, and revealed a cylindrical bronze tool with a dozen tiny apertures in the top.

Fascinated, Syla lifted her spectacles and leaned in for a better look, her nose almost to the instrument.

Among her abler-eyed kin, censorious aristocrats, and especially attractive men, Syla was self-conscious about her nearsightedness and thick lenses, but here... Here it was different. Much like puppies and kittens, antiques did not judge a person.

"It's not as aged as many of the instruments you prefer," the clerk continued, "and such tools are still in use on some of the islands, especially where actual leeches are rare, but it was recently dredged out of the deepest part of Sky Torn Harbor, pulled up from a wrecked warship that was destroyed centuries ago by dragons and their foul riders."

"Oh, in the Battle of 873? I've read all about that and how the dragons created a barricade just outside the sky shield to keep our ships from coming and going. Our forces had to leave the magical protection to confront them, and many were lost."

"It must have been a dreadful time, yes." The clerk made the eyes-of-the-moon symbol, two fingers tapping his chest, followed by a circle traced over his heart.

Syla rotated the instrument to study the back. "Is that the mark of Henis the Godcrafter? Goodness, what an *exquisite* specimen."

Reminded that the clerk always thought her wealthy and asked outrageous prices, Syla leaned back and wished she hadn't shown such interest. Now, he would try to gouge her.

"I thought it might appeal to you." Yes, he sounded smug, as he always did when he believed he would wheedle money out of a patron.

Since Syla had walked to his shop of her own accord, procrastinating on her way to the castle for the dreaded weekly family dinner, she couldn't pretend to be a victim.

"What is it?" her bodyguard, Sergeant Fel, rumbled in a suspicious bass from his position near the door.

"A spring-loaded scarificator." The clerk demonstrated its function by tapping a small button on the side of the cylinder. Tiny scalpels inside sprang out, protruding from the apertures. "Some call devices like this artificial leeches."

Fel, a twenty-year fleet veteran, who'd served another twenty years as a bodyguard for the royal family, drew back, as if he hadn't seen and experienced much worse during his career. He curled a distasteful—maybe even *horrified*—lip as he regarded the scarificator, as well as the antique ecraseur and speculum the clerk had first laid on his counter for Syla to consider.

With a shudder of his broad shoulders, he stated, "This place is unholy," then turned to look out the window and regard whatever threats he envisioned creeping down the cobblestone street. In the process, he stuck one of his legs out to stretch his calf. He flexed and grimaced at his muscle tightness. "I thought you were looking for *herbalism* antiques."

"I do adore the history of herbalism, but other than pointy gathering sticks and occasional decorative cases, there aren't a lot of antiques associated with the craft. There *are* a lot of old books." Syla lowered her spectacles to eye the shelves, wondering if any new tomes had come in. She longed to find a copy of *Aramon's Herbs and Lore of the Rainforest Continent* for her collection.

The clerk, who was glaring balefully at Fel, didn't mention if he'd received any books lately.

"Not everyone is as fascinated by the history of healing as I am," Syla said apologetically to him.

She eyed the scarificator again, contemplating making an offer —a *low* offer to counter whatever ridiculous price the clerk would quote. But her room at Moon Watch Temple already overflowed with healing and history tomes, drawings of medicinal plants, and antiques related to her profession that were tucked into every nook and cranny, not to mention mounted to the wall, stacked under her bed, and overflowing from the dresser drawers. She didn't *need* anything else, but...

"Is your bodyguard all right?" The clerk's baleful glower had turned to one of concern.

Likely, he worried more about the many breakable items around the shop than the sergeant's well-being. Even *without* the dour grimace, Fel always looked dangerous and on the verge of violence. Head shaven—to hide how gray his hair was, he'd once admitted—broad face scarred, and his tall frame still well-muscled, despite his years, he intimidated many people. The crossbow slung across his back, bandolier of quarrels and daggers, and heavy mace at his belt all suggested he was a man capable of doing a lot of damage to enemies—and perhaps sensitive antiques as well.

"That dour frown is part of his normal expression." Syla

nodded as Fel switched legs, his grimace deepening when he stretched the other calf.

The clerk looked at her with a furrowed brow. Maybe she hadn't answered his question sufficiently?

Syla held up a finger. "How much longer until your retirement, Sergeant Fel?"

"Seventeen days, eight hours, and..." Fel drew a pocket watch from his blue uniform trousers. "Thirteen minutes."

"That's when he'll *truly* be all right," Syla told the clerk, not minding Fel's gruffness or even that he didn't want to be at her side any longer than required.

After a lifetime of body-guarding her older and more politically important siblings, he deserved retirement. And she... Well, she'd never believed herself in need of a protector. Who would try to kill a healer? The youngest by far of five children? Syla kept waiting for her oldest sister to have children so that she would no longer be directly in line for the throne and an even less likely target, but the gods hadn't blessed any of her siblings with children yet, an absence the newspapers noted often.

Fel leaned closer to the window, frowning as he tucked his pocket watch away. His hand strayed to his mace, and was that a *growl* that emanated from his chest? He sounded like a gargoyle.

"Maybe he should wait outside." The clerk must have heard the growl. He lifted a fragile, decorative dragon egg and two glass vases from the counter, then tucked them safely underneath it.

Syla joined Fel at the window, wondering if she'd been too quick to dismiss the possibility of trouble in the street. But here in the capital city, on the most protected island in the Garden Kingdom, muggers wouldn't ply their trade. And, thanks to the magical sky shielder, people didn't have to worry about dragons, wyverns, or other aerial threats.

Syla peered at the one- and two-story shops lining the wide street, horses hitched at mounting posts outside. "Sergeant, are you growling because your calf is knotted or because you spotted trouble?"

She felt diminutive standing next to her bodyguard. At five-and-a-half feet in height, she wasn't *short* for a Kingdom woman, but her head only came to the top of his shoulder. Even if she'd worn her shoulder-length auburn hair in the currently trendy beehive style, instead of clipped back over her ears, Fel could have seen over her head.

"My calf is knotted, my arches ache, my heel feels like it's being stabbed, *and* my knee is throbbing, but it's the *dragon* that just flew overhead that's making me growl." Fel pointed toward the cloudy gray sky.

Syla didn't see anything but the promise of evening rain, but she didn't doubt the sergeant. His body might hurt from a lifetime of hard work, training, and wounds received in battle, but he'd never indicated any failings with his eyes.

"Just one soaring above the shield, right?"

"It looked lower than that." Fel held up a finger. "Stay here."

Syla blinked. *Lower* than the sky shield? That wasn't possible. Dragons couldn't pass *through* the magical barrier. None of the storm god's creations could.

"Dragons?" The clerk tucked more fragile antiques out of the way, as if damage to a few gewgaws would be the main concern if deadly predators made it through the shield.

Syla, neither a warrior nor even well-endowed with athleticism, obeyed Fel's command to stay inside, but curiosity prompted her to lean through the doorway for a better look.

Once out in the cobblestone street, clear of the shop's awning, Fel surveyed the sky, then turned toward the castle on the bluff that overlooked the harbor and capital city. Whatever he saw up there made him widen his eyes and curse.

At first, he reached for his crossbow. Then he looked at Syla and swore again. When he rushed toward her, screams came with him. Two horses pulling carts raced down the street, wheels rattling as the drivers cracked their whips and shouted for greater speed.

"The castle is under attack." Fel gripped Syla's arm. "Dragons. A whole wing of them. We have to get you to a bunker."

Though stunned, Syla let him drag her into the street. Sticking to the side, they ran under awnings and overhangs whenever possible. She glanced back toward the castle, half-believing he had to be mistaken. The sky shield had successfully protected the islands for *centuries.*

But dozens of green, gray, and blue dragons circled the castle, spewing fire at the towers and battlements. The only defense came from archers, crossbowmen, and Royal Protectors manning cannons. Smoke roiled from the courtyard and the high windows of the keep, promising great damage had already been done. Horrified, Syla stumbled, almost falling to the cobblestones.

Her entire family was in the castle; they'd been partaking in the very dinner she'd been on her way to attend. But nobody would be dining now. They had to be rushing to the underground tunnels for protection. No, wait. Was that her mother and older sister, Nyvia? Out on the ramparts with their weapons, helping the defenders?

Fel tightened his grip, keeping Syla on her feet and running.

"This way," he urged. "One of the ancient bunkers is off Three Fountains Street. The Royal Protectors will fight off the dragons."

"I should go to the temple. There'll be wounded."

"Later. Once the attack is over. You have to survive first to heal people."

Someone in the street ahead screamed, startling Syla into tripping again.

Dozens of people were out now. Maybe hundreds. They were running away from the dragons—or so they thought.

A great blue-scaled beast swooped toward the street. Its wings tucked in close as it dove, and its maw opened, its fangs dripping saliva. An icy-faced rider with a gargoyle-bone bow rode on the dragon's back, no saddle or harness keeping him in place. Dagger tattoos on his hollow cheeks gave him a fearsome visage.

The man glanced at her but focused on a horse-drawn cart full of wooden kegs, its driver the only person heading *to* the castle instead of away. The rider nocked an arrow, but it was his powerful mount that represented the greater danger. Smoke wafted from the dragon's nostrils an instant before fire roiled out of its maw.

Fel still had a grip on Syla's wrist, but he wrapped his arm around her waist and hefted her from her feet as he sprang into a doorway. More curves than leanness, she wasn't light, but he carried her over his broad shoulder without slowing.

Scant feet away, in the center of the street, the fire struck. It enveloped the cart and rider, the man screaming. An instant later, the cart—no, the *kegs*—exploded.

Black powder, an analytical part of Syla's mind processed, even as utter terror gripped her and Fel carried her deeper into a carpenter's shop. The shockwave from the explosion struck the buildings on either side of the street, blowing out glass and knocking down walls. Roofs caught fire, more people screamed, and the dragon... Syla couldn't see what happened to the dragon, but she imagined it flapping casually away while its rider grinned with pleasure at the kill.

Cries of pain grew audible once the explosion faded. For the first time, Syla squirmed, trying to escape Fel's grasp.

"I need to help," she said.

Overhead, a beam snapped. Not five feet away, a flaming section of the ceiling fell to the floor, hurling sparks over furniture and workbenches.

Swearing, Fel spun to put his back to the fire to protect her. "I'm getting you to the bunker."

"I appreciate your adherence to duty, but—" Syla squirmed

again, wanting her own two feet under her, longing to do her job, not run away when people were in pain, "—I'm a healer. A *gods-blessed* healer." She waved the back of her hand at him, as if he might have forgotten the quarter-moon-shaped birthmark that she and her close relatives had, hereditary gifts that imbued them with the power to help the Kingdom when needed. "I can keep people from dying," she added as Fel dragged her toward a back door.

"There'll be plenty of people who need that at the bunker."

Between his arm around her and the smoke and heat in the shop, she felt frustrated and claustrophobic and tried again to free herself. She might as well have been attempting to escape iron shackles.

Fel thrust open the back door and started into an alley but halted abruptly, swearing again.

Thanks to whatever distracted him, Syla twisted free and set her feet on the floor. His arm tightened around her waist, but he didn't lift her again. Instead, he unhooked his mace from his belt and glowered across the alley toward the rooftop of the building behind theirs. Flames leaped from the gutters of both structures, but Syla saw what he saw.

A green dragon even larger than the first perched atop a chimney, its size dwarfing it and the building underneath. Its scales gleamed, reflecting the dancing flames all around it, but the creature seemed impervious to the heat. As did its rider, an athletic-looking man in black leathers, including fingerless black gloves. He was striking, with bronze skin and wild, windswept black hair framing a lean, angular face. His emerald eyes matched the scales of the dragon. She had no trouble noticing those eyes because the man was staring down at her. His *dragon* looked toward the castle, and its muscles bunched under its scales, as if it meant to spring into action at any moment, but he... his eyes locked not onto her face but her hand. The moon-mark.

Realizing it would make her a target, Syla tucked her arm behind her back. But it was too late. He'd seen it.

Fel raised his mace and crouched, prepared to defend her, even against a rider and a dragon. Even if there was no chance that he could survive the encounter.

The dragon's head swung around on its long neck so that it also looked at Syla. Terror gripped her, and she wished she hadn't slowed Fel down, that they'd already reached the bunker. As he'd pointed out, she wouldn't be able to heal people if she were dead.

"That's Captain Vorik Wingborn," Fel growled, drawing her back through the doorway and under cover, out of the line of sight of their enemies.

She could still see the bottom of the dragon, those talons gripping the chimney.

"Warrior, archer, and storm-possessed bastard," Fel continued, "whose hobby has been sinking every third cargo or merchant ship that's sailed beyond the protection of the sky shielders these last ten years."

Syla doubted they would make it to the bunker. The captain hadn't yet attacked, but more dragons flew overhead, their roars drowning out the screams of fear and pain coming from all over the city.

Would anyone in the capital survive this?

A war horn blew in the distance, from across the sea. The green dragon shifted on the chimney, as if the call beckoned it, and crouched to spring. Before it did, its great tail lashed out like a whip, long enough to cross the alley and slam down onto the carpentry shop. The roof above Syla and Fel collapsed.

As stone and wood crashed down, Fel sprang atop her, using his body to protect her as the great weight crushed them to the floor and buried them.

2

A HARD PIECE OF RUBBLE JABBED PAINFULLY INTO SYLA'S RIBS, AND Fel's oppressive and unconscious weight crushed her from above. In the darkness after the building's collapse, she lay trapped, unable to see anything, barely able to breathe. Tears leaked from her eyes as overwhelming despair crushed her as surely as her bodyguard's weight.

Her family had been in the castle and fighting back, but Syla worried her mother and her siblings wouldn't all survive the onslaught of dragons. What if... *none* of her family survived? What if *she* had to take her mother's role as queen and leader of the Kingdom?

No, she couldn't. She wasn't qualified. She'd even avoided suggestions that she apply for a leadership position in Moon Watch Temple. She didn't have the aptitude to be in charge of people, certainly not people who had just been devastated by a dragon attack.

And what if more than the capital had been targeted? There were twelve islands in the Garden Kingdom. What if the other shielders, the artifacts that powered the sky shields, had also stopped working?

The question brought her back to the most pertinent one, at least for her at that moment: what had caused the shielder for Castle Island to stop working?

The magic infused in the devices, devices that had been built long ago by the gods themselves, had never failed before. She'd read enough history books to know that for a fact. There'd been an instance in the third century of a spy finding and sabotaging a shielder, which had briefly let dragons in to attack Vineyard Island, but an engineer in the Moonmark family had been able to repair the artifact. None of the shielders had simply stopped working on their own.

Could the one under the castle have been sabotaged? By a spy? Only her own kin could enter the shielder chambers. And of those with the magical moon birthmarks, hardly any had been entrusted with the locations on each island where those chambers were. Those were closely guarded secrets among those in line for the throne. Those like her.

Always before, she'd scoffed at the idea that she might lose her older brothers and sisters and have to worry about inheriting the throne, but now...

"No," Syla whispered, her hoarse throat coated in dust. "At least *some* of my siblings have to be okay. I'll find them and heal them."

Except, at the moment, she couldn't move.

Something warm and damp dripped onto the back of her neck. Fel's blood.

By the eyes of the moon, she had to heal her poor bodyguard first.

Summoning what energy she could, Syla pushed and squirmed. Not only his weight lay atop her but the fallen roof had settled upon them. Grunting, she attempted to shove from different angles. Her knuckles smashed against wood and brick, but she managed to free one arm, improving her ability to move, to dig.

A piece of tile moved, clunking as it shifted. She dug at that spot, hoping...

A soft tink sounded, like glass hitting rock, and she abruptly remembered her spectacles. She reached for her face to make sure she hadn't lost them, but the frames weren't on her nose.

Fresh fear lurched into her. Smashed in the darkness, with so little room to maneuver, she hadn't realized she wasn't wearing them.

As she patted about underneath her, hoping they'd landed close by, her fear threatened to turn into panic. Not being able to find her spectacles at home, in the safety of the temple, was alarming enough. But out here? With enemies all over the place and the city half-razed? How would she find her way home without her spectacles? Her vision was too poor for her to see sharply for more than a foot. Even if the city hadn't been a mess made unfamiliar by all the rubble and carnage, she doubted she could have navigated the streets.

The sound of ragged breathing in her ears, echoing strangely in the tomb of rocks, made her aware that she was hyperventilating. *Panicking.*

Being aware of it didn't make it easy to stop, but she attempted to calm herself, to smooth her inhalations and exhalations. For the moment, nobody was attacking her. She was in a better position than some. But not being able to find her spectacles gave her more reason than ever to climb out of the rubble and heal Sergeant Fel. She needed his help to get to the castle and figure out... whatever they could figure out.

Digging more carefully now, she pushed away broken tiles, wood, and stone. Soon, a hint of smoke reached her nose, trickling in through the rubble. It reminded her of the fires in the city but also promised that she was close to escape.

The sound of someone crying in the distance floated to her. Fel wasn't the only one who needed her.

As she moved about, he groaned and shifted slightly. He remained unconscious, but with less of his weight atop her, Syla dug and pushed more effectively. More smoky air flowed into what had almost been their tomb.

Fury simmered in her veins as she dug. Fury toward the collected tribes—the stormers, as they called themselves—and all dragon riders and everyone else who'd been involved in this attack. Especially that captain whatever-his-name-had-been. If he'd shot her with his bow, it would have been less ignoble than having his dragon casually flick its tail and destroy the building above her head.

The desire to live long enough to see Fel drive a crossbow quarrel through the captain's heart renewed her strength. Finally, she pushed enough rubble aside that she could move fully out from under the sergeant and sit up. Pervasive smoke overrode the pleasant sea breeze that usually caressed the city, and she coughed, wishing for fresh air.

"Sergeant Fel?" Syla glanced about as she pushed part of a broken beam off him.

Everything around her was blurry, but in the dimness of encroaching twilight, there might not have been much to see anyway. If enemies were creeping about, who would know?

The alarming thought made her heart thump rapidly in her chest. Dare she go into a meditative trance and use her magic to heal Fel's wounds? Normally, she wouldn't think twice about it, but if ever she'd needed a bodyguard to watch her back while she worked...

She strained her ears, trying to detect threats nearby. Other than the sounds of a few people crying in neighboring buildings,

buildings she had no doubt had also been destroyed, the city had grown quiet. Had the attack ended? She could hear the roar of the sea beyond the harbor.

Fel groaned again but didn't open his eyes.

Syla shifted more rubble away from him and rested her hand on his side. Her arm brushed his mace. He'd been gripping it when the ceiling fell and half lay on it.

"Sergeant Fel, do you give me your permission to use my power on you?" Syla uttered the question formally, but she doubted he was conscious enough to answer.

The law required her to seek permission from him, or someone who could speak for him, since magic tended to bind those who'd been healed to the healer for a time. This was, however, an extenuating circumstance.

"I have a feeling we're going to be bound together for a while anyway," she murmured, shaking her head bleakly as she thought of his retirement countdown. For some reason, the thought prompted more tears, the certainty that he wouldn't be able to retire now.

More tears flowed after that, tears for her family, for the city, for all those in pain or worse. It took her a few minutes, the darkness deepening, before she could get herself together, stare at the back of her hand, and reach for the meditative trance from which she accessed her healing magic.

With her fingers splayed across Fel's chest, the moon-mark started glowing silver, and energy hummed through her. The magic of her gods-sense allowed her to see his body from within and find all the injuries, including one causing swelling against his skull, the likely reason he was unconscious.

A quiet clatter came from somewhere nearby. The alley outside?

The memory of the dragon and its fearsome rider swept into her, interrupting her concentration, and her magic faded. Just before the silver glow disappeared from her hand, she spotted its reflection glinting on something nearby. Glass. Her spectacles?

She lunged for the spot and patted around. Yes, there were the frames. Terribly bent. When she lifted them to see if they could hook over her ears, more glass tinked, pieces falling out. With dread sinking into her stomach, she realized she might cut herself if she donned spectacles with broken shards sticking out of the frames.

When she probed the eyeholes, her finger went through on one side. No glass remained. In the other... The lens was there but shattered.

"Dear departed gods," she muttered.

After making sure no glass would jab her in the eye, Syla straightened the frame as much as she could and hooked it over her ears, hoping she would get some vision through the shattered lens. Sergeant Fel's body came more into focus, but it was distorted, with a crack right in front of her eye.

Shaking her head, she turned her attention back to him. She had spare spectacles at home, but she needed help getting there.

"Another reason to heal you whether you can give permission or not," Syla murmured, resting her hand on his chest and willing her power into him again.

As she focused her magic on lessening the swelling and repairing what turned out to be a crack in his skull, she sliced off a modicum of her attention to continue inspecting the rest of his body. His arms and limbs appeared hale, but he had cracked ribs and bruised organs. Healing external wounds, those she could see with her eyes, was always easier than fixing interior damage, but she'd had plenty of practice in her more than ten years as a healer.

She had to be careful, however, about how much she did here, while in this vulnerable predicament. Since the healing magic relied on her own energy and stamina, as well as the power gifted by the gods, doing too much could leave her crumpled and unconscious herself.

A rustle and a clunk came from the alley, and she paused. A dog sniffing about? An enemy?

She peered into the blurry gloom, afraid.

When the noise didn't repeat, she bit her lip and hurried to send power into Fel more swiftly than was wise. With her senses and her magic, she finished working on his skull, then knitted the broken ribs together while sending energy into his organs to reduce the swelling and encourage the body to apply its own healing power to them.

Fel stirred, groaning, and that gave her hope. Hope that he would wake soon, that *his* eyes would be fine and he could get them back to the temple. There, she could grab her spare spectacles, and then they could go to the castle and... find out who remained alive.

Even grim and afraid, she couldn't keep from yawning as she worked, fatigue creeping into her body. The sense of being watched came over her. Again, she looked toward the alley, but it was too dark to see anything. No, wait. Was that a hint of movement? Something in her periphery?

"Go away," she whispered and gripped Fel's mace, drawing it out from under his body to brandish it toward the alley.

He groaned again.

"Wake up anytime, Sergeant," Syla said. "I need you more than ever."

She was close enough to see his face when he winced. Soon, he would rouse from unconsciousness, but when he did, he would be in pain from the wounds she hadn't yet attended. They were less grievous, and she told herself he could function with them, but she wished she could do more.

Unfortunately, more yawns stretched her mouth, and her

eyelids wanted to lower. She didn't have the energy left for more healing.

A horse whinnied in the street.

"This is looting, you know," someone outside whispered. The male voice was close enough for the words to be distinct.

"If we didn't do it," another man said, "the dragon riders would. Just find what's valuable."

"Check that building." Were the men right outside the front door?

The shadows stirred, and a clunk sounded.

Syla gripped the mace and tried to stand up. But the healing had taken too much out of her. Lightheaded, she collapsed and lost consciousness.

3

THE WAR HORN BLEW AGAIN, THREE SHORT NOTES TO SUMMON officers, and Agrevlari flew across the sea toward it without input from his rider.

"I'm sure General Jhiton appreciates your swift obedience." Captain Vorik patted his bonded dragon on his scaled back as he looked over his shoulder, toward the fiery remains of Garden Castle and the Kingdom's capital city.

Some dragons continued to attack, killing and razing for pleasure, but Vorik and his wing mates had taken out the key military officers and members of the royal family, those with the ability to find and operate the sky shielders. Had the horn not summoned him, Vorik might have attempted to call off the other dragons, but he only commanded the riders, not their kind. Dragons worked with the human tribes when it suited them, but never did they take *orders* from the puny two-legs, as the wild ones called men.

Jhiton can clip my talons, Agrevlari spoke telepathically into Vorik's mind. *It is Wingleader Saleetha who commands my loyalty.*

"Still hoping she'll invite you into her nest, huh?"

She would be a most appealing partner, but you know the wild dragon for whom I pine.

"Is it still that pretty red one? Wreylith?"

Wreylith the Graceful and Beautiful and the Utterly Magnificent.

"That's a long name." Vorik spotted a black dragon in the distance, he and his rider standing atop a rock formation in the middle of the sea, waves crashing around the base.

A few other dragons with riders circled the formation, wings spread wide as they rode the air currents, but they didn't land. It appeared this would be a private meeting, at least in the beginning.

General Jhiton's gaze shifted from the burning castle in the distance to Agrevlari's approach. Muscular arms folded across his chest, stance wide against the wind, and a griffin-fur cloak flapping behind him, Jhiton intimidated most people, but Vorik saw his older brother, the person who'd raised him after their father had died, and he flew closer without concern. Gray flecks in the short black hair at Jhiton's temple were the only suggestion that he'd seen well over forty years and had been using his twin swords, one belted to either side of his waist, to slay enemies for decades.

When their gazes met, Vorik lifted his bow in the air, a salute and also a signal to indicate success, though he suspected the general had heard all the details. For the beginning of the battle, Jhiton had been there, leading the attack on the castle, the need for vengeance burning in his green eyes. Later, he'd leaped off his dragon and into the courtyard, chasing down specific enemies with his swords, relentless in his desire to slay every moon-marked scion of the royal line.

When Agrevlari alighted atop the jagged rock formation, Vorik hopped down, finding a flat spot on which to land. As always, he gave a wide berth to his brother's surly black dragon, Ozlemar, who tended to snap at anyone who strayed too close.

"Mission accomplished, eh, General?" Vorik asked, addressing his brother formally, as Jhiton preferred.

"This stage, yes. The battle was glorious, Captain." Jhiton's gaze locked with satisfaction on the smoldering castle.

"I'm looking forward to getting my hands on the crops. All those juicy and delicious fruits and vegetables that grow all over the islands, half of them wild and untended, just *there* for people to feast on, to eat without having to chew a thousand times. Jhiton, it's been *years* since I had a strawberry. Remember that battle? When we were lucky enough to find that merchant ship meandering out from under the shield with that most wondrous of bounties in its hold? Oh, and we can hunt with the dragons on Castle Island now. *Easy* hunting of fat and sumptuous prey. Have you seen the ungulates that wander the grassy hills of the pastures with barely any means to defend themselves? Cows and sheep and balsinor. Their meat is *so* succulent. I can't wait. Do you think strawberries are in season now? Do you think one could smother a balsinor tenderloin in berries, and it would be good? I've heard of sauces one can make from them. And *jams*."

Jhiton gave him a sidelong look. "Only you would go to war for *fruit*."

"Well, that's what this is all about, isn't it? Access to resources that the entitled gardeners have kept from our people for centuries?"

"Resources like strawberries."

"Apples are good too. I wonder if they're in season yet. Summer is a ways from over."

"You know what I want. What we all want." Jhiton pointed at his chest and at Vorik's but didn't indicate the dragons, though they had expressed longing for the delicious ungulates that the shields denied them. But other things motivated dragons, and humans didn't presume to know all that mattered to them. With their great power, they could compete with their fellow predators and hunt the dangerous prey found in the seas and on the desert and rainforest continents. Unlike the humans living outside of the gods' protection, dragons didn't need to worry about losing family members to ferocious predators every time they left their caves. "A better life for our people," Jhiton added.

Despite their victory, a familiar haunted expression lurked in the general's eyes.

As always, Vorik was sympathetic—he missed his little nephew and couldn't imagine what it had been like for his brother to lose his only son—but he also flirted with the idea of pointing out that war wouldn't bring Jebrosh back. Since Jhiton was, in addition to everything else, his superior officer, Vorik didn't do that. He merely nodded.

"I have a mission for you." Jhiton pointed to a blue dragon flying toward them, a female rider on its back.

Captain Lesva from the Moonhunt Tribe.

Vorik straightened, bracing himself for whatever sarcastic comments his rival and former lover would have for him. Despite a few feminine attributes bound tightly by riding leathers, Lesva didn't have many soft aspects about her. Maybe the general's presence would inhibit her snark.

Wishful thinking, Agrevlari's telepathic voice rose up from below, the words for Vorik alone. *Her tongue is sharper than her dragon's talons.*

Is her tongue sharper than your *talons?* Vorik replied silently.

Few humans had the gift of telepathy, so they couldn't broadcast their thoughts, but dragons never seemed to have trouble reading Vorik's mind and catching all his words. For dragons bonded to their riders, such communication was particularly easy.

Of course not. My talons are sharper than the lost swords of the gods. I tend them exquisitely to ensure their deadly edge.

Vorik had lost sight of Agrevlari and peered over the side of their perch. Fifty feet below, the magnificent green dragon floated on his back in a pool formed by the curvature of the rock formation and protected from the surging waves, though a few splashes made their way to his belly and agitated the water around him. His eyes were closed, and he looked as content as a mountain lion sprawled on a sunny outcropping.

Is that what you're doing now? Vorik asked.

Now, I'm letting the surf massage my muscles, which were taxed somewhat by all the twisting and diving I had to do to avoid cannonballs and harpoons, a task that I handled with great aplomb.

Yes, I recall. You flipped upside-down three times despite our previous agreement that you wouldn't do that when I'm on your back, not unless you let me put a saddle on you.

Though Agrevlari didn't roll over or otherwise move from his comfortable floating position, he did open one eye to gaze balefully up at Vorik. *Only sycophantic lesser dragons allow such undignified contraptions to be buckled around them like chains. As a rider, it behooves you to have strong leg muscles with which to clamp on.*

My leg muscles are exquisitely honed. However... I don't know if you've checked yourself out in a mirror lately, but you're a lot of dragon to clamp onto.

Like all riders, Vorik had to find the minuscule gaps between the scales of his mount to help hang on when a dragon's flight grew erratic and involved barrel rolls, dives, and exuberant undulations. It was his *finger* muscles that were exquisite. When he was hanging on that way, he couldn't fire his bow. Not that he was truly complaining. To be permitted to not only ride but bond with a dragon, and receive some of his power through their magical link, was the most wondrous honor there was.

I am a lot of dragon. Agrevlari sounded smug.

Captain Lesva's blue dragon, Verikloth, landed on the far edge of the rock formation from the surly black, wings spread to come down lightly. Prematurely silver hair pulled back in a tight braid that accented her prominent cheekbones and jaw, Lesva eyed Vorik before hopping down and saluting General Jhiton.

"I have the information from our spy, sir." She reported to Jhiton, but she gave Vorik a sidelong look. "I stayed to obtain it, even after I slew two of the Moonmark Clan and helped Verikloth defeat the castle defenders and take down one of its towers."

The brag was directed at Vorik; he had no doubt.

"You're an asset to the stormers and a capable officer," Vorik stated, keeping his expression neutral and tamping down the sarcasm that always wanted to come out when he dealt with her.

When they'd been lovers, he'd delivered insults as often as she, always feeling the need to compete with and defend himself against her. *She'd* gotten turned on by it, and their verbal sparring had led to sex more often than he could remember. He'd felt more disgruntled than satisfied by the encounters, as if snapping at her hadn't been honorable, but she'd always seemed to *want* to fight with him. The sex hadn't been bad, but he hadn't found the relationship relaxing. Whether Lesva wanted sex now, he didn't know, but he'd made a conscious decision, after they'd broken up, to stop being lured in by her bait.

Lesva squinted suspiciously at his comment. "Does that mean that you and your lazy dragon didn't get *any* of the Moonmarks?"

Verikloth peered over the edge at Agrevlari, his blue tail going rigid. They were probably also insulting each other. Their relationship was almost as contentious and Lesva and Vorik's, though Vorik didn't think they'd ever mated. Agrevlari, when he wasn't busy tending to his muscles and talon sharpness, always pined for Wreylith.

"We battled many castle and city defenders and helped Lieutenant Navor take out their stockpiles of explosives," Vorik said.

Fortunately, that was what his orders had been. He'd objected to outright assassinating members of the Kingdom's royal family. Oh, Vorik had no reason to adore the Moonmarks, those ultimately responsible for not allowing the stormers access to their ancestral lands, but he believed in facing opponents in fair and honorable fights, not slipping through the shadows to stab daggers into their hearts from behind.

"That means no, then. Really, Vorik. I don't know how you got your rank." Lesva glanced at Jhiton but didn't do anything to suggest that it might have been nepotism. That would have been insulting to Vorik *and* his brother. If anything, Jhiton had always worked Vorik harder than anyone else, ensuring he grew up to become a warrior their father would have been proud of. And Vorik, who knew how many enemy ships he'd sunk and duels for rank he'd won over the years, didn't have any self-doubt. He'd earned his position and knew it. Lesva knew it, too, and was just trying to get a rise from him. Maybe she did feel randy after the battle.

"What did our spy report, Captain?" Jhiton's tone suggested he didn't want her to waste more time sniping with Vorik.

"He wasn't sure where Lieutenant Mavus was, but, as far as he was able to determine, all except one of the royal family is dead."

"One escaped the attack?"

"She wasn't at the family gathering, as our spy had predicted. Had she been at the castle, per the royal family's own plans, we would already have gotten her."

"Is that the youngest princess?" Jhiton asked. "Syla Moonmark?"

"Yes. Our spy is looking for her. The moon-god temple where she lived and worked was destroyed, and he thinks she may have died inside when it collapsed."

Vorik blinked, realizing he'd seen that girl. Not in a temple but in a shop in the merchant section of town.

"She's not dead," he said. "Well, I'm not actually certain of that. Agrevlari flicked his tail and brought a roof down on her and what was probably her bodyguard. It just wasn't a *temple* roof." Before they'd disappeared under the rubble, he'd glimpsed the bodyguard throw himself onto the princess to protect her. "She's probably not dead."

Jhiton flickered an eyebrow at his uncertainty.

"Why didn't you *ensure* she was dead?" Lesva asked. "The whole point of this attack was to kill the Moonmarks."

Vorik shrugged. "The war horn called."

Lesva gave him a scathing look.

Vorik shrugged again. He'd been half-glad Agrevlari had been the one to take the initiative. He'd known the mission and its goal as well as anyone, and he'd spotted the birthmark on the princess's hand, but he hadn't wanted to attack her. On the plump and curvy side, she hadn't looked like a warrior, especially not when she'd peered up at him through those thick-lensed spectacles. Trying to kill such a weak opponent wouldn't have been honorable.

"If she's alive, she has the power to activate the shielder," Jhiton said.

"It's been destroyed, hasn't it?" Vorik asked. "That was Lieutenant Mavus's mission, right? Why he spent months wooing the older princess?"

"It was his mission," Jhiton said, "and the shield dropping suggests he completed it, but we won't know the details until he arrives to report."

Lesva lifted her chin. "I volunteer to go back for the princess, to find her and kill her."

Jhiton started to nod but paused and gazed thoughtfully toward the city. "Neither our spies nor Lieutenant Mavus have learned where the shielders on the other islands are. Harvest and Vineyard Islands are the true gems that our people seek to acquire. Not only could the crops there feed all our people, but the dragons seek to hunt prey found only in those sheltered locales. Lieutenant

Mavus hoped to unearth a map or instructions on how to reach the shielders on those islands, but, the last I heard, he had not. To truly fulfill our mission and nourish our people for generations to come, we'll need access to the prime agricultural islands." Jhiton cocked a somewhat amused eyebrow as he looked at Vorik. "Castle Island isn't where the majority of the berry patches and orchards are."

"I do long to stroll through the rows and rows of pear- and apple-filled trees on Harvest Island," Vorik allowed himself to say wistfully before remembering Lesva's abrasive presence. He eyed her, expecting more sarcasm.

Surprisingly, she looked wistful too. Maybe it was simply human nature to desire sweet things, a change from the meat, fish, and various fibrous plants and seaweeds the stormers scrounged from the harsh world they lived in.

"From the pictures I've seen of the youngest princess," Jhiton said, "she's not a threat, not a combatant like her older siblings and the queen were. Reputedly, she's a healer and uses her hereditary magic for that."

"I'm sure she can still activate the shielders, sir," Lesva said.

"I have no doubt of that. But she doesn't sound like someone capable of rallying a nation or rebuilding a kingdom."

Lesva snorted. "No, sir. I've seen the same pictures. She's chubby and soft and probably blind, or close to it, without those weird things on her face." She waved to her eyes. "She would be easy to kill anytime."

No dragon riders, and very few stormers, had poor vision, so Vorik didn't know much about what the spectacles implied, but the princess certainly hadn't had the mien of a warrior. He wouldn't have called her *chubby* though. Voluptuous, maybe. She had the kind of curves that a man would enjoy exploring.

"I could go kill her tonight." Lesva leaned forward. Eager for the assignment, was she? "That would bring my kills of Moonmarks up to three. More than anyone else." She shot a look of superiority at Vorik.

Jhiton, gazing toward the mainland, didn't respond to the captain's offer. "As a direct descendant of the throne, however low she was in her family hierarchy, it's likely she knows the locations of the rest of the shielders."

Lesva blinked. "Oh, do you want her captured? To interrogate? I could get that information out of her without trouble." She flexed her hands in the air, as if demonstrating strangling.

Apparently, *she* had no qualms about killing—or torturing—a weak opponent. Vorik knew from experience that Lesva liked to challenge herself with duels and athletic competitions against strong adversaries, but she'd never been that bogged down by the need to be honorable. In some of the stormer tribes, that was more ingrained in the psyches of its members than in others.

"Those with the magic of the moon-mark," Jhiton said, "are as susceptible to pain as anyone, but they can supposedly use their power to lock off their minds and keep from uttering truths when under duress. Reputedly, moon-mark healers even have some power to control the minds of others. Of course, that's supposed to be only those they've healed, but I've heard tales of them *healing* someone who didn't wish it and didn't have significant injury, and then gaining sway over them."

"Like when we were young and that spy got information from one of *our* people?" Vorik asked.

Jhiton nodded. "Exactly like that. I'm surprised you were old enough to remember, but the healer treated our chieftess after a battle, and then she, for weeks afterward, wanted to be with him. To *please* him. In bed and elsewhere. Even though she had a mate back home."

"It would be easy enough to keep a soft princess from using her magic on me." Captain Lesva patted her sheathed sword.

Jhiton's thoughtful gaze swung toward Vorik. "I believe... I have another idea."

Vorik raised his eyebrows.

"Captain Lesva," Jhiton said, "I do not want the princess slain at this time. You did excellent work today, though, and I'm making note of your dedication to your duty. The Storm Guard and Sixteen Talons will combine to host a great celebration once we finish here and return to the caves. For now, you're dismissed."

Lesva opened her mouth, as if she might object, or request again to add a third Moonmark kill to her list, but Jhiton's eyes closed to slits in a silent warning. He was a powerful warrior, and Lesva had never challenged him in practice or in truth. Vorik, who'd sparred often with his brother, wouldn't have challenged him either. Even among the sometimes-reckless riders, few were that suicidal.

"Yes, sir." Lesva bowed to Jhiton, then headed toward her dragon, managing to pick a path that let her swat Vorik on the butt in passing. The smile she gave him before mounting managed to be superior, snarky, and inviting all at once.

"Guess that answers my question about if she still wants to have sex," Vorik muttered.

"A brazen woman," Jhiton stated as Lesva flew off.

Despite the somewhat approving tone accompanying his words, he didn't gaze after her or appear sexually interested. As far as Vorik knew, his brother hadn't taken another lover since he and his previous life mate had parted after their son's death.

"She is that," was all Vorik said. "What's your plan?"

"*You* are my plan."

"I know you don't want *me* to capture and interrogate the princess."

Actually, Vorik *didn't* know that, but he'd made his feelings on honor clear over the years and doubted Jhiton would send him on such a mission when there were others more willing. He *hoped*

Jhiton wouldn't. Ultimately, Vorik's loyalty was to the tribes and the Sixteen Talons, and he'd long ago sworn to obey his commanding officers, so he had to do what they wished. It wouldn't be the first time he'd been forced into something distasteful.

"If your reputation is to be believed—" Jhiton waved toward Lesva's receding form, "—you wouldn't *need* to interrogate a woman to get information out of her."

"Well. I guess I have been known to have them burble involuntary details while in the throes of passion."

"Even gardener women." Jhiton's eyes narrowed with judgment, even if he didn't say more.

"From time to time, yes." Vorik shrugged, not caring to explain that he sometimes liked a woman who *wasn't* a warrior, who had more soft parts than hard parts and who rarely wrestled for dominance with him under the furs.

"I've seen your face draw tribeswomen of all kinds. Even of all ages. The *grandmothers* flirt with you."

"It's my devastating smile. Grammies can't resist it. You'd get more of the same kind of attention if you hadn't allowed yourself to be so scarred up and uglified over the years." Vorik smirked. He would never tease his older brother in front of the troops, but he couldn't always resist when they were alone. They'd both teased each other when they'd been younger, before Father had died and Jhiton had gotten so serious.

"Does your dragon appreciate your wit?"

"Yeah, it's what drew him to me."

I was drawn because you fed me delicious smoked salmon and read poems to me while I ate. Even from far below, Agrevlari was apparently following the conversation. One sometimes wondered how keen dragon ears were.

They were the lyrics of a manly ballad I was composing, not poems.

You know we're an oral people, and songs are how we pass down history and lessons.

It was a ballad about the might and magnificence of dragons. I approved.

Of course you did.

You remarked on my grace in the sky and the speed with which I can swiftly descend to annihilate my enemies.

I didn't realize you'd memorized the lyrics.

Impressive, yes? You don't sing it to me nearly often enough. Your human voice lacks the appealing screech of a dragon vocalization, but I've over the years grown to find it less distasteful than the voices of many of your kind.

What expression Vorik wore, he didn't know, but his brother raised his eyebrows. "Is your dragon being snarky with you?"

"Usually, yes. Though that may have been a compliment. What exactly do you want me to do with the Moonmark princess?" Vorik already had an inkling and had conflicted feelings about it. "Seduce her?"

It was hard to imagine seducing a woman when he'd just partaken in an attack on her people. No, not only her *people*. They'd been targeting the princess's mother and siblings specifically. If she'd been at the castle, she would be as dead as her kin. Knowing that, how could Vorik make a pass at her?

Oh, he was sure he could manage the sexual interest—the glimpse he'd caught of her had included appealing curves, lush auburn hair, and a cute face, but after what he and his people had done, he couldn't imagine luring her under his furs.

"Find the princess and win her trust," Jhiton said, oblivious to Vorik's contemplations. "Tell her you're one of the Freeborn Faction." He sneered at the mention of the former stormers who'd left the tribes to supposedly find a peaceful future with the Garden Kingdom. "Promise to protect her from dragon-rider assassins. After you've gained her trust, get the information about the other shielders from her. I want their locations. *All* of them."

"I'm sure her deepest family secrets will come up during our first post-coital chat."

Jhiton's eyelids drooped, no humor on his face. "As the sole remaining member of the royal family, she should feel obligated to protect her people. I suspect she'll realize they should remove one of the shielders guarding a less populated island—nearby Harvest Island, perhaps—and bring it back to the capital to restore a barrier on Castle Island."

"Will that work?"

"It might. All that matters is that she thinks it will and takes action. In the process, she can lead you to another shielder. If she doesn't come up with the idea on her own... perhaps you can encourage it."

"*Perhaps* she will know exactly who I am and not trust me in the least."

"Your face isn't as well-known as mine."

Vorik thought of his brief view of the princess—and the sturdy old warrior who'd stood beside her. "I'm certain the bodyguard recognized me. He'll have told her."

"Even trusted officers can leave and join that faction." Another sneer promised that Jhiton hadn't forgiven the lieutenant who'd done exactly that the winter before. "And perhaps, we..." Jhiton gripped Vorik's shoulder. "Perhaps we have recently had a falling out."

"It's against the stormer code to fall out with the brother who raised you after your father died."

Jhiton smiled sadly and turned the grip into a friendly pat before releasing Vorik. "Had he not been weakened from a lack of food during the famine year, he wouldn't have fallen so easily to disease. Even the dragons suffered that winter."

"I well remember being hungry."

"Our people are *often* hungry. Think of gardener root cellars stuffed with apples and carrots as you befriend the princess and win her trust."

Vorik couldn't manage a faithful smile at the thought. He wished farms and orchards were easier to start and maintain elsewhere in the world, but even in the areas where the soil was hospitable enough, deadly predators sprang at anyone who attempted to set up agriculture, and pest animals and insects razed the crops, as hungry as humans for food on the harsh continents. Only the Garden Kingdom's islands were protected enough and in a suitable enough climate to foster lush farms and orchards. It didn't hurt that the earth god had supposedly added enriching magic to the soil before leaving the mortal world, a reparation to humanity for letting the mad storm god unleash his deadly creations.

"It is through shared struggles and overcoming adversity that bonds are forged." Jhiton nodded to himself. "I'll help convince her that you and I have had a falling out."

"How?"

"Keep your sword and bow at the ready."

Vorik sighed, imagining his brother sending fake assassins—or maybe *real* assassins—after the princess. After both of them. Might he even tell Captain Lesva that Vorik had joined the Freeborn Faction and was to be dealt with? The notion was troubling, but the thought of battles didn't bother Vorik as much as something else.

"I don't care to lie even to enemies," Vorik said, aware of his brother's intent gaze upon him.

Jhiton hadn't yet made this a direct order. Thus far, it felt more like they were brainstorming a possible plan. That made Vorik feel he might have leeway to suggest something else. But what else might work? If Lieutenant Mavus and the rest of the spies hadn't learned the locations of the other shielders, who but the only remaining direct Moonmark heir would know?

"It isn't honorable," Vorik added quietly.

"I know. I once felt the same as you about honor, but, whether for good or ill, desperation allows a man to bend his compliance to the rider code. I've had visions about our people and the future. The world is changing, the winters growing longer and harsher, the summers drier. A famine year, like the one that took our father, will come again. Many more times. We must do this for the future of our people." Jhiton softened his voice, the words barely audible over the roar of the sea. "We must do it for the memory of Jebrosh, for all the other children in the tribes and the survival of our people."

Vorik closed his eyes. "Are you making this an order?"

"I must, Captain. Find the princess, win her trust, and get her to tell you the locations of the shielders. You needn't destroy any of them yourself—she would find that suspicious and not fall for it more than once. Just find out where they are. I'll send in people afterward to handle the destruction."

"And if I fail?" Vorik would do what he was ordered, as he always did, but he doubted it would be as easy to *win the trust* of the princess. A handsome smile could only get a man so far with a woman.

"Then Captain Lesva can try her idea. One way or another, we *will* complete this mission. We'll change the future of our people forever." Jhiton's eyes narrowed. "Agreed?"

Vorik nodded. "Yes, General."

4

When Syla woke from unconsciousness, her head pounded, and she didn't want to open her eyes. But she was swaying back and forth in someone's arms and worried she'd been captured. When she pried her lids open, the blurry view wasn't illuminating. Smoldering fires provided ambient light, and she could tell she was outside, but it took her a long moment to make out that she was staring at the side of someone's thick neck.

"Sergeant Fel?" she whispered, *hoping* that was who had her.

"Yes," he said, a hint of relief in the single bass note.

Thank the sun and moon gods.

"I'm glad it's you." Syla peered uselessly around, the looming shapes of buildings impossible to identify. "Are we going..."

Home, she wanted to say, but the memory of all that had happened came crashing back to her. The castle wouldn't feel like home anymore. And Moon Watch Temple? Had it made it through the attack? Were her friends and colleagues there safe?

"We're almost to the castle," Fel said.

"The temple might be a better spot." She thought of her spare spectacles in her room there and touched her face, though she already knew she wasn't wearing the broken ones. "If you need more healing—"

"I'm fine. *You* were the one I was worried about when I woke up with you collapsed on top of me."

"Sorry about that. I, uhm, got tired."

"You healed me. Magically." His tone was hard to read.

Did he disapprove? Or feel dread knowing her magic might bind him to her for some time going forward?

"I did," Syla said. "I'm sorry I couldn't get your permission first. You were unconscious, and I needed you. I couldn't see, and there were men scrounging for valuables, and— Wait, what happened to them?"

"*I* happened to them. When I woke up. They were patting us down, looking for items to steal. I knocked their asses into the street, left them bloody, and didn't care in the least that they were Kingdom subjects."

"I… found the thought of them looting distasteful as well."

"Yes." Fel shifted his grip on her, balancing her briefly in the crook of one of his big arms, and she tightened her grasp around his shoulders while he drew something out of his pocket. "Here. These look like they were stepped on by a dragon, but I'm sure you need them."

Syla held out a hand, and Fel pressed her bent spectacles frame into it. Unfortunately, the lenses were as broken now as they had been before and would do her no good.

"Thank you, but I'm going to need another pair. They're at the temple. Can we—"

"It's gone," he said grimly.

"Gone?"

"Flattened."

"Flattened," Syla mouthed. "But… the stormers honor the same gods we do. To destroy a place of healing…"

"A dragon did it. I don't know if it had a rider, but those scaled monsters don't care about our gods. They don't even honor the mad storm god who created them and all the other unnatural beasts in the world."

"No."

Syla slumped against his chest, not trying to put the spectacles on. With the lenses broken, what was the point?

"There were injured and ill in there recovering," she whispered. "And my colleagues were there. I'd *just* seen them not hours before this started. Larvee brought honeyberry streusel in for us today, and we were sharing it for an afternoon snack." The words sounded inane coming out, but just that afternoon everything had been *normal.* "I showed her an old foraging map from my collection that points out the location of some of the best wild berry patches and bogs in the Kingdom."

How had everything fallen apart so quickly? Had any of her friends escaped the destruction? Since most healers lived and worked in the temple... they would likely have been present for the attack. It was only chance that she'd neither been at the castle nor in the temple. No, not chance. Her dillydallying because she hadn't wanted to attend a family gathering. If she had been at that dinner on time, the way she was meant to have been...

A hiccup of emotion came out, sobs threatening. Fel turned his head toward her.

"Sorry," Syla whispered, trying to swallow down her grief. She wiped her eyes. Now, more than ever, she needed to hold herself together. She was alive, even if she shouldn't be, and that meant she had duties. "This is all just so awful."

"It's outrageous," Fel said. "This never should have happened."

"No."

"The dragons are monsters."

"So are the *riders.*" Syla thought of that captain they'd seen. "They're the ones who were behind this. They had to be. A *dragon* couldn't have gotten through the barrier and somehow sabotaged the shielder."

"Agreed." Fel nodded toward the route ahead.

In the blurry dark, Syla couldn't see much, only that they were climbing the road that led up the bluff to the castle.

"I think I can walk," she said as the route steepened and the sergeant's pace slowed. She sensed more than saw the tautness of his muscles and clenching of his jaw. Though she'd mended some of his wounds, he ought to be resting in bed, not carrying her.

"You are injured."

"Not badly. I just passed out." Deciding that sounded pathetic, Syla added, "Due to the effort required from using my magic."

"From healing *me*."

"You were the focus of my magic, yes."

"I will carry you. As far as you need me to." Was that his loyalty as a bodyguard speaking? Or some compulsion he felt after being healed?

Syla didn't ask. If it was the latter, she didn't want to know.

"Just to my bedroom in the keep, please, to find an old pair of spectacles." By the time they reached it, she should have recovered enough to stand on her own and convince him she didn't need to be toted around.

Fel looked up, seeing something in the dark sky that she couldn't. A dragon flying high overhead?

"I'll take you there," he said, "but unless the Royal Protectors have restored order, we dare not stay long. I've seen surprisingly few Kingdom enforcers in the streets, and those looters weren't the only people taking advantage of the chaos. I spotted a couple of fleet ships in the harbor, the military helping put out fires, but they looked busy with that and watching for more attacks. I've glimpsed dragons now and then, not only over the city but farther inland. Hunting or lighting homesteads on fire. Who knows?"

"Did they have riders? Do you think the stormers will attack again? Is there..." Syla's throat tightened, and she had to once more blink away tears. "How much of the city and castle are *left* to attack?"

"I haven't seen much more than you have, but not all neighborhoods were damaged. The castle and areas around it were most directly targeted." Grim, Fel lowered his voice to add, "The castle especially."

Syla, remembering the way the dragon-rider captain had focused on her birthmark, didn't need to ask why. "Do you think the stormers will be back to occupy the island? Was this just a raid or... part of a larger plan?"

"I don't know, but their people have never been populous. A lot of them die because of the dangers of the world out there. It's unlikely they have the numbers to occupy the Kingdom, even an island."

Syla believed the various stormer tribes, if they were all working together, could field more people than he'd suggested, but she didn't argue. He had far more experience when it came to military matters. Whether it had been a raid or invasion, the results were the same. Her people had been decimated.

"We'll have to find and join the Royal Protectors to ensure you're properly guarded going forward," Fel added.

Syla rubbed her face. That made sense, but... "What about the shielder? If it can be fixed... we should figure out how."

"Do you know where it is?"

She started to answer but hesitated. Many years ago, when her mother and father had shown her and her siblings the locations of all the sky shielders in the Kingdom, they'd sworn them to secrecy. More than that, Syla and her siblings had needed to promise that they wouldn't reveal those locations to anyone, even under duress of torture. At the time, she'd been twelve and laughed away the notion that anyone would bother torturing her. Now... now it was all far too real.

"As your mother's daughter, you should," Fel added, "at least according to the legends. The locations and how to use the devices are supposed to be passed down to those in line to inherit the throne and protect the Kingdom."

"I know where they are." Whether her mother would approve or not, Syla didn't know, but she had to trust Fel. Depending on what they found in the ruins of the castle, he might be the only one she had left who she *could* trust. "I've been to the ones on Castle, Harvest, and Vineyard Islands, and I had to memorize the locations of the others on maps."

"Do you have any idea how to fix a shielder that's broken? Or has been sabotaged?"

"No."

"Ah. I thought your love for heinous medical tools might hint of mechanical aptitude."

"Sorry. I just put the tools on my shelves to enjoy looking at. Also, they're fascinating, not heinous."

Fel's deeply dubious grunt aptly conveyed his opposition to that opinion.

The road leveled, and he nodded toward the dark remains of the castle wall and gatehouse ahead. With the rambling ancient structure mostly made from stone, fewer fires burned up here, and the air was clearer, smelling more of the briny sea than of smoke, but Syla didn't doubt that it was as damaged as the city. Probably more so. Even with her poor vision, she could make out huge gaps in what had been a solid wall around the courtyard, keep, barracks, and ancillary buildings inside. And was the southeast tower missing entirely? She squinted but couldn't make out the details of what had to be rubble where it had stood.

"There's nobody guarding the gate," Fel said as he walked through the entrance and looked around. "Where *is* the gate?"

Syla imagined a dragon ripping the great wrought-iron portcullis from its mount and hurling it into the harbor.

"Something for a future wreck diver to find, perhaps," she said without humor, remembering her discussion with the clerk.

Fel had to walk around huge mounds of rock and wreckage in the courtyard. The stables were completely gone. No, *flattened.*

Had the poor horses escaped? Syla hoped so. It was too dreadful to imagine them being snatched up and eaten by dragons.

And was that a body lying mangled amid the rubble? She couldn't tell. Maybe she should be thankful that her spectacles were broken.

"I don't see many wounded among the dead," Fel said. "The dragons were either very thorough, or people escaped into the city or the tunnels under the castle. But if they did... I would have expected them to come out by now." He looked down at something.

Another body? Though the sea breeze mostly kept Syla from smelling the odors of carnage and death, she caught a whiff of it for a moment, and her stomach twisted.

Fel glanced at her and moved quickly past the spot. "We'll check the tunnels while we're here. It's possible people escaped down there but were then trapped, like we were under the roof of that shop."

"Yes." Dare she hope that her siblings were alive in the tunnels? Even her mother?

More and more, as Fel navigated around the wreckage and toward the keep where the royal family had their suites, Syla grew certain that she needed to find and fix the shielder. She didn't have mechanical aptitude, but she knew engineers. There were even some in the family who used their moon-mark magic in the field.

Her aunt Tibby came to mind. She even lived in the area. Had she survived?

Not unlike Syla, her father's sister had eschewed politics and having anything to do with governing the Kingdom, and she worked on agricultural machinery, keeping everything in order on the farms that fed the royal family and staff. Fixing magical devices left by the gods wouldn't be Aunt Tibby's specialty—since the shielders never needed repairs, that wouldn't be *anybody's* specialty—but she would know more than Syla.

Unaware of her planning, Fel circled the keep, looking for a way in. Only portions of it still stood, and Syla didn't know if her room had survived, especially if the riders had been targeting the royal family. But everyone should have been at dinner, and if the stormers had somehow known about the gathering—if they'd had a spy—they would have attacked the dining hall specifically.

Before stepping through a doorway that remained standing, Fel halted and looked back at the courtyard. Long seconds passed as he stood still, head cocked as he listened, then squinted toward the sky. He shifted Syla in his arms and set her down so he could draw his mace. He kept one hand out to support her.

Fortunately, her body had recovered enough from her healing exhaustion that she could keep her legs under her.

"Someone is nearby," Fel said quietly. "I haven't heard anyone, but I've glimpsed a few shadows moving in the courtyard."

"Staff who survived?" Syla asked. "The Royal Protectors?"

"It's possible." Why did he sound skeptical? Because allies would have called out to them?

"You think there may be spies or riders lingering?"

"Or assassins." After another look around the courtyard, Fel gripped her arm, turning to lead her into the building, intending to keep her close.

That was fine. Assassins or not, Syla needed a guide until she found her spectacles.

Screeches came from the sky, and Fel swore and released her. He spun and sprang past her to return to the doorway.

"Wyverns?" Syla guessed, having heard the smaller cousins of dragons before. But she'd never had to worry about them in the past. The shield had kept them away.

"The scaled scavengers have been circling." Crouched in the doorway with his mace, Fel peered skyward. "At least a dozen of them. They must have been drawn by the scent of death, but they'll happily kill and eat the living too."

His hand strayed to the crossbow strapped to his back, but maybe he didn't think its quarrels would be sufficient against scaled enemies. He stuck with the hefty mace.

"We'll be safe inside, won't we?" Syla rested a hand on the stone wall. "They're too big to come through doorways, right?"

"I wouldn't bet on that, but better inside than out." Fel pointed his mace toward something.

One of the wyverns landing on the courtyard wall? All Syla could glimpse was blurry movement.

"As much as I'd like to drive them away so they can't harass the dead, I don't have any way to do that. Their scales are as armored as those of dragons, and they're hard to kill." Fel's grim voice lowered as he glanced back at her and added, "Everything that survives in the wilds outside of the shields is."

"A reason for us to get the shielder working again." Syla lifted her chin and waved for him to guide her to her room.

Movement in the courtyard—something landing on the ground—made Fel turn away from her again. But the wyvern, if that was what it was, had found something to occupy it.

Fel lifted a hand, as if to shut out the death and danger of the courtyard, but the door was gone. Ripped from its hinges. If it lay somewhere nearby, Syla couldn't see it.

Fel grunted and pushed something heavy in front of the doorway—one of the marble pedestals she remembered from the hallway?—to partially block the entrance. That done, he turned and guided her down the hall.

The sounds of flesh being torn from bone followed them and

horrified her. She'd known the staff all her life. If they and possibly even her kin were part of the wyverns' feast...

Dear departed gods, she wanted to throw up.

"There were more wyverns landing," Fel said quietly as they moved deeper into the keep. "We may have trouble leaving."

"Let's deal with one thing at a time." The words came out sounding calm and reasonable, but Syla almost felt as if someone else had spoken them. Someone less numb and horrified.

Fel nodded and, when they reached an intersection, turned to lead her toward the royal suites. Now and then, he glanced down at rubble or maybe more bodies of the slain. Everything remained dark and blurry to Syla, and, for the first time in her life, she was relieved she couldn't see better.

Despite her attempts to focus on what she needed to do, tears trailed down her cheeks as they walked, and her chest tightened with the need to break down and sob. She didn't allow herself to but couldn't keep from stumbling often. Each time, Fel was quick to steady her. What would she have done without him?

"How much can you see without your spectacles?" Fel asked after guiding her over a pile of stone half-covered by a smoldering tapestry that had fallen onto it.

"Very little."

"The gods may have blessed you by taking away your eyesight tonight," he said, maneuvering her past another obstacle.

A body that time, she feared.

"I was just thinking that," she murmured.

"That one was stabbed. There must have been riders or other enemy agents inside the keep." Fel gazed down a hallway and didn't suggest that some of those enemies might remain, waiting to pounce on survivors. They both understood that without words.

As they neared the queen's suite, an enormous pile of wood and stone from a collapsed ceiling blocked them. Fel found another route, leading Syla past a window, the shutters torn free, the sounds of screeches and squabbling entering from the courtyard. The wyverns fighting over who got what? When more ripping and tearing sounds followed, Syla stumbled a few more steps, then threw up.

This was too awful. She didn't know if she could go on.

Fel rested a hand on her back. "That's your room up there, isn't it? The way is clear."

Syla gripped her stomach, gulped in air that she wished were fresher, and managed to continue on. When they entered her old bedroom, it was almost laughable how undamaged it was. Maybe because she hadn't lived there for years, no enemy had thought to target it.

Though she'd rarely spent time in the room the past ten years, she knew it well enough to find her way around without a guide. The ornaments and tools of her various childhood collections hadn't even been knocked off the shelves.

"I'll find a lantern," Fel said.

Outside, full darkness had fallen, but Syla didn't have trouble locating the cabinet where she'd tucked her old pairs of spectacles.

"There's one on that shelf by the door." Syla trusted her family hadn't come into the room and moved things around in her absence.

"Found it. I'll only put up a small light." Fel covered the window before doing so, maybe worried about the wyverns. Or... whoever or whatever he'd glimpsed earlier, when the shadows had been stirring.

Syla found her spectacles and, despite Fel's suggestion that the gods had been sparing her from the details of the carnage by removing her eyesight, put them on with vast relief. Not being able to see, especially when she was in such a vulnerable position, was awful.

Her room and Fel became clear with only a slight blur to the hallway behind him. He had set the lantern on the desk and stood in the doorway, keeping an eye on that hallway.

"Thank you for your help, Sergeant." Syla waved to indicate she meant for everything.

Fel nodded solemnly at her. His stomach rumbled, reminding her of the dinner hour they'd missed.

Thanks to her queasiness, she had no desire to eat, but with all the rubble piles blocking routes, it might take hours to reach and then study the shielder. And if it was destroyed and they had to go to another island to find another? Syla shook her head, hoping the rest of the Kingdom had been spared, that this hadn't been a concerted attack with multiple sky shields failing at once.

"Let me grab a few things." Syla plucked a bag out of one of the armoires. "Then we'll see if we can find some food to take, and I'll be ready to go."

"From the outside, the kitchen looked badly damaged. Part of the roof came down. At the least, the doors are blocked."

"Oh."

Fel waved toward the courtyard, the wyverns. "Once we're somewhere safe, I'll find provisions."

Somewhere safe. Where on Castle Island would that be?

As she packed, her scattered mind thinking it practical to tuck in such items as an antique venom extractor and hernia tool, Syla shared her thoughts about checking the farm outside the capital where her aunt lived and worked.

"Your aunt?" Fel asked, as if he were trying to place her.

"Yes. She looks like me except older." Syla pointed at her spectacles. "She's moon-marked but uses her power as an engineer. She'll be perfect to help with the shielder."

"I've seen her around the castle, but doesn't she build... tractors?"

"Her specialty is agricultural engineering, yes, but she went to school and apprenticed for years, studying widely before going to work on the royal farm."

"So... yes to tractors?"

"*Magical* tractors, Sergeant. Supernaturally sturdy."

Judging by the twist to Fel's lips, he didn't think the maker of such implements would be useful in their quest. That was only because he didn't know Tibby well. She was versatile.

The challenge would be to get to her.

Syla glanced toward the shuttered window. Would they be able to escape through the courtyard past the wyverns? Or—her gut clenched—would they need to wait until the creatures feasted their fill and left? The idea of having to walk past the half-eaten bodies of people she'd known threatened to make her throw up again.

"We'll check the shielder first," she decided.

If all they had to do was flip a switch to turn it back on, they wouldn't need Aunt Tibby.

While packing, Syla found two more old pairs of spectacles and tucked them away. Her corrections hadn't needed to be as strong back then, so there would be more blurriness, but anything was better than her horrible vision of minutes before. On a whim, she tucked a couple of treasures into the pack, including her favorite book on the history of the Kingdom and how it had been established. Unlike the things she read as an adult, it had beautiful painted pictures and maps of current places and those that had once been. Even though she largely had the information memorized, she'd always loved that book.

Maybe it was silly to take so much with her—since the riders had achieved their objective, they wouldn't likely return to further raze the castle—but who knew what other scavengers would come along before order could be established? *If* there was anyone left to establish order. She couldn't help but wonder since they hadn't encountered anyone from the fleet or Royal Protectors yet. Of course, if the wyverns had been circling all along, she could hardly blame the military for waiting.

She paused at a fist-sized, red glass figurine of a dragon. Given the day she'd had, she ought not to want anything to remind her of their kind, but her father had left her the antique. Even though the great scaled beasts were a constant threat to the Kingdom, he'd always found them beautiful. Once, he'd taken her to Eyrie Point, a rock formation perched above a beach miles east of the capital, where dragons fished just outside of the shield. Breathtaking, he'd called them as they'd soared and dove. Back then, she'd also admired them and found the idea of riding one wondrous, but now...

Her fingers clenched, and she almost threw the ornament across the room. But she couldn't destroy something that had been special to her father. Besides, it had some magic about it. He'd never told her what it did—maybe he hadn't known himself—but through her moon-mark, she'd always sensed its power.

"Maybe it'll help somehow." That was wishful thinking, but Syla tucked it into the bag with her other belongings.

"Lighter than books, anyway." Fel had watched her pack.

"Books are wondrous founts of knowledge that can either guide us in the world or enrich our imaginations while allowing us to visit other realms." She wished she could take more of her old tomes; in the coming days, she would need an escape for her mind. She had no doubt.

Fel grunted. "They're heavy."

"They're worth their weight in gold, diamonds, and sapphires."

"That'll soothe my mind when I end up carrying your pack."

"You won't have to do that." Syla adjusted the straps and snugged the bag on her back. That old book *was* a touch heavy, but she lifted her chin, determined to carry her own load.

"Unless you heal someone and faint?"

"Well." Syla noticed he was leaning so that one of his legs took more weight than the other. She might have healed his acute wounds, but she remembered his earlier strains and grimaces. He endured a number of chronic issues. "Maybe you could find a horse with a cart to haul me and my books around."

Fel took the lantern and stepped into the hall. "Sergeant Horiks, the man who drilled all the bodyguard rules into me, said we must do what we can to ensure a royal's comfort while simultaneously prioritizing their safety. *Carriages* were mentioned, not carts."

"You can throw me in a sledge fashioned from whale bones," she said, following him, "as long as I can keep my book."

He glanced over his shoulder. "You're quirkier than your siblings."

Yes, and she'd never fit in with them. Part of it had been the seven-year age gap between her and the next youngest of her siblings, but part had been that they'd been athletic, outgoing, and at ease in their bodies. She'd always been the opposite: awkward, introverted, and more at home in a library with her books.

"Is that why you don't call me *Your Highness*?" Syla had always heard him use that deference when he'd been Nyvia's bodyguard, but she was heir to the throne and naturally exuded authority.

Was or *had been*? The unsettling reminder made her shoulders slump. What she packed was hardly important in light of everything else.

"No. That's because I'm almost retired, and I don't care that much about pomp and propriety anymore." Fel hurried her past a body, maybe realizing she could see them now.

Doing her best to avoid looking down, Syla was relieved when the doorway to the courtyard came into view. Until she spotted the green wings of a wyvern feasting on the dead.

She groaned and halted. The creature lifted its reptilian head, slitted yellow eyes turning to peer through the half-blocked doorway. The nostrils at the end of its long snout twitched.

"Is there another way into the underground tunnels?" Fel asked. "I know of the routes from the queen's suite and the stables, but neither are easy to reach now. The tunnels would be our best chance for escaping."

And finding the shielder. Fel didn't yet know it, but the hidden doorway to its chamber lay under the castle.

"There's an access door in Serk's suite," she said, naming her oldest brother.

"The way to that was blocked too."

"I know."

The wyvern cocked its head, slitted yellow eyes focused on them. Those eyes looked hungry. Clearly, the beast hadn't yet eaten its fill and wanted more.

Though wyverns weren't much taller than men when they stood on the ground, with wingspans of ten or twelve feet, they were lean and powerful with dense muscles under their scales. The fangs weren't quite as long as those of dragons, but that didn't mean they weren't deadly. And this one stepped toward them, looking far too interested in devouring them.

Fel held up a hand, though they'd both already stopped. "That's what I was worried about."

"That we'll have to wait for them to go away?"

The wyvern took another step, wings flexing, nostrils twitching again.

"That they *won't* go away," Fel said, "and they'll prefer fresh prey over the dead."

The wyvern crouched and sprang, arrowing straight for the doorway. For them.

5

"STAY BACK," FEL BARKED AS HE LEAPED INTO THE DOORWAY TO MEET the wyvern.

Syla's earlier belief that the scaled creature wouldn't fit through proved wrong. It simply tucked its wings against its body. But the pedestal Fel had pushed into the doorway impeded it.

When he swung his mace toward its snout, the wyvern accepted the powerful blow as though a mosquito had stung it and nothing more. Long fangs leering, it snapped its jaws at Fel.

Syla gasped, certain the wyvern would wrap its deadly maw around his shoulder—or his neck. But Fel was more agile than his age suggested. He leaped lightly back, and the jaws snapped at empty air inches from his face.

Again, he swung his mace, smashing the metal head between the creature's yellow eyes. That was enough to make the wyvern jerk back, but it didn't retreat. Muscles bunching, it lunged for the doorway again. The pedestal skidded back and toppled to the tile floor with a thunderous *thunk*.

Feeling foolish for having grabbed tchotchkes instead of a

weapon, Syla looked around for something she could use to help Fel. Or… in case he went down… she needed to defend herself.

"Not that I kept *weapons* in my room," she muttered, spotting nothing useful in the wreckage.

Mace met fangs with a loud clink. Again, the wyvern backed away, but, again, it didn't retreat. It screeched, the piercing sound supernaturally loud, and another winged predator landed beside it. Damn it.

"I'm a healer, not a warrior," Syla snarled in frustration.

She lifted her pack, thinking she might throw *it*. If Fel had complained about the heft of the book, maybe a wyvern would too—if she could smack it in an eye.

"Back up." Fel kept his mace raised to defend their retreat. "We're going to have to go another way."

Though she doubted there *was* another way clear, Syla nodded and crept backward. If that mace scarcely bothered the wyverns, her book would do even less.

As the two creatures advanced through the doorway, a massive splitting of stone came from behind Syla and Fel.

Debris rained down, and Syla halted, gaping as a huge chunk of the ceiling over the hall was torn free, revealing the night sky above—and another great scaled beast.

At first, she believed it a third wyvern, but it was too large. A huge green dragon flexed its neck and flung the section of roof aside.

Fel swore, pushing Syla against the wall as he tried to keep his mace up toward the wyverns *and* the new threat.

The dragon roared, the sound thunderous in the night. The wyverns paused, peering at the larger creature, and didn't charge into the hallway. That was no reprieve, however, when the dragon's huge horned head swept down through the hole it had made.

Fel sprang past Syla to meet it with his mace.

"Watch out for fire!" she yelled, terrified that her only ally would be incinerated.

When Fel swung his mace toward the dragon's scaled snout, the weapon struck, thudding against the armor-like scales, but it did even less than it had against the wyvern. Almost casually, the dragon head-butted Fel, sending the forty-year veteran tumbling away. As he rolled cursing down the hallway, he clipped Syla.

Knocked off balance, she couldn't spring away when the dragon's maw stretched toward her, more chunks of the ceiling clattering down as it encroached. Terrified, she swung her pack at their enemy. Impervious, the dragon clasped its jaws around her.

Syla screamed, expecting excruciating pain. The fanged maw did wrap around her with alarming pressure, but the beast didn't tear her to pieces or fling her away as it had done the roof.

No, it pulled her out of the hallway—out of the keep entirely—and lifted her into the air. She screamed again and clamped her hand to her face to make sure her spectacles didn't fall off.

As if *that* would matter if the dragon intended to eat her.

After flying into the air twenty or thirty feet above the keep, the dragon twisted its neck and tossed her. More terror rushed into her, and she flailed with her free hand, imagining flying all the way over the courtyard wall and off the bluff to land in the rocky sea far below.

Instead, she came down on the dragon's back with a startling thump. Someone grabbed her to keep her from bouncing off. Powerful arms manipulated her, maneuvering her into a position astride the dragon, as if she were mounted on a horse. A horse with a *very* broad back.

A rider, came the observation from the tiny part of her mind that remained capable of rational thinking. This dragon had a rider.

That did nothing to comfort her. When a strong arm wrapped

around her to keep her in place, she knew she was imprisoned, not saved.

"Greetings, Princess Syla," a ridiculously calm baritone voice said. The rider.

She squirmed in his grip, though the last thing she wanted was to fall off and break her neck. Through the distorted corners of her spectacles, she could make out the castle courtyard far below. No, falling would *not* be good. But she couldn't let the rider take her away and abandon Fel. Those wyverns would get him—if they hadn't already.

"I got it right, didn't I?" the rider asked. "Princess Syla? I'm here to take you somewhere safe, Your Highness."

"Like where?" she demanded. "A torture chamber?"

"No, my mission is to keep you from that fate."

The dragon had been circling above the courtyard, but it banked, wings flapping to take off in another direction.

"Fel!" Syla craned her neck to look down, her hand still pressed to her spectacles.

For the first time in her life, she was flying, riding a dragon, but there was nothing delightful about it. And wyverns lurked all over the courtyard below, blood dripping from their talons and fangs. They'd paused to eye the dragon warily, but its arrival hadn't scared them away.

"Is that the soldier?" the rider asked.

"My bodyguard. He's in danger." Syla thrust her hand toward the ruined castle below. She couldn't see Fel, who was presumably still in that hallway, but she *could* see the two wyverns that had been attacking them. One disappeared into the building. "Help him!" she urged, though she doubted her captor would.

If anything, he had to be pleased that she was alone and utterly defenseless. Her bag had fallen, so she didn't even have her book to throw at him.

"Very well," the rider surprised her by saying.

The dragon glanced back. It had been angling out toward the sea, but the rider must have communicated with it—she'd read about the telepathic link that dragons and riders shared—for the creature banked again, and it flew back toward the courtyard.

The wyverns must have believed the dragon intended to leave them to their business because they weren't looking up at its approach. Not until the great green creature soared low, wings stretched out in a glide that took it over the ruined courtyard wall to skim the ground. It snapped up a wyvern that had been about to enter the keep.

Fangs crunched audibly through scale and bone, and the smaller beast screeched. The wyvern twisted and tried to claw at its captor, but the dragon had it around the back of the neck, and the smaller beast couldn't reach it with talons or fangs. More crunches sounded, more bone breaking. The vertebrae in the wyvern's neck?

As if its prey weighed nothing, the dragon flung it over the wall and toward the edge of the bluff, as Syla had earlier imagined it would throw *her*. Limp, with its neck broken, the creature tumbled out of view, already dead.

The remaining wyverns, having realized the threat, took to the air. Their chaotic flight reminded Syla of when she'd seen someone's wolfhound barking and running down the beach, seagulls scattering. The dragon roared instead of barking and sprang for another wyvern, one that had lingered, trying to take its meal with it.

Syla, still horrified that the scavengers were eating the remains of her people, looked toward the castle instead of at the body that dropped. She tried to spot Fel near the doorway, but the shadows were deep in that hallway. The lantern he'd carried had gone out. Even the courtyard was dim, with no moon visible through the clouds and few fires remaining burning, so she couldn't make out much. Nor could she see the face of her rider when she glanced back at him.

The dragon finished the second wyvern it had caught, breaking its neck, the same as the other, and flung it aside. Briefly, their mount landed, but only, Syla sensed, so that it could bunch its muscles to spring into the air again.

"Fel!" Syla yelled, afraid they'd been too late to help him—and that her captor would take her away before she could learn his fate. "We can't go yet."

She glanced back. What could she say to persuade someone who was undoubtedly her enemy?

"*He* is not the one I was sent to protect," the rider said.

"I'm not going without him. He's been my bodyguard for—" She stopped herself from uttering the truth, that Fel had only been assigned to her two weeks earlier. "I've known him for *years*." That was true. She'd seen Fel often when visiting the castle.

"The wyverns are gone. He'll survive if we leave him here."

"He's got my pack and my *book*," she said, trying another tactic, but what would a history tome matter to a dragon rider? Those people didn't even *read*.

"Those items sound precious to you."

"*Extremely* precious. The pack has a first-aid kit inside." Technically, it had a random collection of decorative medical items she'd grabbed from around her room, but she *had* thought to include bandages and suture thread. "Oh, and there's a pretty dragon artifact inside. I'll give it to you if you pick up my sergeant." Maybe it was a silly thing to mention, but she didn't have much that a rider might value. What else could she bribe him with?

"What color is it?" he surprised her by asking.

"Red."

"Oh, *red*." The rider patted his dragon on the scales.

What, did that have some significance to him? To *them*?

"Like your *girlfriend*, Agrevlari," he added.

A rumble reverberated through the dragon—Syla could feel it against her thighs. Had that been a growl or a sigh? Did dragons *sigh*?

The rider patted him again. "Check on the old fellow, will you?"

Only when the dragon flew back toward the courtyard did Syla realize the words had been for their scaled mount. Maybe the riders didn't always use telepathy with them.

She pointed toward the doorway, and dragon and rider looked in that direction. Surprisingly, Fel stepped out from another half-crumbled structure in the courtyard. He'd grabbed her pack but dropped it by the door while he focused on the dragon. He'd traded his mace for his crossbow and had it loaded. Even as the rider turned, catching the movement out of the corner of his eye, Fel fired a quarrel.

The dragon's head whipped around, and he spewed fire at the projectile as it streaked toward them. The rider also released Syla to draw a sword, as if he'd planned to deflect the quarrel. Maybe he could have. Syla didn't wait around to ask. She used her brief moment of freedom to jump off the dragon's back.

As the wind whistled past, her shoulder bumped against a scaled flank, and she pitched off-balance toward the ground. She almost shrieked, terrified she'd made a mistake, that she would break every bone in her body. When she landed, she hit hard, coming down on her side and hitting her hip so badly that it jolted her to the core and sent her spectacles flying.

Her fear of losing them overrode the blast of pain that made her want to curl up and cry. Instead, she forced herself to her hands and knees so she could pat around for the spectacles. She couldn't lose *another* pair.

An inferno of blurry orange burned through the air to her left, and she flinched, certain the dragon had decided to torch her. In the blast of light, its green outline was visible even to her poor vision. She realized it faced the opposite side of the courtyard. Toward Fel.

He had to be firing again, buying her time to escape. Determined to use it, she patted around at twice the speed. Where had her spectacles landed? Her knuckles grazed hard rock, drawing blood, and she swore.

"Princess Syla," the rider called from the dragon's back. "That was not necessary. We're here to protect you. I—"

When he broke off abruptly, she hoped he was dodging more crossbow quarrels. No, she hoped he was *failing* to dodge them.

"That's Captain Vorik," Fel yelled from across the courtyard.

The words prompted fresh fear. Wasn't that the officer that Fel had identified earlier? The one whose dragon had smashed the roof onto them?

"You tried to kill us!" she yelled.

A thump nearby made the ground shiver. Had that dragon slammed its tail down *again*?

"Find cover!" Fel yelled.

No kidding.

Syla brushed something small that moved at her touch. Her spectacles. She snatched them up and hooked them over her ears, relieved when the world came back into focus. The lenses weren't cracked. Thank the earth god.

Something big whistled through the air above her. The dragon's tail. The creature was swinging about to face its attacker. Fel had left the cover of a building to run—limp—across the courtyard.

"Look out!" Syla knew he was trying to lead the dragon away from her, but he would get himself killed doing it like that.

"Find cover!" he roared to her again.

He probably hadn't seen that she'd lost her spectacles and that was what had delayed her. Even though she wanted to linger and help him, she didn't have a weapon. The dragon's muscles bunched as it prepared to spring, its tail out rigid.

Surprisingly, the rider—the *captain*—had lowered his sword and patted the creature's side. The gesture seemed more designed to calm the dragon than propel it into motion. As Fel ran away, dodging behind a rubble pile before reaching the gatehouse and crouching there under partial cover, their scaled enemy didn't spring to follow.

Syla didn't know why they were hesitating to finish off Fel, but she obeyed his order and ran toward a doorway that led to the throne room, theater, and the council chambers. Half the building had collapsed, but she remembered there was a tunnel entrance in the back. Maybe she could reach it. If nothing else, she could hide among the wreckage. Unlike the wyverns, a dragon wouldn't fit through the doorway.

Of course, its *rider* could.

As she darted inside, Syla glanced back. Though the dragon remained facing Fel, tail twitching as if it longed to chase after him, the rider had turned to gaze after her. He hadn't yet leaped off to give chase. As she ran deeper inside, she hoped he wouldn't.

She needed a reprieve. No, she amended as she skirted a body. She needed for this day to have never happened. Unfortunately, even the gods could not turn back time.

6

As she sought an entrance into the tunnels beneath the castle, Syla passed two hallways blocked by rockfalls—*roof* falls—and climbed over a pile of wood, tile, and stone higher than her head. She glanced through a hole in the ceiling, half-expecting to spot that dragon peering down at her. Every time a noise came from somewhere nearby, she spun in fear, certain its rider was after her.

Its very confusing rider.

Why had Captain Vorik claimed to have come to help her—to *protect* her, he'd said—when his people had been responsible for the horrible attack? And he'd surely participated. He'd *been* there, smashing a roof onto her head. Had he thought she wouldn't recognize him?

True, she hadn't in the dark, when she'd been in front of him on the dragon, but she would have eventually, even if Fel hadn't warned her. When they had come face to face. And that dragon? In better light, she wouldn't have missed recognizing the color of his green scales, the reptilian coldness of his eyes.

As she approached what had once been the royal theater, a

place the family had gathered to be entertained by traveling and local troupes, she feared it wouldn't remain standing. Surprisingly, however, the arched ceiling had held up under the attack. The tall windows were broken, with shattered glass littering the flagstone floors and rugs, but the rows of seats and the stage remained intact, barely disturbed.

A *thunk* sounded behind her, followed by softer clunks. A rock in the hallway she'd passed through shifting and falling off a rubble pile?

Syla jumped into the theater, putting her back to the wall near the door. Silence followed the noise, and she could hear and feel her heart hammering. Was it the rider following her?

After a moment of stillness, she heard something else. Boots on the floor, someone walking. Someone with a heavy, uneven gait.

"Fel?" she whispered.

"Yes, Your Highness." Weariness and pain in his voice made her wince in sympathy.

When Fel stepped into the doorway and held her pack out to her, his sooty face was bruised, his shaven head spattered with blood, and he leaned right, favoring the other leg. Emotions constricted her throat, but she didn't want him to think her weak by crying, nor did she believe the gruff bodyguard wanted a display of sympathy.

She swallowed and said, "I thought you didn't use *Your Highness* with me because your upcoming retirement has made you worry less about pomp?"

Fel slumped against the doorjamb. "Something tells me I'm not going to get to retire for a while."

"Maybe we can get the shielder repaired in the next... seventeen days, was it?"

"Even if we're able to do that, there'll be a lot of rebuilding to do." Fel looked out into the theater. "And the succession and who's going to be in charge... Someone's going to have to figure that out."

His gaze settled on her.

"It won't be me. And I'm not deciding who it will be either. But the shielder... I can help figure that out. But first, are you all right? You need healing again. I can tell."

"Not now. The captain and his dragon are loitering in the area, probably doing whatever they came to do. *Spying* probably."

"I thought the rider might come inside after me."

"The last I saw, they took to the air, but they didn't head out to sea. Instead, they flew inland. Off to frolic over the countryside and steal food or raze villages or who knows what."

"How did you escape from them in the courtyard?"

"The dragon wanted to kill me, but Captain Vorik seemed... I'm not sure. They tried to kill us earlier, so I don't know why he didn't finish me off. I can guess why they didn't kill *you*."

"Oh? Why?"

"You know where the shielders are. Vorik must have intended to take you back to his people to question. To *interrogate*."

"I... Yes, that makes sense, but his people must already *know* where the Castle Island shielder is. Or was." Since Fel didn't want healing at that moment, Syla headed up the aisle toward the stage. It was time to see if the shielder remained under the castle and was repairable.

"Agreed." Fel trailed after her, noticeably trying not to limp.

Oh, Sergeant. She wished she could send him to the temple for a comfortable bed in a quiet room looking out over the sea. But the temple was gone. Her *life* was gone.

Pushing the thought aside, Syla climbed the steps to the stage. She couldn't feel sorry for herself. She was alive and others weren't. Still, a small, self-pitying part of her wondered if they were luckier than she. Whatever her future held, it wouldn't be a life of ease.

"One worry at a time." Syla knelt by a large piece of equipment that could swing thespians around in the air so they appeared to the audience to fly. It had been years since her parents—yes, her father had still been alive then—had shown her the location of this entrance, and she had to pat all around before finding a button.

Fel stood guard, his hand on his mace as he watched the doorways. Judging by his expression, he believed the captain wasn't frolicking over the countryside, as he'd suggested, but would return and try again to capture her.

Once Syla depressed the button, the equipment rolled to the side on oiled hinges and revealed a square trapdoor in the wooden floor of the stage. She opened it easily and peered into the empty space under the stage as well as at another trapdoor in the flagstone below.

After she swung down, shadows cloaking her, she knelt on it. Flush with the floor, this door didn't have a handle. She pressed her fingers against the cool stone, willing her magic into it, much as when she sent healing power into a patient. The trapdoor, as old as the castle itself, glowed around the edges, its ancient magic responding to hers. A faint click sounded, and a handle made of a glowing tendril appeared.

She gripped it and lifted. Since the trapdoor was made from the same flagstones as the floor, it should have been heavy, but, for her, it rose with scarcely any effort.

Below, stone stairs led deep into the ground, more than twenty feet down, to one of the ancient tunnels underneath the castle. There were sconces on the walls, but nobody had lit the torches. She looked bleakly at them, afraid that meant what she'd feared. None of her family, or even the closely trusted staff who tended them and knew some of the castle's secrets, had made it into the escape tunnels. At least not the ones near the theater. Perhaps elsewhere...

"Let's hope."

"Princess Syla?" Fel knelt on the stage beside the first trapdoor. "Do you need light?"

"Yes."

"Let me see what I can find."

"Thank you."

"Don't go anywhere. There may be dangers down there."

Syla hesitated, then nodded. It was wise advice. Besides, where would she go in the dark?

Not far, but she did creep down the stairs, intending to wait at the bottom. And to see... if anything could be seen.

The bleakness filling her at the thought that nobody had escaped was so overwhelming that she couldn't help but hope for at least *some* sign that she wasn't alone, that she wasn't the only surviving member of her family.

At the bottom of the stairs, the tunnel stretched in two directions. Down one way, a hint of light came into view, a torch or lantern burning. It was so far off that Syla suspected it near an entrance across the courtyard in one of the other buildings. In the other direction lay the stables, and Fel had mentioned that entrance was blocked off. That way was dark, regardless.

A shadow passed through the light at the end of the tunnel, and she jumped.

Had that been her eyes playing tricks on her? Or was someone else down there? And, if the latter, was it friend or foe? As much as she wanted to find living siblings or her mother, the dragon riders might be down here, some having lingered to explore.

"I can tell I'm going to need to find more of my bodyguard brethren to keep an eye on you," Fel grumbled, coming down the steps behind her with two lanterns.

"Because enemies are going to keep trying to capture and question me?"

"Because you're a pain in the ass who wanders off after agreeing to stay put."

"I didn't *wander off*. I came down the stairs. And I see you're back to eschewing pomp and propriety."

"My sore knees, feet, hips, shoulder, and everything else are making me grumpy."

"And prone to call a princess a pain in the ass?"

"Yeah, my left knee specifically suggested that." Fel handed her one of the lanterns, then, less gently than he might have, pushed her against the wall so he could step past her in the tight tunnel.

Syla smiled, not offended, not in these circumstances. Fel frowned balefully toward the distant light, then looked wistfully in the other direction, as if he would prefer to go down the dark tunnel. Maybe he, too, believed they would be more likely to run into enemies than allies down here.

"I thought I saw movement in the light that way. Just for a second. It might have been nothing though." Syla waved to her spectacles to indicate the unreliableness of her vision, though she had a feeling her *brain* rather than her eyes would be to blame if she was seeing things.

"Which way to the shielder?" Fel didn't comment on the rest.

Syla pointed toward the light.

"Naturally." He grunted and then led off in that direction, lantern in one hand and crossbow in the other. In the narrow tunnel, he had to work to keep from scraping the edge of it on the stone walls.

When they reached the light, which marked a four-way intersection, a single lantern burned in a sconce at the corner. The cross tunnels soon turned around bends, so they couldn't see far in those directions or tell if more lights might be burning. They couldn't see anyone anywhere, but Syla had the sensation of being watched.

"Do some of the staff have orders to keep lanterns burning down here?" Fel pointed at the light.

"No. There are some other tunnels above these that the family uses to get around when they don't want to be seen—"

"—or to foolishly go places without their bodyguards," Fel grumbled in a tone that suggested that had happened during his time working with Nyvia.

"Yes. Those are more often used, but, even then, nobody leaves lanterns burning all the time. Someone is down here."

"Right."

"The hidden chamber is that way." Syla pointed toward one of the tunnels that disappeared around a bend, and Fel took the lead again.

He paused when they heard a distant *clink*. The metal of a sword or other weapon hitting one of the stone walls? Syla didn't know, but it was so quiet underground that any noise stood out. It had seemed to come from the direction they were going.

Probably thinking the same, Fel loaded a quarrel in his crossbow before continuing on, the tunnel sloping downward after the bend, taking them deeper into the bluff under the castle. They were, Syla was fairly certain, heading away from the harbor and the sea. One of the tunnels at the intersection they'd passed led to an underground lagoon that always had a boat in it, one seaworthy enough for the royal family to escape in if need be. On the way back, she would look to see if the boat had been taken, if anyone had slipped away.

Fortunately, there weren't many places one could turn, so the tunnels weren't a confusing maze. Had they been, Syla would have struggled to remember the way since it had been years since her parents had shown her these passages. As it was, she could easily have missed the hidden entrance that led to the shielder. The stone door matched the tunnel wall and was set dozens of yards before the passageway ended at an ancient catacomb from a time when burials had been more common than the current day's funeral pyres. But... the door to the hidden tunnel stood open. And lights burned in that direction.

Syla stared, a feeling of ominous foreboding filling her. Maybe it was silly since she'd logically *known* someone had been down here, sabotaging the shielder, but seeing the evidence was still unnerving. Thoughts that the magic of the device had simply failed after so many centuries departed her mind.

"Whoever did it may still be down here." Fel stepped through the doorway but didn't yet continue on, instead regarding her grimly over his shoulder.

"Are you thinking again about how I'm a pain in the ass?"

"No, that I wish more of the bodyguard contingent were here so I could have someone watch you in a safe spot while I investigate."

"Oh, I see. Does that mean your knee is feeling better?" Syla smiled but lamented that he considered her to be in the way, or at least a burden that was keeping him from a greater duty.

"It's feeling dreadful, but other concerns are distracting me."

She touched her chest and raised her eyebrows.

"Exactly. Stay close."

Shoulders set, Fel continued forward.

She glanced toward the end of the passageway, the catacomb that they hadn't yet checked, again having that feeling of being watched, but what could she do? Check it out on her own? No, thank you. She hurried to catch up with Fel and his mace and crossbow.

"There's another catacomb at the end of this passage," she said, "and the shielder is—or should be—mounted in the center, placed close to protect the tombs of the first kings and queens of the Kingdom."

Fel nodded without glancing back, his attention remaining forward.

"Also, it would have taken someone with a moon-mark to open that door." Syla tilted her thumb over her shoulder, wondering if he'd seen her open the entrance under the stage.

"I figured there had to have been an insider involved," he said.

"A, uhm, *very* insider. There are only a few people who have moon-marks and also know about these tunnels." Her direct family members, essentially. She doubted even a close relation, like Aunt Tibby, who'd worked around the capital her whole life, and had visited the castle countless times, had been given the family secrets.

Fel only nodded again.

After another two dozen silent steps, they entered a circular chamber, a single lantern burning near the closest sarcophagus. It was one of twelve, the stone burial places curved to fit along the walls, elaborate statues and chiseled tablets adorning each tomb. The sarcophagi created numerous nooks where people might hide, but Syla's gaze was drawn to a woman's legs sticking out from behind the thirteenth sarcophagus, the only one in the center of the chamber. A pale blue dress was tangled around those legs, blood spattering the fabric and floor around.

Whoever it was had to be dead, and Syla rested her hand on the wall for support while mentally bracing herself for the identification. Her middle sister, Venia, favored dresses over the trousers that their warrior-trained sister, Nyvia, liked. Even though Syla hadn't spent a lot of time studying Venia's legs, her gut churned with a certainty that she couldn't logically have yet. The memory of Venia, seven years her elder, trying to teach her how to properly drink sageberry tea while testing her on the geography of the Kingdom came to mind, a day that had stuck with Syla because it had been the first that she'd memorized everything sufficiently enough to satisfy her demanding sister. Venia had rewarded her with candied walnuts from Orchard Island.

Syla rubbed her face, pushing away the memory and

reminding herself that she couldn't be distracted, not here. They weren't alone.

Fel had to have seen the body, but he hadn't yet moved. His gaze was roving around the sarcophagi—doubtless checking the nooks, though they wouldn't be able to see into all the shadowy corners until they walked toward the center of the chamber. His instincts had to be telling him that danger lurked, and Syla didn't doubt that it did. The sensation of being watched wouldn't go away.

Beyond the central sarcophagus and the body was the shielder. Sitting within its mount, the eight-foot silver orb represented the moon, including the two craters that people called eyes. Comprised of silver branches, the top and bottom of the mount stretched upward and downward, disappearing into the floor and ceiling. Supposedly, those branches not only supported the orb but were conduits for its magic, sending its power out to protect the island from all sides.

But the shielder was far different from when Syla had seen it before. The two other times she'd visited, the whole contraption had glowed silver, the orb itself emitting moon-like light. Now, it not only lay dark, but a jagged hole had been created on one side, baring its core, a tangle of angular and tube-like innards that Syla couldn't begin to make anything of. They looked more machine than magic.

"Stay here." After glancing down the tunnel behind them, Fel moved to the left. He walked slowly around the chamber to check the nooks around each sarcophagus and ensure nobody crouched among them.

Syla couldn't obey. Drawn by a need to identify the body and look more closely at the orb, she set her pack on the ground and let her feet pull her forward. She did glance toward the sarcophagi she passed, also checking for intruders, but she didn't see anyone crouching in the shadows. With the foul sabotage done, whoever had been responsible might have left hours ago.

She had to see the body even as she dreaded seeing it. For support, she rested a hand on the cold stone lid that covered the central sarcophagus, that which contained the remains of the first queen of the Garden Kingdom, a half-god, if the legends could be believed.

The woman on the floor—dear departed gods, it *was* Venia—lay on her back with her eyes open, her blonde hair arrayed wildly around her head like a dandelion gone to seed. The top half of her dress was unbuttoned, as if she'd come down here for a tryst rather than a betrayal. A gargoyle-bone-bladed dagger was thrust into her heart, though she was cut in other places, too, as if there had been a fight first. There weren't any other weapons visible, however, only the dagger that had ended her life. A rider weapon. The magic infused in gargoyle bones made them stronger than steel.

Syla closed her sister's eyes, tears springing to her own at the coldness of Venia's body. Lamenting that her sister would have to lie here on the stone floor a while longer, until a semblance of order could be restored, Syla wished she had a blanket with which to cover her. For now, all she could do was whisper one of the prayers for the dead, requesting a peaceful afterlife for Venia, protected by Venia's chosen deity, the sun god.

After that, Syla wiped her eyes and made herself look away and examine the shielder more closely, especially the dark hole in the side. Had the gargoyle-bone dagger also been the weapon that had damaged the orb?

The magic of the shielders, the artifacts crafted by the gods themselves, supposedly made them strong. *Very* strong. Legends spoke of arrows glancing off instead of penetrating. But... they weren't completely impervious, otherwise they could be on display on the various islands, not hidden away, their locations carefully guarded secrets.

Syla crept closer to the orb and lifted a hand. When she'd been guided down here by her parents, she hadn't presumed to touch the device, but maybe her magic could tell her... something helpful. Something *hopeful.* That the shielder wasn't completely destroyed and could be fixed. It looked utterly dead, with no hint of light, heat, or magical energy coming from it, but maybe...

"You're again not in the spot where I told you to stay," Fel said.

A sarcastic retort came to mind, but Syla couldn't summon the energy for it, not with her sister dead three feet away. She could only shake her head grimly as Fel joined her, and rest her hand on the unbroken side of the orb.

He watched her warily, as if afraid magical energy would hurl them across the chamber, but he didn't try to stop her. If anything, his eyebrows rose with the faintest of hope.

The orb was cool against Syla's palm, the texture grittier than she would have guessed, and she willed her magic to enter it, as if this were a patient with a broken bone she might repair. The moon-mark on her hand glowed, as if the magic would obediently do as she wished, but it didn't leave her body and flow into the orb the way it did when she healed people and animals. For good or ill, the shielder was neither.

Nonetheless, she closed her eyes and attempted to sense what her eyes couldn't see, as she did when she looked with her mind into the bodies of injured people. Was there *anything* inside that she might be capable of repairing? Or was there any hint of magic remaining? When she'd visited the chamber before, she'd been able to feel the shielder's power from across the room. No, even sooner than that. She'd sensed it as soon as that hidden doorway had opened.

But now...

"Nothing," she murmured.

"It's completely destroyed?" Fel guessed.

"I..." As she withdrew her senses, pulling her magic back into her body, the faintest of sensations brushed against her awareness. Like a tiny hint of plant growth on a prairie that had been swept by wildfire. For a brief moment, she sensed magic. Power. Something alive. But when she tried to examine it more closely, it retreated. Had she imagined it? Or was she simply not attuned to this kind of power? "I'm not sure. We need an expert."

"*Are* there experts on the shielders? The legends don't suggest they break or need any kind of maintenance."

"I don't think they do, but there's Aunt Tibby."

"The tractor engineer."

"She's moon-marked."

"I'm sure the tractors like divine attention."

Before Syla could retort, stone scraped nearby, startling her.

She sprang back from the orb as Fel whirled toward the central sarcophagus scant feet away. The lid crashed to the stone floor, and a warrior wielding a gargoyle-bone sword leaped out of the interior. A *stormer* warrior.

Raising the blade, the man leaped straight toward Syla.

7

Fel reacted instantly, intercepting the warrior as he leaped from the sarcophagus, swinging his bone blade toward Syla's head. She scrambled back but crashed against the shielder and wouldn't have evaded death if not for her bodyguard.

Fel knocked the warrior to the ground, but their opponent was agile and twisted in the air to land on his feet. With grace Syla would have admired if the man hadn't been trying to *kill* her, he switched the swing of his sword toward Fel.

Using his mace, Fel parried the blow while ordering, "Take cover," to Syla. "Out of the way."

As the magical bone blade met the steel of Fel's mace, clangs ringing out in the chamber, Syla ran around the back of the shielder. She looked for a makeshift weapon or any way to help, irritated to *again* be a liability instead of an asset to her bodyguard.

If the fierce warrior, who had to be half Fel's age, bested him, he would come after her. Judging by the glances the man sent her way, *she* was his target. With flowing black hair, sun-tanned skin, and deep brown eyes, he would have been strikingly handsome if he hadn't come to assassinate her.

And had he been the one to kill Venia?

When Syla glanced that way, she cursed in surprise. A second warrior was crawling out of the sarcophagus.

For an instant, indignation filled her—it was blasphemy to open a tomb, much less climb *into* it and onto the remains of the dead—but when the man leaped to the ground, fear over her own predicament replaced the feeling.

With tattooed cheeks and a gargoyle-bone dagger—one identical to the blade in Venia's chest—the man rushed toward her.

Syla ran around the shielder again, darting past Fel's engagement with the first warrior, and sprinted for the exit, but an alarming thought made her lurch to a stop. The stormer would easily run her down in the tunnels, and if she left Fel, she would be on her own. Defenseless.

As the man sprinted after her, Syla spotted her pack on the ground and lunged for it. Her first thought was that she would use her book as a weapon, but there wasn't time to remove it. With the man almost upon her and thrusting with the dagger, she spun and hurled the bag at him.

Even though his brows rose in surprise, he was fast enough to dodge it and lifted an arm to knock it to the ground. The pack skidded into the doorway, stopping at the feet of someone new entering the chamber.

Forsaken by the gods, how *many* enemies were lurking in here? And why were these men trying to *kill* Syla instead of capture her, damn it?

She skittered back but bumped into one of the sarcophagi. There was nowhere to run.

But her opponent hadn't continued to advance on her. He'd spun toward the entrance, his eyebrows rising in surprise again as a black-clad rider strode in, muscled and powerful with a gargoyle-bone sword in his gloved hand. Captain Vorik.

"Sir!" the second warrior blurted as Fel's fight with the first raged on near the wall, the opponents fully occupied with trying to kill each other. The speaker pointed at Syla, but Vorik sprang at him instead of answering, or even responding to the exclamation.

Though startled, the man got his dagger up to defend himself.

The bone weapons clunked together, the noise different from metal striking metal but sharp and rapid as Vorik swept in with slash after slash. The clear aggressor, he pressed the younger man, who barely managed to step onto the fallen sarcophagus lid instead of tripping over it. Unrelenting, the captain kept attacking, the series of blows so fast that Syla didn't know how anyone could have defended against them. Throughout, his face remained masked, his jaw set. He wasn't even breathing through his mouth.

His opponent was, the man's eyes wide and confused as he panted, struggling to keep his fellow stormer from killing him. *Why* Vorik was trying to kill the man, Syla had no idea, but she glanced to the tunnel, wondering if she could slip past all the fighting and escape. But she couldn't leave Fel. He was—

A cry of pain came from his fight, and she turned, afraid he'd made the noise. But it was the younger man who'd dropped to one knee, struggling to keep his blade up as Fel swept the mace toward his head. Blood streamed through the man's fingers as he gripped his side with his free hand. Powering past a weak defense, the mace smashed into the man's skull.

Movement pulled Syla's attention back to the other battle.

The younger man had also crumpled to the ground, his back to the sarcophagus, his dagger clattering onto the lid. Vorik bent, grabbed his shoulder, and thrust his sword into the man's heart. His opponent didn't scream, only gasping and stiffening with his back arching before he collapsed onto his side. Without a change in expression, Vorik pulled out his sword.

"Come." Not hesitating or sheathing his weapon, Vorik looked at Syla, though he also glanced at Fel. "More stormers may be down here, looking for the moon-marked. I'll help you escape the city."

"We're not going anywhere with you, rider." Though blood streamed from a gash at his temple, and his face was bruised from his previous battles, Fel stood straight and snarled, mace at the ready in case he had to fight again.

"It is I who will go with *you*." Vorik kept Fel in his peripheral vision, but he focused on Syla. "As I was attempting to say before you flung yourself off my dragon's back, I'm here to protect you."

"Your *dragon* dropped the roof on us and almost killed us," Fel said.

Syla nodded and walked gingerly around the fallen men to stand not at Vorik's side but at Fel's. She needed to stick with her bodyguard and find a safe place where she could use her healing magic on him again. Only grit was keeping Fel upright; she was certain.

"That is true, but it was an accident," Vorik said. "Agrevlari was unaware of the orders that I received. He knew only of the attack orders from the general."

"The general who is your superior officer?" Fel asked.

"That he is. He's quite the grouch though. I can't recommend serving under him if it's not a familial duty."

"We don't need stormer help." Fel pointed at the doorway. "Go away."

"Do pardon my bluntness, but I believe you may have both perished if I hadn't arrived when I did." Vorik spoke in a calm tone and didn't appear harried—he wasn't even sweaty from his battle—but he did glance toward the tunnel now and then.

Were there more stormers roaming about under the castle? These had been lying in wait for Syla. Or for someone, anyway. They might not have known that she specifically would come but must have expected someone in the royal family to do exactly what she'd been attempting, fixing the shielder. Or at least trying to determine if it *could* be fixed.

"I could have handled them both." Fel lifted his chin, though he had to know that was bluster. Even without his injuries, battling two extremely capable stormer warriors at once would have killed him.

Syla almost wished she'd learned how to fight along with her siblings but couldn't imagine driving a sword into anyone, even a loathed enemy. As a healer, that was anathema to her. Though, if these men had killed her sister, maybe she could have made an exception...

"You can handle the next two by yourself if you wish." Vorik gestured to the tunnel. "I'll be magnanimous and let you lead while I walk beside the princess."

"I'll bet." Jaw clenching, Fel strode toward him with his mace raised. "I can imagine what you want to do with her."

Vorik's eyes narrowed, and he lifted his sword, a silent promise that he would defend himself. Reminded that Vorik hadn't wanted to collect Fel back in the courtyard, Syla feared he would kill her bodyguard without batting an eye.

"Stop, Sergeant," Syla said. "He helped us, so we won't fight him, but we won't join him. We'll—"

Fel did *not* stop. With his mind perhaps full of imagery of vile atrocities he imagined a dragon rider would inflict on a princess, he swung the mace in a combination of feints and legitimate attacks, an attempt to brain the captain, just as he had the other stormer.

Vorik ignored the feints, somehow reading them easily, and parried the real attacks. He was shorter than Fel, only a few inches taller than Syla, but fast, agile, and strong. In between his parries, he gave Syla long-suffering looks. Fel was unrelenting, his bruised face red as he threw all of his frustrations into the attack.

"Sergeant, stop," Syla tried again, striding toward them,

though she dared not get close to the swinging weapons. With certainty, she sensed that the younger captain—the younger and *uninjured* captain—could kill her bodyguard whenever he wished.

Indeed, when one of Fel's attacks swept perilously close to Vorik's face, the rider lost his patience. He parried twice more, then stepped into Fel, distracting him with a high attack while he hooked his leg around to slam his heel into the back of Fel's knee.

Her bodyguard, who'd complained often of his chronic joint issues, couldn't recover from the blow. His knee buckled, and Vorik used his strength to shove Fel against a wall between two sarcophagi. With a wrenching grasp, Vorik yanked the mace from Fel's grip and tossed the weapon away. He raised his sword toward Fel's neck.

The mace clattered and rolled on its round head to stop at Syla's feet. She snatched it up with a notion of slamming it into Vorik's back—or maybe his skull. Anything to keep someone else she cared about from dying this horrible day.

But once Vorik pinned Fel with his weight, the sword resting against the side of his neck, Vorik didn't move. He could have cut deeply at any moment but didn't.

Red face pressed against the wall, Fel snarled and flexed his muscles, as if he would shove away and continue the attack, but the blade cut slightly, drawing blood. Inflicting pain.

"Since you don't trust me to protect your charge, Sergeant," Vorik said calmly, "it might behoove you to keep yourself alive, if possible."

Expression aggrieved, Fel looked sideways as much as he could while trapped against the wall, and met Syla's gaze.

"Let him go..." Syla paused, considering using a derogatory term, but this wasn't the time to antagonize the rider. "Let him go, Captain Vorik," she said, struggling for a calm tone of her own. "Sergeant Fel won't attack you again."

Since she'd thus far had no luck in ordering Fel to stand down, she doubted Vorik would believe that, but what else could she do to win her bodyguard's freedom?

"Is that true, Sergeant?" Vorik asked Fel. "If I release you, will you refrain from attacking me again?"

Fel seethed, lip curling, muscles flexing against the man restraining him. If he could have escaped without making any promises, he would have.

"If you won't give me your word," Vorik said, his tone growing icy for the first time, "then I must kill you. You won't be the first Kingdom sergeant I've put an end to."

"Oh, I know," Fel snarled, hatred in his eyes now.

He either blamed Vorik for everything that had happened in the castle and city above, or... he had some other reason to loathe him personally. Syla couldn't tell, but maybe they'd met in battle before. After all, Fel had identified Vorik on that rooftop without hesitation.

"Your status as our enemy is what prompts us not to believe you have good intentions now," Syla offered, though neither man was looking at her. They were too busy glaring at each other now.

"That is understandable," Vorik said, his tone back to being calm and reasonable instead of cold and terrifying. "If we can depart this dangerous place, I'm willing to explain everything, Your Highness."

Syla *did* want to depart, but it had more to do with finding her aunt and trying to engineer the repair of the shielder than listening to explanations from a stormer.

"Are you done trying to kill me, Sergeant?" Vorik asked again.

Fel opened a hand, as if to show he was without a weapon, but he said, "If you place a single finger on her, I will strangle you until your head pops off."

Vorik looked at Syla, a hint of a rueful smile on his face. "I'm unclear on whether he acquiesced to me or not."

His face had been handsome before, but the smile made it

even more so. Much like the first warrior, he was striking, the kind of man a girl would swoon over in normal times.

The thought made Syla rock back with a realization, and she looked toward poor Venia's body. Earlier, she hadn't seriously been thinking that her sister—her *married* sister—had come down here for a tryst, but maybe that was exactly what had happened. Somewhere along the way, she'd met that beautiful warrior, and he'd wooed her, maybe talked her into meeting in secret in these tunnels for sex. Would the intelligent thirty-three-year-old Venia have *fallen* for something like that?

Syla shook her head, having a hard time believing that her sister would have done anything to betray their people. Her marriage to the much older Lord Telenfar had been arranged, and there hadn't been a child yet, so it was possible a young and handsome suitor might have tempted Venia, but... there was no way Venia would have led a lover—led *anyone*—to the shielder. She wouldn't have betrayed the Kingdom for lust—or anything else. It was a foolish hypothesis.

"Sergeant?" Vorik prompted into the silence.

"I won't attack you tonight unless you attack me," Fel finally said, "but if you touch Princess Syla, I, as her bodyguard, will be *compelled* to come to her rescue."

"I can't touch her at all? What if she trips and falls?"

"*I* will catch her."

"I see. Very well." Vorik stepped back, releasing Fel.

Fel flexed his shoulders and shook out his arms as he turned. He didn't put his full weight on the knee Vorik had kicked, but he did walk toward Syla without limping.

She stepped toward him, lifting his mace to offer to him, though she expected Vorik to stop her, to want Fel to remain unarmed. Vorik watched them but didn't object as Fel clasped the handle of his weapon.

"This way." Vorik tilted his head and walked into the tunnel.

Syla had no intention of going anywhere with him, no matter what *explanation* he offered, but there was only one way out of the chamber.

With Fel at her side, they walked out after Vorik. At the tunnel entrance, Syla paused to take one last look at the shielder so she could etch the details in her mind and better relay them to her aunt. As she did, she noticed the fallen warrior that Vorik had battled. He lay on the lid of the sarcophagus where he'd dropped. It occurred to her that someone ought to put that lid back on, that leaving the tomb open was a disservice to the dead. But would she ask the injured Fel? Or Vorik? It would involve shoving the dead stormer aside, so she hesitated, but something told her to put that lid back on, that nothing good would come from leaving a tomb disturbed.

"This way, Your Highness." Vorik had paused a few steps ahead. "I'm eager to give you the explanation for my behavior so that I may gain a modicum of trust from you."

"This should be good," Fel muttered darkly.

He hadn't paused to look back and didn't appear concerned about the open sarcophagus. He walked with determination after Vorik, doing his best to mask his injuries.

With Fel in need of healing, Syla didn't want to linger. She would have to return later to retrieve her sister's body, and she could tend to the sarcophagus then.

"Your Highness?" Vorik prompted.

He watched Syla intently, waiting for her to join them.

"I'm coming," she said.

"Excellent," Vorik said.

Syla was certain it wasn't.

8

"You've heard of the Freeborn Faction?" Vorik asked, not hesitating to launch into the explanation he had promised to Princess Syla as they walked painstakingly slowly through the tunnels under the gardener castle, her injured bodyguard ensuring they couldn't assume the brisk pace that Vorik wanted. Through his link with Agrevlari, he'd learned that, with the dragons gone and wyverns no longer feasting in the castle above, the local military had regrouped and marched in to look for survivors. Some of them had to know about the tunnels and would descend into them to search for any of his people who lingered.

"I haven't. I've read widely enough to be aware of some of your history, but if that's something that's developed more recently, I've been busy at Moon Watch Temple." A pained wince crossed Syla's face. "I am—was—a healer there."

That temple must have been destroyed. A number of them had been. Vorik hadn't been responsible, but the dragons, always prone to the predatory savagery inherent in them, hadn't been as pinpoint in their attacks as the riders themselves.

Vorik looked at the bodyguard, suspecting him more worldly.

It made his shoulder blades itch to have the armed and vengeful man walking behind him, but he would have to show some trust to them if he had any hope of doing as his brother wished and earning the trust of the princess.

They were, of course, as suspicious as Vorik had expected. He didn't blame them and couldn't help but think the general had given him an impossible task. When he'd tried a slight smile on the princess, aware that she had suffered great loss and wouldn't be in the mood for *flirting*, she'd drawn back in what he guessed was stunned horror. After so many generations drifting apart, the gardeners and stormers had many cultural differences, but he suspected *stunned horror* looked like *stunned horror* across all human civilizations.

When Fel, who was probably distracted by his pain, finally noticed Vorik looking in inquiry, all he did was grunt. Whether that meant *yes*, he'd heard of the faction, or *no*, Vorik couldn't tell.

"Ah, I'll explain briefly. As you're aware, if you've studied history, Your Highness, the stormers never started out as a large cohesive unit. We come from people who were exiled or voluntarily left the protected Garden Kingdom islands in fits and spurts over the centuries. Those who went solo into the dangerous world didn't live long, so many banded together in small tribes, but my ancestors wanted freedom, not to suffer the rule of a king, so nobody sought to set up a central government. But now... Well, since you've been sheltered, you may not be aware that the number of scaled predators and other creatures capable of devouring humans whole has increased as the climate around the world has grown harsher, with storms, droughts, and even volcanic eruptions more frequent. We've always had to be careful to survive out there—there's a reason we call people we trust *sky watchers* and warn each other to *watch the sky* when they depart—but it's gotten harder to survive in recent years. There have been precious few edible things to forage on the mainlands and less sheltered islands, and the skies are more full of predators than prey."

Though he had to watch and listen for other threats in the tunnels, Vorik glanced back often, hoping Syla was listening intently. He didn't expect a gardener to be sympathetic to his people, especially when the stormers had *just* destroyed so much of the Kingdom's capital and killed her entire family, but he hoped she would at least understand some of what motivated them. That would make it easier for her to be sympathetic to him, to believe he might prove an ally.

"Get to the point, rider," Fel growled.

That the bodyguard said the noble profession like an insult, as if riders were pirates or brigands, made Vorik bristle. He was honorable, damn it. He'd only attacked military ships or cargo ships with armed escorts, and he'd always battled them openly, not striking in the night. But... he admitted that some other riders used more guerrilla tactics. Especially those from tribes on the brink of starvation. It was hard to resist a cargo ship full of freshly harvested crops.

"In recent decades, the tribes have banded together for common purposes," Vorik said, keeping his voice calm, trusting he wouldn't win regard from the princess by sniping at her injured bodyguard, "and created a loose coalition. None of the tribes rule over another, but all who want to be allied send soldiers to be trained, either as part of the Storm Guard or, for those who have great aptitude and can entice a dragon into allowing itself to be ridden, the Sixteen Talons Air Fleet. Our goal is—"

"We *know* what your goal is." Grim-faced, Syla looked past him toward an intersection.

As of yet, it was empty, and Vorik didn't hear anyone elsewhere in the tunnels, but his dragon's warning made him want to hurry.

"Yes, we soldiers have not hidden our goal." Enticed by the thought of the wondrous fruits and vegetables and delicious flesh of livestock that had never known a life of tension and terror, Vorik had been known to cry out for the destruction of the sky shields more than once as he'd battled ships navigating from island to island, out from under the magical protection as they carried supplies throughout the Kingdom. "But the Freeborn Faction is different. They—*we*—" Oh, how painful it was to touch his chest as he uttered that *we* and pretend his allegiance, "—have attempted to open negotiations with your queen in recent years. Those of us in the faction seek *permission* to return to the Kingdom and are willing to obey its rules in exchange for the easier life found under the sky shields."

From what Vorik had heard, the king had been more open to negotiations, but the queen ruled—*had* ruled—without sympathy for outsiders. She hadn't wanted to allow stormers under any circumstances to visit the Kingdom. Ever.

Syla's eyebrows drew together, and she looked to her bodyguard.

"That faction's envoys haven't been trusted when they've shown up," Fel said, then lowered his voice. "You'd have more details than I if you'd gone to more family dinners."

Thanks to his keen hearing—it was one of the magical attributes that his bond with Agrevlari lent him—Vorik didn't have any trouble hearing the man.

Syla looked toward the tunnel's arched stone ceiling, or maybe she was looking through it with her imagination to the castle above. "I... haven't decided yet whether it's fortuitous or dreadful that I didn't arrive at tonight's dinner in time."

The bodyguard opened his mouth but didn't seem to know what to say and closed it again.

Vorik stopped in the intersection, a single lantern mounted there burning low. He doubted his people had lit the way and suspected the now-dead princess, who he knew had been lured down for a tryst with Lieutenant Mavus, had been responsible.

Vorik regretted that Mavus had died to the bodyguard's mace but didn't know how he might have stopped that. It had been bad enough that Anok had blurted *sir* and been startled when Vorik rushed in. Neither of the men, of course, had been filled in on General Jhiton's recently formed plan. Vorik was glad that Anok had caught onto his eye-widening signals and had figured out to play dead when Vorik thrust his sword between the soldier's arm and chest instead of, as he'd attempted to convey, through Anok's heart.

Princess Syla had seemed a little suspicious as they'd walked away from the chamber, but she must not have figured out the ruse completely, or she would have ordered her bodyguard to finish the man off. She certainly wouldn't have left Anok there with the shielder. Oh, the thing had looked utterly destroyed to Vorik's eye, but he trusted Anok would *ensure* it was before slipping away. Vorik hoped he would also be able to take Mavus's body with him so the lieutenant could have a proper funeral pyre, incineration by a dragon, as all who served in the Sixteen Talons wished to be in the end. If not... Well, he'd been willing to give his life—and risk unrest in the afterlife—to ensure the stormers finally, *finally* had access to the lands under the shields.

"What matters is that the Freeborn Faction wants peace with your people, not war," Vorik said, drawing their gazes back to him. He didn't add that those belonging to the treacherous little group were willing to undermine the Storm Guard and even the Sixteen Talons by passing information along to gardener spies. It had only been by extremely careful planning and letting only the most trusted officers know about this day's attack beforehand that the riders had been able to keep the details from leaking out. Success had not been certain, not in the least. "We have so many taloned and fanged enemies in the world that we in the faction believe humans should work together going forward. *We* didn't want this attack." Again, Vorik made himself touch his chest to imply he was a part of the faction, though it galled him to claim that allegiance.

It also bothered him to lie to the princess. Oh, he didn't care to lie to anyone, under any circumstances, but she hadn't done anything to earn his deceit or the implied disdain that went along with being mendacious with a person.

Vorik didn't feel disdain for her. He even smiled at the memory of her hurling her pack at Anok.

His first assessment of Syla had been that she wouldn't be the type to leap into a fray—for a healer, that made sense—but she also wasn't one to quail in shock and fear at the first sign of a threat. There was a determined sturdiness to her, despite the lack of lean athleticism he was used to in stormer women, and he found the juxtaposition intriguing.

"We didn't see you stopping it," Fel stated.

Since they'd spotted him on Agrevlari's back and possibly helping destroy munitions, Vorik couldn't deny that. He wished he'd known that his brother would come up with this scheme *before* the riders had descended upon the capital. He could have been less brazen about showing himself.

"No. It's complicated. At this point, I still have General Jhiton's trust. In order to ensure he stays in the dark, I've hidden my allegiance to the faction from all but a few of its key leaders. Currently, the general is likely to share intelligence with me, which I then share with the faction leaders. Unfortunately, I didn't learn of the attack on your people until it was too late to warn you. Even if I had known... the faction is small. There is little we can do against the Storm Guard and the riders. What I'm doing now..." Vorik waved to himself and then back the way they'd come, toward the chamber and the men he'd left behind. "I risk Jhiton finding out about my divided loyalties. If I can, in secret, help protect you, that would be ideal."

"Do you need to protect me because your people are planning

more attacks?" Syla scrutinized him through her spectacles. "On my people? And me specifically?"

Those lenses, Vorik was certain, did nothing to indicate a lack of *mental* acuity. He would have to be careful not to inadvertently give away intelligence, at least not related to anything important. Even through the spectacles, Syla's eyes, with dark-gray depths that reminded him of storm clouds at sea, had a captivating intentness that made him *want* to answer her questions. Was it because there was magic about her? His own power allowed him to sense it radiating from her. He also caught himself wanting to see her eyes —see *her*—without the spectacles. The frames were large enough that they almost kept him from noticing the curve of her cheeks, the gentle outline of a cute nose, and the fullness of her lips. They were quite kissable lips.

"Captain?" Syla prompted.

"There will be more attacks." Vorik realized he'd been staring openly at her—and her lips.

"Are your people going after *all* of the shielders?"

"The leaders of the tribes want more than Castle Island."

"They can't know where the other shielders are," Fel said.

"I'm uncertain what General Jhiton and the other high-ranking officers know, but in the last meeting I attended with him, he was confident that his plan would result in the stormers gaining access to *all* of the islands." An image of an apple floated into Vorik's mind, dew droplets beading on its perfect red skin, and his empty stomach grumbled as he imagined flying over Orchard Island and harvesting the fruit.

He shook his head. His brother was right. It was foolish to allow such little things to motivate him. They were fighting for the future of their people, not only the quick satisfaction of their tastebuds.

"Have you heard anything about attacks elsewhere, Fel?" Syla asked.

He shook his head. "Not yet, but the stormers *can't* know where all the shielders are."

"How did they find out about *this* one?" Syla looked at Vorik.

Hadn't she guessed? Maybe she knew and was testing him to see if he told the truth.

"Princess Venia." Vorik tilted a thumb back toward the hidden chamber. "I wasn't included during the planning of that, but I believe Lieutenant Mavus has—*had* been—meeting with her in secret for months, and their trysts were always down in these tunnels."

Vorik more than *believed* that. He knew it. He'd heard a lot more details about that scheme than he would admit. It had been General Amalia who'd come up with it, not Jhiton, but Vorik had been at some of those planning meetings. It was because of the intelligence Mavus had gathered from the princess and seen himself during his visits that Vorik had learned about these tunnels and known where to find Syla when she'd disappeared.

"Venia wouldn't have betrayed our people." The princess didn't sound that confident in her assertion, and Vorik believed he'd guessed right, that she'd already figured it out by the grisly scene in the chamber.

He regretted that she'd had to see that. It also didn't sit well with him that Mavus had killed the woman he'd been seducing for months. Maybe she'd realized what he was up to and had confronted him and tried to kill him first. Either way, Vorik hoped the kill hadn't been done in cold blood.

"I do not know the details," Vorik said again, aware of the suspicion in Syla's eyes as she waited for him to respond. "Only that they were having sex, and she came readily to him each time."

That was true, but, from what he'd heard, Mavus—and General Amalia—had been frustrated that he couldn't tease any secrets out of the princess. Specifically, the location of the shielder and how to gain access to it, the one thing the stormers had been trying to learn for years, if not decades. It had sounded like, in the end, Mavus had used a drug to make her speak truths she would not have otherwise shared.

"Did he pretend to be a member of a peaceful rebel faction?" Syla asked.

Vorik laughed to cover his alarm that she saw so easily through him to the truth. "Perhaps he did."

"Venia is not—wasn't—" Again, Syla winced with emotional pain, "—a dummy."

Seeing a woman in such distress made Vorik want to gather her in his arms and comfort her, not continue to deceive her, but the princess would not appreciate that. And Fel, who still gripped his mace while sending glowers at Vorik's skull, had made his position on touching her clear. Vorik looked at the moon-shaped mark on Syla's hand, reminding himself that it made her an enemy, that his ancestors might have long ago left the Kingdom of their own accord but that it had been *her* ancestors who'd forbidden them from coming back.

"I'm not a dummy either." Syla pointed down one of the tunnels. "You will go that way until you reach a dead-end wall that you may push on to gain access to an underground lagoon that will take you out to sea. There, you can find your dragon and leave Castle Island. I don't need you or any of your people to *protect* me."

Vorik almost pointed out again that she *did* need a protector, but her voice lowered to a whisper as she added, "I just need you all to go away."

Such sorrow and pain and lament filled her eyes as she looked away from him, blinking, that he felt like an ass.

Vorik, Agrevlari spoke into his mind from whatever perch he'd found. *The soldiers that have returned to the castle mentioned checking the tunnels underneath it. I believe many are heading down there now. Have you acquired your new female?*

She's not my new female. Vorik had briefly explained his orders to Agrevlari but didn't know if the dragon grasped the nuances of the plan. It was possible he was being snarky. It was also possible that, his kind being straightforward creatures who rarely thought of deceit, Agrevlari didn't get it.

You said you would return with her and that I would have to endure her riding on my back, even if I have no bond with her and she's unlikely to be strong enough and adequate enough that a dragon would normally accept her as a rider.

I just said she was coming along. You inferred all the rest.

Dragons are excellent inferrers.

Uh-huh. Vorik caught voices in the distance. The soldiers, presumably.

He didn't worry about defending himself against them, but he didn't want the princess caught in the middle of a fight. Also, if he had to kill people—her own allies—at her feet, she would be less likely to ever trust him. It had been difficult enough to subdue the bodyguard without hurting him. Doing so with a whole squadron of troops...

"I'll happily take your suggestion," Vorik said, aware of Syla continuing to point toward the lagoon. "But I suggest you come with me. In the castle above, the wyverns may have returned. They have no qualms about feeding on..." He caught himself before saying *the kills of others*. That was too callous. They were her people.

"I'm aware," Syla said, "but we'll avoid them on our own."

"Our people should have gathered troops and be searching the castle by now," Fel said.

Since that was exactly what was happening, Vorik had a hard time arguing harder—*lying* further—to them.

A clink sounded, and the voices were growing louder as the soldiers headed toward the intersection. Before long, their lanterns would be visible.

Fel and Syla might have lacked his magically keen hearing, but the noises were now loud enough that they turned in that direction.

Syla looked at Vorik and opened her mouth, calculation in her eyes. Was she going to scream for help? For her troops to rush forward and try to kill or capture him?

Vorik lifted his chin, ready to fight if need be.

But she made an exasperated sound and pointed again for him to go in the direction of the lagoon.

"This way, Your Highness." Fel gripped her wrist and led her toward the voices.

She went willingly with him. Vorik hadn't expected anything different but found himself calling softly, "If you change your mind about wanting my protection, I'll wait for you until dawn at the lighthouse along the coast beyond your castle."

The frown that Syla cast over her shoulder suggested she thought he was stupid for believing she would have anything further to do with him. Or stupid for giving her his future location. Perhaps some of both. But if she sent troops after Vorik, Agrevlari could easily leap into the air so they could fly away.

Vorik backed out of the light of the intersection, letting himself watch her for a moment before turning away. The curves he'd noticed earlier were quite appealing from the rear perspective, the fabric of her dress hugging her hips and buttocks, and he caught himself wishing she would look back at him.

She did not, merely walking away with determination. Sighing, Vorik turned and trotted in the opposite direction.

"Princess Syla," came a relieved cry, the male voice of a soldier or castle staff, Vorik assumed. "Are you all right?"

Vorik paused to listen, certain he could outrun the soldiers if Syla sent them after him—keen hearing wasn't the only superior attribute his bond with Agrevlari gave him—and that he might learn something from eavesdropping.

"No," she said grimly. "But I have a plan."

Vorik blinked. What plan had she been thinking up during the chaos of the evening?

"Take me to your superior officer, Lieutenant," she added. "Whoever is in charge now."

"General Tox was unfortunately slain, Your Highness, and General Dolok was badly injured, but I'll take you to Colonel Mosworth."

"Thank you, Lieutenant."

"Wait," Fel said. "There's a dragon rider down here in the tunnels, Lieutenant. Captain Vorik. We saw him only a moment ago, and he went that way."

Vorik had expected them to send the soldiers after him and nodded to himself as he departed. Thanks to Mavus's intelligence reports, he knew the princess had sent him in the right direction and that the tunnel did indeed lead to an underground lagoon through which he could escape.

Given her opinion of what she believed to be a ruse, it was surprising that she hadn't tried to trick Vorik and send him down a true dead-end. And what if the bodyguard hadn't told the troops about Vorik? Would Syla have?

It had sounded like she wanted to leave and carry on with her next steps, not that she'd longed for his death. Maybe, even though they were enemies, she'd felt beholden to him for rushing in to save her from Mavus and Anok. If that was true, there might be hope that Vorik could eventually win her trust.

As shouts followed him toward the lagoon, he nodded to himself again. For the sake of his people, and because the general had commanded it, he would find a way to succeed.

9

"We're so relieved to find you, Your Highness," Lieutenant Lonx said, more than a few tearstains marking his soot-streaked face.

With torn and burned uniforms, bruises, gashes, and limps to rival those of her bodyguard, the entire squad accompanying Syla and Fel out of the tunnels was so battered and beleaguered that they didn't look like they should be upright.

"So far, we've only found..." Lonx glanced at Fel, as if to ask if he should give Syla his bad news.

Fel only grunted and glanced back again. He'd told the lieutenant about Captain Vorik, prompting the less injured half of the squad to take off to hunt the rider down, but Fel looked like he wished he could have accompanied them, that he felt he'd failed by not finding a way to kill Vorik.

Syla was too tired to care that the rider had escaped. She wasn't even sure... Oh, she didn't believe his story about being part of some obscure faction that wanted an alliance with her people, but since Vorik had helped them in the shielder chamber, she had conflicted feelings about longing for his death. If he got away and didn't pester her or the Kingdom again, she wouldn't mind. Of course, what were the odds that he *wouldn't* pester her people again? Maybe she should have schemed with Fel to help her bodyguard kill him. Her healer's heart shied away from the notion though. She struggled to want death for anyone, no matter how vile they were.

"The rest of my family... They didn't make it, did they?" Syla asked the lieutenant when he didn't continue on his own.

Even with the direct question, he winced instead of answering right away.

"I already know about Venia. We... Her body is in..." Syla caught herself from saying *the shielder chamber*, reminded that its location was still a secret to most of the world, and she'd vowed to keep it that way. She would have to return later with a small group of trusted people to assist in opening the hidden passageway so that the body could be removed. Her gut churned at the thought, and she longed to foist the duty off on someone else. "She died in the tunnels. I'll help someone find her body later."

A sergeant walking at Lonx's side cursed. "She was one of the ones who was unaccounted for. We were hoping..." He shook his head and swore again.

Lonx sighed. "The queen and Prince Serk are without question dead, Your Highness. I'm sorry. They fought bravely and died among many of our men on the castle walls, trying to keep out the dragons who were flying low with their riders firing upon the defenders. I was assigned to the gatehouse and saw a lot of it." With a firm nod, he again emphasized, "They fought and died valiantly," as if he wanted the words to reassure her.

Though Syla wasn't surprised that her mother and eldest brother had battled to the end, she wished they hadn't, that they'd escaped into the tunnels. That was what the royals were *supposed* to do. The soldiers had orders to keep them alive at all costs, so they could, in the event that something like this happened, survive and continue to rule and guide the Kingdom and the military.

"What about Nyvia and Gylonar?" she asked after her oldest sister and other brother.

"We..." Lonx glanced at his sergeant, but the man only shook his head grimly. "We're not positive, but people have reported seeing them, ah... Some of the bodies were too charred by dragon fire to be recognizable."

They were nearing the stairs that led up into the castle, but Syla had to pause and rest a hand on the cool stone wall. Queasiness at the thought of being burned alive swept over her, and she closed her eyes, trying *not* to imagine what bodies would look like after that. As a healer in the temple, she'd seen people burned by dragon fire before. Some had survived if it hadn't covered too much of their bodies, but most...

Syla wiped her eyes, trying to tell herself it wasn't any more gruesome than the other ways people had been killed. If anything, if they'd been completely engulfed, they would have died swiftly.

"We're not *positive* they're dead," Lonx hurried to say, seeing her distress. "Because we can't identify the bodies. It's possible—we're *hoping*—one or both of them may have moved away from the area where they were seen fighting and made it into a tunnel." He waved to indicate their passageway and the others beneath the castle. "We've been searching and haven't found them yet, but maybe..."

The sergeant gave the lieutenant a grim look, one filled with his belief that, if Syla's other siblings had survived, they would have found them by now, but he didn't voice the words.

Lonx brightened and added, "We didn't expect to find *you*, Princess Syla. We hadn't realized you'd been in the castle. And the temple... Well, I don't know if you know but the Moon Watch Temple was destroyed, so we thought you were dead too."

"I am aware."

"We think… the stormers may have been targeting your family specifically."

Syla thought of Vorik's words—his *warning*.

"I think so too," was all she said.

The group limped and groaned its way up the stairs and into the theater. The pervasive scent of smoke and death lingered there and in the surrounding halls.

"We'll accompany you to your room, Your Highness, and I'll leave several good and, uhm, young men to guard you." Lonx glanced at Fel.

Fel squinted at him, and his lips rippled like those of a wolf as he revealed his teeth. He had to be offended by the insinuation that he was *old* or somehow incapable, but he kept himself from otherwise responding. Maybe he was wounded enough and tired enough to know he needed a break from being her bodyguard.

"I appreciate your offer, Lieutenant, though Sergeant Fel has heroically stood by my side and capably protected me all night, but I'm not going to my room." Syla patted the pack that she was still toting around.

"You must, Your Highness. Especially if… With your mother dead and you the only of your siblings we've been able to find… As strange as it seems, you're in charge of the Kingdom now."

Syla tried not to be offended by the *as strange as it seems* comment—the lieutenant wasn't the most diplomatic officer, was he?—but it made her bristle. It was more the suggestion that she was incapable than disagreement that she didn't have the proper training and wouldn't be ideal.

"Which makes what I need to do all the more imperative. I saw the shielder. It's horribly damaged, and I'm skeptical that it can be repaired, but I want to get an engineer in to take a look. Then, if it's not possible to repair it, I need to travel to one of the less populated islands and figure out how to bring their shielder back here.

Hundreds of thousands of people live here, so it's imperative that we reestablish protection for Castle Island."

"Ah..." Lonx lifted a finger but hesitated again.

A horrifying thought swept over Syla as she slowly followed the squad through a hallway that led to the courtyard. Men and women had appeared since her earlier traverse of the area and were clearing away rubble and carrying bodies outside. "There haven't been attacks on the other islands, have there been?"

What if the dragon riders had somehow learned the locations of *all* the orbs? And what if they'd attacked multiple islands at once? Or *all* of them?

"Not that we've heard about yet, Your Highness, but no ships have traveled here this night, perhaps for obvious reasons. The lookouts in the lighthouses can see with their telescopes to the two nearest islands, and vice versa, so we'd know if there were fires along their coastlines. So far, they're dark and quiet."

"Good." That, at least, was a small relief.

"The thing is that we can't let *you* take off on some... travel mission. You *must* be protected, Your Highness. My superiors have already determined, just as you have, that another shielder must be acquired if ours can't be fixed—thank you for going down to check on it—and we'll take care of all that. You..." Lonx looked sternly at her. "You must stay in your rooms. If not in a dungeon cell."

Syla blinked. "Pardon?"

"Because the dungeon is underground and would be more easily guarded." Fel nodded at the lieutenant.

What, were they going to work together to lock her in a cell? Both determined to protect her?

Lonx nodded back at Fel, eyebrows raising in relief at her bodyguard's support. "It's only luck that your room wasn't destroyed during the attack, Your Highness. Half of your mother's suite was, and the roof fell in over your brothers' rooms. I'm... not sure about the structural integrity anywhere in that wing. Maybe..."

"My room is fine," Syla blurted, alarmed by the dungeon suggestion. At least she might find a way to escape from her room. A dungeon cell, on the other hand... "We were there earlier. It wasn't damaged at all."

Lonx scratched his cheek, soot coming off under his nail.

"The ceiling looked good," she assured him. "Not even a crack."

"Well, you can start out there." As they entered the courtyard, Lonx peered skyward, no doubt looking for dragons, wyverns, and other winged threats.

They would all have to be much more aware of them until the shielder could be repaired. They needed... what had Vorik's term been? Sky watchers.

"After we get more of the chaos cleared, we can find someone to inspect the standing buildings. The few that remain." Lonx gazed bleakly around before guiding Syla outside.

"Yes, of course. But if you would, at your earliest convenience, ask—you said Colonel Mosworth was in charge, right? Please ask him to come see me. I'm the logical choice to find a replacement shielder, especially if..." Syla took a bracing breath. "I may be the only person left alive who knows where they all are."

"That is something we're all keenly aware of and concerned about, Your Highness. It's why you *must* stay here under our protection. You'll have to talk to my superiors and figure out who you can trust enough to provide with maps to the shielders."

"There's more involved than following a map. You must also have a moon-mark and the inherent magic to open the doors that seal the chambers." Syla held up the back of her hand.

"You've other relatives with moon-marks."

Yes, her Aunt Tibby, for one... She'd almost mentioned Tibby as the engineer she wanted to bring in, but... If the lieutenant knew she was an *agricultural* engineer, he might balk.

"Do you know where any of them are?" Syla asked.

"We will." Lonx nodded and assigned four of his men to accompany her to her room and guard the door from the hallway. He also sent one to stand outside her windows.

Her earlier thought that she might escape her room evaporated. Some of the royal suites had secret doors leading down to the tunnels, but, as far as she knew, hers did not.

Fel tramped after the men and walked into her room with her, but he looked like he only intended to make sure she was all right before taking a break. Syla held up a finger to request he wait, then closed the door so they were alone.

"Fel." Even though it was morally questionable, she hoped her lingering healing magic would make him feel compelled to do as she wished, not what the soldiers thought was best for her. Not what *he* thought was best for her. "I need you to get me out of here. I can't sit here in my room, being *protected*."

Fel took a long, slow breath as he regarded her, and a muscle ticked in his cheek. Was he struggling with himself? Trying to fight away the magic that her healing had left behind?

She waited, hoping the magic would win out.

He scowled, straightened his spine, and said, "You're the last of the royal Moonmarks. The lieutenant is doing exactly what makes sense, and Colonel Mosworth will do the same. You won't talk him into something else. You need to be protected. As you yourself pointed out, you know where the shielders are and have the power to reach and activate them."

"That's exactly why I *can't* stay here. I need to find Aunt Tibby and bring her to check the shielder under the castle. And if it's not repairable, we'll need to locate another to bring back."

Syla tried not to think about how hard that might be. The local governments of those other islands would *not* approve. Yes, the queen ruled over them all, but... there now wasn't a queen. There was only Princess Syla, the healer who'd avoided all things political and governmental for her whole life.

"I can find her," Fel said, "and, if she survived, bring her here."

Syla paused. Was there any reason that wouldn't work? The thought of being prisoner here, having other people run off and do her bidding, rankled, but...

"I *will* find her," Fel said earnestly, his tense face relaxing. Maybe he felt he'd found a way to obey what the magic wanted him to do while keeping her safe.

Reluctantly, Syla admitted that he had. And she had to be reasonable, not hare off on a self-appointed mission that would happen to allow her to avoid staying here to tidy a horrible and unappealing mess.

"All right, but rest for a time and get something to eat first, please. And be careful." Syla wrote down the address of the farm where Tibby lived, though she had no idea if her aunt had remained home after the attack. With luck, the rural location outside the city hadn't been targeted by dragons.

"I'm *always* careful." Fel gave her an aggrieved look.

"Are you sure?" Syla managed a slight smile. "You've a lot of old injuries that suggest a possibly reckless youth."

"What they should suggest is that I've *guarded* a lot of reckless youths." His face was glum. Was he thinking even now about how close he'd been to his retirement?

"I suppose I could have guessed that. Sorry."

"It's not your fault." He sighed, waved the piece of paper with the address, then again said, "I'll find her."

"Thank you."

After he departed, Syla paced her room.

As late as it was, she should have slept, and yawns did plague her, but she was too agitated for rest. Besides, after the horrors of the day, her dreams would all be nightmares. She wished she could do something and started to second-guess sending Fel away. If Tibby was out on the farm or in any of the agricultural buildings when Fel arrived, he might not find her. It was also possible that she wouldn't remember him and come when he called. She also might have been attacked and be injured or dead. With a moon-mark of her own, she *would* be a target.

Syla groaned and eyed her pack, wishing she'd tried harder to talk Fel into taking her. She untied the flap, debating if she should remove anything or... perhaps add to it in case she yet ended up going on a journey.

As she poked around, her fingers brushed the hard, glass-like wings of the dragon figurine. She pulled it out, and its magic warmed her hand. Surprised, she almost dropped it. It hadn't done that before. She'd *sensed* its magic but couldn't remember the figurine ever being warm to the touch.

Uneasy, she set it aside.

As she rubbed her palm on her dress, she thought of the strange Captain Vorik and his ploy, or whatever it had been. Was he *truly* waiting nearby in case she changed her mind and showed up? Maybe she should have sent the troops to check the lighthouse. But if his dragon was with him, he would be dangerous, and more people could end up killed. Even *without* his dragon, he was dangerous. She recalled the amazing speed and strength with which he'd fought. It hadn't seemed... human.

She picked up the figurine, intending to set it back on its shelf, but its magic intensified.

She dropped it, pulling her hand back. Goosebumps rose all along her arms. Was it her imagination, or could she *see* the figurine radiating power? In all the years she'd had it, she'd never noticed anything like this from it.

"Are you more active right now because dragons are nearby?" Syla wondered.

Of course, it did not answer. But when she reached out and touched it again, an image came to mind. Or... was it a vision?

In her mind's eye, she saw a great red-scaled dragon flying through a night sky brightened by stars and a half moon. Then, the perspective shifted, and she witnessed the world through the *eyes* of that dragon, the dark waves of the sea far below. How strange.

It—no, somehow Syla knew that the dragon was a *she*—was flying miles out to sea, but lights were visible on the shoreline of a distant island. *Castle Island.* Syla recognized its contours even though far fewer lanterns burned in the streets and houses than usual. Many of those homes had been destroyed.

As the dragon continued on, Syla saw the lighthouse that Vorik had mentioned. It was quite distant, but the creature's keen eyes had no trouble spotting another dragon perched atop it.

Beauteous Wreylith, a male telepathic voice said. Was... it speaking to the red dragon? *Your presence honors me. Do you wish to go on a hunt?*

There is a human on your back, the red dragon said, *and you have been scurrying around doing his bidding. I have no interest in hunting with a dragon who is a peon for humans.*

I am not a peon. I can fly free whenever I wish. It is only because I seek access to the delicious prey sheltered on these islands that I am assisting with the human scheme.

And because you'll do whatever that rider wishes. He is less pathetic than many of his kind, but to lend him your power and let him be your master... It is disgraceful.

Captain Vorik is not my master, most beauteous Wreylith. We work together as a team. You're looking lovely flying out there under the silvery moon with the starlight gleaming on your wings. I would enjoy hunting with you and showing you my prowess. I am a powerful dragon, not a peon.

Hush, Agrevlari. A feeling of startled suspicion came from the red dragon. *We are monitored.*

Syla sensed the dragon looking straight toward the castle, straight at *her*.

Still in her room, she stumbled back, removing her hand from the figurine. Her heart hammered. What *was* this artifact that had allowed her to witness a private conversation between two dragons?

Maybe it hadn't been real, simply her imagination, but enough magic flowed through her veins that she recognized it at play. That had been—

Who dares spy upon a dragon? the female's voice boomed into Syla's mind.

She wanted to quail and maybe to hide under the bed, but dragons respected power and bravery, so she dared not show weakness. But should she tell the truth? Or lie?

No, dragons reputedly didn't respect liars or lie themselves as part of their way. Besides, couldn't dragons read the thoughts of men? Was this one not, even now, communicating telepathically with her? Speaking words straight into her *mind*?

I am Princess Syla, and I inherited this figurine from my father. I did not realize it had the ability to communicate with dragons.

To spy *upon dragons.* The female sounded furious.

Abruptly reminded that the sky shield was down, and the building her room was in would *not* protect her from a dragon, Syla groped for a conciliatory response.

It was inadvertent spying. I wasn't aware that this artifact could allow that. Please forgive my transgression. I would not intentionally disturb your kind. Syla stopped, realizing she sounded obsequious and that a dragon wouldn't respect that.

The silence that followed worried her. What if the female dragon was now flying toward the castle? Intending to end her for her presumption?

Syla rubbed her face. To have survived everything else this night only to be snapped in two by a dragon who wasn't even involved in the conflict...

I'm a healer, she added on the off chance that it might matter. *If you've any wounds or know anyone in need of my services, I would be happy to offer them at no cost. As a means of apologizing for my inadvertent intrusion.*

"Obsequious, Syla," she groaned to herself. "You sound even *more* obsequious."

A healer capable of effectively treating dragons? The female's telepathic voice sounded closer now—maybe she *was* on the way to kill Syla. *It takes magic to heal a dragon in a way that nature and time cannot, and humans are generally pathetic and inept.*

I am moon-marked. In case the dragon didn't know or care what that meant, Syla added, *My ancestors were blessed by the gods before their kind left this realm. Those of us with the moon-mark have the ability to use magic in some way or another.* She didn't mention the shielders. They already had far too much attention from dragons. *I am a healer and have used my power on* many *beings in addition to humans.*

Dogs, cats, horses, a gerbil... She didn't mention those.

Hm.

Syla scratched her jaw. What did *that* mean?

I recently battled a storm yeti and inadvertently stepped in a basilisk den. I have a wound.

I... I could take a look. By the eyes of the moon, Syla hadn't expected the dragon to actually be in need of her services. Could she truly use her magic on a dragon?

If you are able to heal my injury, you may live. Did the dragon sound even closer? Was she coming to pick up Syla?

That's very generous. What if I, uhm, fail?

There is a transgression that must be accounted for.

Does that mean you'll kill me?

I shall make it swift with little pain. Despite being called a wild *dragon, I am more civilized than many of my brethren.*

Good to know.

The dragon didn't answer.

Syla swallowed and stared at the figurine, feeling betrayed by her father's gewgaw. He'd loved her. He surely hadn't meant to leave her something that could offend dragons. He must not have known.

Since he'd passed, she could never ask him.

"Unless the dragon kills me and I meet my father in the afterlife," she said, jumping when a shadow flew across her window.

The red dragon had arrived.

10

Shouts and cries of, "Dragon!" and "Man the cannons!" and "Look out!" penetrated the window of Syla's room.

Her instincts yelled at her to scramble under the bed and hide. As if *that* would keep a dragon from getting her.

But she had, however inadvertently, called for this dragon to come. She had to do her best to make sure it didn't kill anyone in the area.

After gulping in a breath of air that wasn't as fortifying as she wanted, Syla grabbed the figurine and her pack, then made herself open the window so the red-scaled creature could find her.

The dragon came into view, beautiful and terrifying at the same time. Even larger than the big male that Vorik rode, she exuded tremendous power. Her muscles relaxed and flexed as she flew, lingering fires from the harbor and atop the bluff highlighting her sleek belly. Golden eyes reflected the flames, or maybe they even glowed from within, fueled by her magical power. Her great wings spread as she descended in an elegant glide, angling to come over the courtyard walls and right at Syla's room, as if the dragon knew exactly where a princess would be found.

Maybe she could sense the figurine, almost a miniature version of herself. Or maybe not *almost*. Could it possibly have been crafted to *be* a representation of this dragon?

As those slitted golden eyes locked onto Syla, she couldn't help but tremble, both from fear at such an awesomely terrifying predator and from the concern that she couldn't possibly heal a dragon so she wouldn't live to see dawn. She'd meant to find a shielder to help her people, not call down a living nightmare to kill her.

"Your Highness!" the soldier who'd been assigned to guard her window cried, tearing his gaze from the approaching dragon when he noticed that she'd opened it.

Such shock and horror stamped his face that she paused with one foot on the sill. She'd been about to climb out, but she'd forgotten about him.

The dragon descended lower, her glide deceptively fast as she sailed over the wall. The soldier sprang for Syla.

She lurched back, ducking down below the sill an instant before he passed through the window. He clipped her as he twisted in the air, trying to grab her and carry her deeper into the room with him. But she rolled sideways, flattening her spectacles to her face to keep them from flying off. She landed awkwardly, ramming into a bookcase, as he landed deftly on his feet.

"Your Highness," he blurted, reaching for her as he looked toward the window, his eyes widening as the dragon filled the view.

Syla stood and backed away from him, but the bookcase impeded her retreat. The soldier caught her wrist with one hand as he used the other to shut the window.

If there'd been time, Syla would have laughed at the notion that a glass window casement would keep out a dragon.

Their scaled visitor didn't crash through it the way she'd expected. As the red dragon filled their view, Syla realized she was far too large to fly through a window or even a doorway. Instead, she landed on the roof above, and her long tail, as thick as a mature aspen, slapped down. It smashed through the window, obliterating the glass and knocking the soldier halfway across the room. He released Syla or she would have gone flying too.

A deafening screech came from above, followed by snapping and wrenching sounds that sent Syla to her knees. She almost dropped the figurine as she pressed her hands to her ears. A huge section of the roof tore away as beams snapped and wood pieces slammed to the floor. A section of the ceiling crashed down onto the soldier, half-burying him.

Using her maw, the dragon, now visible through a jagged gap above them, flung a huge chunk of the roof into the courtyard. One of the great golden orbs that were her eyes lowered so she could peer down at Syla, not with curiosity or amiability but with irritation.

Syla's urge to dive under the bed returned. Instead, reminded that *she* was responsible for this, she steadied herself on the bookcase and walked toward the hole in the roof.

She opened her mouth to say she was ready, but shouts came from outside.

"Fire!" someone cried from the courtyard wall.

Cannons boomed, and, through the destroyed window, Syla glimpsed soldiers readying crossbows. With her visitor perched on the remains of the roof, Syla couldn't see how many cannonballs and quarrels struck her scales, but the expression on the dragon's face, inasmuch as reptilian creatures *had* expressions that humans could recognize, suggested she was peeved rather than in pain. *Vexed.*

The golden eye turned away from Syla.

With premonition filling her, Syla yelled out the broken window. "Look out! Get back!"

Fire roiled from the rooftop, from the dragon's maw, and

blinding light filled the courtyard. The heat reached Syla even through the wall, and she backed several steps away. Behind her, the soldier groaned from under the rubble. At least he was still alive.

The troops in the hallway must have heard the commotion inside. Someone tried to open the door, but the collapsed roof had fallen in a way that blocked it.

"Help me!" came one of the men's muffled yells.

"Push!"

In the courtyard, the soldiers ran in the face of such a powerful opponent—and the deadly inferno that the dragon was spewing. Some fumbled and dropped their weapons as they sprinted away. Others retained their crossbows and were more controlled and thoughtful, running for cover, then turning to try to shoot again. The dragon roared and sent another inferno into the courtyard, igniting what few flammable structures remained. Surprisingly, her fire hadn't yet engulfed any humans, and she soon turned back to Syla, her tail flicking in annoyance.

"I'm ready," Syla called up to her.

When the fanged maw descended through the roof, smoke wafting from huge nostrils at the end of her snout, Syla decided she'd lied. Whatever she was, she was *not* ready.

But another groan from the rubble pile reminded her of the lives at stake. She made herself step closer to the hole so the dragon could reach her without further destruction. Even so, the size of the creature's head knocked more of the ceiling down as her jaws parted. Pointed fangs longer than swords reached for Syla, and she squinted and looked away, afraid the dragon had lied, that she didn't want healing. Maybe she'd decided to immediately kill Syla for her insolence.

For the second time that night, a great maw fastened around her body, covering her from knees to shoulders. Syla had meant to be brave, but she shrieked as those dagger-sharp fangs clasped her less gently than the other dragon had. They tightened, to *crush* and *pierce* her, she was certain.

Her feet lifted from the ground, her entire weight suspended between those jaws—those fangs. She shrieked again.

Rubble shifted, and the bedroom door shoved open a couple of inches with another cry of, "Push!"

The dragon lifted Syla toward the hole in the ceiling. The door opened farther, and a soldier squeezed in, his sword raised. Fel shoved his way in behind the man. His gaze darted immediately toward Syla, but their eyes only met briefly before the dragon lifted her out of view.

"It's got the princess!" Fel yelled.

"Fire!" someone cried again from the courtyard wall.

Despite the fresh flames blazing all around the castle, more cannons boomed.

It didn't matter. The dragon's powerful legs shifted, and she leaped into the air. Wind from her wings whipped at Syla's dress as she flew higher. No, she was *carried* higher. Like a hapless fish caught in an eagle's talons. Except a fang-filled maw was *worse* than talons. If the dragon shifted her jaw in the slightest—if the dragon *burped*—Syla might be eviscerated.

As the creature rose higher, Syla's heart hammering against her eardrums, the damaged castle grounds came into view. The devastation was as bad as she'd feared. Then they flew over the edge of the bluff, and she dangled over a drop of more than a hundred feet down to the harbor. That was terrifying, but worse was the view of all the carnage, the destroyed and smoldering ships, docks and piers incinerated, and wreckage and bodies floating in the water.

A cannonball streaked toward Syla, and she almost cried out again. The dragon adjusted her grip as she tilted her wings to turn, to fly parallel to the coastline.

The cannonball sailed past inches below Syla's dangling feet. More booms came from the castle walls.

The dragon's wings flapped easily and steadily, and Syla had the impression that her captor was supremely unconcerned about being fired upon.

After a few moments, Syla got her fear under control. The dragon hadn't yet killed her, and they'd flown out of range of the cannons. As she gazed grimly back at the smoldering city, she resolved again to find a way to help her people. More than ever, she knew she had to restore the sky shield so that more predators couldn't take advantage.

If she could get away from the dragon, maybe she could yet find her aunt.

"Just one problem," she whispered, all too aware of the fangs wrapped around her, holding her tightly so that she wouldn't fall. "Getting away."

After a journey shorter than Syla had expected, the dragon tilted inland.

Syla had thought her captor would take her to some distant lair, but this... She twisted her neck, careful not to prong herself with unnecessary body movements, and peered in the direction they were going.

The lighthouse. She blinked. Captain Vorik had said *he* would be there, but why would this red dragon take Syla there?

This red dragon, she reminded herself, had been chatting with Vorik's dragon.

"Oh."

As they approached the lighthouse, the fire still burning in the top, sending a beacon out to sea, Syla could make out a huge dark form resting on the ground beside it. The green dragon.

Her vision wasn't strong enough to see in the gloom if Vorik was also down there. In the tunnels, the soldiers had chased after him, so it was possible he hadn't made his way out here yet. It was also possible he was dead.

Her captor flapped her wings and angled toward the top of the lighthouse. Before reaching it, the dragon flexed her neck and startled Syla by letting go.

Syla shrieked, arms flailing, as she plunged toward the ground. She was still twenty feet in the air!

She flapped her arms as if *she* might fly, but she plummeted like a rock. The dragon on the ground lifted its head but did nothing to intervene. Syla squinted her eyes shut, expecting to hit so hard that she broke her neck.

But a man darted from the dragon's side. At the last second, he positioned himself underneath and caught her under her knees and shoulders. Even so, her weight and momentum almost carried her to the ground. But he compensated and kept her from injury.

With terror surging through her body, Syla gripped his shoulders, half afraid he would do as the dragon had and cast her away. The cliff above which the lighthouse perched wasn't that far away...

"Your Highness," Captain Vorik said in surprise. "I didn't expect you so soon."

Syla groaned.

11

VORIK HELD THE STUNNED PRINCESS SYLA IN HIS ARMS, LOOKING back and forth between her and Wreylith the Red, the powerful and aloof female dragon perched atop the lighthouse.

He felt almost as stunned as the woman in his arms. Since Agrevlari had pined after Wreylith from afar for years, Vorik was aware of the dragon, and he'd listened in on a few of the telepathic conversations they'd shared when they'd passed in flight before, so he knew that the independent female cared nothing for humans, whether gardeners or stormers.

Why had she flown to the castle and plucked Syla away from her people? Why had she even known who Syla was?

Oh, Vorik had no doubt that Wreylith could sense which humans had magic, either granted via bonds with dragons or by birth because of their gods-touched heritage, but the wild dragons cared about neither.

"Put me down, please." Syla watched Vorik warily, though *Wreylith* should have concerned her more. Her grip on his shoulders lessened, and she glanced down.

"Are you certain?" Vorik asked. "That dragon attempted to toss you to your death, and she's still eyeing you."

Not that Vorik, even with all his battle experience and fighting prowess, could do much to protect the princess from the powerful red dragon if she attacked. Judging by the way Agrevlari was gazing up at the lighthouse—was that what *enraptured* looked like on the face of a dragon?—he wouldn't be any help if a battle with this particular individual ensued.

"She... wants me to heal her." Syla looked toward the lighthouse. "Though she doesn't seem very injured, and I... didn't expect to be dropped from such a height."

Vorik shifted his grip, intending to settle her onto her feet, but the curves of her body pressing against him had some appeal, and he was reluctant to release her. The memory of the general's orders popped into his mind.

Find the princess and win her trust.

Jhiton hadn't ordered that seduction be used, but it had been implied. Too bad Syla's frown didn't imply that she was in the mood for an amorous display of gratitude. Maybe, later on, after she recovered from the start of being tossed, she would feel more inclined to thank Vorik. Perhaps with a kiss on the cheek. Surely, he deserved that. Especially considering that he'd been distracted by picking the deliciously tart blackberries that grew wild around the base of the lighthouse. A few thorns among the brambles had scratched him, but those had been such minor assaults, well worth enduring to fill his pockets with the juicy treats.

His eyes widened with the realization that Syla might have squished the berries when he'd caught her. Yes, he could smell their fruity scent more strongly than before. At least a few had been crushed. Disappointing. He would have to gather more when he figured out what to do with the princess—and the dragon who'd dropped her into his arms.

"Captain," Syla said. "Set me down."

The tension in her body didn't suggest that she had *kisses* or gratitude of any kind in mind. More likely, she believed she was surrounded by enemies and was afraid.

"Of course, Your Highness."

Sighing, Vorik eased her to the ground and released her, though relinquishing her was almost as disappointing as losing the berries. Her curves were, after all, quite intriguing. Unlike the strong but often painfully lean stormer women—memories of sex with the athletic and aggressive Captain Lesva came to mind—Syla had zaftig appeal. Thanks to her sheltered existence as a gardener, she'd been permitted a gentle femininity, a life of ease.

No, Vorik decided as she stepped back, her jaw set, her gaze determined through her spectacles. A healer didn't likely have a life of ease. People were always getting ill or injured, so she'd probably worked long hours at her temple. As one of the few humans in the world with magic and healing training, her skills had to be in great demand. And, as he knew from personal experience, wielding magic was draining.

After the atypical method of travel, Syla's dress was askew. She straightened it, though she gripped something in one hand, and wasn't as effective at smoothing the fabric as she might have been otherwise. Also a pack on two straps over her shoulders inhibited her effort. For a moment, Vorik, thanks to his sharp night vision, got a glimpse of bare flesh. He made himself look away, though a stirring in his groin promised that his body would happily lend itself to the seduction scenario, should that be needed.

Unfortunately, Syla wasn't interested in that. Not *yet* anyway.

"If the mighty Wreylith wished you to heal her," Vorik said, delving into his pockets to check the status of the berries, "that was a surprising way to initiate a temple session."

"I thought so." Syla gave her dress a final smoothing and faced the dragon atop the lighthouse.

I did not intend to wound the female, Wreylith spoke telepathically, the words for them all. *I've interacted with few humans and am not that familiar with the durability of the species on average. I did not know that so slight a drop might harm this one.*

Wreylith looked at Agrevlari as she spoke, and Vorik wondered if he'd been the one to inform her that falls of twenty feet could break human bones. Ah, some of his berries had survived. Wonderful. The others... Well, if stains to his riding leathers were the worst he returned home with, he would count himself lucky. He couldn't resist popping a couple of the berries into his mouth as Syla considered the dragon.

"I... would have needed a healer myself." Syla lowered her voice to mutter, "Or a gravedigger."

From her elevated perch, Wreylith cocked her head. She had such power that her eyes glowed slightly, as if the magic inside her could not be fully contained by her body and had to flow out. Vorik had seen that effect on only a handful of dragons he'd encountered in his life and rarely those who deigned to align themselves with humans and take on riders. It indicated great power.

"Never mind." Syla's words came quickly, nervously, but she didn't stumble over them. If this was her first time communicating with a dragon, Vorik was surprised she managed to hold eye contact and speak at all.

He was as used to dragons as a human could be, and he still found himself awed by the raw power that Wreylith exuded.

"How may I help you, uhm, what's the appropriate way to address a dragon?" Syla asked. "Do you have a name or title that I should use?"

Your sublime magnificenceness, Agrevlari suggested.

Vorik rolled his eyes. "She asked what title *she* should use, not what you call Wreylith in your fantasies."

Both dragons gave him baleful looks, and Vorik reconsidered his choice to be sarcastic in this situation. Even though he always teased Agrevlari, something that went both ways, his dragon might not appreciate it in front of witnesses. This witness, in particular. Indeed, an irritated grumble emanated from the green dragon, and a tendril of smoke wafted from his nostrils.

Vorik folded his arms over his chest and raised his chin, also feeling compelled not to be humble—or humbled—in front of a strange dragon.

I am called Wreylith Descended of Wrathadori, Matriarch of the Stormchosen.

Syla hesitated, looking at Vorik. Yeah, the female hadn't exactly told them how she preferred to be addressed.

"Riders sometimes call dragons chieftain or chieftess, per our conventions among our tribes, but I've heard gardeners use lady or lord or even king or queen, though dragons don't have royalty. They're hierarchical, yes, but it's all about who's strongest and defeats others in battles. I've heard, and can see from her scars, that Wreylith has survived a lot of battles and defeated many challengers." Vorik waved toward the female.

That is so, Wreylith said.

She slew the pompous but powerful Bisarak the Starchaser just last year, Agrevlari said.

Yes. Wreylith made the telepathic statements matter-of-factly, without the pomposity that so many dragons that bonded with riders had.

Vorik, who almost considered it a hereditary dragon trait, regarded her curiously. "Whatever you use, Your Highness, I wouldn't shorten it or make it flippant."

"Princesses are never flippant. And did you mean my people when you said *gardener*?" Syla touched her chest. "Or... actual gardeners? Like farmers?"

"It's our term for your people," Vorik said, surprised she hadn't heard it before. It was a logical term, after all, since they called this the Garden Kingdom.

"Because we're so heavily agricultural?" Syla guessed.

"That's right." Vorik didn't mention that it had negative connotations among the stormers and implied people who were too soft and civilized to survive beyond their sky shields. Since he was, even at that moment, enjoying berries that some gardener must have planted once, he couldn't feel too superior to her people. If there were other areas in the world where such delectables grew without being destroyed by storms, eaten by birds and animals, or surrounded by poisonous plants... he might have gardened too. At least when he wasn't busy flying, fighting, and hunting.

Wreylith hopped down from the lighthouse, the drop not fazing a dragon in the least, though she did land mostly on three legs, favoring her right forelimb. *This is what I require healed.*

She lifted that limb toward them, and Syla jumped when the dragon extended her talons, the moonlight gleaming off them. With the deadly appendage so close, Vorik twitched too. Wreylith *was* a formidable dragon, and he had no idea how to read her moods. She was reputedly mercurial. At the least, if she was like most dragons, she would grow extra savage and deadly when she lost her temper. Dragons had been known to fight with each other to the death simply because one woke up grumpy.

Despite being startled, Syla didn't skitter back from the extended foot, the glinting talons. She walked forward to investigate the injury but shook her head.

"It's a little dark for me to see the problem, I'm afraid." She looked around as if a lantern might be waiting in the grass.

Vorik was disappointed that he couldn't provide one for her. Since his night vision was keen, he never bothered traveling with such items, but he would have to do her a lot more favors if he intended to gain her trust. Yes, he'd kept her from splatting on the ground, but, if she was like other women, she might appreciate it more if he could help her with the small things.

Wreylith's maw parted, and Syla stiffened. Vorik stepped

forward, his hand going to his sword in case he needed to protect the princess.

But a touch of magic flowed from the dragon, and only the smallest ball of fire rolled up her gullet and out of her maw. It drifted through the air until it floated to the side of Syla's head, illuminating Wreylith's foot as well as the lush green grass and a few boulders littered around the area.

Heat as well as light emanated from the sphere, and Syla eyed it with concern. Since numerous of her people had been slain by dragon fire, Vorik suspected she was thinking of that.

He shook his head bleakly, well aware that he and the riders had been behind that. He feared there was too much between them for him to win her trust in any capacity. Jhiton had asked too much.

If you ever raise a blade to a dragon, Wreylith told Vorik, having noticed his grip on his sword, *it'll be the last motion you ever make.*

"I've raised my blade to fight many dragons." Vorik had always done so from astride Agrevlari's back, but he knew better than to be meek in front of their kind, so he didn't admit that. Nor did he yank his hand away from the hilt, though he realized Wreylith had never intended to hurt the princess. "I yet live," he added.

They must have been extremely runty dragons.

"Well, certainly. I would be a fool to challenge a *powerful* dragon."

What a strange human you are. Healer. Wreylith focused on Syla again and flexed her talons.

What looked like a giant thorn was embedded in the flesh of her foot. Or maybe that was a fang that had come away after something had bitten her? She must have incinerated whatever creature had been so foolish as to bite a dragon.

"Yes, I see now." Syla turned her full attention to it. "You said you tangled with a basilisk?"

Yes. While I battled another foe, I stepped upon the lair of a giant blue basilisk. Usually, their venomous fangs cannot pierce a dragon's scales, but this one lucked upon a less armored spot. Wreylith glared at the maligned foot and bared her own fangs in displeasure.

And maybe in pain? From what Vorik knew of basilisk fangs, which were designed to come off and quickly grow back afterward, they could keep oozing their venom into the bloodstream of their target for hours or even days afterward. And that venom was potent enough to kill even large creatures. If not for a dragon's inherent magic, Wreylith might have died from the wound.

"Let me... see what I can do." Judging from the way Syla wiped her palms on her dress, she remained nervous.

Vorik didn't blame her. "Have you healed anything besides humans before?"

"Yes." She nodded and approached the injured foot but also whispered, "Cats, dogs, and horses. And a gerbil."

"No chickens?" Vorik asked. "They're closer to dragons than hounds and horses."

Chickens! Agrevlari rose to all fours, so indignant that his tail straightened, smacking against the side of the lighthouse. Fortunately, it was constructed from solid stone and didn't crumble.

"Anatomically speaking," Vorik said, "you're closer to a chicken than you are a dog."

Dragons are like neither of those inferior animals. *I shall make you walk back to Sixteen Talons headquarters, Vorik.*

"Since there's a lot of water between here and there, walking would be difficult."

Most difficult.

Syla had removed her pack and rummaged in it. She appeared to be ignoring the conversation. Vorik thought she was younger than he—perhaps twenty-five or twenty-six years of age to his thirty?—but wondered if she might be more mature. Probably. Many people were.

Our anatomy is closer to lizards, Wreylith stated, *but since we were, like wyverns, yetis, yarveni, and takrons, designed by the storm god, and we didn't evolve naturally on this world, we have no direct relatives on a phylogenetic tree.*

Lizards. Agrevlari huffed, but when his tail smacked the lighthouse again, it was with less force.

"Ah, here we go." Syla pulled out a small cylindrical tube. "I almost didn't grab it. It'll be useful, of course, if I visit, ah..." She glanced at Vorik. "Other islands with venomous snakes. But perhaps it can be useful here."

She had travel in mind, did she? To acquire a shielder from another island? As the general had suggested?

"There are venomous snakes on the gardener islands?" was all Vorik asked. "I didn't think there was anything dangerous here in paradise."

"They live among the rocks in some places."

"Death strikers? Basilisks? Murder asps?"

"Rattlesnakes, mostly."

"Oh." Vorik laughed and waved a hand. Such snakes hardly counted as dangerous.

Syla bristled at his dismissal. "As a healer who's treated rattlesnake bite wounds when I've traveled to other islands, I assure you, they can kill."

Realizing he'd offended her, Vorik bowed an apology. "Yes, of course."

What is that? Wreylith asked as Syla popped the lid of the cylinder and withdrew an instrument.

"An antique vacuum venom extractor. I have three in my collection." Syla hesitated, then softly corrected, "I *had* three."

She blinked away tears, then shook her head. After all the people she'd lost, a collection of physical items couldn't be as devastating, but the reminder had to rub sand in the broken blister on one's sword hand.

Vorik bowed another apology, but she'd turned back to the

dragon. Closing her eyes, she lifted the tool and her hand to Wreylith's exposed foot.

Vorik sensed her drawing upon power, and the birthmark on the back of her hand glowed slightly, but he couldn't tell how she was applying it. Could she remove the magically tenacious basilisk fang? If Wreylith hadn't been able to take it out, doing so couldn't be easy.

As he watched the glow of her moon-mark, his fingers strayed to the back of his hand, to the spot where a dragon-shaped tattoo lay hidden under his black glove. His mark didn't glow when he drew upon his power, but it was the sign of his link to Agrevlari and the dragon power that had infused Vorik since they'd bonded. Only some riders, those who'd been invited by a dragon to go through the bonding ceremony, had such tattoos, but all of those who flew in the Sixteen Talons wore the fingerless black gloves. It had started as tradition and then become a part of the uniform, a way to keep those with tattoos from being singled out by enemies. It also ensured that enemies never knew for certain if the rider they faced had enhanced abilities, often not until it was too late.

Are you not concerned about allowing one with healing magic to tend to your wound, Mighty Wreylith? Agrevlari asked.

Certainly not, the red dragon replied.

You're aware of the gods-gift that the line of those humans marked by the moon have, aren't you?

Gods-gift. What a term for such puny magic.

As the dragons conversed telepathically, including Vorik and presumably Syla, Vorik watched her, wondering if it concerned her to be at the center of their discussion. She'd closed her eyes behind her glass lenses, and her face was set with concentration. If she could ignore them while focusing on healing, that was impressive. It had to be hard to concentrate with a dragon scant feet away, breathing hot air around one's head.

The magic, Agrevlari continued, *that is used for healing is known to be particularly powerful. It can bind a being to the healer for many days or even weeks until the effects wear off.*

Not a dragon, Wreylith said. *Another puny and insignificant human, perhaps.*

I've seen it work on hounds too. Even more so. For life, they give their loyalty to the healer.

Hounds! Wreylith issued a snort that stirred Syla's hair and made her open her eyes. *Hounds give their lifelong loyalty for a cube of meat. As we've recently discussed, dragons are not kin to weakling and pathetic hounds. Nor chickens!*

"Do you wish me to continue?" Syla's palm was on the embedded fang, but she'd paused funneling magic into the injury. The dragons were probably distracting her. "It is easier to focus without patients nattering."

Wreylith flexed her sharp talons. Syla watched them but didn't skitter back. Many people would have.

Nattering! A wisp of smoke wafted from her left nostril.

"Nattering," Syla said firmly. "Shall I continue?"

A rumble—a growl?—emanated from the red dragon's chest, but she kept her foot raised. *Do so.*

Vorik smiled as Syla closed her eyes again. Maybe it wasn't wise, but he was starting to like her.

I don't think there's any chance of a dragon feeling bound to a human, gods-gifted magic or not, Vorik told Agrevlari. *Especially one as powerful as Wreylith.*

Correct, Wreylith said, even though Vorik had meant to send the words only to Agrevlari. He supposed he shouldn't be surprised that the powerful red dragon could intercept private telepathic communications. *Should she attempt to enact her puny magic on me in any way,* Wreylith continued, *or should she vex me in any way, I shall slay her.*

Syla's lips twitched, but she didn't draw back or even open her eyes. Once again, her face was set with concentration.

Sensing the healing might take a while, Vorik sheathed his sword and walked to the base of the lighthouse. Dawn wasn't that far off, so he knelt to gather more berries. Under the light of day, it would be easier to avoid the thorns. Not that he minded a few scratches. For such delicious treats, he would endure everything from sword wounds to Agrevlari's sarcasm.

Many minutes and many consumed berries later, a roar of pain made Vorik spring to his feet, drawing his sword again. Fearing Syla had inadvertently hurt—or *vexed*—Wreylith and roused her ire, he ran toward them in case he needed to protect her.

But Wreylith was turning away from Syla and flinging her forelimb toward the cliff overlooking the sea. Something flew away, blood droplets arcing through the air as it descended over the edge. The fang. Syla must have cut it out with her magic. Or maybe she'd used another tool from her kit. Did she also have antique tweezers to go with the venom extractor?

Syla lowered her arms and backed a few steps from the snarling dragon. Wary, she asked, "How does that feel?"

If the roar of pain had been any indication, the fang's removal hadn't been a delight. But surely the injury would bother Wreylith less going forward. She had to appreciate that.

That dreadful fang left its venom scorching my veins, and there is a hole in my foot. Wreylith turned toward Syla again. *How do you think it feels?*

"Painful, I'm certain," she said.

Though he didn't wave his sword threateningly, Vorik continued forward to stand at Syla's side.

I should have slain the basilisks for presuming to attack a dragon, a dragon with far superior might and power than they.

Vorik, reminded that Wreylith had intercepted his comments before, refrained from saying to Agrevlari that she was as pompous as he was. *Later*, he might mention that.

"I did my best to remove the venom near the wound, and then

use my magic to break down that which remained in your blood, altering it into an inert substance that your body can eventually excrete, but you are..." Syla hesitated as Wreylith's head lowered, her glowing golden eyes boring into her, "large," Syla finished.

I was not the runt of my clutch, Wreylith said.

"I assumed not," Syla said blandly. "Should you chance upon mugdart root, you could make a paste that would soothe the wound."

Dragons are powerful beings with sublime constitutions. We do not need soothing.

"I have an herbalism book along with maps of prime areas around the world. If you like, I could show you where medicinal plants that can ease pain can be found."

I don't need my pain eased. Wreylith bared her fangs.

"All right." Syla looked a little disappointed that the dragon didn't show interest in what was apparently a passion for her—who brought *herbalism* books along when escaping from an attack zone?

Wreylith lowered her lips to hide the fangs. *You have removed the nettlesome tooth, and the wound will heal. I will not slay you today.*

Syla hesitated again, probably wondering if that meant the dragon might slay her if they ran into each other again. "Thank you," was all she said.

But you will not use that trinket to spy again.

"I did not intend to do so, and I apologize," Syla said.

"Trinket?" Vorik thought of the venom extractor, but that wouldn't be used for spying.

Syla drew something from a pocket in her dress, a red dragon figurine. It appeared fragile, like blown glass, but Vorik sensed magic in it and knew it was sturdier than it appeared. He'd seen such items before, though never linked to a wild dragon. How odd.

"This was my father's, and he left it to me," Syla said to Wreylith.

I am aware.

Syla blinked. "Did you… know my father?"

One before him.

"My… grandfather?"

Do you know nothing of your own history, human? Your ancestry? Wreylith lifted her unwounded forelimb and used a talon to scratch her long neck.

"Uhm, I know quite a bit, but not about people's… collectibles." She sent a wistful look in the direction of the city.

Collectible. Wreylith grunted. It almost sounded like a scoff.

"My father passed earlier than any of us expected. He didn't mention anything about this item to me while he lived." Syla leaned forward, maybe hoping the dragon would share more.

You will not use it to spy on dragons. Wreylith lowered all four feet to the ground and stared intently at Syla. *And you will not summon me with it. I am not, as we discussed, a pathetic hound.* Her jaws parted, her sharp fangs scarcely two feet from Syla, and Vorik tightened his grip on his sword. *Your healing magic has done nothing to* bind *me to you.*

Again, Syla didn't skitter back, though Vorik wouldn't have thought any less of her if she did.

"I didn't think it would," she said.

If you vex me again, Wreylith stated, *I will slay you.*

With those final words, the red dragon sprang into the air. The wind of her wings battered at them as she flew off over the cliff and out to sea.

"Dragons aren't known for being the most grateful of beings," Vorik said, doubting Syla had interacted with them often.

"At least she didn't kill me." Syla grimaced. "Today."

She had to be wondering if she'd made a mistake in coming to the red dragon's awareness. Vorik wished he could assure her that Wreylith wouldn't hold a grudge, but the wild dragons weren't predictable. They weren't like the familiar dragons who worked with humans. Vorik wouldn't say that Agrevlari didn't have any mercurial moments, but he was easier to predict. He was—

Vorik looked around, realizing his dragon had moved away from them. He was near the lighthouse, lying in the lush green grass with his legs crooked into the air.

"What are you doing, Agrevlari?" Vorik asked.

Scratching an itch and enjoying how cool and soft this vegetation is. The dragon swished his hips and shoulders back and forth, tail moving from side to side.

"Is that dragon... rolling in the grass?" Syla stared, her mouth dangling open. In shock?

Maybe the gardeners weren't familiar with the less serious side of dragons. Or that at least *some* dragons had them. Vorik had a feeling Wreylith didn't roll in the grass. His brother's dragon, Ozlemar, *certainly* did not.

"He has an itch," Vorik said.

"Oh."

"And he likes your grass. The stuff that grows out in the dry Desert Mountains, Scorched Islands, and on Juniper Flats is anything but lush. You can braid it to make switches to spank your children with." Vorik patted his backside, well remembering lashings given to him and his brother by their stern mother.

Syla blinked, either at the imagery of him being spanked or at the notion that lush grass didn't exist in many other places in the world.

Vorik opened his mouth to say more, but a distant screech came from the sky. He lifted his sword again as he scanned the predawn clouds, worried Wreylith had changed her mind about sparing Syla's life.

But it wasn't a red dragon that he spotted. The outlines of a gray and a green dragon, each carrying a rider, were visible out over the sea. They were flying straight toward the lighthouse.

In the growing light, Vorik could see the faces of the men, even from the distance, and he recognized those dragons as well. They and their riders were in the Sixteen Talons.

Beside him, Syla followed his gaze and spotted the threat. She tensed and swore, looking around.

Vorik opened his mouth, intending to say that he recognized the newcomers and that they were allies. But, when one lifted a gargoyle-bone sword, and pointed it at Syla, he realized that wasn't true. *She* wasn't an ally of the Sixteen Talons or any other stormer.

The other rider pointed his sword at Vorik and shouted a single word.

The wind and roar of the sea muffled the sound, but it didn't matter. Vorik read it on the man's lips and knew what it was.

"Traitor!"

As promised, his brother had sent men to help along the ruse, men who might, if Vorik wasn't careful, kill Syla.

12

WHILE SHE'D EXTRICATED THE VENOM-FILLED FANG FROM THE fearsome red dragon, Syla had remained calm, fighting down her instinct to run each time the powerful creature twitched a limb or spoke of slaying. But now, with two new dragons flying toward the grassy top of the bluff, her calmness fled. Both of their riders waved swords while glaring at her, their intent clear. Surprisingly, they glared at Vorik too.

When the gray dragon angled toward Syla, descending rapidly with talons outstretched, she sprinted for the only cover on the clifftop, the lighthouse.

"Hide inside!" Vorik yelled after her.

Meanwhile, he ran to his winged ally and sprang high into the air, landing astride its broad back, as if it were a pony instead of a huge dragon. Never had Syla seen anyone capable of such a great jump.

Something that doesn't matter in the least right now, she thought as she ran, wishing she'd stayed closer to the lighthouse while healing Wreylith.

The enemy dragons were coming in fast, and she wouldn't

make it in time. Even if she did, was the stone structure enough to protect her from such powerful enemies? After all, the buildings in the castle had fallen...

As the gray dragon swept closer, it opened its maw, and flames roiled in the back of its throat. It would torch her *and* the lighthouse.

No, a green dragon arrowed in from the side, colliding with the gray and knocking it from its flight path. Vorik riding on his mount. Agrevlari. That had been the big male's name.

The wingbeats of the two dragons battered the air as they twisted and dove right above Syla's head. The wind they generated tugged at her dress hard enough to send her stumbling sideways. As she flailed for balance, she gaped at the sight of the battling dragons. They twisted, bit, and clawed at each other, somehow remaining aloft as they gyrated about, even lashing out at each other with their thick and powerful tails.

"Traitor!" the rider of the gray dragon yelled.

Syla reached the door of the lighthouse and should have run inside, but she paused with her hand on the latch. She couldn't keep from watching as the wind created by the dragons' wings tugged at her hair and made the grass flutter. The display of gravity-defying power and agility from both creatures as they rolled and twisted in the air was mesmerizing.

The battle took place near the lighthouse, more than thirty feet up, but Vorik leaped from the back of his dragon to land on the spine of the gray, as if there were no danger of falling to one's death.

His rider opponent didn't appear surprised, merely spinning around to meet him with a swinging sword. Vorik struck quickly, deflecting the blade with his own as he balanced on the back of the gyrating dragon. He even managed to kick the other rider, a strong blow that took the man square in the chest.

His opponent flew off his mount and tumbled past the edge of the cliff and toward the sea below.

The gray dragon roared and extricated itself from the biting and slashing Agrevlari. Neck snapping around, its fanged maw whipped toward Vorik who still crouched on its back.

"Look out!" Syla caught herself yelling.

Somehow, Vorik leaped over the snapping jaws, avoiding them and coming down farther back on the dragon, just above the base of the tail.

Agrevlari flew in again, but the gray dragon, incensed by having an unwanted rider, bucked and snapped wildly. Twice more, Vorik jumped to avoid those deadly fangs, once somersaulting in the air and swinging his sword at one of the beast's horns, clipping off the tip. Somehow, he landed again on the dragon's back.

Agrevlari flew in close to help—or maybe retrieve his rider.

Captivated by Vorik's sheer acrobatic skill, Syla almost missed the shadow that fell over the lighthouse. The other green dragon was arrowing straight down toward her, its maw parted and hatred burning in its rider's eyes.

She lifted the latch, but the door was heavier than she expected and stuck as it scraped over an uneven stone floor. Terrified, she shoved her shoulder against it. It ground open, and she leaped inside as the dragon landed, head snapping toward her. It missed her but caught the hem of her dress, the rip of fabric echoing loudly in the hollow stone lighthouse.

The yank as the dragon pulled at the captured hem almost pulled Syla off her feet—and back through the doorway. But she lunged away, losing the bottom portion of her dress, then raced for the stairs.

A thump sounded behind her, the rider dismounting. A big muscular man, he'd landed in a crouch right in front of the doorway. He lunged to follow her, to *kill* her, his swinging sword promised.

But something caught him from behind. Vorik had also jumped down from who knew where—forty feet in the sky?

Before the rider could turn to face him, Vorik leaped upon the man, snaking a muscled arm around his foe's neck from behind.

Vorik dragged the man out of the lighthouse and away from the doorway. Syla glimpsed a boot as the rider kicked, trying to escape from Vorik. Then they both disappeared from her view, though thumps and grunts continued as the two fought.

Several steps up, Syla paused, her heart racing, the bottom of her dress shredded. She was tempted to keep running to the top of the lighthouse but had no idea where the dragons had gone. What if they were waiting at the top for her?

A loud snap came from outside near the doorway. It sounded like a bone breaking. Or... a neck?

Silence fell, save for the roar of the sea, and Syla waited, afraid of who would come into view. The last she'd seen, Vorik had held the advantage, but the riders were all so well-trained. It was possible their enemy had managed to get the best of Vorik, especially if one of the dragons had returned to help.

A screech sounded from the sky, but it was farther away than she would have expected. Had the battle between the dragons moved out over the sea?

A dark figure stepped into the doorway. Vorik.

Never would she have thought she would let out a breath of pure relief at seeing him. He was a dragon rider himself. An enemy.

But... was that true?

He'd just fought his own people to protect her, as he'd said he would. Those dragons had been trying to kill each other, and she'd seen that man go over the cliff. He'd probably died on the rocks below. With a fall so far, how not?

"Are you all right, Your Highness?" Other than his clothing being rucked up, his hair tousled, and a gash along his jaw, Vorik appeared fine, his voice calm.

"I... yes." Syla smoothed her dress as much as she could with the lower half in tatters. She tried not to think about how many inches away she'd been from being crushed in a dragon's jaws.

She stepped down the stairs toward him. "Are you?"

When she faced him from the ground, she reached toward his jaw, prompted by her healer's instincts to inspect the wound. It wept blood down the side of his neck and looked painful.

Vorik caught her wrist gently but firmly. "I'm not as impervious to magic as Wreylith believes she is. Please forgive my rudeness, but I'll pass on accepting healing from you, Your Highness."

"Oh." Her cheeks heated. "I wouldn't have used my magic on you without asking for permission. I was just looking to see how deep it is. Sorry. It's a habit."

"I understand." Vorik released her wrist, bowed to her, and stepped outside.

Agrevlari waited in the grass, as if nothing eventful had happened. He didn't appear to have even a cut. She looked for the other dragons and spotted the pair flying away, side by side and already far out to sea.

"What happened to their riders?" Syla had seen the first fall over the cliff, but what of the second? Had Vorik broken his neck?

The grass was flattened where the two men had fought, but she didn't see a body.

Wordlessly, Vorik pointed to the cliff, then walked to the edge. It was only a few yards from the lighthouse, and she eased up beside him to peer over herself.

The rocks jutting from the churning white water below looked as deadly as she'd believed, but she didn't see either of the men's bodies. Had they been dragged under by the tide? She spotted something black—a boot—upon one of the rocks.

"They may be down there, swimming away." Vorik was also looking about, seeking sign of them. "Riders are tough to kill."

"I... would imagine." Syla looked at him, tempted to ask about the superhuman fighting prowess he'd shown. He was clearly fit and trained hard, but only magic could have allowed such feats. "I know why they want *me* dead, but why did they attack you?"

The memory of the man shouting *traitor* rose in her mind, answering her own question.

Vorik shrugged, as if the attack hadn't surprised him. "They must have figured out that which I've tried to keep hidden."

"Your... allegiance to the Freeborn Faction?" Syla hadn't believed that story before, but as blood trickled from Vorik's wound, she started to wonder if he'd told the truth. Maybe it *wasn't* a ruse.

She couldn't deny that those men—and especially that gray dragon—had tried to kill Vorik. They'd glared at him with even more hatred in their eyes than when they'd looked at her.

"Yes. When I return, I'll have to tell Chieftess Atilya. She'll be disappointed to learn that my cover has been blown and I can't be a spy for her anymore, but..." Vorik shrugged again. "I figured that would happen anyway when I came here to protect you."

"I don't know what to say."

"Just tell me where I can find more of those fabulous blackberries."

Syla blinked. That wasn't what she'd expected him to have on his mind right now. "If we find an oven, I'll bake you a cobbler with them."

"Really?" His ears perked, and an expression of wonder and delight stretched his lips, almost startling on the face of such a savage warrior. But, by the moon, he was striking when he smiled. "I've heard of such things but never had one. They're sweet, yes?"

"Yes. It's a dessert."

His smile turned a little sad. "My people don't have desserts."

It was ridiculous, given the situation, but Syla had the urge to hug him. His people had just decimated hers and killed her family. Feeling *sympathy* for them—even for Vorik—would be ridiculous. But... he kept saving her life. She couldn't help but feel... something.

It didn't hurt that he was handsome—*very* handsome—with those keen emerald eyes and cheekbones that couldn't have been more perfect if a sculptor had carved them from marble. And the strong, muscled arms that had so easily caught her when she'd dropped? Though it was undoubtedly unwise, she longed to step closer to him rather than drawing away.

Lorengarth has warned me, Agrevlari said, letting Syla hear his words, *that he intends to return with more riders after he's reported to his superiors about the princess's whereabouts and your betrayal.*

Vorik nodded. "We'd better not stay here. Your Highness, my faction leaders would like me to bring you to their hideout, the better to protect you—"

Syla shook her head and stepped back, her hackles rising. She wouldn't let anyone lock her in a *room* again, not her own people and not his.

"—but you look like you were packed for a trip?" He cocked his head and waved at her pack in the grass.

"I..." Syla wasn't as suspicious of Vorik as she had been twenty minutes ago, but she dared not speak of the shielders to a rider.

It would be safest to tell him to leave her be and that she would go her own way. But, logically, would she survive another day without a protector? If those dragons returned with new riders, they would be looking for *her*, and she didn't have the power to stand up to even a rider, much less a rider with a *dragon*.

"I need to visit my aunt," Syla said.

That wasn't a great kingdom secret that she couldn't let out.

Vorik raised his eyebrows at her vagueness.

She groped for an explanation that would satisfy him without giving away anything important.

"Does she have an oven?" he surprised her by asking.

Syla almost laughed. "Yes."

"Then please allow Agrevlari and me to escort you to her kitchen." Vorik bowed and extended a hand toward the dragon.

Syla looked toward Agrevlari. He wasn't rolling on his back in the grass now but watching her intently.

If she got onto the dragon's back with Vorik, she would essentially be his prisoner, helpless and unable to escape. Even though she wasn't as suspicious of him as she had been, her gut warned her not to put herself into a situation from which she couldn't extricate herself.

But when Vorik cheerfully added, "I'll gather more berries for the cobbler," and jogged to the bramble patch, Syla snorted, again almost laughing. The night had been far too grim for laughter, but, thanks to Vorik, she was still alive, and she could pursue her mission to save the Kingdom.

Maybe it was foolish, but she walked toward the dragon to get on.

13

VORIK TRIED NOT TO FEEL TRIUMPHANT AS PRINCESS SYLA SETTLED astride Agrevlari in front of him, offering directions on how to find the farm where her aunt resided, but it seemed like the general's plan might actually work. Syla was going off with him. *Alone.* There were no soldiers protecting her and no scowling bodyguard to threaten Vorik if he touched her or even smiled at her. Which, after the battle at the lighthouse, she might not mind as much. Maybe Vorik had a chance of gaining her trust, enough to fulfill his orders.

At first, there was space between them on Agrevlari's back, and Vorik didn't presume to scoot close, but when the big green dragon bunched his muscles and sprang into the air, Syla slid backward. She let out a startled exclamation, leaning forward and clasping one hand to her face to keep her spectacles in place while trying to find a spot to grab on a dragon's back.

As Vorik well knew, there wasn't one, only the slight creases between the scales. It took strong and agile fingers to make a handhold out of them.

As Agrevlari ascended, his back tilted enough that Syla slid farther, only stopping when she bumped into Vorik. His leg muscles were practiced at tightening just so to remain in place on a dragon, and he didn't budge, only acting as a wall for her. A wall who abruptly noticed the feel of her weight settling between his thighs, the way her backside molded to him. She stiffened, doubtless not wanting to be so intimately close to him, and he resisted the urge to wrap his arms around her and pull her snugly against his chest.

"I won't let you fall," he said quietly instead.

She eyed the ground as Agrevlari climbed higher into the sky. "I don't know if this is better than dangling from Wreylith's maw or not."

"There aren't any fangs around you."

"No, but—"

Agrevlari banked to turn inland, and his back tilted slightly sideways.

When Syla stiffened again in alarm, Vorik gave in to his earlier urge and wrapped his arms around her. He kept his grip light, not wishing to alarm or offend her, but tight enough so that she would feel safe.

Tension radiated from her body, and he decided not to ask if his arms were more or less appealing than Wreylith's fangs. It wouldn't be encouraging if she said *less*.

As Agrevlari straightened again, Syla relaxed an iota. She even leaned back a little, more of her weight settling against Vorik, her buttocks against his thighs, her back against his chest, wisps of hair that had escaped her clips brushing his nose.

Damn, that was appealing. He fought down the urge to wrap his arms *tightly* around her instead of lightly, and he definitely didn't let his hands roam, though they might be able to distract her from her worries... to soothe her concerns. Or maybe she would find his touch more stimulating than soothing. Might it arouse her carnal interests?

He rolled his eyes, telling himself not to take advantage of her. That wasn't a way to win her trust. He would simply enjoy this moment, having her warm curves pressed appealingly against his body. And maybe she would come to appreciate him behind her, as well.

Though, judging by the way Syla kept glancing nervously at the ground far below, she probably was barely aware of him behind her, much less *appreciating* him. Unless one counted their extremely brief jaunt around the castle courtyard, this was likely only her second time flying with a dragon. Since the first had involved being carried in Wreylith's jaws and *dropped*, her nervousness was quite understandable.

"Agrevlari," Vorik said, "is a mature dragon and rarely prone to impulsive rolls and dives—unless he spots one of his favorite prey in the waves below, a fang-toothed walrus—so he's generally a smooth ride. But even if he does take off after something, I'm practiced at staying on and will keep you in place."

Vorik didn't mention that the magic he received through his bond with Agrevlari gave him, among other powers, the ability to adhere, almost like glue, to a dragon's back. Even though it was possible the gardeners already knew about his magic, and there was no point in wearing the gloves that hid his dragon tattoo, he, like most of the others of his kind that were so marked, didn't announce his power to strangers. And only rarely to friends and lovers.

"Good," Syla said, looking back, "because I'm planning to grab onto you in any and every way I can if I start to lurch sideways."

"You're welcome to do so any time you wish." Vorik, finding her response somewhat promising, tried his devastating smile on her. "I enjoy being grabbed by beautiful women."

A startled flash in her eyes suggested it wasn't the time for flirting. Her earlier suspicion stampeded in behind it.

"My apologies," Vorik said. "I should have realized it wasn't an appropriate time to be playful."

"No. And I'm not..." She shook her head.

Interested? That would make seducing her difficult.

Vorik's ego was such that he also had a hard time believing she didn't find him even remotely attractive, but if she associated him with the devastation to her people... he supposed he understood. Women, he'd learned over the years, seemed to link their attraction far more strongly with feelings. He, on the other hand, could feel desire and long even for an enemy, even for someone he knew he should stay away from. Maybe women were brighter in that respect.

"Nothing is going to happen between us," Syla finally settled on.

The suspicion lingered in her gaze as she turned her face away from him, focusing on the countryside below as full daylight came over the island, revealing agricultural fields inland from the city. And were those dragons atop some of the barns, with stormers filling bags and boxes with produce? Yes, Vorik's keen eyes could identify them. He hoped Syla's gaze wasn't as sharp.

"That's understandable," Vorik said, then lowered his voice to murmur, "if regrettable."

He thought the wind would keep her from hearing the rest, but her puzzled glance back made him wonder if she'd caught it. She adjusted her spectacles and peered toward fires burning on a farm at the outskirts of the city and shook her head. And were those tears glinting in her eyes behind the lenses?

Lament seeped into him. He shouldn't have attempted to flirt or even be thinking of sex.

"Even if I thought you had some... interest in me," Syla said quietly, "it would be a betrayal to my people—my *family*—to have anything to do with you."

"I understand. It's important to honor one's family, whether they yet live or not."

"Yes."

"And it's always hard to lose kin." Vorik thought of his deceased father and a brother he'd also lost several years earlier. And then there was Jhiton's son. There *had been* Jhiton's son. Vorik had adored his little nephew, and he understood perfectly the angst that motivated Jhiton now.

"Yes," was all Syla said, her damp-eyed gaze toward the fields below.

Do you wish me to fly farther than is necessary, Agrevlari asked, *to reach the destination the princess gave to me?*

I don't think so. Why do you ask?

You have not yet engaged in activities that I've come to recognize as necessary for human intercourse.

Ah. That's not going to happen for a while. Vorik kept himself from saying, *if it happens at all.*

Most likely, he *would* need to seduce Syla eventually. For his mission. This just wasn't yet the time. Even if her body might have been receptive, her mind wasn't, and he didn't want her to resent him. Or herself. She had enough to worry about.

Are you certain? She is leaning back into you, much as Lieutenant Avarzy used to before you engaged in coitus. On my back, I'll remind you, as if I were a dumb horse with no feelings on the matter.

I've apologized many times for what I didn't realize at the time was an insult. You and I were newly bonded. To me, having sex on the back of a flying dragon seemed exotic and appealing.

It is neither for the dragon.

I understand that now. Do you want me to write another ballad about your magnificence to apologize for my egregious behavior? I was only twenty-two then, you know. Quite ignorant and naive.

You may always serenade me with ballads. Shall I fly a scenic lap around that butte before taking you down, or not? I can pretend uncertainty of the area.

This is her home. She might get suspicious if you—

Agrevlari banked, and Syla slipped sideways a bit, prompting Vorik to tighten his arms around her again. She nestled back into his grip, not as stiff as she had been before.

You did that on purpose, didn't you? Vorik asked.

Certainly. Human women find you and your musculature appealing. I am helping you use that to your advantage. Perhaps you should sing a ballad to her while you gently hold her so.

I don't think she's in the mood for that.

Syla sneaked a finger up under her lens to wipe tears from her eyes.

No, she was *not* in the mood to be serenaded.

"Were you close to your older kin?" Vorik asked, wondering how insurmountable a task lay ahead. And also hoping that Agrevlari would stop giving advice if Vorik was engaged in another conversation.

"Not as close as they were to each other—I was a surprise child born seven years after my parents had decided not to have more kids—but I loved my older brothers and sisters."

"I regret that you were hurt, that they were taken from you."

She didn't look back at him. She probably didn't believe him—or care if he had regrets or not.

"I lost my father in a battle with your Royal Fleet," Vorik offered. "I was young then, and my older brother took care of me afterward, but it was hard on both of us. We'd both wanted to grow up to be just like him. He was a rider and a great warrior."

Syla looked back at him, scrutinizing his face. Trying to tell if he was lying? He couldn't imagine lying about something like that.

"I lost my father too," Syla admitted. "Not yesterday but several years ago. He was... I was closer to him than to anyone else in my family. He was easier to love than my mother. Even though he was king, he always made time for all of us. Even his youngest and... quirkiest." She said the last word in almost a whisper and adjusted her spectacles before shifting to look forward again.

Perhaps, Agrevlari said, *because of the seeing device she wears, she believes she would not be an appealing sexual partner, and that is why she has not instigated an engagement with you.*

She hasn't instigated an engagement because she's mourning, and I'm from the enemy nation.

Shall I bank and tilt her back into you more?

No. Just... take us to her aunt's farm. She'll need more time.

The more time this takes, the more dragons your brother may send at you—at us. So that you and the princess may bond *over shared struggles and adversity.*

Vorik grimaced, remembering Jhiton speaking of exactly that. Would the attacks come daily? More often?

"You don't seem that quirky," Vorik offered and brushed his fingers along the side of her neck.

Just in case she turned out to be more receptive than he suspected she would.

Syla didn't pull away from him but didn't lean back either.

Would the seeing device be required during mating? Agrevlari wondered.

I'm sure she doesn't need to wear her spectacles in bed. It's not like you need to see anything during sex.

I am certain I do not know or wish *to know the particulars of the mechanics of human intercourse.*

Well, the eyeballs aren't usually involved. The mouth maybe. Vorik smirked.

You are imagining things I do not *desire to see.*

If you're seeing what I'm envisioning, that's what you get for peering into my thoughts.

Through our link, it is sometimes difficult not *to be aware of your thoughts.*

Sorry. I'll try to keep my imaginings involving... mouths to myself.

"I do not trust you, Vorik," Syla stated, looking forward instead of back at him.

"You're wise not to," he offered, not offended.

He was a little amazed she was speaking to him at all and brushed her neck again. To be agreeable and let her know... oh, he didn't know. That if she changed her mind about being interested, he would *also* be interested?

The mission and his brother's plans lurked in the back of his mind.

Vorik sighed, regretting that he had to be anything other than honorable with Syla, but... his people had worked so long for their chance to gain access to these islands. And he'd sworn his oath to the Storm Guard and the Sixteen Talons long ago. He wouldn't allow himself to do anything but obey his commander's orders to the best of his abilities.

As Agrevlari banked, flying over a patch of cultivated land divided by irrigation canals, the wind tugged a lock of Syla's hair free from the frame of her spectacles. Vorik caught it lest it tickle his nose, and his fingers brushed the side of her jaw as he attempted to tuck it back in.

She twisted to look back at him, and he lowered his hand, certain she would let him know she was irritated with all his unnecessary *touching*.

"Your hair is wayward," he informed her.

Her eyes narrowed slightly as she regarded him. With suspicion?

"*You* smell like blackberries," she said. "Did you smear them on your clothes instead of eating them?"

He almost laughed. When daylight had arrived, he'd noticed the stains the smashed berries had granted his tunic. Fortunately, riders wore dark clothing, so they wouldn't be that noticeable.

What kind of warrior flew into battle with purple blotches all over his shirt?

"I told you I'd collect some for the cobbler. More than the handfuls I gathered earlier. I may have gotten enthusiastic with my gathering." He didn't mention that she'd crushed his pockets when he'd caught her.

"I can't believe half the Royal Protectors were searching for you, and you were foraging for berries."

"It was only a few men, and I evaded them easily before leaving the tunnels. Only *then* did I forage." Vorik cocked his head, reminded that it had been her bodyguard who'd told the troops about him. Syla hadn't mentioned him at all. "You're not the one who sent them after me, are you?" he asked quietly, though he already knew the answer.

She shrugged, a troubled crease finding her brow, and looked forward again. Maybe she felt she *should* have sent them?

"Thank you," he said quietly, wanting to encourage such behavior.

She only shrugged again, but she let herself lean back into his arms. He had a hunch she wasn't as offended by his touching as she believed she ought to be. He ought not to take advantage of an attraction her body might feel that went against what her mind wanted, but... he had to keep the mission in mind.

Before he could second-guess himself further, Vorik lowered his lips to the side of her neck, letting them linger, a sensuous touch this time. He brushed them lightly over her warm skin, hoping she would find it appealing. Besides, he wanted to show her that he appreciated the choice she'd made back in those tunnels. It was logical to thank a woman with a kiss, wasn't it?

Syla grew utterly still, but she didn't tense or shift away.

Vorik turned the lip brush into a kiss, then trailed his lips lightly along the side of her neck, tasting her, breathing in her scent. After her night of terror, she smelled of travel and sweat and weary determination rather than the perfumes and soaps he associated with more pampered gardener women. Again, he regretted that she, through no fault of her own and entirely because of her heritage, was at the center of all this, that she'd been hurt.

Syla shifted her weight. Not away from but *toward* him.

A surge of excitement swept through him at this confirmation that her *body* wanted him, even if her mind didn't, even if she didn't trust him. Along with the excitement came arousal, hot blood racing through his veins to his groin as he let himself again notice her appealing weight against him. Vorik nuzzled her ear, tasting her lobe, taking it gently between his lips and grazing it with his teeth.

A slight gasp escaped her lips, and she turned toward him, her lips parting. To speak? To invite a kiss?

She might not trust him, but if she was attracted to him... that was a start.

As he'd been wanting to do earlier, Vorik let his grip around her tighten, pulling her closer to him, *molding* her soft curves to his hard—

That is the farm you desire to visit, is it not? Agrevlari asked, the words for both of them.

Irritation flashed in Vorik. *Now*, the dragon stopped meandering and banking about the area?

"Yes," Syla blurted with relief.

She pulled away from Vorik and shifted forward, almost scooting up the dragon's back to put space between them.

Vorik sighed and resisted the urge to pull her close again. She pointedly didn't look back at him, and he suspected she thought she'd made a mistake in allowing that intimacy, however appealing she might have found it. *He'd* certainly enjoyed it and wished he had indeed told Agrevlari to delay. A longer flight might have led to...

What, Vorik?

He lifted his eyes skyward as the dragon descended toward croplands surrounding a dwelling, a bunkhouse, multiple barns and storage buildings, and two silos. Certain that Syla had no intention of leading him to a bed in one of those buildings when they landed, Vorik blew out a slow breath. He needed to tamp down his arousal.

Besides, as he'd been thinking earlier, his brother might send more troops at any point. Vorik needed to be ready. Who knew how many times the general believed Vorik would have to fight off enemies to prove to Syla that he was on her side?

He rubbed his face as Agrevlari spread his wings to land in a field, chilled by the memory of the word *traitor*. It had all been a ruse, one that those men had known and that he'd known, but it had bothered him nonetheless, the mere suggestion that he might ever betray his people. It would *not* happen.

14

When Agrevlari landed, Syla slid off in such a hurry that she stumbled in the uneven grass and had to reach out to steady herself on a scaled forelimb. Captain Vorik landed lightly beside her, as graceful as ever. As graceful and amazingly athletic as he'd been while battling those riders, protecting her, as he'd promised he would. His face had been nothing but determined when those men had cursed him for turning traitor, for belonging to that faction.

Vorik looked at her, and Syla dropped her hand, not wanting him to think she needed help in any way—not wanting him to have a reason to step close and put his arms around her again. She'd liked that far, *far* too much. At first, it had simply felt good to be embraced and supported after the horrifying day and night she'd had. But then... when he'd kissed her neck, that had sent startlingly intense pleasure throughout her whole body. And those nibbles at her ear? They'd lit her entire being with desire.

Which was ridiculous. She had a mission, she was in mourning, and there was way too much to worry about. There was no way she, or her treacherous body, should be thinking about sex.

Especially with *him.* Vorik was a stormer, from the enemy people who had attacked and *killed* hers. They'd killed her *family.*

She would not allow herself to have any kind feelings, and definitely not *attraction,* toward him. For many reasons, that would be foolish.

It was *possible* he was what he claimed to be, but her instincts told her that she'd better remain wary. It had been useful to receive a ride to the farm, but, as soon as she could, she would slip away from Vorik. She had to. Strolling around the countryside with a rider and his *dragon* felt like a betrayal to the Kingdom, no matter what allegiance he claimed.

Syla walked toward the gate of a wooden fence that surrounded the house, carving out a yard and garden space from the rest of the farm. In one of the barns, horses neighed and whinnied. They sounded nervous. Because something had happened and their handlers hadn't brought breakfast? Or because they sensed the dragon outside?

Syla looked around, seeking signs of her aunt or the laborers who worked here, providing pork, beef, lamb, fruit, vegetables, honey, and herbs for the castle. The gate was ajar, but that wasn't that surprising. People had probably run outside to look toward the sky when the dragons had arrived in the capital. The farm lay more than twenty miles from the castle, but the fires must have been visible on the horizon during the night.

Fortunately, this area didn't appear to have been attacked or damaged in any way. But the workers might have fled, regardless. If dragons had even flown over the area, it would have alarmed those living below, whether the creatures had started fires or not.

Syla didn't think everyone had abandoned the farm though. She sensed that someone was in the area. Watching them.

Hopefully not seeing *everything.* Such as her letting Vorik wrap his arms around her, then leaning back into his hard body and inviting...

Storm's teeth, she hadn't meant to *invite* anything. Letting him touch her had been a mistake.

When she reached the gate, Syla paused, afraid she would find Vorik trailing right behind her, close enough to embrace her again, to pull her back against him.

No, he wasn't there. She told herself that was a relief, then looked around for him. His dragon remained, now lounging in the grass by the road, but where had Vorik gone?

A soft *ah* led her gaze to him.

"Is this a *pear*?" Vorik's soft words held wonder, as if he could hardly believe it, and he plucked one from a low-hanging branch and bit into it. He slumped against the tree trunk and groaned with delight. "It *is* a pear."

Syla stared over the fence at him, reminded of the berries he'd picked. There was something incongruous about such a fearsome warrior having a sweet tooth. A *fruit* tooth.

She'd watched him kill someone and defeat several others with such physical prowess that it was breathtaking, if not terrifying. But he looked positively harmless leaning in the orchard, noshing the pear.

"Something I must not allow myself to think," she murmured, walking up the flagstone path to the porch. "He may be the most dangerous person I've ever met."

"Don't worry," Vorik called to her around a bite of pear. "I'll watch the sky for you." He raised the fruit in a salute.

She waved vaguely, not certain if he'd heard her words and was responding to them, or was simply letting her know he would keep an eye out while he raided the fruit trees. Either way, it wasn't as reassuring as he'd possibly meant it to be.

She started up the wooden steps but halted. The front door stood open. Yes, it was as she feared. Something was amiss. Leaving the gate open seemed a simple enough mistake but the front door?

Worry sank into her gut. What if dragon riders had been here earlier? What if they'd known about Aunt Tibby and her moon-marked magic, and they'd come here to kill her? Just as Syla's mother and siblings had already been killed?

She lifted her hand toward the door, but the fear of walking in and finding another body on the floor—her aunt's body—froze her in place. And what if some greater threat lingered? Should she call Vorik to walk in with her?

No. As she'd just been thinking, she couldn't depend on him. She needed to continue forward on her own.

By the road, Agrevlari grunted and rose to all fours. His nostrils flexed as his head went up.

Are there sheep in this area? Delicious sheep with meat soft and juicy from a life of ease, never having had to flee predators?

Syla tightened her jaw at the thought of Vorik's dragon—of *any* dragons—taking advantage of the shield being down to raid pastures around the island. But that had been their whole plan, hadn't it? To destroy the shielders and devour that which her people maintained. Vorik's eating of the pear took on a more sinister connotation for her, reminding her that he and his people had attacked so that they could plunder.

If Vorik answered the dragon, she didn't hear the response in her mind. After a few more sniffs of the air, the creature sprang into the air and flew in the direction where she knew pastures lay. She wanted to object but didn't. If workers were in hiding, they would be more likely to come out if the dragon was gone.

Syla called a soft, "Hello?" and pushed the door farther open.

A creak came from the back of the house, and the hair stood up on the back of her neck.

"Aunt Tibby?" She kept her calls soft, doubting her relative was the one skulking around. "Is that you?"

Syla took a couple of steps inside, the front room dim thanks to shutters covering the windows, and she eyed the floor between the sofas and chairs, still worried about bodies. And also the feeling that she was being watched. The farmhouse had been used by numerous generations over the years, and the hodgepodge of furnishings filling the living area offered numerous hiding spots.

Another creak came from the kitchen just visible through a doorway at the back of the room. It sounded like someone's weight shifting on a wooden floorboard.

A soft thump from the porch behind made her jump and spin around. Vorik stood on the steps, pears and apples gathered in his tunic as he fished in his hip pocket with one hand. He'd sheathed his sword behind his shoulder and looked more like a shopper visiting the produce market than a fearsome dragon rider.

"How much do these items cost?" Vorik retrieved silver coins from his pocket and laid a couple on the porch railing. "I gather these trees are tended and that the delicious fruits don't grow wild."

"I…" Syla didn't know what to say.

His people had attacked the capital and left bodies everywhere, and he thought someone would be worried about being paid for produce? This farm didn't even sell at the market; its food was used to feed the royal family and castle soldiers and staff.

Vorik cocked his head, studying her in a look of earnest inquiry.

"I pay a copper a pear at the market." Syla spread a helpless arm and pointed toward the kitchen, tempted to ask him to check it out, but if a worker spotted him before her, the person might attack.

Vorik nodded and added another silver coin to the railing. "And how much for a… I believe Agrevlari is singling out a sheep."

"Uh, those are a lot more."

"I was afraid of that. Riders aren't paid that much, and it's more often in salt or edibles than coin, so I'm not certain I can afford to cover what he consumes. I will, however, suggest that *he* pay. Or that he seek animals that aren't raised and tended by people." Vorik frowned into the distance, in the direction the dragon had gone. "He doesn't always listen to me though. Dragons do whatever they wish, even those bonded to humans."

Despite suggesting he couldn't afford to pay for livestock, Vorik placed a couple more silver coins on the railing. Since Syla usually only paid for a portion of meat from the butcher, she had no idea what an entire sheep cost.

Vorik started to say something else, but his gaze snagged on the garden area in the side yard. In the morning sunlight, butterflies flitted from sunflower to marigold to zinnia; the flowers clustered near vegetables in various stages of growth. An attractive clump of eral pods waved in the breeze on their stalks, the versatile herbs a staple in Kingdom gardens, thanks to their healing properties. More than once, Syla had used the milk of the pods to create a salve that neutralized rattlesnake venom.

"Is that a garden?" Vorik asked. "I see zucchini and cucumbers, and are those *strawberries*? This late in the season?"

Syla grimaced, reminded of her older brother's love for the berries with his oatmeal and insistence that the farmers plant varieties that produce as late into the year as possible. Unfortunately, Serk wouldn't be around to enjoy them any longer.

Tears threatened Syla's beleaguered eyes again.

Oblivious, Vorik shuffled the fruit in his tunic, then decided to set the pears and apples on the porch railing, so he could trot over to investigate the garden.

Syla headed toward the kitchen. Strawberries had to be the least likely thing she ever would have expected to distract a deadly dragon rider, but as long as Vorik was preoccupied, she would check out the rest of the house. She grabbed a fireplace poker on the way past the hearth. Just in case.

Warily, she stepped through the kitchen doorway. Another hearth with an oven and cooking spits and racks took up much of the wall beside the door, leaving an island with a pot rack above it in the center. She crept around it with the poker in hand, but it was from behind a hutch that a threat leaped.

Syla opened her mouth to shout as a big man sprang upon her, and she swung the poker. He caught her wrist and flattened a hand over her mouth before she could utter her cry. Snarling, she tried to bite that hand.

"Your Highness," a familiar voice whispered. "Ssh, please. It's me."

Sergeant Fel's face came together for her in dim light coming through a shuttered window. He glanced between her and the doorway leading to the living room—and the garden.

Syla nodded to indicate she recognized him and wouldn't yell, and he released her, drew his mace, and stepped back to guard the doorway.

"What are you doing here?" Syla also whispered, afraid Vorik would charge in and attack Fel.

As Vorik had pointed out, Fel had sent the soldiers after him in the tunnels. Vorik hadn't seemed particularly affronted—or wounded in the least—by that, but he might try to take revenge on the bodyguard.

"I thought you were dead, Your Highness." Despite remaining ready to deal with Vorik if he charged in, Fel took a moment to look her up and down. His expression was aggrieved when he added, "I was too late to keep that dragon from getting you, and it carried you off in its *jaws*. I thought it would eat you."

"It was a *she*, and I… do have a few bruises from being carried that way, but she needed the services of a healer." Syla waved toward herself.

Fel's mouth dangled open. "A *human* healer?"

"I think we're the only kind. At least I've never heard of dragon healers. They probably have a tough time applying bandages with their talons."

She meant it as a joke, but he only stared at her. Shocked that she'd survived?

"What are you doing here?" she asked again, glancing toward the window. With the shutters closed, she couldn't see Vorik, but she worried about him hearing them.

"I… came to fulfill your request. To find your Aunt Tibby."

"Did the soldiers send you? Colonel Mosworth?"

His mouth closed, jaw tightening before he answered. "No. *He* thought I was too old and injured to be of use, especially after we —after *I*—let the dragon take you."

"The dragon would have killed you if you'd reached her. It wasn't your fault."

Fel shook his head glumly. "Colonel Mosworth ordered me to go to the temple on Fountain and Fourth for healing, but I knew that would be packed with truly injured people, especially since Moon Watch was destroyed."

Syla winced at the reminder.

"Besides," Fel said, "your instincts were right. We need to find someone who can fix the shielder or put in a replacement. We can't simply *regroup*, station troops around the capital, and wait for the next attack."

"Is that what the colonel is ordering be done?"

"For now, yes. They're still looking for survivors and hoping to find one or more of your siblings yet alive. The word has gotten out that the entire royal family may be dead, and people are… Well, the Kingdom subjects aren't interested in listening to authority figures right now. Not military ones, anyway. They're crying that the Kingdom will be dissolved and everyone is on their own. People are either fleeing into the hills, afraid there'll be more attacks, or hunkering down to defend what they've got from unscrupulous people preying on the weak instead of banding together." Fel curled his lip in disgust.

Syla thought of the looters and imagined the chaos that must be descending on the city.

"Come with me." Fel pointed toward the back door. "I'll get you away from your captor, and, once we retrieve your aunt, I'll see you back to the castle. I've got a couple of horses."

She almost said that *she* had a dragon, but that was... complicated. She'd voluntarily gone with Vorik, and he wasn't her captor, but trying to explain everything by whisper before he finished picking strawberries sounded daunting. Besides, it would be best to get away from him, not continue on in his presence.

When Fel tried to lead her out the back door, Syla lifted a hand. "We do need to find Aunt Tibby, but I'm not going back to the castle to be locked in my room." What was left of it. "And imprisoned by guards."

"The people need to see that one of the royals is left."

"I really doubt *the people* are going to stop looting and fleeing the capital because a healer shows her face."

"A moon-marked healer descended from the gods-chosen." Fel pointed at her hand, and then toward the door again.

"I'm not going be a figurehead for Colonel Mosworth or anyone else. If we get the shielder fixed, *that's* what will stop the anarchy."

"I don't disagree with that." Fel flexed his shoulders, as if he might step forward and hoist her over one of them. "And I know where your aunt is. We can take her back to the castle too. That's what you want to do, isn't it?"

"Yes. Of course. Where is she?" Syla glanced at the hutch as if her aunt might also be crouched behind it.

"Barricaded in a barn."

She blinked. "What?"

"I found her, but she wouldn't come out for me. I gather some soldiers came through and stole horses, so she's irritated with everyone in uniform right now."

"Why would soldiers steal horses?"

"It sounded like they were deserters." Again, Fel curled his lip. "They probably wet themselves when the dragons showed up, and fled without helping. Cowards."

Syla rubbed her face again. She couldn't believe how quickly the Kingdom was falling apart. "The leaders from the other islands should send troops to help establish order soon. My cousins and aunts and uncles hold positions of power elsewhere in the Kingdom, and I'm sure someone will come here to lend the authority the military needs to get the capital back in order."

Unfortunately, she *wasn't* sure about that. The other islands might hunker down, worried they would be targets next.

"Take me to Aunt Tibby, please." Though Syla doubted they could slip away without Vorik noticing, she nodded to indicate she would follow Fel.

"This way," he said.

Leading, Fel stepped out onto the covered back porch, looking all around before heading toward steps that led into the backyard and toward an open gate. The garden wasn't in view, so Syla couldn't see Vorik. Was he still there? Munching down strawberries? She didn't know but hoped he wouldn't be angry if she left without him.

Once he was convinced the way was clear, Fel, his mace in hand, eased down the back steps. He waved for her to follow and captured her wrist to lead her, as if she might dart around the house and into Vorik's arms if left unmonitored. She bristled at that notion but didn't want to make unnecessary noise by protesting.

At the bottom of the steps, before starting down the path to the gate, Fel once more looked left and right. The threat came from above, Vorik crouching on the edge of the roof.

Fel must have glimpsed him out of the corner of his eye because he released Syla and spun back toward the house while raising the mace. He wasn't fast enough. Vorik kicked the weapon out of his hand as he dropped from the roof.

Fel sprang for him, but Vorik ducked and dodged so quickly that Syla couldn't track his movements. Between one blink and the next, Vorik got behind Fel, immobilized his arms by yanking them behind him, and shoved at the backs of his knees to buckle them.

With a snarl of frustration, Fel found himself twisted about and kneeling before Syla. His strong shoulders flexed against the fabric of his uniform, but he couldn't escape Vorik's powerful grip.

Syla froze, worried about how the rider captain would react to her attempt to sneak away. And what he would do to Fel.

When Vorik met her eyes over Fel's head, his face was cool and hard to read, far from the enthusiastic fruit picker she'd left out front. She feared her earlier thought was wrong, that she *was* his captive and that a captor had no use for a captive with a bodyguard.

15

THE BIG SERGEANT SEETHED, MUSCLES TAUT AS THEY STRAINED FOR freedom, but Vorik, with strength enhanced by his dragon bond, kept him subdued. Irritated that the bodyguard kept popping up, he didn't manage to keep a neutral expression on his face, and he read the concern in Syla's eyes as she watched them.

"Release me," the sergeant snarled.

What was his name? Fel. That was it.

"I haven't attacked you," Fel added.

"Because you didn't see me." For the princess's sake, Vorik smoothed his face and made his tone light. Well, maybe lightly sardonic. "Not because you didn't want to."

"That's the truth," Fel muttered and again strained against Vorik's grip.

"If I let you go, will you refrain from attacking me?"

Vorik doubted it. The bodyguard was casting longing looks at the mace lying in the grass beside the path.

For an answer, Fel snarled.

Nobly tamping down his irritation, Vorik looked to Syla for help or at least a suggestion of how to go forward. He'd been listening in on their conversation and had heard that the aunt Syla sought was on the premises. Though she hadn't explained her interest in finding the woman to Vorik, he believed it had something to do with repairing the shielder, or perhaps finding another one. Could the aunt be one of those entrusted with the locations?

Vorik doubted it could be repaired—even if it hadn't been completely destroyed when he'd been there with Syla, the man he'd left alive in the chamber would have finished it off. Once Syla learned that, she would continue on with the next part of what he believed to be her quest: heading to another island to retrieve another shielder to bring back. Vorik would find a way to accompany her and achieve what his brother wished. Either he could destroy it, robbing another gardener island of its defense, or he could mark its location and relay it to Jhiton. That would be ideal and allow Vorik to continue to appear to be a friendly protector to Syla. Through her, he might locate even *more* of the shielders.

It was exactly what the general wanted, and the thought should have pleased Vorik. But he couldn't help but feel regret that he would have to betray Syla. Multiple times if his people got their way. Unfortunate, but... he would do his duty, as he always had. Too much was at stake for him to let concern about a woman divert him.

"Maybe you can explain to the sergeant that I'm not a captive," Syla suggested, looking intently at Vorik, her eyes silently asking if that was true.

"You're not *my* captive." Vorik tilted his chin toward her wrist where Fel had gripped her. "I'm less certain about whether your bodyguard is giving you any freedom."

"I'm here to protect her, not imprison her." Fel spat in exasperation. "Release me, and face me like an honorable man so I can do my duty and slay you."

The suggestion that Vorik wasn't being honorable vexed him

anew. He'd merely wanted to get Fel away from Syla before starting a confrontation so she wouldn't be hurt.

Still, the appeal to his honor always got to him. He released Fel and stepped back, bracing himself to be attacked again.

Fel snatched up his mace but backed toward Syla, as if to defend her from Vorik. As if that was necessary.

Vorik clenched his jaw, but he reminded himself that the man *was* Syla's bodyguard. Since Vorik's goal was to keep Syla alive while he learned the location of all the shielders... he should want the man here as backup. He had a feeling, though, that having the bodyguard along would cause nothing but trouble. He would far prefer to be alone with Syla.

"Your last fight with him didn't go well," she whispered to the sergeant.

Fel didn't look like that would stop him from trying to knock Vorik's head off. "We're not letting an enemy trail along with us."

Syla eased down the steps to stand at his side. Though bespectacled, in a torn dress, and a head shorter than the man, she didn't hesitate to reach out and push Fel's mace arm down. His eyes narrowed, but he did let her do so.

"I wouldn't suggest letting an enemy trail along either," Vorik said. "But I'm not an enemy to you. As I told you before, I'm here to protect the princess." Then he offered something he'd managed to keep safe in his hand while jumping from the roof and restraining the bodyguard. Since the treasure was fragile, it had taken quite the effort to do so. "Strawberry, Sergeant?"

"What?" Fel asked in a flat tone, though he couldn't have missed seeing the offering.

"I sampled a few while you were skulking in the kitchen and whispering to the princess. They are *amazing.* So sweet and juicy." Vorik eyed the large berry, thinking of retracting the offer and popping it into his mouth.

Fel eyed it like it would be poisoned.

"Maybe you should eat it, Vorik," Syla suggested. "You paid enough for the fruit you took—though the hypothetical sheep is more questionable—and you're... Well, your people are all so lean. Maybe you could use some sweets."

That was the gods-known truth. If only leanness was where it ended. His people needed the nourishment that these islands provided.

Fel shifted his suspicious eyes from the strawberry to Syla. He probably didn't want the princess sympathizing with rider *leanness*.

Vorik walked closer, aware of Fel tensing but not letting it deter him, and offered the strawberry to Syla. "I've had my fill. You take it if he won't."

"I... all right." She accepted it and smiled at Fel, as if to say, *I'll show you that it's not poisoned*, and nibbled a bite from the bottom.

Vorik approved of the sign of trust, since it boded well for his mission, but he caught himself watching her lips more closely than he should have as she chewed, then ate the second half of the berry, the pink of her tongue briefly visible. He knew she didn't mean anything erotic by the way she ate, but his libido found the sight quite interesting regardless.

With the scowling sergeant standing beside them, Vorik made himself look away and step back. "I'll accompany you to find your aunt. It sounded like your bodyguard needs help with whatever barricade the... I gather somewhat aged woman put in place." He couldn't keep from smirking his amusement that the sergeant hadn't been able to handle the situation.

Syla frowned at him. "Aunt Tibby is in her fifties and doesn't seem aged at all to me. She's smart, a hard worker, and resourceful. I'm sure there's more than a chair leaned up against a doorknob."

Vorik bowed an apology. Maybe he'd meant to take a dig at the sergeant, but he didn't want to offend Syla.

"She has a pack of magical *machinery* guarding her," Fel said. "I'd never spoken to the woman before this, but I can already tell *resourceful* is an understatement."

"There's a reason I want to find her." Syla stepped past Fel and Vorik to lead the way.

Fel rushed to follow right behind her, glowering at Vorik, as if that would keep him away from her if Vorik chose to make an issue of their walking order. He did not. Besides, he'd received an update from Agrevlari on the deliciousness of the not one but *two* sheep—and a goat—that the dragon had hunted down and was in the process of devouring. Before following Syla, Vorik left most of his month's salary on the porch for the aunt or whoever did the books for the farm.

16

THEY PASSED THE STABLES AND A BARN FILLED WITH HAY BEFORE approaching what Syla thought of more as a machine shop than a barn. Since she'd visited the farm before, she knew that a variety of magic-powered farming equipment was stored and worked on inside the building, so she had an inkling of what they would find.

"How do we get rid of him?" Fel whispered as they walked toward the closed double-doors of the structure.

Two huge tractors had not only been parked outside but idled, a hint of magic emanating from under the hoods. Perhaps because of Fel's earlier words, Syla had the notion of guard dogs rather than corn harvesters.

"For now, I think we shouldn't try," she whispered back.

Vorik was strolling behind them, surveying the farm and the sky—did he expect his dragon to return soon?—and appeared to be giving them the privacy to speak, but she wondered. If he'd heard the whispered conversation they'd had in the kitchen, with the exterior door closed and the windows shuttered, he had keen ears.

"If he helped you, it was because he needs you for some

reason." Fel had listened as she'd given a brief accounting of the battle at the lighthouse and how Vorik had saved her life—again—but it hadn't swayed him from believing Vorik was an enemy.

"If I'm a target for stormer assassins right now... we may need *him* for a reason."

"I won't let myself be parted from you again."

"I..." Syla groped for a tactful way to say that two dragons and riders would have been more than a match for Fel.

But a window in the loft slid open, saving her from needing to explain that diplomatically.

Vorik surged forward, startling Syla as he leaped in front of her, his sword in hand. The barrel of a hand-cannon thrust through the open window, and she understood what had prompted him.

"Trespassers will be shot!" a woman yelled through the window, peering out enough to reveal red-gray hair drawn back from her face and thick spectacles reflecting the landscape. "Especially overly belligerent trespassers who belittle a woman by not believing her capable of taking care of herself."

Vorik raised his eyebrows, as if wondering if the words were meant for him.

But Fel sighed as he massaged what was probably a sore hip. "We had a previous conversation."

Increased rumbles came from the idling tractors, and Syla sensed magic flowing down from the loft and into them.

"I take it that your conversation didn't go well." Syla, realizing her aunt wouldn't be able to see her well through Vorik, stepped up beside him.

He lifted a hand to stop her, but she swatted it away. His eyebrows arched, but he didn't grab her or push her back.

"Aunt Tibby? It's Syla. We... need to talk."

"Syla! You're a prisoner!"

"No, but I—"

The tractors surged from the door, much like the guard dogs Syla had imagined. Each on four huge wheels, one roared toward Fel and one toward Vorik.

"Aunt Tibby!" Syla called. "Stop your machines, please."

"I'm saving you!" Tibby called. "Run toward the door."

Fel trotted to the side of the road, probably thinking the machine would have more trouble navigating through the grass after him. Syla doubted it. Vorik ran straight toward the other tractor, his sword still in hand.

As if *that* would stop the thing. It had to weigh tons.

Someone inside pushed open one of the large shop doors.

"This way, Your Highness." A boy of fourteen or fifteen leaned out and waved at her.

Syla hesitated, not wanting to abandon the men. Either of them.

As the tractors pulled away from the building, they increased in speed. The one after Fel charged off the road without trouble, tearing into the grass and angling straight for him with the unerring aim of a hawk. Vorik crouched, prepared to spring atop the other machine, but a shadow swept over the road. The dragon.

Agrevlari swooped down with his talons extended. As big as the dragon was, the core of his body not much larger than the tractor, Syla didn't expect what came next.

With a great flexing of the muscles in his back and legs, Agrevlari plucked up the machine before it reached Vorik. Wings flapping so hard that the nearby grass flattened to the ground, the dragon rose into the air with the tractor.

A *boom* came from the loft window, Tibby firing the hand-cannon.

"Look out!" Syla yelled to Vorik.

But her aunt had aimed at the dragon. Propelled by black powder, the ball slammed into Agrevlari's flank.

Unlike the red dragon, who'd seemed impervious to all

attacks, he screeched in pain or fury—or both—and dropped the tractor. He'd carried it high enough that when it crashed down next to an irrigation canal, it landed on its side with a thunderous *crunch.* After that, it didn't move, other than the wheels spinning uselessly in the air.

Flames shot from Agrevlari's maw, though it seemed a reflexive part of his rage, for he didn't have a target. Not until he banked and started back toward them.

"Hurry, Syla!" Tibby yelled. "Get inside."

As if a wooden *building* would stop dragon fire.

But Syla obeyed, partially out of fear of Agrevlari but mostly because she wanted to convince her aunt to stop attacking the men. As she darted toward the door, she spotted Fel dealing with the other machine. He'd managed to clamber onto it and into the driver's seat. After having no success using the steering mechanism, he started pounding on the control panel with his mace. The tractor continued to run, circling the shop as it weaved and sped up and slowed down, as if some intelligence guided it.

Syla reached the open door, and the kid guided her into the dim interior, few windows brightening the way. Even with her spectacles, her vision wasn't as good as other people's, and with the light change, Syla almost crashed into another giant machine scant feet inside.

"Is that... a catapult?" Syla peered around it, seeking a ladder to the loft.

"Yes, we drove off another dragon with the magical exploding ammunition that your aunt made. Lady Tibaytha, do you want me to roll out the catapult to use on this dragon?"

"Yes!" Tibby yelled. "Hurry, Terrik."

"No." Syla gripped the boy's arm to keep him from throwing the doors open wide to do exactly that. "That dragon is..." She groped for a way to explain Agrevlari and Vorik, who would probably charge into the shop any moment.

"Spitting up bones!" Tibby cried from the loft.

Syla looked back outside. She'd expected Agrevlari to light the area on fire, but he'd landed on the road near Vorik, who held his sword at his side as he watched Fel riding around on the tractor while ripping pieces from it. Hacking noises came from the dragon. Muscles in his neck undulated, and, like an owl regurgitating the bones of its prey, Agrevlari threw up in the grass.

Abruptly, the rumble of the remaining tractor engine stopped.

In the silence, Vorik's voice was audible as he mildly said, "I told you not to eat the second sheep."

"My sheep!" Tibby said. "That dragon is eating my sheep? I'll shoot it again. And— *you*. You pompous bastard, what did you do to my tractor?"

It took Syla a moment to realize she was yelling at Fel now instead of the dragon.

"Aunt Tibby, please come down. We need to talk. These men are... uhm..." Syla almost said allies, which Fel certainly was, but what exactly Vorik was, she hadn't decided.

"I'm here to protect Princess Syla," Vorik stated, striding through the doorway.

Eyes round, the kid—Terrik—skittered back.

Vorik still carried his gargoyle-bone sword, though he kept it at his side as he strode in. That didn't mean he didn't look intimidating. This time, he wasn't proffering strawberries.

Aunt Tibby peered down from the top of a ladder. "You're a dragon rider."

"I am, yes." Vorik bowed to her. "Thank you for noticing. I strive to maintain my physique in a manner appropriate for the elite Sixteen Talons warriors. Might I suggest that it's neither wise nor health-inducing to attack dragons? If Agrevlari hadn't had a... digestive incident, he would have torched your barn."

"You're an *impertinent* dragon rider." Unlike the kid, Tibby glowered fearlessly down at Vorik. Possibly because she'd reloaded her hand-cannon.

"Yes, ma'am." Vorik gave her a dazzling smile.

She pointed the hand-cannon at him.

"Aunt Tibby." Lifting a hand, Syla ran toward the ladder.

Vorik crouched in case he needed to spring for cover, but he didn't appear alarmed by having a firearm pointed at him.

A wrenching came from behind as fangs wrapped around one of the doors and ripped it free. Light flooded into the shop as Agrevlari hurled it into the field. The door sailed over the head of Fel, who was limping toward the barn, having finally defeated the aggressive tractor. The sunlight was soon blotted out as Agrevlari thrust his head through the doorway, his snout coming in beside Vorik as he glowered up at Tibby, his jaws parted to reveal his fangs.

After a moment of consideration, Tibby lowered the hand-cannon.

Giving the dragon a wide berth, Fel stopped in the road to look in and meet Syla's eyes. Pain hooded his own, but he saluted her, as if to say he was ready to fight again, if necessary.

Syla's heart went out to her bodyguard. If not for all the family she'd lost, she would think Fel was having a much rougher time than she.

The sobering thought brought her back to Tibby. Her aunt probably hadn't heard the details yet about the deaths. Even if Syla's father—Tibby's tie to the royal family—had passed years earlier, her aunt would be devastated by the loss of her nieces and nephews. Syla's stomach knotted at the idea of having to tell her about the losses.

"You say we need to talk?" Tibby adjusted her spectacles and looked down at Syla.

"About much, yes." Tears pricked at Syla's eyes, and she

removed her own spectacles and used her frayed dress to clean the lenses.

Tibby eyed the dragon. "It feels wrong to give up the high ground."

"Do you want us to come up there?"

Tibby pointed at Syla. "I want *you* to come up here. *They* can wait outside." She lowered her voice to a mutter. "Or in an active volcano."

Syla looked at Vorik and Fel.

Fel sat down in the grass and stretched his leg out so he could rub his hip. He appeared relieved not to have to deal with Tibby.

At first, Vorik didn't move, his eyes slitted thoughtfully as he considered Tibby. But when Syla made a shooing motion toward the door, he bowed toward her and walked out, waving for his dragon to withdraw his head.

"You have wool in your teeth," he told Agrevlari as they departed.

My meal was interrupted when I had to come save your life, the dragon replied, surprisingly sharing the words with Syla as well. Or was he including everyone?

"My life wasn't in danger from a ponderous mechanical construct. Even the wounded bodyguard was able to defeat that foe."

Your gratitude over the ever-heroic feats I engage in to assist you is noted.

"I don't know *how* you're going to explain all that," Tibby said from the loft, "but I am most curious to hear you try."

17

Syla sat on a toolbox in the loft and told Aunt Tibby everything. Down below, Fel leaned against the door jamb, giving them their privacy for the conversation but insisting on keeping an eye on Syla.

Since Tibby had shooed Vorik outside, he hadn't attempted to return to the machine shop, but Syla kept her voice low, reminded of how much he'd heard when Fel had spoken to her in the kitchen.

"You saw it in detail?" Tibby asked at the end. "The shielder under the castle?"

"Yes. It looked very destroyed, but I sensed... the faintest of magic about it. I thought it might be possible for a qualified engineer to repair it." She gazed at her aunt.

Tibby blinked. "I *am* an engineer, but... I've never been invited to work on one of the shielders. I've never even seen a schematic."

"I don't think they've previously *needed* working on. It's not like there's a note on my mother's desk with the address of a shielder repairman she had summoned on a regular basis." Syla regretted the flippant words as soon as they came out. It was too soon for jokes involving her mother—anyone who'd passed—and it had only been minutes since she'd informed Tibby of their relatives' deaths. Tibby had, however, taken that without surprise or much of a reaction at all. She'd either already known, or she'd suspected.

"I suppose not. They're reputedly sturdy. I've never been invited to look at any of them though, not even the one under the castle."

"I don't know anyone else who could help."

"I don't suppose you brought me a schematic."

"Sorry. I don't know if such things exist."

"They'd be on your mother's desk." Tibby smiled sadly. "Or in a cabinet, anyway. Maybe framed and pinned to the wall." She touched her chest, as if to say that was what *she* would do with such a schematic.

"My mother mostly has—had—maps, spreadsheets, and notes related to enemy movements up there." For all the good that last had done her...

"May I see your thoughts?" Tibby lifted the back of her hand, showing her moon-mark, and pointed to Syla's.

"Pardon?"

"Telepathically. Just related to what happened in that chamber. If I can see what you saw, it might help me to guess if the shielder can be repaired."

"I didn't know anyone but dragons could speak telepathically. Or share experiences through a mental link."

"You've never moon-linked with your siblings?"

Syla shook her head.

"Hm, I did with mine when we were children. I thought all of the family knew about that."

"Maybe they did with each other when they were young. The difference in ages between me and the others... Well, they didn't play much with me when we were children."

"Hm. Here." Tibby pointed at Syla's hand. "You don't have to do anything. Just don't try to block me. It sounds like going to the castle would be dangerous, both because of enemies we might meet along the way—if not on this very farm—" she glanced toward the front doors, though Vorik and his dragon weren't visible at the moment, "—and from those who would imprison us in the castle for our own good."

She'd been sympathetic when Syla had shared that. Aunt Tibby wasn't one who would put up with being locked in her room—or a dungeon cell—either.

"All right." Syla didn't know what to expect but held her hand out toward her aunt.

Instead of clasping it, Tibby angled hers so that their birthmarks came to rest back-to-back. She closed her eyes, and, a moment later, Syla sensed a tingle of magic. First, it felt like it was on the surface of her skin. Then, it flowed into her and up her arm and toward her head. Like healing magic but lighter, it brushed her nerves, and she sensed that it wouldn't alter her brain or body in any way. Had an enemy been doing this, she would have been alarmed, but she'd known her aunt all her life and trusted her.

The magic tickled her thoughts, stirring up some of the events of the trek through the tunnels. Tears flowed from her eyes as she, once again, experienced walking into the chamber and finding her sister's body. Tibby leaned over and squeezed her shoulder but didn't stop sifting through Syla's memories. Time seemed to slow during the moments when Syla had been investigating the shielder, even freezing at one point when she'd gazed into its innards.

"Hm," Tibby murmured, letting time flow forward again.

The link started to fade, but Tibby paused when the stormer warrior sprang out of the sarcophagus, and she watched the ensuing battle, including the arrival of Vorik, before pulling away. After the two enemies had been killed, the memories stopped playing in Syla's mind.

Tibby leaned back, gripping her chin and studying the wooden floor of the loft. "It may have an inkling of magic in it, but I wouldn't begin to know how to repair it without a schematic. Even then... the engineering the gods did is nothing like what humans base everything on. I'm daunted at the thought of... *tinkering*."

"But you will try, right?" Syla asked.

It wasn't like it could get worse.

"Yes, but I think the other part of your plan is what we should pursue next."

"Retrieving a shielder from one of the other islands?"

"Harvest Island makes the most sense. It would be a shame to remove the protection from all the farms, orchards, and fisheries, but, thanks to the oft-smoldering volcano, it's always been lightly populated when compared to the others. Fewer lives would be at stake."

"We get our cantaloupes from there." It was a silly thing to think of, but the melons were Syla's favorite fruit, and she didn't want to imagine hordes of Voriks descending upon the fields to harvest them while dragons denied the farmers access. No, Vorik had at least paid for what he'd taken. It was the other stormers she imagined being less fair. And what if they and their dragons wreaked havoc in addition to taking the crops? As they'd done to the capital and the castle?

"Fewer *human* lives would be at stake." Tibby smiled faintly.

"Yes, of course. I only meant that it's a shame we'd have to leave any of the other islands unprotected. I do agree that it's for the best."

"With a working shielder to study, I might have better luck repairing the first, so it's possible it would be temporary."

"Ah?" That was encouraging, and Syla nodded.

"Do you know how to find the shielder on Harvest Island?" Tibby asked.

"I know where they all are. My siblings and I visited several one summer, and memorized maps and instructions on how to reach the others. Mother made sure we could recite precise instructions, and I haven't forgotten. We went to Harvest Island personally."

"Good. None of the rest of us, those who weren't direct heirs, were told the locations. I always thought it was foolish that so few people knew, since exactly what happened could happen—assassins could have taken out the entire family at any point. But... if what you were thinking is true, that Venia betrayed our people..."

"I don't think it was on purpose," Syla hurried to say.

She hadn't *said* she thought that might have happened, but Tibby must have seen it in her thoughts.

"Even so," Tibby said, "it shows how dangerous it is for people to know the locations. Maybe it would have been better if the gods hadn't shared that knowledge with your ancestors before they left. If nobody had ever known, there wouldn't have been a secret to lose, and the shielders might have gone on working undisturbed for another thousand years."

Syla could only spread her hand.

"All right." Tibby pushed herself off a stack of drop cloths on which she'd been sitting. "We'll have to get to the harbor and hope there are ships about—ships that haven't been destroyed by dragons. We'll need transport to Harvest Island."

"I... think someone right outside might transport us." Syla pointed in the direction they'd last seen Vorik. Specifically, the dragon. Agrevlari.

Tibby arched her eyebrows. "I was going to ask what your plan is to get *rid* of them, not suggest we ask them to fly us to another island."

"It would be a fast way to get there, whereas a ship..." What were the odds that they could even *find* a ship right now? From what Syla had seen, the dragons had targeted all the vessels docked there. "I saw the harbor. It's not in good shape. The ships... The ships are in worse shape. I don't think we'd find one capable of taking us over there."

"Well, we're not riding with your spy." Tibby pointed toward the door. "Especially not when we're planning to go to the secret location of a shielder. That's probably why he's lurking here. To learn where the other shielders are so that his people can destroy them."

Syla opened her mouth, thinking to go into more detail on the faction and how many times Vorik had come to her rescue in less than a day, but didn't she yet have reservations about him herself?

"How else would we get there then?" was what she asked. "Look, I don't know if he's lying to me or is what he claims to be, but... unless one of your tractors can float, we don't have another way to reach Harvest Island."

Tibby pushed her spectacles higher on her nose, lifted her chin, then crossed her arms over her chest. "The aquatic weed harvester is waterproof and can dredge the irrigation canal."

"Sounds very seaworthy."

"As long as the shielders are still protecting the other islands, a dragon wouldn't be able to take us there anyway."

"Not... all the way, but they can fly to within a mile of the shoreline. We've always seen them out here, fishing and keeping an eye on us." Syla waved in the direction of the sea.

"So, a mile away, the dragon would dump us into the ocean and tell us to swim?"

Syla pulled up one of her mother's maps in her mind. "The Savian Shallows on the west side of Harvest Island are somewhat protected. If we were dropped there, we could make it to shore without being pulled out to sea."

Tibby dropped her arms to her sides. "You're serious."

"It's my duty to protect our people. It always has been." In the past, Syla had been able to do it as a healer, not an adventurer, but if this was what the Kingdom needed to end the anarchy and return safety and hope to the people... so be it.

Tibby shook her head. "Come with me."

She walked across the loft to the window she'd used earlier for firing her hand-cannon. Syla joined her, looking down at the road and the croplands beyond. Agrevlari lay on his belly in the grass, his tail curled around his body. Vorik sat, leaning his back against the dragon's flank, his eyes closed, as if he were napping.

Like Syla, he'd been up all night, but something told her he was awake and much more alert than the position implied. Indeed, as they looked down at Vorik, one of his eyes opened, and he looked right at her.

She kept herself from jumping, but how had he known? He had magic, too, she reminded herself, and she didn't know what all it allowed him to do. As she'd been thinking earlier, he was dangerous. Very dangerous.

"That body in the chamber didn't have any blood around it," Tibby said. "Did you notice?"

Syla's first thought was that Tibby meant Venia's body, and she looked at her aunt in confusion. There *had* been blood around her.

"The body of the assassin that your ally supposedly killed," Tibby clarified.

"Oh." Syla had taken a good look at that area since the man had died on the sarcophagus lid, and she'd wanted to put it back on, but she hadn't been thinking of blood—or a lack of it. Her aunt must have had something else on her mind when she'd witnessed that moment in her thoughts. "You're right," Syla said slowly, mulling over her memory. "I saw Vorik run him through, but..."

"There should have been blood if he'd *really* run that man through. As a healer, you of all people should have thought of that."

Syla's cheeks flushed. "I had something else on my mind."

Maybe she should have said that the man *could* have died without spilling a lot of blood, that if the cut had been clean and straight through the heart, only some might have seeped out on the back side, but she felt flustered and didn't get that out before her aunt replied.

"Was it how handsome that rider is?" Tibby pointed at Vorik, who'd let his eyelid shut again. "That smile he gave me could have melted the ice off a frost harpy."

"That's *not* what was on my mind." Syla's cheeks heated further. It wasn't a lie. At least, she hadn't considered that in the chamber. Later, when he'd rescued her from the riders and had his arms around her on his dragon... By the eyes of the moon, she didn't, on some subconscious level, want to ride with him again so they could relive that moment, did she?

No. She wasn't a fool. She didn't trust Vorik—or his smile.

"If it's true that Venia fell for a handsome stormer spy and all these people died because of it..." Tibby waved toward the capital and the castle. "The last thing you want is to repeat that mistake."

"I know. And I won't. I want to use Vorik for transportation. That's all. Besides, as you pointed out, his dragon wouldn't be able to fly to the island with us. Only *he* could swim after us. And without his mount, Captain Vorik is..."

Tibby raised her eyebrows as Syla trailed off.

"Still dangerous," Syla admitted.

"I'm glad you see that. I only glimpsed some of his athleticism through our link, but he's bonded with that dragon; I'm sure of it. That makes him powerful."

"I'm aware," Syla said.

Down by the road, Vorik's eyes opened again, and he gazed at her. A little shiver went through Syla as she wondered what exactly his powers entailed. Was he, even now, able to hear everything they said? Did he know Tibby suspected his story? Suspected *him*?

And did Syla also suspect him? Yes. But...

"Vorik," she called.

"Yes?" he answered promptly.

"Is your dragon willing and capable of giving us a ride to Harvest Island?"

There wasn't any surprise on Vorik's face. Maybe he *had* been able to hear their conversation. Or had some other way of monitoring enemies from afar.

"Dragons are very strong," he called, "but one of Agrevlari's size would only be able to carry two riders such a distance."

The words were issued matter-of-factly and without any smirk or hint of smugness of plans falling into place. Even so, Syla had a feeling that Vorik liked relaying that particular information, that he *wanted* to go on this journey alone with her.

"That's not going to work. Unless the dragon is willing to take the two of us and leave *him* here." A hint of thoughtful speculation entered Tibby's eyes as she imagined the scenario.

"A dragon will only accept humans on his back if one of them is his chosen rider," Vorik said.

Tibby hadn't spoken loudly. Vorik's response verified what Syla had been worrying about. He either had extremely keen hearing, or he *did* have another way of monitoring conversations from afar.

"You're not going off alone with him," Tibby said.

"I... agree that's not a good idea." And Syla did, but would she do it anyway? For the sake of her people?

She planned to find a way to depart from Vorik's company once she reached Harvest Island, but she would need her other allies when she arrived. She wanted Fel to protect her and Aunt Tibby to know what under the stars to do with the shielder once they found it. Besides, what were the odds that Syla could even manage to swim a mile to shore without losing her spectacles? Her aunt wore a strap around her head to keep hers in place. Maybe she could find something similar before they left.

"We'll find a ship to take us," Tibby said.

"All right." Whispering, Syla added, "We'll depart Vorik's company here, but it might be better to avoid returning to the harbor if we want to retain our freedom and not be swept up by the military. There must be a ship in a cove somewhere and a captain willing to take us."

"Yes." Tibby patted her on the shoulder. "Thank you for not being..."

"Foolish and impulsive?" Syla poked into her bag for a map that she'd packed, thinking to look at the coastline for coves they could check, but her knuckles brushed the dragon figurine, and a new thought popped into her mind. Hm.

"I was going to say horny and smitten, but your words work too, I suppose."

"I'm not a teenager who can't control her libido, Aunt Tibby."

"I'm glad to hear it." Tibby patted her again and headed for the ladder.

When Syla looked back at Vorik, she found him watching her with alarming intensity. Would he *allow* her to depart his company?

18

I don't think I'm going to get a blackberry cobbler, Vorik said telepathically to Agrevlari as he watched Syla pace back and forth on the road while the engineer—Aunt Tibby, as she'd called the mid-fifties woman—examined the ambulatory machine that the bodyguard had destroyed. Vorik wasn't that concerned about her. Though the woman was moon-marked, Vorik had gathered from what he'd overheard that she didn't know where the shielders were. His focus remained on Syla—and the steam coming out of her ears.

Oh, not literal steam, but he imagined he could see it wafting up, her brain boiling from all the concentrating she was doing. Or was it... scheming? If she'd been Vorik's poor deceased nephew, he would have been certain of it from that expression. The kid had been a thinker and a schemer.

A twinge of sadness and nostalgia swept over him at the memory of Jebrosh.

A cobbler... Agrevlari mused. *Is that not a human occupation?*

It's also the name of the dessert Syla said she could make if she had access to an oven and, presumably, the proper ingredients. Vorik remembered the tangy taste of the tart berries he'd eaten and grew wistful for another reason.

Ah. Given what I know about you, it makes more sense to desire a dessert than the flesh of a human.

Yeah, I'm not interested in eating my own kind.

This interlude has been satiating—an image of a sheep accompanied the words—*but is it not time to resume the pursuit of our orders? It is possible I could carry three, if that would sway the princess to ride with you on my back. The Island of Eliok is not far.*

Elioks are animals, right? Vorik hadn't previously heard what he assumed was the dragon name for Harvest Island.

Most delicious prey that have been hunted to extinction everywhere but on a handful of Garden Kingdom islands. They are known to be particularly populous in the wilderness near the volcano and away from the cultivated lands there. Our kind crave the opportunity to hunt them again and enjoy their sumptuous flesh.

Which was probably why Agrevlari was offering to carry the heavy burden of extra riders. He hoped the shield would be taken down so he could hunt. Dragons had singular ambitions.

Thanks for offering, but I don't want *you to carry three, especially not if one is the tedious bodyguard. I need to get the princess away from her allies if I'm going to...* Vorik remembered riding to the farm with his arms wrapped around Syla and her warm body between his thighs.

Seduce her?

Win her trust and locate the other shielders. The bodyguard and aunt are suspicious of me and want to get rid of me.

The princess is also *suspicious of you and wants to get rid of you,* the dragon said dryly.

Less so. Her mind and instincts warn her that I'm a dangerous enemy who is not to be trusted, but her body craves my touch. It hadn't been Vorik's imagination that Syla had melted back into him when they'd ridden together.

Right now, she's touching the statuette of Wreylith.

Vorik frowned at Syla. When had she pulled out that figurine?

Even though Syla had survived her encounter with the red dragon, it wouldn't be a good idea to intrude upon Wreylith again in the same day. Or the same *year.*

Where did she get that, do you think? Vorik asked. *It's a krendala, isn't it? I've only heard of them before, not seen one. Nobody left in this era knows how to make them, do they?*

I've seen a few of the magical tools that allow bonded humans and dragons to communicate from across great distances, but I believe you are correct that centuries have passed since new ones have been made. As far as I'm aware, the knowledge of how to craft them has been lost. Wreylith, however, is not the youngest of dragons.

You'd better not call her old when she's close enough to overhear, or she'll light your tail on fire.

I did not say she is old, Agrevlari said. *Dragons may live many centuries; some have even reputedly survived for a thousand years. Wreylith is not old but mature, which makes her wise and powerful and extremely...*

Sexy?

She is that. Agrevlari rose from his reclining spot in the grass and stretched like a cat, his tail swishing back and forth. *She sets the libidos of many male dragons ablaze.*

Despite her aloofness?

Perhaps that is part of the appeal. That which is not easy to obtain is valued greatly. Did you know she reputedly killed the last male who sought to court her? She mated with him to sate her urges, then slew him, like a black-widow spider or the legendary female morisaka.

I know the possibility of being killed afterward gets me eager for sex.

I think it's possible your Captain Lesva would slay a mate who didn't satisfy her.

Vorik snorted. *That* is *possible.*

My point in bringing up age is that Wreylith may have been bonded to a human in the time when makers with the knowledge to craft krendalas still existed. That figurine is most certainly linked to her.

Vorik watched Syla turn it over and over in her hand. He didn't sense her using her magic to activate the power within the figurine, but might she be contemplating it?

Wreylith couldn't ever have been bonded to a human, Vorik replied as he debated *why* Syla might want to reach out to the red dragon again. Wreylith had, however inadvertently, almost killed her. She would be foolish to want to interact with the dragon again. *She has utter scorn for riders—and those of your kind who allow themselves to be ridden.*

I've, alas, been the recipient of many of her comments on that and agree that it does seem unlikely, but... the krendala exists.

Yeah. Vorik sensed a trickle of magic flowing from Syla and into the krendala.

Bloody daggers, she *was* trying to draw the red dragon's attention.

Vorik jogged over, hoping to stop her before it was too late. Syla had her shoulder toward him and didn't seem to notice his approach until he reached out to touch her hand.

Syla jumped, dropping the figurine and spinning toward him with alarm widening her eyes.

"I apologize." Vorik stepped back. He'd meant to interrupt her but not startle her. She must have been quite focused on the figurine not to have noticed his approach. "I didn't mean to scare you."

"You didn't *scare* me." Syla scowled at him and picked up the krendala to hold protectively to her chest. "I didn't see you coming."

Her spectacles had slipped down her nose, and she pushed them up as she took another step back from him. A touch of enlightenment came to him as he realized they might affect her peripheral vision—or maybe it was that they couldn't correct for eye weakness to the sides.

"I didn't mean to *startle* you," he said, hoping she would object less to that word. "But I was concerned by... Ah, did you *intend* to draw the red dragon to you again?"

"Yes. There are four of us, and your dragon can only carry two."

Vorik gaped at her. "*Wreylith* isn't going to carry you. She scorns all dragons who bond with humans or let themselves be ridden at any time."

Agrevlari let out a mournful rumble.

"I didn't presume it would be easy to talk her into it," Syla said, "but I want to try. It would be faster to ride from here to Harvest Island than to find an undamaged ship and a willing captain to take us aboard."

The aunt headed in their direction. Tibby, Vorik reminded himself. She scowled at Fel as she approached. Even though Agrevlari had destroyed the other machine, Tibby seemed less inclined to glower at him. The bodyguard, who was keeping an eye on Vorik while discussing lizards with the stableboy or whatever that kid was, didn't acknowledge the aunt's ire.

"If she comes at all, it might be to kill you," Vorik warned Syla. "You may think you did her a favor by pulling out that fang, but the wild dragons never feel beholden to humans. If anything, they think we should serve them and give them offerings since we're supposedly a lesser species."

I do enjoy when you give me smoked salmon. Oh, and the whale-blubber pemmican that your people make in the winter. What is that delightful seasoning you put in it?

Pepper.

Since Tibby had drawn near, Vorik waved to invite her to listen to his conversation with Syla. Hopefully, she would advise her niece that summoning a wild dragon would be a *bad* idea.

"If I had an offering for her, do you think she would give us a ride?" Syla asked.

"No. If you knew what kind of offering she liked and had one, she might spare your life, but she's probably going to kill you for using that." Vorik pointed at the krendala.

"Is that your father's little statue?" Tibby looked at it.

"Yes," Syla said. "He left it to me when he passed. Do you know anything about it?"

"Just that he inherited it. It's been in the family for several generations."

"I…" Syla trailed off, her gaze shifting toward the northern sky. Her jaw sagged, and her face grew pale. "The dragon is coming. She said…" She looked at Vorik. "She's not happy with me for using the figurine again and plans to kill me and take it."

"Using the figurine?" Tibby mouthed.

She must not have had any knowledge of its power. Had these people even heard of krendalas?

"You'd better find an offering for her." Vorik pushed his hand through his hair. He and Agrevlari might need to once again protect Syla, this time from herself rather than the general's plot.

Did they have the combined power to stop Wreylith? Vorik doubted Agrevlari alone would be her match and didn't know if his smitten dragon would raise a talon toward her, regardless.

"I noticed eral pods in the garden," Syla said. "My plan was to offer to make a salve for her wound from them."

In the distant sky, the powerful red dragon grew visible. She was flying fast, her hard face set with irritated determination. Already, Vorik could tell her icy gaze was locked upon Syla.

"Maybe you should have made that salve *before* summoning her." Vorik, worried Wreylith wouldn't give Syla time to explain herself, mounted Agrevlari. *We're going to have to protect the princess.*

From Wreylith? Agrevlari sounded stunned at the idea.

I can't seduce Syla or win her trust if she's dead.

Agrevlari eyed Syla, who was, instead of wisely taking cover as the dragon approached, walking out to stand openly on the road with her arms spread. *The general may have underestimated the magnitude of effort that would be required to achieve that goal.*

Tell me about it. Vorik patted Agrevlari, urging him to take to the sky. It would be easier for the dragon to maneuver and fight once he was airborne.

Reluctance seeped from Agrevlari's muscles, but he sprang into the air and started circling the area. Wreylith was approaching fast.

"Does the eral-pod venom salve *work* on dragons?" Fel asked as he came to stand by Syla with his mace in hand.

As if *that* would do anything against a powerful dragon.

"I have no idea," Syla said.

Agrevlari remained close enough that Vorik could hear the conversation from above.

"But it shouldn't *hurt* one," Syla added.

"If dragons are like lizards," the stableboy offered from the doorway of the machine shop, "they might like tangtor grass."

Syla looked curiously at him.

"When snub-nose lizards lose their tails to predators," the boy explained, "they've often been observed rubbing the bloody stump against macerated tangtor grass. It's supposed to help with the regeneration."

Syla's gaze shifted to her aunt.

"Terrik has numerous books on lizards as well as a taxidermy collection of species from around the world. It's one of his passions." Tibby wavered on the road, not looking like she knew if she should stand beside her niece or run into the machine shop.

You dare intrude upon my thoughts again, human! Wreylith boomed into all of their minds, ending other conversations.

"I'm in need of a favor," Syla said, her arms spread, "but it also occurred to me that you left before I could apply a healing salve to help your wound. I'm aware of numerous kinds that assist with venom."

Wreylith flew over a canal and angled toward Syla. Agrevlari flapped his wings, as if he might intercept her, but her eyes flashed with power and irritation as she glanced at him, and he diverted.

Maybe Vorik should have stayed on the ground to face Wreylith without Agrevlari.

Put me down if you won't fight her, he urged.

She's irked. It would be suicidal for either of us to fight her.

Dragons have great regenerative powers, Wreylith boomed. *We don't need* salves *or other worthless human concoctions.*

"I can make one specifically designed to help your kind with venom." Syla's glance toward the stableboy suggested she'd taken the lizard-tail-stump plant to mind. "If your foot aches at all, it would help."

It does not ache! Such a feeble wound inconveniences a dragon not at all. Wreylith swooped low, talons stretching toward Syla.

To her credit, she didn't flinch. Maybe she knew that showing fear to the dragon would be far worse than being bold.

But Vorik worried that boldness would get Syla killed. Though Agrevlari hadn't put him down, as he'd wished, he jumped off, dropping twenty feet. He landed in a crouch with his sword in hand and sprinted toward Syla.

The dragon flew over Syla's head, showing her close-up the foot that had been injured, the talons spread wide. Fel leaped and took a swing at the dragon, and Vorik could have lashed out at the tail, but Wreylith swooped back upward, avoiding striking weapons. She landed at the apex of the machine shop, talons scratching the roof.

Did she favor that injured leg as she landed? Maybe her foot did ache.

"It would not take long to make," Syla said, as if the dragon hadn't been six inches away from tearing her head off with those talons. "I noticed the ingredients in the garden."

I do not need your human concoction. Wreylith glowered down at her.

"Give me a half hour in the kitchen," Syla said and started walking up the road toward the farmhouse.

Vorik looked at Fel, wondering if his charge was always like this. The older man appeared as nonplussed as Vorik.

Wreylith sprang from the rooftop. Vorik whirled, raising his sword again, but the dragon soared past too far overhead for him to reach. Talons outstretched, Wreylith flew right at Syla.

Vorik charged after her, but Wreylith reached the princess first. Only when her shadow fell across Syla did she show fear, her arms jerking defensively upward.

Wreylith didn't slay Syla, instead plucking her up and drawing a startled gasp from the princess. Syla flailed as the dragon carried her off, and her spectacles fell to the ground.

Vorik ran and picked them up, but, noticing the direction the dragon took off, had an inkling about what Wreylith intended, so he didn't sprint after them. Fel *did* charge after Syla, but he was far too late to reach the princess. Wreylith swept her over fields on the way toward the farmhouse.

Reminded of when Wreylith had dropped Syla, not realizing that normal humans couldn't fall from great heights without injury or death, Vorik realized the danger wasn't yet over. He cut across the fields to run after them.

Wreylith did drop Syla when they reached the house ahead of him, but, this time, the dragon descended to five or six feet off the ground before opening her talons. Syla wasn't the most athletic—it couldn't help that her spectacles had fallen off—and didn't manage to keep her feet when she landed, but she stood up right away. With determined steps, she strode toward the garden. Meanwhile, Wreylith alighted on a nearby silo and glowered defiantly at the surrounding farmland.

This is fascinating, Agrevlari observed.

I wasn't that fascinated to learn that you wouldn't help me attack a threatening dragon, Vorik replied as he continued toward the farmhouse, doubting Syla could make salves without her spectacles.

Only certain *threatening dragons. As you well know, I've aided you in battle against* many *fearsome enemies.*

Just not the sexy ones.

Correct. You are fortunate that I categorize so few dragons so.

Apparently.

Tibby rode on yet another wheeled magical machine, stopping to pick up the limping Fel along the way, and arrived at the farmhouse at the same time as Vorik. The bodyguard jumped off, grimacing as he landed on the leg he favored, but strode over to stand beside Syla as she plucked plants from the garden. Mace still in hand, he alternated between glowering at the red dragon and at Vorik—as if *he* had anything to do with this. He also sent a few glares at his wayward charge.

Ignoring him, Vorik walked to the garden and handed the spectacles to Syla.

"Oh, thank you," she said with such relief in her voice that it clued him in to how poor her eyesight had to be without the implements.

An unfortunate handicap, though he'd observed that gardeners were often afflicted with it. Myopia was rare among his people; stormers were more likely to lose one or both eyes in battle, leaving a vision deficiency that spectacles couldn't help.

With hers secured over her ears again, Syla efficiently collected the ingredients she needed and turned for the house. Before she headed that way, Vorik handed her his collection of blackberries. He didn't have much hope of her making that cobbler now, but if she was going to be in the kitchen anyway…

Her expression was bemused, but she accepted them, then headed toward the house. Vorik started after her, but Tibby had parked her machine and stepped out to intercept him. Maybe she'd seen the blackberry exchange and didn't approve.

"You are not needed, rider," Tibby said, "and we would appreciate it if you would leave our island. Your people have done enough damage here."

"I'm not needed? Surely, you don't think you've made an ally of that dragon." Vorik waved toward Wreylith, noticing that Agrevlari had alighted on another silo.

Wreylith was ignoring him utterly. Poor fellow. He needed to stick to flirting with females who didn't scoff at bonded dragons.

"I do not believe that, no." Tibby eyed Wreylith warily. No, she was eyeing *both* dragons warily. "I would like to encourage them to leave as well. *My* plan is to find a ship for our journey." Her gaze swung back to him, her eyes cool behind her glass lenses. "A journey on which you are not invited."

"Princess Syla has found me useful. *She* may invite me."

"If she wanted to go off with you, she wouldn't be trying to woo a different dragon to help us."

"I'm certain she's simply attempting to arrange transportation for you and her bodyguard. She was most pleased to ride with me earlier. Agrevlari is a far more agreeable dragon than that one. Far less likely to *slay* those he allows to ride him."

"I'm sure he slew plenty of Kingdom subjects last night."

Vorik hesitated. He couldn't deny that. Those had been their orders. Never would he have guessed that his brother would come up with this plan.

"Last night, my status as an agent of the Freeborn Faction had not yet been discovered by the rest of my people," Vorik said quietly, aware that Syla had shared his story with her aunt. "I understand why you mistrust me, but I've been commanded to protect the princess, and, since you are moon-marked, I will protect you, as well, if you'll let me."

"You wanted to take Syla and leave her bodyguard and me behind, not *protect* me."

Vorik spread his arms. "I only said that my dragon can carry at most two riders."

"We know *which* two he intended to ride on that dragon," Fel grumbled.

Tibby nodded at him, and they locked similar suspicious glowers on Vorik. Maybe she'd decided to forgive the bodyguard for his transgressions against her machine.

Clinks and clunks came from the kitchen as Syla prepared whatever she needed to make the salve. She was either oblivious to the argument outside or doing her best to ignore all of them. Probably a wise choice.

Tibby said something about packing a bag and getting some books, then strode inside, leaving only Fel glowering at Vorik.

"I admit I didn't expect her to call a second dragon. Or stand fearlessly while she approached." Vorik flexed his fingers in the air to mimic talons, and he smiled, though he'd not often observed that men found the gesture as charismatic and appealing as women did. Most women. The aunt hadn't been noticeably affected by his smile. "Considering she's not a trained warrior, she has... nerve."

The compliment only made the bodyguard's glower deepen. Maybe he didn't want an enemy rider admiring his charge's nerve.

So be it. Vorik collected the fruit he'd picked earlier and waited to see if Syla would succeed in talking Wreylith into offering a ride.

If she did... Vorik would have to find another way to get rid of the bodyguard and aunt. He had no doubt that they were scheming to get rid of *him*.

19

While the salve simmered in a pot and a berry cobbler baked in the oven, Syla found twine and did her best to tie it to the frames of her spectacles. She had a spare pair in her pack, but they were older, the lenses even weaker than the ones she was wearing. She didn't want to lose these, something that might well happen if *dragons* kept plucking her up to carry.

Even though she'd asked for Wreylith to return, she'd nearly fainted when the dragon had come at her with her talons outstretched. She hoped her plan would work, that Wreylith would agree to carry at least two of them to Harvest Island. She would need Aunt Tibby to help her remove the shielder when they found it and then to install it under the castle back in the capital. And they would need Fel to protect them along the way.

And Vorik? Once they arrived, they needed to find a way to escape Vorik. As helpful as he'd been, Syla couldn't let him trail her to a shielder. She wouldn't make the same mistake that her sister had. As horrible as Venia's death was, it might have been a blessing for her. Better to die than to live with the knowledge that one had betrayed one's people and caused the deaths of thousands.

While the salve and the cobbler cooled, Tibby entered the kitchen with a backpack so stuffed the seams bulged out. Hers looked to contain even more books than the one that Syla had packed. Maybe it was a genetic tendency?

"We're going to have to swim," Syla reminded her.

"The pack has been oil-skinned, and I've further wrapped everything inside." Tibby pointed at the cobbler. "That's not for the dragon, is it?"

"No." Syla hadn't *intended* to make the dessert, but Vorik had given her the berries, and most of the ingredients had been sitting out on the kitchen counter, as if the gods themselves had wanted him to have a cobbler. More likely, someone had been in the middle of baking preparations when the attacks had started. Since the salve had needed time to simmer anyway... "Vorik requested it."

Tibby's eyebrows flew up. "You're *baking* for him?"

Syla lowered her voice though she hesitated to speak any of her plans aloud since Vorik had a knack for overhearing everything. "Let him think he's winning me over. Then it'll be easier to slip away later."

"We need to slip away *now*. How can we get rid of him?"

"Well, as we talked about, the dragons won't be able to reach land with us. It'll be easier to get away from him when he can't mount Agrevlari and fly after us."

"He's still going to be faster on foot than we are. Did you see him jump off his dragon's back from twenty feet in the air? And land like he'd hopped down *two* feet?"

"I've observed that he's athletic, yes."

Tibby gave her an exasperated look. "That's a lot more than *athleticism*. As I told you before, he has magic. Powerful magic. You of all people should recognize it." She pointed to the back of Syla's hand.

Syla sighed and scooped the salve into a bowl. "I do recognize it."

"He could kill us easily. Any time he wishes." Tibby pointed at her chest and Syla's, then waved toward the garden outside as well. Including Fel?

"Yes, and he hasn't. That's not what he wants."

"What do you think he wants? You're a comely girl, but I'm positive he's not here because he's smitten with you."

Syla's cheeks heated as the memory of riding with Vorik again popped into her mind.

"He wants the shielders," Tibby said. "And he thinks you'll lead him to them."

"You said that before, yes. And I haven't discounted it. But that faction he told me about... Fel has heard of it. It apparently *does* exist, so it's possible..."

"It exists. I've also heard of it. But *he* isn't in it. It's mostly women who are tired of scavenging for their food and constantly being threatened by predators that can bite one of their children in half if they're careless outside of their caves for even an instant."

"You don't think some men are also tired of scavenging and threats to their children?"

"Not him."

"We'll escape him on Harvest Island." Syla grabbed a large wooden spoon, then took the cobbler pan and the salve bowl and headed for the door.

Tibby intercepted her, leaning close to whisper in her ear. "Does he trust you enough to eat that without question?"

Syla shook her head in confusion at the question. "I don't know."

"There's some dried zalok in the root cellar."

Syla froze. Since she knew herbs well, she recognized that one and what it did.

It was a potent poison, one that was taken to the castle so that anyone who knew Kingdom secrets, which included her, could consume it if they were traveling between islands and captured by stormers. It was supposed to be one's godly duty to kill oneself to keep from divulging vital information.

"You can easily mix some into the topping, and he wouldn't taste it," Tibby added.

Syla couldn't keep from giving her aunt an aggrieved look. While she understood the logic, she was a healer, not a murderer. She couldn't contemplate poisoning someone.

"Or I could do it," Tibby said, her voice low. "So you wouldn't have to. I know it would be hard for you."

"I would hope it would be hard for you too."

"Not after what he's done. What they've *all* done. You were there. You have to know even better than I the horrors."

Syla closed her eyes, tears threatening as the words brought to mind her sister's body and all the other dead she'd seen in the courtyard, the pure horror of the wyverns feeding on them.

Throat tight, she whispered, "I do."

"I'm sorry," Tibby said. "I know what you lost. What *we* lost. I just... This may be the only chance to get rid of him."

Syla shook her head. "Even if I could, he doesn't trust me *that* fully. He's aware that I'm suspicious of him. I don't know if he'll even eat this."

Was that true? Vorik's eyes had lit up at the idea of a blackberry cobbler, and he had been so delighted to have found simple pears and other fruit in the orchard.

But he might even now be listening to them. If she *had* been willing to do this, she should have done it on her own, without saying anything. Hell, she didn't even know if *thinking* was safe around those dragons.

"No," she said and walked outside.

Her heart almost stopped when she found not only Vorik standing on the path in front of the porch but the red dragon waiting on the other side of the fence. Sweat broke out under her armpits, and she forced a smile.

"This is for you." Syla handed the spoon and pan of cobbler to Vorik, forcing herself to meet his eyes, if only briefly, then hurried past him toward the gate. She half-expected Vorik to grab her and confront her about the discussion, but he didn't, and she made it past the fence to stand in front of the stern-faced Wreylith. "I, uhm." She held up the bowl of salve, like the offering Vorik had mentioned.

Of course, the dragon didn't have thumbs and fingers and would struggle to apply such a thing.

Wreylith lifted her forelimb and spread her talons. The deep gouge that the fang had left was already healing, appearing less inflamed than it had that morning, but the flesh around it remained swollen and red. Despite the dragon's words, Syla had no doubt that it continued to hurt.

Human concoctions can do nothing to aid dragons, Wreylith stated, though her foot remained raised. *And dragons do not need slimy slop smeared on their toes. With our great power and stamina, we can regenerate from all but the greatest of wounds on our own.*

"I'm certain that's true." Syla dipped her fingers in the salve—she would consider it *unctuous* rather than slimy—and gently coated the gouge.

The dragon stood so still, her wings and tail out rigid, that she might have been a statue. Tendrils of smoke wafted from her nostrils, and Syla swallowed, worried the pain of the application would cause fire to spontaneously flare from Wreylith's maw.

When did my world become so insane? Syla wondered and smeared more salve.

A blurry shadow appearing to her side made her twitch. Vorik.

He moved without making a sound, seeming to pop up out of nowhere. He wasn't holding his sword, and he stopped a few feet back, but she sensed that he was letting Wreylith know he would fight to protect Syla if necessary.

The dragon gave no indication of being worried or even caring about him.

Syla decided not to look at him either—she didn't want him to see that he'd startled her again—and finished applying the salve. Per Terrik's suggestion, she'd mixed in some powdered tangtor grass. She knew nothing of lizards and what natural medicines they favored but doubted it would do anything to diminish the potency of the salve. Besides, it added a pleasant, almost minty, scent to it.

You have called upon me and made this offering as a bribe. Wreylith set her foot down.

Syla thought about feigning innocence—no, *lying*—to the dragon but doubted Wreylith would fall for that. If dragons could read minds, she definitely would not.

"I did hope for a favor," she admitted.

I have not slain you despite you not once but twice impertinently and unwisely using the magic of that statuette to spy upon me.

"It was never my intent to spy."

I know this, else you would already be dead. But you've invaded my privacy nonetheless.

"I apologize for that, especially the first time. That was an accident."

But this time, you want something.

"For you to carry me to Harvest Island."

"To carry *two* of us there," Fel said.

He and Aunt Tibby stood side-by-side in front of the gate, not far behind Vorik.

"It can be in your maw," Syla made herself say, though that

had been a dreadful means of transportation, "if you won't allow humans to ride on your back."

Fel issued something between a groan and a grunt to opine on that.

"I'll ride with the enemy captain," Tibby said faintly.

"It's not that long of a trip." Syla gazed into Wreylith's faintly glowing golden eyes, though it was unnerving. Everything about the huge muscular dragon and the power she emanated was unnerving. "We can find our own way back."

Where did you get the krendala? Wreylith looked toward the pocket where Syla had tucked the statue.

"From my father, who apparently got it from his mother." Syla glanced back, and Tibby nodded.

You are descended from Queen Erasbella?

"Uhm, yes." Syla blinked in surprise that the dragon knew anything about her lineage. "She would have been my great-great grandmother. She passed long before I was born."

Long. Wreylith's eyes slitted, and she snorted out a breath. Was that... a laugh? Maybe the dragon equivalent?

"To humans," Syla said, reminded that dragons could live for centuries.

Humans are so inferior. Why the gods deemed them important enough to give them wondrously fertile islands and protect them, I cannot imagine. Wreylith looked at her foot, flexed it, then sprang into the air, wings flapping.

Syla stepped back before remembering that Vorik was behind her. He lifted a hand, stopping her with a light touch before she would have stepped on his foot. Oh, if she had but half the coordination and athleticism of a rider. She would even delight in Fel's somewhat aged and injury-affected athleticism.

"I don't think that dragon is carrying us anywhere," Tibby said.

"Good." Fel grunted. "Ships don't have fangs."

But could they *find* a ship? Exhaustion made Syla's shoulders slump as she imagined having wasted the last hour.

"This is magnificent," Vorik said.

She looked at him and realized he was holding the cobbler rather than his sword. It was still sheathed in its scabbard on his back while he wielded the spoon, the dessert half gone.

"Stormer cultural norms would suggest I share it with the others of the tribe, but nobody here is of my tribe, and I don't feel kinship to your aunt or bodyguard." A baleful glower toward them should have accompanied the words, but Vorik smiled at them instead, as if the dessert was putting him in too amiable a mood for harsh gestures.

A little zing of awareness went through Syla even though his gaze wasn't directed at her. As she'd noted before, Vorik was striking when he smiled, the gesture softening the hard, lean lines of his face.

"I don't think they feel kinship for you either," she said.

They nodded.

Unconcerned, Vorik turned his smile toward her and gazed at her through his eyelashes. Her awareness of him intensified. More than that, she felt drawn and wanted to step closer, to rest her hand on his chest. The word *striking* floated through her mind again.

But even if Tibby hadn't warned her about what Vorik was likely up to, Syla wouldn't have let herself act on her attraction. She stepped back, not even wanting to acknowledge it. There could be no attraction. He was the enemy. She couldn't forget that.

"I appreciate you making this for me," Vorik said, ignoring or unaware of her reaction to his smile. "We don't have any of the ingredients in it, I don't think. Is it honey that makes it so sweet? It's more than the berries themselves, though they are amazing."

"Sugar. We grow beets on several of our islands and process

them for it. I do have recipes that use honey too. We have a lot of hives throughout the Kingdom."

"Hives that aren't raided relentlessly by honey-loving predators?" Vorik brought his berry-stained fingers to his lips, bits of the sugary crumble from the top of the cobbler on them. "That's amazing too. I only once ever found a beehive in the wild, and it was way up in a tree. I climbed up and got stung repeatedly before I got a taste, but it was worth it." He licked the crumbs off his fingers, his tongue sliding along them as he closed his eyes, visibly enjoying the treat.

Syla stared, almost hypnotized at his tongue dancing along his fingers. She didn't think he meant the gesture to be sensual, but it made her think of what else he might do with that tongue, and her body tightened. Storm-cursed seas, she *was* attracted to him.

His eyes opened again, still slitted as he watched her through his lashes. Maybe he *had* meant the gesture to be sensual. An... invitation?

"How old were you?" she asked.

"Eleven or twelve, I think. I haven't spotted such a delight since. As I said, hives are rare out there." Vorik didn't quite polish off the entire pan, leaving a third of the dessert and setting it on the fence before waving that Fel or Tibby could finish it if they wished.

Belatedly, it occurred to Syla that Tibby's idea that they poison it might have worked. He'd not only eaten it, but he'd not hesitated to do so, at least not that she'd seen. Did he *trust* her? Or simply not think she was the kind of person who might poison someone?

"I'll take you to Harvest Island if you wish." Vorik pointed at her and waved at Agrevlari. He didn't look at Fel or Tibby. Nothing had changed. He couldn't—or *wouldn't*—take them.

As much as Syla wanted to hurry up and find a shielder to

protect her people, she couldn't go without her aunt, and she didn't want to go without Fel either.

"And once we're there, I'll protect you from whatever threats may await," Vorik added.

"It's *my* job to protect her," Fel said. "We're finding a ship."

Vorik's gaze remained on Syla, intent. He wanted badly to take her away from her aunt and bodyguard. She had no doubt. Whatever the reason—maybe it was exactly what Tibby suspected—that alone ensured she couldn't go off with him by herself.

"Would you take me to see the leaders of your faction?" Syla asked.

His eyebrows rose. "What?"

"I think I'm going to need more allies for my quest." Earlier she hadn't had any interest in being flown off to meet any stormers, and she still didn't want to go, at least not until she had the shielder installed under the castle, but she asked it as a test. If Vorik *was* working with them, he wouldn't object to taking her to see them, right?

He scratched his jaw. "They do want to see you alive and even wanted me to bring you."

Oh, right, he had mentioned that before.

"But I thought you were set on visiting Harvest Island."

"I am, but perhaps we should see your people." She'd hoped to catch him in a lie, but, so far, he hadn't reacted as she'd thought he might. Was it possible that, despite what Tibby believed, Vorik *was* working with that faction?

"That's fine. Agrevlari and I will be happy to take you to see them. But—"

Wreylith returns, Agrevlari said to all of them.

The red dragon was flying back in from the sea, zigzagging through the sky and even rolling and diving, like a dolphin frolicking in the waves.

And is playful, Agrevlari's telepathic voice came across as shocked.

Syla had a feeling *playful* wasn't an adjective often attributed to the red dragon.

And beautiful, he added wistfully.

"My dragon is pining," Vorik noted.

"Will that affect his ability to fly?" Syla asked.

"I don't think so."

She didn't get to find out. Wreylith arrowed down and caught Syla in her jaws, just as she'd done back at the castle. Syla gritted her teeth at the pressure from those fangs, but they didn't pierce her skin. To her surprise, Wreylith tossed her into the air.

Utter fear clenched her for a moment, and she flailed, spectacles sliding down her nose despite the twine, until the dragon's broad scaled back came into view. More through luck than adroitness, Syla managed to land stomach-first atop it, arms and legs splayed for balance.

Wreylith banked and came around again, this time plucking up Aunt Tibby.

Tibby yelled in alarm as she, too, was tossed into the air. She managed to twist and come down astride Wreylith, her backpack still on her shoulders. Terror widened her eyes, however, and she sent a few quick prayers to the sun god.

Without waiting for them to settle themselves, Wreylith took off to the south, in the direction of Harvest Island.

On the ground, Vorik and Fel gaped after them. It didn't take Vorik long to recover. He sprang atop Agrevlari's back. Fel shouted something. An entreaty to take him along?

After the cross words—and crossed weapons—they'd shared, Syla expected Vorik to embrace an opportunity to abandon Fel. To her surprise, his dragon banked and came back, plucking up Fel, much as Wreylith had plucked up Syla. A moment later, he rode behind Vorik on Agrevlari's back, and the green dragon flapped after the red dragon.

After adjusting her spectacles—thank the gods she'd thought to secure them with twine—Syla met and held Vorik's gaze.

He looked more amused at everything than angry at how things were turning out, and she wondered... was it possible he *was* on her side? Maybe she *could* trust him. She bit her lip. If only she knew.

20

As Agrevlari flew after Wreylith, the afternoon sun gleaming on Syla's auburn hair, Vorik wished she were on the same dragon as he. Instead, the odious *Fel* sat behind him, the bodyguard doing his best to stay astride without touching Vorik. That suited Vorik fine, but Fel didn't have any experience riding dragons and kept sliding sideways whenever Agrevlari banked. Each time, he would have to clutch Vorik's waist for support.

Vorik only sighed, wondering what impulse had prompted him to collect the bodyguard. Only a vague sense that Syla would be pleased if he brought the man along. The aunt had been talking to her, telling Syla that she couldn't trust Vorik, and she had been unsettlingly close in her guesses about his true intentions. He'd been careful when Syla had questioned him about the faction and relieved when Wreylith had shown up. What under the moon's eyes would he have done if he'd actually had to take Syla to the leaders of the Freeborn Faction? He didn't even know where they lurked these days.

Agrevlari flapped his wings faster to catch up to the powerful Wreylith, and Fel had to clutch Vorik's waist again.

Had *Syla* been doing the clutching, Vorik wouldn't have minded. She'd made him a blackberry cobbler. He would have cheerfully invited her into his furs, regardless of his general's orders, simply because of that. The dessert had been *amazing*. And that she'd made it for him had been even more amazing. Why had she bothered?

Oh, Vorik was aware that Tibby had wanted Syla to poison it—Agrevlari had telepathically monitored that conversation and let him know—but Syla hadn't considered it for long. And it hadn't been on her mind at all when she'd decided to make the dessert.

Maybe she wants to seduce me, Vorik mused telepathically.

What? Agrevlari asked.

Syla made me a dessert.

Oh, I'm aware. You've wiped your grubby blackberry-stained hands on my scales twice.

Sorry about that.

You can wash up when we aren't able to fly all the way to shore and have to dump our riders into the ocean.

Yes, that will be an opportunity for a thorough bathing.

You could use it. After the night's many battles, you're aromatic. Dragons have keen senses of smell, you know.

It's a great sacrifice your kind makes to bond to us lowly and odorific humans.

It is indeed. You should give me smoked salmon more often.

Noted.

Vorik looked toward the red dragon. Tibby lay on her belly, her arms tight as they draped Wreylith's back, the side of her face pressed to the scales and her eyes squinted shut behind her spectacles. In front of her, Syla sat straighter, peering curiously to the left and right at the ground below as they flew over her homeland. Soon, they sailed over the southern coast and out to sea, heading for the next island, one of two in the chain that were visible on the horizon.

Wreylith was still sashaying back and forth, banking and almost dancing in the air, no doubt feeling good since her wound was healing. Her vigor didn't make the easiest of flights for a new rider, but Syla hung on, her enthusiasm for the experience seeming to override what would have been natural fear. Even many stormers, who grew up climbing cliffs and trees to scavenge for food, were terrified during their early rides and worried about falling. Maybe Syla was less concerned since she'd ridden once with him. Or maybe it was that she had, as he'd been thinking earlier, a lot of determination and confidence for a healer.

Or for anyone. Vorik smiled, thinking of her facing Wreylith as the great dragon approached, intent unknown. Syla must have been worried, but she hadn't stepped back either time the dragon lifted one of those deadly taloned feet.

His groin tightened, the memory stirring arousal, and Vorik rolled his eyes at himself.

It would be useful for this mission if he was genuinely attracted to Syla, but he didn't want to let sexual interest develop into feelings. He already found his orders morally ambiguous. He was a warrior, not a spy, not someone who seduced women for their secrets. He preferred facing opponents openly, honorably. This rankled.

Other dragons are circling the Island of Eliok, especially the north end, Agrevlari said. *They are from Captain Lesva's squadron.*

Vorik sat straighter, peering over the twin horns on his dragon's head as he pushed his musings aside.

My brother must have sent them so that I could defend Syla again. Vorik grimaced and rotated his shoulder. He'd wrenched it during his *last* battle and wondered how many more fights against his own people he would have to endure.

Since he hadn't slept the night before, the idea was more wearying than usual. Further, it was hard to feel zeal for attacking his comrades. Vorik believed the men who'd targeted Syla at the lighthouse had both survived their falls—he'd done his best to make sure they dropped into the water instead of hitting the ground—but it had been close. What if he had to kill his own tribesmen for the sake of this ruse?

There is confusion among the dragons, Agrevlari added. *I'm close enough to hear some of their thoughts, and Pomplinor spoke directly to me. They know Wreylith, of course, and she's always made her feelings on riders clear.*

Seeing her with one must be puzzling. Vorik glimpsed two dragons angling in from the west. They were on a course that would intercept Wreylith. Was that Captain Lesva's Verikloth?

There is debate going on about that very subject. Pomplinor wants to know if the female—the princess—has been chosen and how it could be possible that a gardener could bond with a dragon. Verikloth likes the idea of attacking and defeating Wreylith. More, I believe, because he thinks showing his greater fighting prowess would make her want to mate with him than because he cares that she's taken a rider.

He and Captain Lesva aren't a match for Wreylith, Vorik said.

Normally, I would agree, but Wreylith carries two females who are not warriors. She will be hindered in a battle if she tries to keep them from falling off.

Vorik frowned, remembering how the red dragon had tossed Syla to the ground the first time. *I don't think she* will *worry about keeping them on her back. I'm surprised she's carrying them at all.*

As am I.

Worried at the prospect of Syla being tossed into the sea to drown, Vorik touched Agrevlari's scales. *Speed up, if you can, please. We need to be there to help if they attack Wreylith.*

Agrevlari flapped his wings harder, the briny breeze tugging at Vorik's clothes. *From their conversations, I sense... I'm not certain those dragons and riders know that if they attack the princess, we will defend her and that it would be part of a ruse.*

No, Lesva knows. She was there for that meeting with General Jhiton.

Of course, Lesva hadn't heard the seduction plan. She'd been dismissed before that. All she should know was that Jhiton had said no when she'd volunteered to capture Syla and bring her back for interrogation. What if that was her plan now? Maybe she even intended to do that interrogation herself, whether the general wished it or not. Maybe she was acting on her own. Taking... initiative.

Vorik grimaced. *Catch up, Agrevlari.*

I have been attempting to do so. You may have noticed that Wreylith isn't old or infirm, despite her mature years.

I did notice.

Vorik also noticed when Syla spotted the threat, her gaze swinging toward the approaching dragons. She glanced back, saying something to her aunt, though it was so windy that Vorik wondered how well they could communicate with spoken words. White-capped waves frothed below. They were about halfway to Harvest Island.

More dragons came into view, also flying toward Wreylith and her riders. As Agrevlari had said, they were all a part of Lesva's squadron. That meant they would follow their captain's orders. The rider flying beside Lesva, her first lieutenant, Talvaya, especially would.

Vorik touched his sword, fearing he would have to use the blade today and that it might not be a ruse. He might be fighting for his and Syla's lives against an ambitious captain on her own self-assigned mission.

He wished he had the power to speak telepathically with Lesva and learn her intentions, but the magic that came from his bond with Agrevlari only allowed him to communicate that way with his dragon—and other dragons in the area who might be using their innate power to listen to his silent words.

Maybe it didn't matter. As Lesva and her lieutenant arrowed intently toward Wreylith on their mounts, Vorik believed he'd guessed their intentions.

They were going to try to capture Syla to interrogate her. And if she didn't survive the fight they started... they wouldn't care in the least.

Flying on a dragon's back was the most wondrous thing Syla had ever experienced, and she dearly wished the circumstances were different and that she could enjoy the salty breeze tugging at her hair and the amazing view from high above. Ahead, the somewhat lopsided Harvest Island, with its volcano on one end and lush verdant croplands stretching toward the other, was striking from the air. Black cliffs alternated with black-sand beaches interspersed with inlets and coves all along the north side of the island. A hint of green south of the volcano promised untamed forestlands where wild animals browsed. It was all beautiful.

What would it be like to live in Vorik's world? To get to ride a dragon *all* the time? To swiftly be carried about the world on the back of such a magnificent creature, one lesser predators wouldn't dare bother?

"Where did all those dragons come from?" Aunt Tibby asked from her position behind Syla.

Since Syla had been watching them approach, the question wasn't a surprise. Though Wreylith hadn't altered her course or said anything telepathically to them, she had to be aware of the dragons too. Likely, she'd spotted them long before her human riders had.

Of the two in the lead, one was blue and one gray. They were flying hard toward Wreylith with riders on their backs. It looked like they wanted to intercept the red dragon before she reached the island.

As powerful as Wreylith was, Syla worried about being outnumbered. She could make out two more dragons in the distance, also heading in her direction.

"It's almost like they were waiting for us," Syla said, but how could the stormers have anticipated that she would leave Castle Island and that it would be by air?

Unless... could Vorik have somehow told his people?

Syla looked back, half-expecting to find him and Agrevlari on a leisurely flight, having anticipated the arrival of these dragons. But no. Agrevlari was flapping his wings hard, his tail streaming straight out behind him as he sought to catch up with Wreylith. And on his back, the grim-faced Vorik leaned forward, his gargoyle-bone sword in his hand. They were trying to catch up so they could help if a fight broke out. Syla silently apologized to Vorik for doubting him.

Impudent human-hugging dragons, Wreylith boomed telepathically, *why do you fly to intercept me?*

Why do you carry two human runts on your back? one replied promptly. The voice seemed to originate with the blue dragon. *They are enemies to our kind and to wild dragons as well.*

Wreylith digested that for a moment. *One is not an enemy to our kind. One has assisted this dragon in a minute but not insignificant manner.*

"She's grateful to you," Tibby said.

"I wouldn't assume that from those words."

The princess of the Kingdom is desired by General Jhiton, a significant *ally to dragons.*

Only to dragons who fawn at the boots of humans. Wreylith managed to flick a dismissive wingtip without missing a beat. *He is not significant to wild dragons.*

Syla peered toward the cliffs along the northern coast. They were getting closer, but would they reach the invisible shield around Harvest Island before the dragons reached *them*?

All dragons will appreciate being able to hunt and fish on the teeming shores of these islands, the blue dragon said, *once the shielders have all been destroyed.*

Even though Syla had suspected that was the stormers' plan, she found the naked statement chilling. Even more chilling was that they had dragons on board with their plan. Not only that, but those dragons were trying to woo Wreylith to their side. And Wreylith, though she was helping now, had no reason to love humans. Might she not be tempted by *teeming* shores?

Give us the one you carry, the blue dragon continued when Wreylith didn't respond, *and we will not harm you.*

Harm me? You spineless dragons haven't the ability to harm me.

The jaws of the blue parted, and it spewed fire. The gray flapping its wings beside it did the same, their gouts of flame mingling to form a cloud that they flew through, impervious. The fire didn't seem to touch their riders. The enemy dragons had drawn close enough now that Syla could see those riders, both female, both wearing the same black riding leathers and gloves that Vorik wore.

One woman pointed at her. Was she the leader?

"They're out for you," Tibby said. "They seem indifferent to me."

"You're lucky then."

"If I were *lucky*, I wouldn't be riding immediately behind you."

"We're not far." Syla nodded toward the black cliffs growing more distinct along the shoreline ahead. This wasn't the spot she'd thought they should angle for, with protected shallows that would make for an easier swim, but with Wreylith adjusting her flightpath to maneuver away from the oncoming dragons, Syla wouldn't attempt to direct her. She didn't want to risk Wreylith deciding that her passengers were too much work—or too annoying—and should be given to the other dragons. "I'm not sure exactly how far out the shield extends here, are you?"

"I only know that it's not a precise distance. In some places, it's a mile or more. In others, the dragons can get within a quarter mile of shore. *They* can sense it. I've seen them flying along its borders."

Syla nodded. She had too. In the past, on one of the handful of trips she'd taken to other islands, she'd sensed the magic, rippling like a curtain, when her ship had passed through. The shields only kept dragons, wyverns, and other powerful predators away. Humans were always welcome, no matter who they were aligned with.

Last chance, the blue dragon said, close enough now that its yellow slitted eyes were visible.

They didn't glow the way Wreylith's did, but Syla didn't presume the dragon wasn't powerful. Very powerful. And there were two of them. With two more on the way.

You are the one interfering with my *flight,* Wreylith replied. *It is not my last chance but* yours. *My ire is roused.*

Flames spewed from her open maw, brilliant and intense. Syla lowered on her back, afraid the wind would send the fire in her direction.

The other dragons weren't deterred. Maws open and fangs on display, they flew straight toward Wreylith's flank.

Hold on, humans, Wreylith warned. *I will attempt to get you close to the barrier, and then you will have to depart, but I believe you would find it difficult to swim to shore from here.*

"That's an understatement," Tibby muttered. "Is that a shark fin down there?"

They were too far above for Syla to make out such things, and she only said, "A rock formation, I think."

"Ah, that'll be pleasant to fall on then."

After Wreylith's advice, Syla tightened the straps of her pack around her shoulders and sank lower, but she didn't know what they could hold on *to*. It wasn't as if there was a harness or reins, and the scales were slick, not rough, with only the faintest of grooves in between each. All she could do was attempt to hug herself to the dragon's back.

"Is there anything we can do to help?" she asked, though she had no weapons.

Many riders shoot arrows or wield swords if the fighting draws near enough.

"I, uhm, don't have either. Only some suture needles in my pack. They're more effective in the aftermath of battles." Feeling useless, Syla glanced over her shoulder, but it wasn't as if her aunt would whip out a rapier.

"I have books," Tibby said, but she was busy hugging the dragon, her cheek pressed to the scales, and her eyes squinted shut.

Simply stay on then.

Did Wreylith sound disgusted? Or was Syla imagining that?

Agrevlari had nearly caught up with Wreylith, and Vorik shouted something to the lead female rider. Thanks to the wind, Syla couldn't make it out, but the rider pointed her sword at him and flicked a finger toward her female ally, who had a bow with an arrow already nocked.

This is turning into a dreadful flight, Wreylith said. *I'd hoped the barrier might be down on this island, as on the other, and I might hunt the fabled elioks. I remember their wondrous meat from my distant youth.*

"Sorry." Syla thought about mentioning that the barrier *might* drop on this island, should she be effective in her mission, but she didn't want rows of dragons lined up to take advantage. Besides, speaking of her mission to strangers wouldn't be a good idea.

The rider with the bow rose up, aiming over the horns of her dragon toward them.

With an irritated roar, Wreylith banked hard. She didn't veer away from the archer and other dragons but *toward* them.

The movement caused her to tilt. Tibby cursed, and Syla gripped even more tightly to Wreylith's scaled back, willing herself to stick like a spider to a wall.

Breathing fire, Wreylith flew toward the blue dragon. Nearby, Agrevlari adjusted his flight and also angled toward the blue. The four dragons came together with screeches and bursts of fire. Heat roiled off a gout that streamed past only a foot to Wreylith's side, skimming the top of her wing. The red dragon dipped into a short dive before flying upward, wings flapping hard. She came up to bite at the underbelly of her foe.

Again, Tibby swore, struggling to stay on.

Suffering the same problem, Syla fought to keep her fear from turning into panic, but she knew she would inevitably fall, and they remained far from shore. Even if sharks and other sea predators hadn't been a problem, the currents at this distance would keep even a strong swimmer from reaching safety.

Syla willed the magic in her moon-mark to somehow help her, to lend her power to strengthen her grip on Wreylith. But all she'd ever learned to do with her magic was heal people. She'd never longed for battle and certainly never dreamed of riding on a *dragon*.

Agrevlari screeched as he also bit at their blue foe, then headed for its ally, the gray dragon carrying the archer. Somehow, Vorik had no trouble staying on his twisting and diving mount. He was even on his feet and swung his sword at the archer loosing arrows at Wreylith—and Syla and Tibby. The female rider ducked, but Vorik managed to slice through her bowstring as Agrevlari carried him past.

Behind him, Fel had pulled his crossbow off his back, but he merely clenched it as he stayed low. Much like Aunt Tibby, his face was a rictus of concentration as he fought to keep from falling off.

Once more, Wreylith banked hard, swinging her body around as she bit at the tail of the blue dragon. The twist almost threw Syla off. Tibby did lurch sideways, but she managed to scrabble back astride though one leg dangled precariously.

The moon-mark on Syla's hand warmed, the way it did when she drew upon her magic, but it didn't seem to know what to do. *She* didn't know how to use her magic to help with flying.

As Wreylith dove again, Syla glimpsed the other two dragons approaching. For the moment, the battle was evenly matched, but that pair would arrive soon, and what then?

Tibby hollered as she again scrambled to stay on. The huge gray dragon flew right over their heads, maw opening and roiling fire visible in the back of its throat.

Syla swore even more than her aunt. There was no way to take cover.

Before the flames would have struck, Wreylith rolled away. Gravity threatened to dump Syla into the ocean far, far below, and she started falling, but the roll was so fast that Wreylith's back returned to an upright position before her riders tumbled away. Only Syla's heart seemed to pitch into the ocean below.

By the moon god, she *had* to find a way to use her magic to stay on. Wreylith had dodged the fiery blast, returning to flying upright several yards ahead of the other dragon, but it veered to follow right after her. When Syla glanced back, she glimpsed blood flowing from a gouge in Wreylith's tail.

That she could at least use her magic to help with. Maybe it wasn't the time, but she willed her power into the dragon.

A tendril of her magic flowed from her hand, through scales, and toward the wound in the tail. As the healing power knitted the gouge together, Syla realized she could anchor herself via that tendril. Her palm flattened to Wreylith's scales, and the next time the dragon moved quickly, her neck snapping like a whip to allow her to bite into the gray dragon's flank, Syla's hand didn't budge.

The rest of her body tried to pitch off, but through that link, she remained anchored.

"Hold on to me," she yelled to her aunt.

Tibby's face was flushed red, terror making the whites of her eyes visible around the irises.

"Or find a way to use your power to hang on," Syla added.

If she could figure out a way, Tibby might be able to as well. Could she *engineer* something in a dragon? Wreylith might object to that more than healing.

Movement to the side caught Syla's eye. The lead female rider was falling, rage more than fear contorting her face as she tumbled toward the sea. Sword in hand, Vorik crouched not atop his dragon but on the one she'd ridden. The blue. And that dragon wasn't happy about it. It twisted in the air and snapped at Vorik, trying to bite him in half.

Vorik leaped off an instant before those jaws would have crushed him. He also plummeted toward the ocean, and Syla gasped. It was so far below that hitting the surface of the water could kill him as surely as hitting the ground.

But Agrevlari flew in from the side, Fel balanced precariously on his back, and angled to catch the falling Vorik. Another dragon was chasing Agrevlari—the gray carrying the female archer. She yelled at Vorik as he settled astride Agrevlari in front of Fel. Like the other woman, fury raged in her eyes, and she waved, as if commanding others to get him.

Syla realized that was exactly what she was doing. The other two dragons had caught up, making the odds four to two. The fact that one dragon had lost a rider meant nothing. The blue dragon flapped its wings, its eyes almost as furious as those of the humans as it smashed into Agrevlari's side. The other dragons focused on helping their ally more than going after Wreylith, and blasts of fire hid the battle from Syla's view.

She couldn't tell if the flames seared through the space

between her and Agrevlari, or if they struck his riders straight on. Vorik might have magic to let him survive that, but Fel didn't.

We near the sky barrier, Wreylith said, diving toward the ocean below.

"We have to help the others," Syla blurted, twisting to try to see the other battle, but with the new angle, a red dragon tail blocked her view.

"It's too far to shore!" Tibby called.

Though she didn't want to abandon the others, Syla made herself look forward. Tibby was right. It had to be more than a mile to the shoreline. The *cliff*-line. Worse, an obstacle course of rock formations jutted out of the sea between them and the uninviting shoreline, and white water churned dangerously around those rocks.

"Can you get closer?" Tibby pointed toward a beach in the distance.

"The water doesn't look as rough there," Syla added, hoping Agrevlari could escape the others and drop Fel off too. But when she looked back, the green dragon was struggling to evade their enemies. *Three* dragons bit and clawed at him, and was that an *arrow* through Vorik's shoulder? As strong as he and Agrevlari were, they couldn't fight off so many.

What Vorik had done or said to draw all their enemies from Wreylith, Syla didn't know, but he was buying time for the red dragon to fly close to the shield. Had that been his intention? That Syla escape, even if he didn't?

Wreylith glanced back with one eye, enough to convey a baleful expression. *Pesky humans, you will get off where I drop you. I do not know why I did not give you to the human-tainted dragons. You are insufferable.*

"I healed your foot. And your tail!" Granted, Syla hadn't finished mending the tail wound and was using that tendril of magic as much to hold on as to knit the gash shut, but it had at least stopped bleeding. "And I'll happily heal any more wounds you receive."

I am only receiving wounds because I'm helping you.

"Didn't you get in trouble with the basilisk on your own?"

Maybe it wasn't wise to point that out because Wreylith gave her another baleful look.

Tibby poked Syla in the back. To tell her to shut up, Syla thought at first, but her aunt was pointing upward and behind them.

Syla looked in time to see Vorik, his face drenched with his own blood, falling, and Fel tumbled off the dragon right behind him. Agrevlari was too harried by the others to fly down and catch his riders.

"You have to help them!" Syla yelled, willing Wreylith to turn around.

She and Tibby could wait if need be—storm god's madness, she didn't know if she and her aunt could even survive that swim. Through her tendril of magic, Syla tried to influence the dragon, desperate not to let Vorik and Fel die because they'd been helping her.

But Wreylith snarled, probably sensing the attempt at manipulation. She twisted and bucked in the air, the powerful whipping of her body breaking Syla's bond and hurling her and her aunt toward the frothing white water and rocks below.

21

Fear filled Syla as she flailed with one hand and clasped her spectacles to her face with the other. As she plummeted toward the sea, the clear sky contrasted starkly with the dark-blue water and frothy white waves. When she plunged in, frigid water jolting her body, the force wasn't as great as she'd expected, but she barely managed to keep her spectacles from flying off as the sea flooded her mouth and nostrils. She sank deep but didn't hit any rocks.

One-handedly, she clawed her way to the surface, her clothes and pack making movement awkward. A wave smashed into her face and hurled her body several feet. She tried to get her head up, to look for her aunt and Vorik and Fel, but the sea taunted her. Another wave batted her like a crinkled ball of paper at the mercy of a playful cat. Would the current send her toward shore? Or farther out to sea?

For a second, as a wave carrying her crested, her face was toward the sky, and she saw someone plummeting downward, just as she had. She also glimpsed the red dragon flying in the other direction. Wreylith was done with her.

But was that Vorik? Or Aunt Tibby or Fel?

Another wave smashed water into her face, again trying to wrench her spectacles away and drown her, but not before she spotted someone splashing down. Vorik. He appeared unconscious. Or worse.

Again, Syla clawed her way to the surface. Vorik hadn't fallen into the water far from her, but in the powerful current, she didn't know if she could swim toward him. Still, she tried, willing whatever magic her birthmark would lend her to help her. Too bad she couldn't heal the *ocean* to anchor herself or do something that would aid her.

But desperation lent her strength, and she managed to paddle in the direction she wanted. When the wave carrying her crested again, she spotted Vorik floating atop the water near a log. Beyond it, the jagged black cliffs were in view. From above, they hadn't appeared so high and forbidding. At least they could guide her to shore.

Kicking and paddling, Syla angled toward Vorik. She had no idea what had happened to the others. She prayed to the earth, moon, and sun gods that luck would favor them. She even would have sent an appeal out to the deranged storm god if it might have helped.

Another wave brought Syla closer to Vorik. She reached him and the log at the same time. After flinging an arm over it for support, she gripped his shoulder and called his name, but his eyelids were closed. Though the water had washed away his blood, she could see numerous tears in his tunic and trousers, deep red gouges visible beneath, and a broken arrow shaft protruded from his shoulder.

And his head? He must have hit that as well. It was probably where all the blood had come from. Why had the riders all leaped onto him in the end?

Because he had, in their eyes, turned traitor? Maybe it had

been revenge since he'd knocked the female leader off. If she'd fallen from a great height—and Syla believed she had—she might have died.

In that moment, as she clung to Vorik and the log, Syla realized that Vorik might have been telling her the truth all along. He'd turned on his own kind and chosen a faction that wanted peace between their two peoples. And he was risking his life at every turn for that.

"I'm sorry I didn't believe you," she rasped.

His eyelids didn't so much as flicker.

Syla attempted to kick in the direction of the cliff, but she barely could have swum against the current by herself. With Vorik's dead weight along with her, she didn't know how she would make it. That was even more true when a wave sent the log smashing into a rock formation. It struck with a *bang*, the force knocking it out of Syla's grasp. She scarcely managed to retain her grip on Vorik as the water tossed them about.

He coughed, and she hoped he had woken, but it was his body's involuntary reflex to spew out water that went down his trachea. He remained unconscious.

When she glimpsed the cliff, Syla couldn't tell if it was closer or farther now, but she paddled and kicked in that direction. She had to make it, or she would be swept out to sea and die.

That concern reinvigorated her, and she kept going. Unfortunately, even with the buoyancy of the saltwater, Vorik's lean muscled body wanted to sink, and her pack dragged at her as well. Even in the icy water, her efforts left her hot and panting.

Her spectacles fell around her neck, only the twine keeping her from losing them completely, and the cliffs turned into little more than a dark blur. A wave smashed her against a rock formation. Again, she almost lost her grip on Vorik, but she managed to clutch a protrusion on the barnacle-covered surface.

Needing a moment to rest, she hung on and found a foothold

underwater. She used it to push upward, trying to get her bearings, but she couldn't grip Vorik, the rocks, and raise her spectacles to her face at the same time.

In the sky farther out to sea, a dragon flew past, its outline as blurry as everything else. All she could tell was that it was green. Was that Vorik's Agrevlari? Or one of the enemy dragons?

It didn't matter. The barrier kept it away.

"As long as we're not swept out to sea and into their reach," she rasped.

"Your Highness," came Fel's gruff call from nearby.

Thank the eyes of the moon.

"Here!" Syla hoped Tibby was with Fel and that she was all right. But she worried for her aunt, who would have as much trouble seeing out here as she. And her pack was even *more* full of books.

Fel navigated to her rock formation, dashed water out of his eyes, and scowled at Vorik.

"He's out?"

"Yes. Bleeding from many wounds, including at least one on his head."

Fel's grunt sounded a lot like *good.* "Let him go. That'll solve one of our problems."

Yes, but...

"I can't," she said.

"Why not?"

Syla struggled to explain her feelings. "If it were the other way around, he wouldn't let me go."

"Yes, and don't you find that suspicious? You're his enemy."

"I don't know if that's true."

"It's true. Trust me." Fel pointed toward the cliffs. "Come on. I'll help you, but leave him. If he survives floating out there, his dragon can collect him." He squinted toward the one she'd spotted. "Actually, that might be one of the dragons that was trying to kill us."

"That's what I was afraid of."

"His dragon might be dead. I don't see the red one either."

"I doubt they slew her. She... considered her duty done and left."

"You mean she hurled you and your aunt into the ocean. I spotted Tibby swimming over that way, by the way." Fel pointed again toward the cliffs.

"Good. We need to catch up with her."

"I'll help you." Fel gripped her arm lightly.

"I'll accept your guidance, since I can't see well, but Vorik is coming too."

Fel issued an exasperated grunt but didn't force her to release him. When he pushed off the rock formation to swim for the cliffs, Syla did her best to paddle along so she wouldn't be dead weight, but she kept one hand firmly on Vorik.

Doing their best not to kick each other or crash into rocks, she and Fel swam awkwardly toward shore. When they reached a small beach of black pebbles and agates between two sections of the cliff, Fel released her and climbed to dry land.

Vorik still hadn't woken. Syla did her best to tug him up, but the waves that kept crashing onto the beach made it difficult. Further, as soon as his weight wasn't supported by the water, she couldn't budge him.

Blood ran not only from the side of his head, mingling with water as it dripped onto the dark sand, but from the numerous gouges in his torso and a long one in the side of his thigh. His breathing, though even, had a pained hitch, and she worried he'd broken ribs and bruised organs. Once she had him safe and stable somewhere, she needed to heal him. Unfortunately, she was so exhausted that she doubted she had the power at the moment.

Hopefully, his hardy rider constitution would keep him from dying before she could rest up.

"First, we've got to get out of the water," Syla said and heaved, trying again to pull Vorik up the beach.

After watching her for a moment, Fel grumbled under his breath and helped her. As battered as he was, he had the strength to drag Vorik up above the tide line, though the pained expressions that twisted his face suggested the effort hurt him. Syla would have to offer him healing again too, as soon as she was able.

Seagulls squawked from perches on the great black cliff that loomed behind the beach. Syla hoped they could locate Tibby and find a way up. She also hoped there would be a road leading to civilization. They hadn't come ashore where she'd wished, and she didn't know how far it was to the small harbor city that housed the local government and most of the island's non-farming population. She did know of a temple perched along the cliffs of the north shore and wondered if they might be near it. Ships wrecked in this area from time to time, so the healers kept trained men and women in the area to handle the wounded.

"Syla," Tibby called, waving from farther up the beach. Clothes sodden and torn, her tunic half-fallen off one shoulder, she picked her way past algae-blanketed rocks toward them. It looked like she'd lost her pack, or maybe cast it aside to keep from drowning. "Thank the moon god for blessing our ancestors. You're alive!"

Syla waved at her aunt, though so many water droplets dotted her spectacles that she struggled to see her well. With a damp sleeve, Syla wiped them. The effort removed the water but left sand on the lenses, and she sighed in frustration.

"I'm alive too," Fel remarked.

"My machines wouldn't have mourned your passing," Tibby said.

Worried about all the blood seeping out of Vorik, Syla tore

pieces from his shirt and attempted to staunch the worst of the wounds. But he needed real bandages. *Dry* bandages. Somehow, through all the swimming, she'd managed to keep her pack over her shoulders, but everything inside would be soaked.

"If they've the capability of mourning *anything*, I'm concerned," Fel said.

"There's a path up the cliff over there," Tibby said. "I think we're within five or ten miles of Lavaperch Temple. If so, I have an engineering friend who retired from the capital to work there and be close to his wife's family. If he's at the temple now, he might be willing to assist us with our quest." Calculation gleamed in her eyes as she looked out to sea.

"Retired to... *work*?" Fel scratched his head.

Maybe Fel had no plans to ever again lift a finger after he turned in his uniform.

"Instead of designing shipyards, piers, and boat lifts around the Kingdom," Tibby said, "he now lends his engineering expertise to fermentation projects. Lavaperch is known for its beer and ale as well as being a home of healers."

"I'm more ready than ever to visit the place then," Fel said.

Tibby stopped beside Vorik and frowned down at him. "We're leaving him here, right?"

"That was my suggestion." Fel crossed his arms over his chest.

"If we're not far from the temple, we can get help for him there." Syla brightened with relief, hoping her aunt was right.

"Help for him?" Tibby asked. "This is our chance to get rid of him. Why did you bring him ashore?"

"He helped us with the dragon battle," Syla said. "And he's helped me *numerous* times this past day and night. I can't intentionally let him die."

Judging by the long look that Tibby and Fel exchanged, they felt differently.

Syla stood. Too bad. "Sergeant, I must ask a boon. Will you help me carry him up the cliff to the temple?"

Fel scowled his opinion on that. It was a lot to ask—that path had to be steep, and the temple would be a long walk. Maybe she could ask Tibby to go ahead and send back help?

Syla was about to do so when Fel grumbled again and asked, "Can I bash his head against the rocks a few times on the way?"

"He's already concussed."

"Then he won't feel more bashing." Fel lowered his arms and hefted Vorik up over his shoulder, staggering and wincing before adjusting his load enough to find his balance.

"You're going to carry him up that cliff like that?" Tibby asked him.

"Someone healed me yesterday, and I'm feeling magically compelled to help her." Fel glowered at Syla.

Hm, maybe she *wouldn't* offer to heal Fel again later. He wouldn't want to feel further bound. For that matter, if Vorik remained unconscious, how would she get his permission to use her magic on him?

"Does your compulsion preclude you from making a travois or a stretcher?" Tibby asked.

Fel looked around.

"A cart would be better," Tibby said, "but it's hard to make wheels out of driftwood."

Without waiting for agreement or permission, Tibby walked about, finding long pieces of wood that they could use. When Syla got the gist of what she intended to make, she helped, pulling kelp over to use as ropes. Perhaps thanks to her engineering background, Tibby laid out a design that looked like it would be quite sturdy, despite the substandard materials.

When Fel set Vorik down to help tie the frame together, Vorik groaned faintly.

Syla looked at him, hoping he would waken, though even if he did, she doubted he would be able to walk. His eyes didn't open, and he didn't groan again. She patted his hand, in case he sensed it on a subconscious level and found it comforting.

Though his clothing was torn, the black leather gloves that he always wore remained unscathed, other than sand stuck to them. Curious, she let her fingers linger on one. Though the power she'd witnessed suggested it, she wanted to see for herself if he had a dragon tattoo. While the others weren't looking, she tugged the glove down to reveal the back of his hand.

Yes, the likeness of Agrevlari in flight, wings outstretched, was magically inked into his skin in almost the same place that the family moon symbol forever marked her hand. She'd been born with her mark, but, from what she'd heard, the riders were granted theirs in a ceremony with the dragons who deemed them worthy of being bonded. Reputedly, only one in six or seven riders had the mark and the power granted by their kind. The rest were simply allowed to ride and serve in the Sixteen Talons because they had goals that aligned with the dragons' goals. But Vorik… he had a stronger link. And greater power.

Syla nodded to herself. She'd known. No mundane human fought with the prowess that he possessed.

When Fel returned with more wood, Syla tugged the glove back into place to hide the mark. Her bodyguard probably suspected too, but she didn't need to intentionally give away Vorik's secrets.

When it was done, they lifted him onto a travois made from driftwood and kelp. Fel took the lead, dragging it toward the path, and Syla and Tibby did their best to help lessen his burden. The bumpy ride couldn't have been comfortable for Vorik, so maybe it was for the best that he remained unconscious.

At one point, however, Syla caught his eyelids flickering. As they neared the top of the cliff, he blinked and looked blearily around. He focused on her, his pupils uneven, and she wasn't sure if he was present in his head or not.

Chance did not favor him because the travois bumped hard against a rock. Vorik slumped, his eyelids closing as he lost consciousness again.

"Rest for now," Syla murmured, her own exhaustion making her wish that she could. "I'll heal you later."

She'd spoken softly and doubted Fel or her aunt had heard more than a mutter, and she didn't think they'd noticed Vorik's eyes opening, but Tibby looked over at her. The slump to her shoulders promised she was also exhausted.

"I admit I've not needed healing that often in my life," Tibby said. Maybe she'd caught that word and had injuries she hoped could be tended later. "How long does the magical compulsion that someone feels toward the healer last?"

"Some people don't feel anything at all," Syla said, "and since you're also moon-marked, I think you'd be protected. But some people will feel… kindly toward the healer for weeks afterward."

"*Kindly.*" Fel grunted.

"With some people, it's more that they feel compelled to obey," Syla admitted. "Sergeant Fel is the first person I've witnessed feeling resentful because of the compulsion."

"I think that's just his normal personality. He's an abrasive sort, isn't he?" Tibby hadn't lowered her voice, and she glared at the back of Fel's head as she spoke.

"He was supposed to retire this month."

"We're *all* inconvenienced—or much worse—by these awful events." Tibby glared at Vorik again, but she didn't suggest leaving him behind. She did quietly mutter, "I hope you know what you're doing, Syla."

"I do too."

Even though her beliefs and vows as a healer told her that tending the wounded was *always* the right thing, Syla did worry that it was a mistake not to take this opportunity to get away from Vorik. Would she regret it later?

22

Twilight approached as the black stone walls of Lavaperch Temple came into view. Two wide towers with slate roofs rose from either side of the walled keep, the windows gazing out over the sea from atop the cliff. Its windows also overlooked the road that Syla, Fel, and Tibby had found, making the going easier as they'd taken turns dragging the unconscious Vorik in the travois.

Someone must have been on watch, because the gate opened as Syla and her bedraggled allies approached. The smell of hops wafted out, mingling with the briny sea air.

After not sleeping the night before, such deep exhaustion had set in that Syla couldn't speak. She dropped onto a bench near the gate as three people walked out wearing the blue robes of a healer. For a moment, she wished to be a child again, with her father still alive and willing to carry her to bed. He'd done that often when she'd fallen asleep staying up too late, tagging along after her older siblings.

Aunt Tibby sank down beside her, slumping against the backrest. Only Fel had the stamina to remain standing and address the three healers, two middled-aged men and an elder female who looked familiar. Syla believed the woman had visited Moon Watch Temple for lectures and training several years earlier, but she was too tired to dredge up the name. As Fel and the elder spoke, Syla caught her eyelids drooping shut. The last thing she was aware of as she nodded off was Tibby snoring beside her.

How many hours passed before she woke again, she wasn't sure, but she found herself in a small stone-walled room in a narrow bed, so someone must have carried her after all. Fel? The healers? She didn't know, but when she turned toward the window, she could make out a gray sky through shutters that were parted enough to allow the sea breeze in. And was that rain pattering outside?

It was daylight, but Syla was confused since the sky had been clear the last she'd seen it. She must have slept through the entire night. Or... *multiple* nights?

She sat up with a start, hoping she hadn't lost days. She had too much to do.

Her sudden movement made her body protest, and pain announced itself from at least a dozen spots, everywhere from a knee to a hip to her shoulder to blisters on her feet from walking in soggy shoes. A groan escaped her lips. She might not have received the grievous injuries that Vorik had, but that swim and helping drag his travois for miles had left her battered and sore.

"Vorik," she whispered with alarm, looking around, as if she might find him in the room with her.

She did not. Worry made her forget her wounds. What if the healers, not realizing he was an ally, had done something to him? With all the injuries he'd received, he might have died if they'd only done *nothing* to him. But, surely, the tenets healers swore to abide by before joining a temple would have prompted them to treat him.

A knock sounded at the door. Had someone heard her groan?

"Yes," she rasped, her voice stiff from disuse, and her throat dry.

Noticing a cup and ceramic jug of water by the bed, Syla poured herself some as the door opened. The elder she'd recognized the night before—Jemla, that was her name—stepped in, her gray hair pulled back in a braid and her blue eyes concerned as they raked over Syla.

"How are you, Your Highness?" she asked.

"I don't know." Syla gulped water, relieved the elder recognized her so she wouldn't have to produce coins for the offering urn and she would hopefully be granted help when she explained what she could of her quest. "How long have I been sleeping?"

"It's afternoon, so about sixteen hours."

"That explains why I need to pee." Syla managed a quick smile and spotted a screen in a corner, presumably with a chamber pot behind it. The castle back home had indoor plumbing, but that was rare in the temples, which had all been built in past eras and rarely renovated.

"I imagine so." Jemla managed a brief smile, but it didn't last. The concern remained. "As soon as you're able, we need to speak with you. I'll wait outside."

She must have heard about the fall of the capital. At least, as of the day before anyway, the shield here on Harvest Island remained in place.

Syla grimaced as she headed to the chamber pot, realizing her entire mission was to take the shielder from this island, which would leave the inhabitants vulnerable. When she'd come up with the plan, it had made logical sense to shift the protection to the island with the much greater population, but leaving these people unprotected would be difficult. She realized she had better keep that plan to herself. Even if she was the current heir to the throne, she couldn't presume that people would do as she wished—or go along with plans that would endanger them.

"This is going to be hard." Reminded that she needed to worry about Vorik too, Syla hurried to dress in a temple robe and soft shoes that someone had left. Her own clothes must have been taken to be washed. Fortunately, someone had brought her seaweed-draped pack and left it by the window to dry out.

Outside, rather than Jemla, a gray-haired temple guard waited for her. Dressed in a blue uniform, with a sword at his hip, he bowed deeply and extended an arm toward a hallway with doors on one side and windows overlooking the sea on the other.

"This way, Your Highness. I'm Flaron. We're relieved to learn that you're alive. The scattered reports we've received here... Well, we're almost twenty miles from town, so things don't get reported that promptly, but... we could see the fires from here the night before last." Flaron nodded toward the windows as he led her down the hallway. "At one point, it looked like all of Castle Island was burning."

"It seemed like it, but the fighting focused around the capital, I think." Reminded of her lost family, Syla murmured, "Around the castle."

"That's... what we've heard. We were led to believe that *none* of the royal family were left alive, and then, when the assassins came for Lyvenia..." Flaron shook his head gravely, leading her up stairs that turned twice, taking them to another hallway a level up.

"Lyvenia Moonmark? My cousin?"

The older cousin who'd visited the castle a few times when Syla had been growing up? Who'd healed squirrels and stray cats and dogs as well as people? Who'd made Syla want to investigate healing as a career?

"Yes. An assassin got her, I'm afraid to report. There have only been a handful of deaths that we've heard about on our island, but they're going after..." Flaron waved toward the mark on the back of her hand.

"All of us?" Syla whispered, though in her heart, she'd known.

"Everyone with the power to use the sky shielders is what is being speculated."

"Yeah."

"Anyone who would target a *healer*, moon-marks regardless, is lower than a snake's belly." Flaron stopped in front of a stout teak door with an anatomical picture of the human body carved into the wood, but he curled his fingers into fists and flexed his shoulders instead of knocking. Anger gleamed in his hooded eyes, and he took a breath to get control of himself. "I hope the dragons turn on the stormers and kill them all, the heinous bastards."

Unfortunately, the dragons had all seemed to be on board with the riders' plans. They'd wanted to recruit Wreylith too.

"When the Kingdom enforcers get here," Flaron continued, "they can question your prisoner, maybe figure out where the tribes are headquartered right now. We *have* to find a way to retaliate."

"Uhm, prisoner?"

Dread trickled into her anew. He could only mean Vorik.

"The rider that you brought with you. Sergeant Fel said the rider has been trying to—uhm, no offense meant, Your Highness—trick you into believing he's turned sides, but that's *Captain* Vorik. He's a hero among his people and the left hand of General Jhiton, one of the highest-ranking officers in their Sixteen Talons and Storm Guard. Vorik wouldn't turn. He's got to be working for them. Everyone agrees."

Syla rubbed her face. Who was *everyone*? How many discussions among how many people had gone on while she'd been sleeping? And why hadn't *Fel* been sleeping too instead of yapping about Vorik? He must have been as tired as she, damn it.

"Where is he now?" Syla asked. "He needs healing."

"To survive long enough to be interrogated?" Flaron nodded.

Syla barely kept from baring her teeth at him.

"He needs healing because it's the humane thing to do," she said firmly.

Flaron opened his mouth but must have read some of the irritation on her face because he paused to consider his answer. "He's being guarded in a cell in the east tower. He's got water and smoked fish. We don't torment our prisoners, not like *they* surely would if they got one of us." Flaron gave her an aggrieved look. "If they'd gotten *you*."

"I need to see him." Syla needed to *heal* him. Especially if... "Did you say enforcers are coming?"

"A messenger went to town to request their assistance. We've a few guards, but holding a rider—especially one with the mark of the dragon—might be beyond us. Besides, the island lord will know best how to use any information we can get out of him."

Syla debated how long it would take a messenger to ride the twenty miles to town, find and talk to the right people, and return with troops. A while, especially given all the other chaos going on, but probably not as long as she needed.

She was tempted to sprint to the east tower and start healing Vorik right away, but the teak door opened. Inside, Jemla and a white-haired man Syla didn't know waited at a stout wood table. A platter in the center held smoked salmon, crackers, cheese, fresh sliced apples, and was that a ramekin of hazelnut butter?

Her empty stomach growled vociferously.

"Come in, please, Your Highness." Jemla bowed her to a chair in front of the food. "This is our temple leader, Huzloron. We'll help you in any way we can, but we're also wondering..." She spread her hand.

Huzloron finished for her. "Why are you here, Your Highness? Were you chased off Castle Island by assassins? Or captured by dragons? We saw the battle at sea yesterday and wondered what it was about."

"I... yes. I was in that battle." Hadn't Fel told them about that? Maybe they wanted her version of the story. "Stormers have been trying to kill me. Regularly."

They exchanged looks.

"We should warn you," Jemla said, "that it's not safe here. Oh, our island hasn't been breached by dragons, but rider assassins are striking at..." Her gaze strayed to Syla's hand.

"I heard." Syla nodded toward Flaron, though he'd remained in the hallway outside.

"We were preparing a funeral pyre and time of mourning for Lyvenia when you arrived."

"I'd like to attend that if possible, but I need to see..." Syla hesitated to identify Vorik, since everyone seemed to know of his reputation, but Flaron had spoken his name, so someone had already recognized his face.

"Your prisoner?" Jemla watched her intently.

Wondering if Syla believed him a prisoner? Or was being successfully *tricked*, as Fel had apparently implied?

"Captain Vorik, yes. He needs the attention of a healer." Syla waved her hand to indicate her birthmark and power. She didn't want to imply the healers here weren't talented, but if Lyvenia had been killed, they might not have anyone else with magic as well as suture skill and knowledge of herbs and potions.

"He's dangerous, Your Highness. It's better for him to remain weakened."

"It's our duty to heal the ill and injured."

"Not him," Jemla said. "He may very well be here to assassinate more of your kin."

"He's not. He's joined a faction and has turned against his people."

Jemla smiled sadly at her. *Pityingly*. "He is a handsome young man. I can see why you might find his words and smile appealing, but—"

"That's *not* it. I'm not so young and naive that I would fall for something like that, but he's saved me from the very assassins you've spoken of. More than once. With my own eyes, I've watched him fight the stormers—his own people—to protect me."

This time, Jemla and Huzloron exchanged even longer looks.

Syla attempted to lower her hackles. She wouldn't convince them. She would have to gain access to Vorik and heal him so that he could escape if he needed to—before the enforcers arrived. And she... she needed to avoid irritating the locals, lest they try to keep her from her path.

"Are Sergeant Fel and my Aunt Tibby—Tibaytha—all right? We've all had a rough couple of days."

"I have no doubt." This time, Jemla's expression was more sympathetic than pitying. "I'm sorry for the great losses that you've suffered. The whole Kingdom has suffered them, but, for you, they're especially keen."

Syla's throat tightened, the emotions she'd been too busy to dwell upon threatening to arise at the sympathetic tone.

"Yes." She didn't trust her voice to say more.

"Do you want us to arrange a ship back to the capital, Your Highness?" Huzloron asked. "They must be missing you there. They'll need guidance from the royal family, surely?"

"What they need is a working sky shielder."

Huzloron and Jemla shared looks again.

"That's why I brought my aunt with me," Syla said, hurrying to explain before they assumed she wanted to take theirs. "She's an engineer, and I think she can study the working shielder here and learn from it. There weren't schematics with the one in the capital, you see. They've never failed before, so it wasn't something we had to worry about."

"You... believe the one on Castle Island can be repaired?" Huzloron asked. "We were led to believe it was destroyed."

"I went to see it myself after the attack. There's a faint hint of magic about it. We believe it might be repairable." Syla made herself meet each of their eyes so they wouldn't suspect her of lying. Technically, she *wasn't* lying, though Tibby hadn't held out much hope for repair. Still, it *might* be possible. "I believe my aunt, by studying a working shielder, may be able to figure out how to repair ours."

Yes, she *did* hope that. But she fully intended to take the Harvest Island one if needed. Castle Island *had* to be protected.

Syla swallowed around a lump, hating that she had to make decisions like this, decisions that would result in the deaths of some of her people.

"I didn't realize there were engineers with knowledge of the ancient gods' artifacts." Jemla lifted her eyebrows, as if she didn't know whether to be hopeful or suspicious.

"It's not Tibby's specialty, but she's smart and versatile." Syla tried not to recall Fel's skepticism when he'd said, *Doesn't she fix tractors*? Besides, Tibby did much more than that. "If anyone can repair a shielder, she can," Syla added sturdily.

"I'm glad she's well then," Huzloron said, "and that our cooks insisted on giving heaping portions of our precious hazelnut butter to our guests."

He smiled, looking a little encouraged by Syla's words, and waved for her to sample the food. She did, but as delicious as it should have been, especially on her empty stomach, it went down like lead weights. She was being dishonest with Kingdom subjects—*her own people*—and it disturbed her greatly.

"May I see Captain Vorik?" she asked when she'd eaten enough to satisfy her hunger.

The elders hesitated, and Syla braced herself for a rejection, but Jemla ultimately sighed. "As far as we know, you are now the heir to the Kingdom. We haven't the right to deny you."

Syla didn't feel deserving of the Kingdom or anything else, but said, "Thank you. I appreciate your cooperation," and was relieved when the guard in the hallway, per Jemla's instructions, led her to the east tower.

Syla hoped she hadn't waited too long, that Vorik wasn't in great pain or in a worse condition than she'd last seen him. If he was still unconscious, the enforcers wouldn't have any trouble taking him away for interrogation.

23

Along the way to the east tower, Flaron stopped at the rooms that Fel and Tibby had been given. Fel had finally fallen asleep, so Syla left him snoring without trying to wake him. Aunt Tibby was being tended by a healer but waved for her to come in.

Syla wanted to hurry to check on Vorik, but Tibby's expression suggested it was important.

"The friend I mentioned is indeed here. I'm going to have dinner with him and his wife this evening. If you don't have any objections, I'll ask if he can arrange... transportation." Tibby widened her eyes with significance.

"To town?" Syla didn't quite catch the significance. "Or...?"

Maybe her aunt meant someone who could port them to the shielder. That made more sense. It lay within the lava tubes underground halfway up the volcano.

"Or." Tibby nodded firmly, then tilted her head toward the young healer rubbing ointment into abrasions she'd probably received from bumping against rocks while swimming. The girl couldn't have been more than fifteen or sixteen, but she might have orders to report what she overheard to the temple heads.

"I don't object. If he can help, that's perfect."

Later, when they were alone, Syla would sum up her meeting with Jemla and Huzloron—and that they were suspicious of what she planned to do with the Harvest Island shielder.

"Good." Tibby winced at ointment being applied to a deep wound.

Syla took the opportunity to depart, not wanting to explain where she was headed next, but called, "Let me know when we can leave."

Tibby waved a curt acknowledgment before telling the healer that she'd lubed engines with less vigor.

Later, Syla would return to check more thoroughly on Tibby and Fel, but she hurried after Flaron, suspecting Vorik needed her most now. Even if his wounds weren't as dire as she believed, she needed to warn him that the enforcers were coming.

Stairs wound toward the top of the tower, and Syla's legs felt leaden, despite the many hours of sleep. She probably needed a week to recover from her ordeal. Or ten years. Every time her thoughts strayed to her mother and siblings, she diverted them with plans for the current mission. Once the Kingdom was safe again, she would allow herself time to mourn—to break down and weep—but she couldn't do that yet.

On one of the landings, Flaron halted with a start next to a window overlooking the sea. He stared out it and swore.

Syla squeezed in next to him, looking past the rain forming puddles on the rocky cliff top and out to the sea. On a formation beyond the breaking waves, a dragon perched. The gray day made it hard to discern its color, but she suspected it was Agrevlari, waiting for his rider to find a way to reach him.

Not surprisingly, there wasn't a red dragon perched out there, a color that she wouldn't have missed, even under the drab sky. By now, Wreylith was probably halfway around the world, eager to put distance been her and the pesky human who'd been responsible for her being attacked.

Syla ought to be pleased that she'd convinced the dragon to help in any way, but she couldn't help but feel wistful at the idea of a companion like Agrevlari, one who could be ridden at any time and one who felt loyalty to his rider. It was a silly thought, since Kingdom subjects didn't ride dragons. Never had such a thing happened, at least not that was mentioned in the history books. She needed to be grateful for the experience she'd had and not contemplate ever touching that figurine again, even though it had, through surprising luck, remained in her pocket through the fall and swim.

"I've seen way too many dragons these past few days," Flaron grumbled and resumed climbing. "People are whispering, saying the stormers might have a plan to steal or sabotage the rest of the shielders, and that those dragons are out there plotting the mayhem they'll loose on us."

Flaron looked at her, as if she might be privy to the plans of the stormers.

"That won't happen," Syla said, determined to keep it from coming to pass even if that *was* what the stormers were plotting.

She immediately felt uncomfortable, though, reminded that she *did* plan to take the shielder for Harvest Island. For the greater good, she had to. That didn't make it easy, especially when she was *on* the island, and its inhabitants were helping her.

"The enforcers will question your prisoner and learn their plans." Flaron nodded as they continued their climb.

"Yes... When do you think they'll arrive?"

He glanced out the next window they passed. "Probably not until tomorrow morning. But don't worry. We've got the rider locked in a sturdy cell with bars over the only window."

"Sounds like a cozy place to recuperate," she murmured.

"Too bad we don't have a dungeon to chuck prisoners into, but this is a place of healing, not internment."

The next landing had a blue rug, two plush chairs, and a small bookcase filled with tomes on healing, making it an appealing spot to sit and read while gazing out to sea. A young guard stood dutifully in front of one of two doors presumably leading to rooms.

"He's awake, sir," the guard reported to his superior.

Flaron nodded to Syla and rested his hand on his sword. "I'll go in with you."

"That's not necessary," she said. "If Captain Vorik wanted me dead, he's had numerous opportunities to kill me. Besides, he's injured. I'm planning to give him medical attention."

"As far as we know, you're the only direct heir to the throne. Keeping you safe is of paramount importance."

"Come in if you like, but he's got internal injuries as well as external ones. I may have to remove some of his damaged organs. Do you have a surgical kit?" Syla made snipping motions in the air. "Are you, by chance, trained to assist with a cholecystectomy or a nephrectomy?"

His face went pale.

"I trust as a trained temple guard, you're not bothered by the spurting and gushing of blood. I'll probably need some cautery irons. Oh, and that arrow. Is it still in his shoulder? I'll need an arrow extractor. Do you keep leeches on the premises? You must."

"Maybe I'll wait out here," Flaron said, eyeing his colleague. The younger man's eyes had grown a little wide too. "Or fetch you someone who can assist with, uhm, spurting."

"That would be wonderful. Thank you." Syla smiled, patted him on the arm, and opened the door, then closed it behind her.

Inside, Vorik sat on the edge of the lone bed, his tunic off as he hunched over and examined a long gash curving around his side.

Beside the bed stood a nightstand with a couple of unlit

candles, a jug of water, and a plate of crumbs that might have held bread or crackers. Not the delicious spread the healers had shared with Syla, and she felt a twinge of guilt that she hadn't wrapped up some fruit to bring. At least they had given Vorik food of some sort.

Her gaze snagged on an armoire against the wall opposite the window, with two huge green Candles of Serenity perched atop it, her nose picking up their distinctive eucalyptus and dragonquell scents even without the wicks lit. Of course, if the wicks *had* been lit, Vorik would be unconscious. Back home, she often used similar candles, the dragonquell oil mixed in a sedative helpful for patients undergoing surgeries. Like many healers, especially those moon-marked, she'd developed a tolerance for the scent, and could stay alert while her patient dozed off.

"It's wonderful to see you, Your Highness." Vorik beamed a smile in her direction.

When she turned her gaze back to him, Syla realized he was doing more than *examining* his wound.

He'd talked someone into giving him a needle and suture—or maybe he'd found medical supplies in the armoire?—and was stitching it himself. That had to hurt. And was that bloody chunk lying next to the plate the arrowhead that had been in his shoulder? How had he pulled it out without *passing* out?

"Vorik." As Syla rushed to the side of the bed, she almost tripped over an iron chain snaking out from a sturdy eyelet bolted to the stone wall. A shackle around Vorik's ankle ensured he wouldn't go far.

"Your Highness." He tied off his stitches, snipped the end of the thread, and set the needle and scissors on the table. When he shifted toward her, the chain clinked on the floor. "It's good to see you, but what is a cholecystectomy? And a... nephrectomy?"

"Your hearing is excellent."

"I think you've learned that already." Vorik looked at his hand.

The black gloves that had covered the dragon tattoo lay on the table.

"I have, yes. Those refer to surgeries, the removal of the gall-bladder and a kidney."

Vorik's eyebrows rose, and his hand strayed to his lower abdomen. "Is there something *wrong* with them?"

She snorted softly. "I hope not. I was trying to convince the guard to stay outside." She tilted her head toward the door. "They think you're a prisoner."

Vorik lifted his leg enough to rattle the chain. "I gathered. I trust they didn't put a shackle around *you*."

"No." Syla turned up the lanterns in the room and sat on the edge of the bed to look him over. Fortunately, he'd only stitched one wound so far, a deep gash that probably *had* threatened his kidney. And he'd pulled out the arrowhead, leaving a deep puncture weeping blood down his torso. "I'm sorry I fell asleep and didn't come sooner. A man shouldn't have to stitch his own wounds." She refrained from commenting on how lopsided and awful the sutures were.

"You were understandably tired." Vorik offered a half-smile. "I woke briefly a couple of times on the way here. Once in the water and once with you helping carry me on a stretcher of sorts."

"Yes." Syla lifted a hand toward his chest, her gaze drawn to an old scar rather than one of the new wounds. With his torso bare, she could see that he'd been injured often in the past. The scars didn't detract from the symmetrical beauty of his muscular physique.

The door opened, and Syla lowered her hand to her lap instead of touching him. Flaron set a bowl of water, towels, a surgical kit, and a few other medical tools on a table near the door.

"If you harm her, we will enter promptly and slay you." Flaron frowned sternly at Vorik.

"I assumed you would, yes," Vorik replied, unperturbed. Maybe even amused.

How could anyone with so many fresh wounds be amused? They all had to be painful. Syla was amazed his body hadn't lured him into remaining unconscious. Especially when he'd started *stitching* himself.

"I'll take some zivorak herb for pain and an antiseptic potion, too," she called before Flaron departed.

He hesitated, glancing at Vorik as if it might be a betrayal to the Kingdom to give him a pain killer, but ultimately said, "Yes, Your Highness," and sent the younger guard off with orders to fetch the items.

Vorik reached for the skein of suture thread, as if he might continue working on himself.

To stop him, Syla rested her hand on his bare forearm. Warmth radiated from his ropy muscles. His eyebrows drifted upward.

"I *am* a healer," she said. "Will you let me tend your wounds?"

"I don't know. Would you be tending them *magically*?" His eyelids drooped, and he watched her through his lashes.

He probably didn't mean the expression to be sexy, but sitting on a bed this close to him, with his bare chest scant inches away, made Syla think of things other than healing. But he'd been the one to warn Wreylith about the potential danger of having one's wounds tended magically, of how one might feel bound to the healer afterward, perhaps compelled to do what she wished. Perhaps even... speak truths that one didn't want to speak.

Did Vorik have truths that differed from what he'd told her? After all the times he'd fought to protect her, she was more inclined to believe he was a member of that faction and wanted her to live, but she wouldn't mind a way to compel him to honesty with her. Just in case.

"That would be ideal," she said, aware of Vorik watching her intently. "Especially since..." She looked toward the barred window. If she warned him about the enforcers, he might try to escape instead of letting her heal him. But she didn't want him to be captured and tortured. Even if she wanted the truth from him. That wasn't the way. "I've learned that the leaders of the temple sent for the enforcers after we arrived. The guard doesn't think they'll arrive until tomorrow, but it's hard to know for certain."

"I suppose your Kingdom enforcers would know not to put me in a cell with a window," Vorik said dryly, "and they would lock me in a shackle that I don't have the strength to break."

"I'm sure you can't break that one."

"No?" Vorik bent and rotated the shackle, showing a gap where the locking mechanism had been pulled apart. After it had broken —after *he'd* broken it?—he'd hooked it back together enough that someone walking in wouldn't notice that he was loose.

She stared at it. "How did you...?"

Was it possible that Agrevlari was channeling power into Vorik from a distance?

"Magic." He smiled, but he also lifted an arm and flexed his biceps.

She swallowed, her gaze drawn to the interplay of his muscles in the lantern light. What would it be like to have sex with someone so lithe and powerful?

Over the years, she hadn't been in many relationships, in part because of the conflicts of interest involved in meeting men through healing them, and in part because... not that many appealing candidates had stepped forward, candidates interested in *her* rather than her status or the access she offered to the royal family. None of the ones she *had* spent time with had possessed a physique like Vorik.

None, she told herself firmly, were as *dangerous* as Vorik. Even if he was loyal to that faction instead of his belligerent leaders, she couldn't have anything to do with him. It would be foolish, if not a betrayal. The memory of her dead kin entered her mind again.

Oblivious to her thoughts, Vorik shifted his gaze to the window, his smile lingering. It looked out upon the roof of the keep and the tower on the other side of the temple, not to the sea or across the countryside, so it wasn't the *view* that prompted his smile.

On a hunch, Syla left his bed and walked to the bars, eyeing them instead of the opposite tower or the road she could see to one side, other than to note that no travelers were approaching in the rain. The bars appeared sturdy and in place, but a few crumbles of stone lay at the base of one of them. When she looked up, she spotted a deep gouge that extended from the top of the bar to the edge of the sill. She gripped the length of iron and found it loose. She could have easily pushed it the rest of the way out and opened the gap enough for a lean man to squeeze through. Of course, once out, such a man would then have to climb down the sheer stone wall of the tower, across the roof of the keep, and jump to the ground. Of all the feats she'd seen Vorik perform, that one wouldn't rank near the top.

She sensed him approach, stopping close enough behind her that she imagined she could feel the heat emanating from his body. She *could* feel his power in the air about him and imagined him breaking iron with his hands. That shackle lay open on the floor by the bed. Bonded riders apparently got more magic from their dragons than she'd realized.

"I have a good constitution," Vorik said softly, looking out the window over her shoulder, though she also sensed him watching the side of her face, "but I'm not immune to infections and complications from injuries. I wouldn't mind having a trained healer treat me."

He brushed his fingers down the back of her head, and a heated tingle ran through her.

Syla swallowed, wondering if sending Flaron away had been a bad idea. But she didn't try to step away from Vorik. "That's why I came."

"Is it? You weren't simply drawn by my allure? I was trying to send it out through this compound so that you would feel it and come see me." His fingers shifted to the side of her neck, pushing her hair aside and gently stroking her skin, as he'd done when they'd ridden together on his dragon. Right before he'd kissed her there, then nibbled on her ear, stirring within her the most amazing sensations.

"I… it's my duty to heal wounded people," she said. "That's all."

"Will you chat with me while you sew me up? I've been lonely."

"I'll need to concentrate. You're a mess." She turned toward him and caught him eyeing her neck, his lips parted.

Had he been about to kiss her? And if he had, would she have stopped him?

Nervous and flustered, Syla licked her lips. It didn't miss her notice that, since Vorik stood so close, she was essentially trapped against the wall. Trapped by a man strong enough to break shackles and rip iron bars from stone, despite his many wounds.

"I am a mess," Vorik agreed, "but will you simply use mundane methods on me? I do not give you permission to use your magic."

"It'll take much longer for the wounds to heal, and the chance of infection will be higher, but that's your choice."

His eyebrows rose, as if he'd expected her to be unwilling to give her agreement.

"I will point out," she said, "that with your magic—your clearly *strong* magic—you probably wouldn't be affected by mine. Even among normal humans, not everyone feels bound to a healer after the healing."

"There are some risks I'm not willing to take."

"That's a surprising statement from someone who leaps about

on dragon backs, jumping from one to another and risking falling to his death in every battle."

"There are things worse than dying in battle."

"Like what?"

Betraying one's people, she thought, somehow certain that was what he worried about. There *were* truths he didn't want to be compelled to speak. She'd been on the verge of trusting him, but now... now she again doubted that she could. Especially when he shook his head instead of answering.

Eyes intent—no, *intense*—Vorik lifted a hand, brushing her cheek gently with his knuckles. The heated tingle returned, running from her face to her core, making her want... what she dared not ask for. What she dared not offer.

"Will you give me your word?" Vorik asked. "No magic."

"You have my word," she said without hesitation.

Maybe she *should* have hesitated, but she'd never contemplated going against his wishes on that matter.

"Thank you." His fingers trailed from her cheek to her jaw, lifting it slightly, and he kissed her.

His lips were warm and gentle, in contrast to the fierce power emanating from his body.

He probably meant the kiss as a sign of appreciation to accompany his words, but it aroused startling desire in her, and she had to flatten her hands against the stone wall behind her to keep from gripping his shoulders, from pressing herself against him and kissing him back. Her body was taut with need, with the steamy attraction she hadn't wanted to admit to but undeniably felt.

A tremble rippled through her, but she told herself he needed healing, not sex. Besides, he was a prisoner, and there were guards outside. They couldn't...

But, by the watchful eyes of the moon, she wanted to, and she caught herself leaning away from the wall and into him. Her body molded to his, and her lips parted, her tongue slipping out to stroke his. Need coiled within her.

His eyelashes flickered, a hint of surprise at her reaction, but it couldn't have displeased him, because he slid his hands down her back and pulled her closer against him. She could feel the scorching heat of his hard body through the healer's robe she'd been lent, a robe with a flap that tied at the hip with a loose knot that could easily come free. Then they could—

A grunt and a clang sounded in the room outside. In a blink, Vorik shifted away from her.

Breathless, Syla wanted to complain, to rush after him, but he'd already sat back on the bed and hooked the shackle so that it appeared to restrain him.

The door opened, and Flaron set several bottles on the table with the other items. He looked suspiciously at Vorik and then over at Syla, his concerned eyes silently asking if she was all right.

No, she thought, craving Vorik's touch and hoping the shadows of the room hid the flush to her cheeks—to her entire body. But she smoothed her face and nodded at the guard.

"Thank you, Flaron."

"Holler if he threatens you in any way. One of us will be out here." Flaron patted his sheathed sword.

"Thank you, but it'll be fine. As you can see, he's too wounded to be a threat." Syla was impressed she got those words out without laughing at the ridiculousness of them. A man who could break bars with his hands was more threatening than any other she'd known, no matter what state of injury he was in.

"He's a rider with a bond mark." Flaron waved at Vorik's bare hand. "He's a threat. Don't let yourself forget it, Your Highness."

Flaron lingered in the open doorway, vacillating. Thinking of staying to keep an eye on her?

She walked to the table, picked up the surgical kit, and opened it. She didn't say *spurting* again, but Flaron eyed the sharp instruments and withdrew, shutting the door behind him. A few seconds later, voices started up. *Both* guards might remain on the landing.

Since half the temple thought Vorik was *tricking* her, Syla had to keep this professional. Besides, if the enforcers showed up at dawn, she wanted him to be fixed up in case he needed to run. She didn't trust him, but she also couldn't bring herself to want him caught and tortured.

"Lie back." Syla approached him. "This will take some time."

"Yes, Your Highness." Vorik smiled a little wryly and did so, locking his hands behind his head, as if to say he wouldn't impede her.

Most people were tense and worried when they came to a healer, but he looked... pleased. Maybe because he'd extracted her word from her not to use her magic.

As she set to work on his wounds, Syla wondered if that had been a mistake. Maybe, for the good of the Kingdom, she *should* have tried to use her magic to bind him.

24

Vorik woke, rain pounding on the roof above and the predawn lighting dim, barely enough to illuminate the arched stone ceiling of the temple room. The *cell.* He reminded himself that he'd already secured his freedom and could escape if need be, but something distracted him from that thought. He grew aware of soft hair fanned out over his bare chest, the weight of Syla's head on his pectorals.

The afternoon and evening before, she'd spent hours stitching and bandaging his many wounds, including removing and replacing the awkward sutures he'd given himself. He'd been lucky he hadn't passed out while trying to tie his innards in. He *had* swooned while pulling out the arrowhead, flesh ripping with agonizing intensity, but he would never admit that.

Night had come before Syla had finished to her satisfaction, carefully tending every wound, even the slightest abrasion, and after he'd extracted the recipe for making blackberry cobbler from her, she'd fallen asleep against him, probably still exhausted from the previous days' horrors.

His body ached in a dozen places, a promise that she had not, as he'd requested, used her magic on him. He'd monitored her the entire time to ensure she didn't, but somehow he'd also trusted that, once she'd given her word, she would keep it. That was a bit of a marvel to him given his previous experiences with gardeners, especially gardeners interacting with *his* loathed kind. They had never seemed to feel bound to act honorably with him.

But Syla was different. She was... much more than he'd expected.

Despite her admission that she wasn't a leader, she was, Vorik believed, more than capable of taking over her mother's role as queen and ruling her kingdom. Of course, if *his* people got their way, there wouldn't be much of a kingdom left to lead. A week ago, that thought wouldn't have disturbed him, but that had been before he met Syla.

Careful not to disturb her, he lifted his left arm experimentally. A twinge came from the now-bandaged spot where he'd removed the arrow. That wound would slow him down for some time.

Maybe he *should* have let Syla use her magic on him, as it would take a long time for these wounds to heal naturally, and they would impede him on this mission. But he hadn't wanted to be bound to her in any way. He'd *dared* not allow that. Not when he'd already developed feelings for her that he shouldn't have allowed. She'd made him that wonderful cobbler and then... she'd saved his life. He hadn't missed that. She probably *shouldn't* have pulled him out of the ocean. He'd heard Fel and Tibby pointing that out, that he might have drowned if they'd left him out there. But, for whatever reason, Syla had made them bring him here.

Why had she done that?

More, why hadn't she used her power on him? Back at the beach, he wouldn't have been capable of objecting to magical healing. She could have taken advantage of him being unconscious. It wasn't as if he would have been able to stop her if she'd used her gods-gift to heal him. But she'd respected his wishes—she'd respected *him*—even though they were enemies. Even though he was working against her.

Damn it, he didn't want to betray her. He wanted... *her*. Especially after that heated kiss the day before by the window.

Perhaps not surprising, given her soft cheek and lush hair touching him, he'd woken with an arousal. He would have laughed at his silly libido, at how it functioned perfectly well despite the injuries the rest of his body had endured, but his ribs ached, and even soft chuckles would have hurt. Sex would *definitely* hurt, though if she woke and offered it, his body might have to suffer for the sake of his cock.

He lifted a hand and stroked her hair, letting his fingers rub her scalp through it. The memory of their kiss returned, how she'd been stiff at first but then... Then she'd given in to her instincts. Instincts that *wanted* him. He'd had no doubt. He didn't think she *wanted* to want him, but bodies often didn't obey their owners' wishes.

The general must have envisioned something like this when he'd sent Vorik on this mission, but had he realized Syla would be so drawn to Vorik?

Her spectacles lay on the table beside the bed, so he saw her face clearly in the brightening light coming through the window. Her round cheeks, a cute nose, and full lips that he could easily imagine wrapping around his—

She lifted her head, eyes opening, and he tried to halt his imagination. Easier said than done. What had been a mild morning erection had grown rock hard at his thoughts and at having her so close. He had to fight the urge to wrap his fingers around the back of her head and pull her down to his chest, where she might be tempted to run her tongue over his muscles, to bring her soft evocative mouth to his nipples and then lower.

Her lips parted as she met his gaze, and he tried to straighten his face, to wipe the lust from his eyes.

"Are you... all right, Captain?" Syla glanced at his chest.

Was it his imagination that her gaze lingered on the swell of his muscles before she averted it?

"I've been better," he said, then cleared his throat. Damn, his voice was husky with need. She couldn't miss it. He swallowed and added, "But I appreciate that you obeyed my wishes and didn't use your magic. Didn't *bind* me with your magic." He checked her face to see if she would deny that her power could do that.

"I always obey the wishes of my patients on that matter." Syla shrugged, as if she hadn't been tempted in the least. The movement shifted the fabric of the simple robe she wore, the flap tied loosely, flesh visible below her neck. "Unless it's an emergency, and I deem they might die if I don't use my power. Then it's a more difficult decision. But you're healthy and fit—*very* fit..." Her gaze strayed to the broken shackle on the floor beside the bed, and then the window. "I figured you would recover."

"Yes." Vorik shifted into a sitting position, which happened to bring them closer together, and lifted a hand to her face. "Though I wouldn't have if I'd drowned in the ocean. I know you fished me out."

Her cheeks grew pink, and she looked away, though she didn't pull away from his touch.

"I know your allies didn't want you to," he added. "They wanted you to let me die."

Vorik didn't feel malice toward them. They were, after all, enemies. Those two sensed it, despite all his efforts to prove himself a loyal ally. Syla... She wasn't the naive innocent that his brother must have imagined, and she didn't trust Vorik either, but she was more conflicted about it. She knew, he believed, that it would be better if she had let him die, and yet...

“It’s not my nature as a healer to abandon people to their death,” she said.

“That’s fortunate for me. I could have easily drowned out there.”

He let his fingers trace her jaw as he admired her profile, the soft appeal of her lips. He wanted to pull her into his lap and kiss her. *More* than kiss her.

“You would not have. You’re harder than that to get rid of.” Those lips he’d been admiring twisted wryly.

“Probably true. I am determined to fulfill my mission.” That was a truth, alas.

“The one to protect me.” Her eyebrows twitched. “For the sake of the rebel faction.”

He smiled and traced her throat to her collarbone, his fingers longing to wander lower. That simple flap would be so easy to shift aside, the knot to untie. Then, he could touch more than her face, her throat. His groin tightened with eagerness as he imagined cupping one of her full breasts, of bringing his lips to it and tasting her.

“If you’d bound me,” he murmured, “you could have forced me to tell you if that’s the truth or not.”

“My magic isn’t *that* powerful.”

“You might not have needed that much to sway me to speak the truth. After all, you saved my life. As I said, I’m grateful.”

He was *more* than grateful. It bothered him that they were at cross purposes. He wanted to reward her for respecting him as much as he wanted to sate his own desire. Well, maybe not *as* much, but he would like to thank her. But, bound by his oath and his orders, he couldn’t thank her by leaving her to fulfill her quest without his involvement. That was, he had no doubt, what she truly wanted.

Her eyes closed, however, as if she was enjoying his touch too much to think about her mission. Good. He *wanted* her to enjoy it. Just as she had by the window.

What would have happened if that guard hadn't returned? He let his hand wander lower, brushing the outline of her breast through the robe as his fingers strayed toward the knot. A soft sound escaped her lips, almost a gasp, and she shifted toward him. He smiled, glad his touch pleased her. Perhaps he could reward her that way.

"Don't make me regret making an honorable choice," Syla whispered. Almost a plea.

Honorable. That was his word. What he always wanted to be. And yet, in this situation, he did not feel honorable. She deserved better. She deserved...

More than him. But what more did he have that he could give? His oath was to the Sixteen Talons, his heart and soul to his people. He couldn't betray them. Physical pleasure was all he could give her, but he vowed to make it something she would remember. Always.

With that thought, he leaned forward and kissed her. By now, it didn't surprise him that she returned the kiss without hesitation, but it pleased him. He wanted her to enjoy this.

When she ran her tongue over his lips and gripped his shoulders with eagerness, he knew she would. It was as if she'd been dreaming of being with him since they met and couldn't wait.

His groin thrummed with excitement and anticipation—his entire *body* did—but he willed his libido to stand down. He wanted to give her more than his selfish lust. After she'd retrieved him from the sea and carried him here, she deserved that. Maybe, afterward, she would find that she craved more of him, but he wanted to give her pleasure first. It would be an expression of his gratitude, and maybe it could also be an apology of sorts, since he knew he would eventually betray her. He had to.

When he pulled Syla into his lap, she came eagerly. She had to feel his desire, but it didn't alarm her. If anything, she wriggled against him, excited to know he wanted her.

He untied the flap of the robe and slid his hand up to cup her breast, its curve as wondrous as he'd imagined. He stroked her soft skin as he kissed her, sliding his tongue into her mouth, reveling in her taste.

Images of pushing her down onto the bed and plunging into her eager core swept into him. With great effort, he thrust them aside, wanting to focus on giving *her* pleasure instead of taking his own.

Later, he promised his hard cock as she shifted in his lap, rubbing against him, building his need without even knowing it. Though he wanted this to be about her satisfaction, he realized he wouldn't be able to restrain himself if she writhed and bucked beneath him, exposing herself and crying out for him. He would have her.

With a growl, Vorik shifted her onto her back, pushing the flaps of the robe fully aside. She touched his shoulders, then his arms, and his waist, her nails grazing him as she hungrily ran her hands over his muscles. One hand brushed his cock through his trousers, and a burst of hot need almost made him reach for the clasp, to free himself and take her. She lay before him, eager and ready.

But no. He remembered his intent and left his trousers on, needing that barrier, that reminder, and lowered himself to kiss her while his fingers explored her body. Oh, but her eagerness made it so hard to concentrate on pleasing her, on stroking her breasts, on making her quiver and twist, trembling where he touched her. It was so erotic. She didn't even mean it to be. It was simply her natural response to him.

He ran his fingers down her stomach as he kissed her, her tongue dancing against his as she reveled in his touch, his taste. He found the slit of her core, already slick, already throbbing for him. Her fingers tightening on his shoulders, she arched up, full of need, her body begging for him.

He rubbed her sensitive flesh, stroking her as he'd done with others, knowing what many liked, what would send wondrous sensations through her entire body. Through Syla. He wanted her to experience such exquisite ecstasy that...

That what? She would forgive him for later betraying her?

No, she would never forgive that. This was simply to give her *something*. The only thing he could offer.

And that she wanted. She gasped, pushing against him, hungry, desperate. Again, thoughts of freeing his erection filled his mind. She wouldn't object. He knew that. She wanted this. And so did he. He longed to touch her and taste her with more than his fingers, to let himself prowl down her body, a suck here, a lick there.

When their mouths parted, her eyes opened and locked onto him. They gleamed with scorching desire, and her grasps on his shoulders turned into a push, guiding him lower.

He obeyed, his own excitement electric when he finally slid his tongue into her. He stroked her as her delicious heady scent wreathed him. And she tasted exquisite. He groaned. By all the gods, he wanted her.

Her head fell back as she pushed up toward him, fingers clenching the sheets now. She groaned and thrust, so hot. And he was so hard. After this, he would take her. He *had* to take her. But first...

Riders approach, Vorik, Agrevlari spoke into his mind from his perch on a rock formation out in the ocean beyond the barrier. *More than twenty men on horseback. They have explosives, armor, an iron cell on wheels, and hunting hounds. I am certain they have come to apprehend you.*

Not now. Vorik remembered that Syla had warned him of the

enforcers. She *shouldn't* have, but she had. He would not leave her bereft of his gratitude.

I do not believe they will pause if I suggest it to them, Agrevlari said dryly.

Vorik growled at the interruption, both from his dragon and the world, but that didn't keep him from stroking Syla as she quivered beneath him. She was close. A little more...

Clanks and clatters drifted through the window. Someone heading to the gate to open it for the riders outside. He didn't have long if he meant to escape, but he wouldn't leave her yet.

"Vorik," Syla panted, fingers twisting in the sheets, sweat gleaming on her skin. "Please."

He slid his tongue deeper into her, then, sensing she wanted it, he nipped lightly at her throbbing clit. She arched wildly and cried out as the gate clanged open and great undulations of pleasure swept through her. She was so sexy, so hot, and he wanted to stay and plunge into her, not flee into the rain like a whipped dog. As he looked at her beautiful body, her eyes full of deep satisfaction and even wonder as she looked at him, his need was so hard and insistent that he almost did something very stupid.

But thumps on the stairway announced men coming.

"What's going on?" someone with a bleary voice mumbled from the landing.

Frustrated, Vorik flung the robe over Syla, as if *that* would quench his need. It would at least protect her modesty from the guards.

"Vorik, you have to go," she whispered, but she gripped his arm, as if she didn't want him to leave. Even so, she waved him toward the window. She didn't want him to be captured either.

Why, he didn't fully know, but emotion swelled within him. Her lips, moist from their kisses, drew his eye, and he wanted so badly to stay, to satisfy himself as he'd satisfied her. But the guards approached.

He couldn't keep from kissing her before rising, and he caught himself whispering, "I'll find you later, and I'll *have* you."

His voice harsh with lust, the words came out sounding more like a threat than a promise, but eagerness and anticipation sparked in her eyes.

That didn't keep her from pushing him out of bed. From trying to protect him. Gods, he wanted her. But he grabbed his sword and his boots, sprang for the window, and kicked the iron bar out so he could escape. He couldn't return to her if he was dead.

25

HANDS TREMBLING, BODY SLICK FROM VORIK'S INCREDIBLE ministrations, Syla barely got her robe fully closed before footsteps thundered across the landing. She flung her legs to the side of the bed, thinking to sit up and look alert—*not* like she'd just experienced the most intense orgasm of her life—but the mattress didn't have a lot of support and she slid off the edge and onto the floor.

At that moment, the door banged open and four guards charged inside.

"Your Highness," one blurted, as if he hadn't expected to find her in their prisoner's room. "Er, are you all right?"

"What did he *do* to you?" another guard roared. Flaron. His hair was mussed and his uniform askew, so he'd probably been off-duty.

"He went that way." Syla pointed toward the window.

Since they would have spotted the broken bar anyway, it didn't feel like a betrayal. And she needed them to go away. She needed a moment to gather herself lest any of them think... Storm god's wrath, she didn't know what they would think. She'd cried out numerous times and had been so lost in her pleasure that she hadn't thought of the guards, hadn't thought of anyone. Had the man stationed on the landing outside fallen asleep? He must have. And maybe the rain had smothered some of the noise. Even so, she feared someone would figure out what had happened.

"The roof!" one guard yelled out the window. "Surround the temple. He's on the roof!"

The men charged out of the room, thankfully leaving her alone. Syla pushed herself to her feet and drank water from the jug, then looked around for a cloth so she could wash herself and get her scattered thoughts in order.

By now, she believed Vorik wily enough—and gifted enough with incredible athletic abilities—to escape the guards, but as shouts rang out and a cannon boomed, she went to the window with concern. Day had come, but the clouds were so dense, the rain so heavy, that it still seemed like night. In the damp air of the courtyard, not a single lantern burned.

That was better for Vorik. He would escape more easily in the dark and rain. Among his powers, he could probably see in the dark. Dragons, she knew, could. And Vorik was...

She didn't know *what* he was.

"An enemy," she whispered, afraid that was the truth, no matter how often he saved her, no matter what pleasure he'd given her in bed.

A tendril of warmth flushed her body at the memory, combatting the chill from the wind and rain outside the window. His parting words came to her: *I'll find you later, and I'll have you.* His voice and his lust-filled eyes had made her body thrum with desire all over again, and she wanted nothing more than to see him once more. She caught herself peering all around the temple, hoping to catch a glimpse of him.

She didn't until she looked toward the cliff and the sea, wondering if his dragon remained out there in the rain. That was when she spotted a shadow, someone who'd run along the rocky escarpment and away from the temple. Vorik.

He crouched, about to slither over the edge of the cliff, but he hesitated. Though he was nothing but a dark distant shadow in the gloom, she could tell when he paused, turning to look at her, to meet her eyes through the rain.

Through some instincts, some magical power, he'd known she was looking at him. His promise to *have her* came to mind again. She had to finish her mission and protect the Kingdom, and it would be far better if she never saw him again, but she couldn't help but long for another night with him. A full and uninterrupted night.

Vorik lifted a hand in parting, and she raised hers in return before he disappeared over the edge of the cliff.

To climb down? A hundred feet and more? Maybe he intended to swim out a mile and reunite with Agrevlari. The healer in her wanted to admonish him for contemplating such a feat before he recovered fully from his wounds, but he seemed so much greater than a mere mortal. Maybe it didn't matter.

The door opened again, and Syla spun in alarm, lowering her arm and trying not to feel like she'd been caught breaking a rule.

It wasn't a guard but Sergeant Fel who strode in.

"Your Highness," he said in relief, looking her up and down. "Are you all right? When I didn't find you in your room..." He looked toward the bed, a crinkle furrowing his brow.

"Yes. I stitched and bandaged Captain Vorik's many wounds." Syla didn't want to be questioned about why that had taken *all* night and groped for a way to explain herself. "He wouldn't let me use magic," was what came out.

It was, after all, true.

Fel grunted. "I'm still regretting that I wasn't conscious enough to make that demand."

Syla winced, feeling guilty again that she'd inadvertently bound Fel.

"I'm sorry, Sergeant. I didn't mean..." She slumped against the wall; her guilt wasn't without reason. "I knew you felt more obligated than your duty would have otherwise demanded, and I asked you to carry Vorik anyway. I didn't feel I had a choice since you and Aunt Tibby weren't going to bring him, but... it was wrong of me to do that."

Fel sighed and met her gaze. "You're the princess, maybe my monarch now, once everything gets settled. I would feel obligated to obey your wishes, regardless."

Syla shook her head, doubting that, if magic hadn't been involved, Fel would have toted Vorik all those miles.

"I just like to voice my disgruntlement when things don't go well," he added, managing a wry smile. "More than I should."

"We all have plenty of reason to be disgruntled right now." New guilt crept into her. For a time, she'd forgotten all her woes—and the horrors that had occurred—and reveled in her own personal pleasure. "I don't blame you for it in the least."

"Thank you, Your Highness. Now, if you've enough clothes for the road..." Fel waved at her bare feet. "I need to usher you out of here while the temple staff are distracted. I already rounded up your aunt and horses and a carriage, though she thinks we'll have to head up to the volcano and abandon anything with wheels."

"I... You want to leave right now? To find, uhm." Not certain if more guards were out there, Syla didn't finish, only waving vaguely toward the distant volcano.

Aunt Tibby might not have known the exact location of the shielder, but she was right. That was the correct direction to go.

"Yes. Huzloron spoke to me only a few minutes before the enforcers arrived. His intention is to send you back with them once they capture Vorik. To go to the capital and speak with the island lord. Huzloron wanted to make sure I wouldn't object."

"Why would he think you would object?" Syla asked, though she intended to find the shielder before visiting Lord Ravoran, a distant relative of her mother's who governed over Harvest Island, reporting to her and enforcing Kingdom law here. Given her plans, Syla didn't know if it was wise to visit him at all.

"I overheard him speaking to the other leader. Jemla, right? I gathered that at your meeting you *didn't* tell them you planned to take their shielder, but they were pretty certain before we ever showed up that someone from Castle Island would come, intending to do so. And then, when you arrived... Let's just say that they might not act openly against you, but they want to impede your quest."

Syla bent forward and gripped her knees. "It's horrible to take it, isn't it? But we have to, Fel."

"My mother lives in Promontory Peak on the south side of Castle Island. I've got cousins over there too. And the woman who was... until she grew tired of me... my wife. I'll do whatever it takes to help you return a sky shielder to Castle Island. You're not wrong to make that choice, Your Highness. The greater population is there. If we have to, we can evacuate Harvest Island."

Yes. Syla had forgotten that was an option. Reminded, she brightened and stood straighter. "That would be hard but doable. We'd probably lose the crops but people's lives are more important."

Fel nodded. "There's room on Castle Island for more, at least for a time. But we have to get a working shielder back over there first. Come. Your aunt is waiting outside in the rain. She, too, knows the importance of this quest. But we have to hurry. Before the temple people realize we're leaving."

"Let me grab my pack out of my room, and then I'll be ready."

Syla started after him but paused to grab two stout Candles of Serenity, thinking they might come in useful along the way. Especially if her own people wanted to throw her in a carriage and imprison her.

With a last look at the bed, she walked out after Fel. She vowed to set aside thoughts of Vorik and the time they'd spent together, other than to silently thank him for providing a distraction so that she could get away from the temple. She might be the rightful heir to the throne, but right now... she couldn't help feeling like a criminal. But Fel was right. This was the logical choice. And the sooner they succeeded, the sooner she could protect the Kingdom as a whole.

26

THE HEAVY RAIN MADE THE ROCK FACE SLICK, AND VORIK, HAVING NO familiarity with the area, climbed down carefully. Actually, halfway down the cliff, he climbed *laterally*. Distant shouts from the temple promised the Kingdom enforcers were still looking for him. Earlier, a couple of men had run to the edge of the cliff and peered down. But he'd had time to climb far off to the side, so they'd looked in the wrong place. At least for now. As the day got brighter, he would be easier to spot.

Are you coming out to reunite with me? Agrevlari asked into his mind.

Not right now.

Are you irritated that I interrupted your mating?

Given the circumstances, no. Vorik hated to admit it, but the dragon might have saved his life.

Even hearing the guards and the danger, how close had he been to ignoring it all? To letting his penis rule his mind and body and take the pleasure it had craved? Too close.

It had been a long time since he'd been engulfed in lust so strong that it made him stupid. Of course, it had been a long time since a woman had saved his life. Even more than that, Syla hadn't tried to poison him when she could have—*should* have. And she hadn't bound him with her magic, again when she should have.

It would have been one thing if she'd believed his tales and grown smitten with him because of his athleticism or good looks, but she *knew* he was trouble. He had no doubt. And yet she wouldn't betray him. He wouldn't blame her if she did, but it didn't seem to be in her nature. She was too... wholesome? Was that the right word?

He imagined her naked beneath him, squirming and panting as she gripped his shoulders and cried out his name, and decided wholesome wasn't a good descriptor. He also grinned at the memory until a rocky protrusion bumped his groin. That poor body part, still half-aroused despite the passage of time and his precarious position, was having a rough start to the day.

I'm going to find the princess, Vorik told Agrevlari.

To complete the mating?

That would be amazing, but he said, *To complete my mission. Our orders.*

Having mating interrupted is unappealing. Dragons are not anatomically like humans, but we do have some similarities, more so than to lizards or chickens. We, too, can experience discomfort if we cannot complete the act.

I'm sure. You needn't give me any details about that. Maybe you can see if your keen eyes can peer into the temple and let me know if Syla leaves.

I will do so. We have been bonded for many years, and I've long learned that you are more agreeable when you've satisfactorily mated.

That's not *why I need to know when she leaves.* Vorik rolled his eyes toward the clifftop high above, though Agrevlari probably knew there was a part of him that was motivated by wanting to *satisfactorily mate.* Maybe it was foolish to deny his feelings to a dragon who could see into his mind. Nonetheless, he said, *I need to track her to the shielder. Once I know where it is, I'll find a way to get it or destroy it, then figure out a way to reach you.*

Vorik imagined himself swimming out to the dragon while pulling an artifact identical in size to the huge glowing orb underneath the castle. How heavy was the damn thing? He would need a raft. Or a barge.

He snorted at himself. He might only be able to return to the general and give him the location. Let *him* figure out how to move it.

Syla would hate Vorik forever if he managed to destroy it. Somehow, giving its location to his superior officer seemed like it would be less of a betrayal to her.

But... would she see it that way?

He told himself it didn't matter. There wasn't a future for them. He shouldn't even pursue her for a single night of pleasure. He should do his duty and get out of her life.

Except... the general's demands wouldn't end with the capture or destruction of one more shielder, would they? Vorik didn't know his exact plans, but Jhiton wanted *many* of the Kingdom islands for their people, if not *all* of them. He wanted the stormers to have access to the bounteous croplands and all that they produced so that their people could survive and thrive.

This mission is turning out to be harder than I thought it would be, Agrevlari.

Since I am nursing a bite wound from one of my own allies, I do not disagree.

We'll finish it up as quickly as possible, and then... The memory of Syla floated through his mind, but Vorik pushed it away. She would not be a part of his future. *Then we'll rest, my friend.*

I look forward to it. Hold. Another dragon approaches.

Another one that wishes to bite you? Vorik paused in his climb, wiping grit from his damp palms as he peered out to sea.

As he'd noticed before, Agrevlari perched on a rock formation beyond the shield. Another dragon approached him, a dark gray one that appeared almost black in the dim lighting.

Is that Tonasketal? Vorik asked.

Yes. He says he's dropped off Lieutenant Wise with a collapsible kayak. The general sent him to spy on the largest population center of this island, but when they learned you were here, they diverted, and the lieutenant is coming to get your report.

I don't have a report. Vorik grimaced, not wanting to explain that he'd not only lost track of Syla, at least as of a half hour ago, but that he hadn't gathered any information on the location of the shielder on this island—or any other island.

Perhaps you should compose something. General Jhiton will wish an update.

It's hard to compose reports while you're dangling from your fingers on a vertical rock face.

Having talons, which are far superior to fingers, I've not experienced such a difficulty.

It must be wonderful to be a dragon.

It's exquisite. Since I'm not actively fleeing hunters or dangling precariously, I can, if you wish, compose your report for you.

Aware that he would have company soon, Vorik picked up his pace, angling toward a black-sand beach in a tiny sheltered cove instead of the top of the cliff. Later, he would find a spot to climb up and start tracking Syla. Ideally, after the enforcers gave up on their search for him.

Would your report include details of my near-mating?

Naturally. Seduction is a part of your mission, is it not?

Well, gaining the trust of the princess and learning information from her.

Likely through seduction, Agrevlari said.

That's optional.

Your tongue was in her sex orifice.

Blazing sun god, don't give a report that talks about that. If Vorik hadn't been busy climbing with both hands he would have smacked himself in the forehead. Who knew a dragon could see such detail from so far away? Maybe their bond was a little *too* strong. *Look, I'll think up something to tell the lieutenant to pass along to my brother, all right? Just... stop trying to help.*

Very well. I will merely wait here in the rain and speak with Tonasketal. He has joined me on this perch. Perhaps we shall fish.

It's good to have company.

Yes. He is also an admirer of Wreylith. We may discuss her.

Not her sex orifices, I hope.

Only her magnificence in battle and her beauty as she dips and weaves in a brilliant blue sky with the sun gleaming off her rich red scales.

That sounds nice.

Indeed. I will keep considerations of her sex orifices to myself.

"I don't know if it's perfectly logical that such a strange dragon chose to bond with me or if it speaks to my oddity as a rider," Vorik muttered.

A seagull perched on a ledge squawked down at him. No, it was looking out toward the sea. Vorik followed its gaze and picked out a lean rider, with prematurely white hair, navigating through the waves in a kayak. Young Lieutenant Wise.

He'd almost died his first year as a rider. His dragon had perished in battle, and he'd dropped from a great height to a tiny, rocky island and broken both his legs. He'd lived on nothing but seaweed, oysters, and other beach detritus he could gather while waiting for his bones to heal. He'd used driftwood to drive away wyverns, cloud strikers, and other aerial predators who'd tried to turn him into dinner. Eventually, his squadron had found him and taken him home to a healer, but he'd lost all his hair during the stressful time. It had grown back white, making him appear prematurely sage. He was still a young goof, but the squadron had given him the nickname Wise anyway, and it had stuck.

Vorik reached the beach at the same time as the lieutenant, one of the most unlikely spies he could imagine. A white-haired twenty-five-year-old didn't fit in among the gardeners *or* the tribes. Maybe he'd intended to wear a hat as he skulked about.

Wise waved cheerfully after pulling his kayak onto the beach. "Hullo, Captain Vorik. It's good to see you."

"You too."

Before speaking further, they climbed the beach and found a sheltered overhang. As soaked as Vorik was, it probably didn't matter if they stood in the rain, but it felt good to be out of it for a time.

Wise scraped dampness out of his short white locks and sat on a rock. "I wasn't certain if we'd find you alive until my dragon sensed yours. We got a garbled report from Corporal Taskan that Captain Lesva was lost at sea and her lieutenant killed. Lesva had been ordered to patrol the sea between Castle and Harvest Islands and attack any ships that might be sent, especially with a shielder, from one to the other."

"Patrol. Right." Vorik didn't exactly feel *betrayed* by Lesva, but it irritated him that she'd presumed to attack Syla after being ordered *not* to capture her.

Her lieutenant's death had been a mistake though. Vorik hadn't meant to strike to kill, and he regretted that deeply.

"We heard she spotted the gardener princess riding on the great wild dragon, Wreylith." Wise looked at him with wide eyes. "That didn't *really* happen, did it? I mean, I don't doubt Taskan or his dragon, but..."

"It happened." Vorik didn't fully understand it himself, other than that Syla had a *krendala* of Wreylith. He didn't try to explain further, instead shrugging.

"That's incredible. Wild dragons *never* let humans ride them, and they scoff at all those who do."

"I'm well aware. The general didn't amend his orders, did he?

I'd wondered... Well, Lesva went after the princess even though Agrevlari and I were right with her. Protecting her to gain her trust and get intel from her."

"Ah, is *that* your mission? I'd wondered. The general was close-lipped about his motivations when he sent men to attack her... while you were watching and could help."

"Yeah, this plan is all Jhiton's idea." Vorik didn't speak about the part that disgruntled him, about having to get close to Syla, knowing he would betray her. He didn't want to say anything about the general or question him in front of other troops. When he got a chance to report in private, he would bring up his concerns.

Vorik leaned out from under the ledge and gazed upward, wondering if the enforcers had given up on searching for him yet. Concerns or not, he needed to return to his mission.

"That's interesting, but he is a crafty one," Wise said. "Have you learned anything from the princess yet?"

"Quite a bit but not the location of the shielder."

"Oh, that's too bad. The dragons are all really excited at the idea of hunting elioks." Wise waved toward the interior of the island.

"Yes, Agrevlari mentioned that. Even Wreylith spoke wistfully of their rarity and delicious meat."

"I'm to head to the major port town here and watch for sign of the shielder artifact on the move," Wise said. "It's believed that the royal gardeners—I guess just the princess is left?—seek to remove it from this island and take it to the more populated capital, most likely on a ship that will leave out of that harbor. It's the only harbor, after all, on this island."

"Yes," Vorik said, remembering that Jhiton had been trying to engineer exactly that scenario.

Would Syla walk into his trap? The thought made Vorik more glum than triumphant.

"I'll head to the harbor soon," Wise said, "but when I learned you were alive, I wanted to come see you and get a report for the general. He'll be relieved that Captain Lesva, who seemed to be letting her ambition guide her into making her *own* plans, didn't succeed in killing you. Jhiton was aghast with worry when he learned you'd fallen and might be dead."

"My brother was aghast?" Vorik asked skeptically.

"Well, his lips pinched together a little at the corporal's report, and that scar above his eyebrow twitched ever so slightly."

That sounded closer to the truth. "I'm touched that he was so concerned that he let himself display such an outburst of emotion."

Wise grinned. "I would be. If Lesva had reported in, I think he would have clobbered her or demoted her on the spot, but she's missing too. The corporal said her lieutenant was for-sure dead, but he only knew that Lesva fell, and the barrier kept her dragon from diving to retrieve her."

"Yes, I'm well aware of how that goes. The currents are such out there that you get swept through the barrier before you know it."

I was electrocuted by its foul magic when I attempted to fly after you, Agrevlari spoke into his mind.

Are you listening in on our private conversation?

Certainly. I cut short my conversation with Tonasketal about Wreylith because his lust for her made him crude. If she heard him speaking so of her appealing attributes, she would bite his neck in half and slay him instantly.

"Do you have any reports you wish to relay through me?" Wise asked.

"Just that I've made progress in gaining the princess's trust, and I believe I'll soon learn where the shielder for this island lies."

"Ah? That's good. Is she..." Wise looked around, but there was little to see beyond rain falling on the waves crashing to their little beach. "I assume she's not with you."

"No. Unfortunately, I had to flee because someone reported my presence on the island to the gardener authorities, and they sent troops. Had they not, I might *already* have fully gained the princess's trust. I was on the verge of it." The memory of her naked underneath him flitted through Vorik's mind once more, but he hurried to refocus on his mission before his libido could flare to life again.

"You think she'll share a confidence like that with you?" Wise asked, sounding awed.

"She thinks I'm handsome and on her side because I'm part of the Freeborn Faction."

Wise's face twisted with disgust, and he spat. "Those betrayers? We were lucky we pulled off the surprise attack without them alerting the gardeners."

"I know." Vorik rose, more than his libido making him want to end this meeting and start his search for Syla. "Head to the harbor, if that's the order you received, and deliver whatever report you wish about me via your dragon. As for the shielder, whether the princess and her allies will be able to carry it miles to a ship in that harbor, I don't know. The one I saw looked quite heavy. For your report, however, Syla *does* seek to take it back to her island and place it there to protect her people. If our dragon allies are ready, they might be able to intercept it."

"Yes, perfect. The general, I gather, would be pleased if Harvest Island were laid bare, but he wants them both exposed for our people and our dragon allies. He wants the islands of the entire Kingdom."

Vorik thought of his deceased nephew. "I'm well aware of what Jhiton wants."

And, no matter how it would hurt Syla, he was sworn to obey.

27

Fel sat in the rain on the driver's seat of the carriage, guiding the horses up a muddy road that wound past blueberry farms, hazelnut orchards, and raspberry thickets, crops the northern part of Harvest Island was known for. Thanks to the weather, they passed few other people. It also helped that they were heading away from the more populated side of the island and toward wilder lands.

Noon approached, and they'd left Lavaperch Temple miles behind, but that didn't keep Syla from glancing out the back window of the carriage. As Fel had suggested, the healers and guards had been distracted by Vorik's escape, and their little group had been able to depart from the stable without anyone questioning them. Before long, however, Syla would inevitably be missed.

As the carriage rocked and lurched, frequently caught in mud puddles before the horses could pull it out, Aunt Tibby sat on the bench across from Syla, a book she'd borrowed from her engineer friend open in her lap. As Tibby had mentioned with chagrin numerous times, she'd lost her pack—and the tomes she'd brought—during the swim to shore.

The schematics and mathematical tables she studied now meant little to Syla, but she hoped the resource would help her aunt when they reached their destination.

Tibby placed her finger to hold her spot and lifted her gaze. "You weren't in your room last night when I came by."

"No, I was sewing up Vorik."

"I suspected. At the dinner I told you about, I spoke privately to my comrade about transportation."

"This isn't it?" Syla waved at their carriage.

"This wobbly-wheeled carriage from the turn of the century? Fel dredged it out from under hay piles in the stable. I'm talking about transportation for the *shielder*. Sea transportation. Do you have a plan for removing it and getting it out of whatever cave it's ensconced in? From what I've read, they're quite large and heavy."

"They are, and I don't have a plan for moving one, no, but I brought an engineer for a reason." Syla smiled at her aunt.

"Ah, is that why you recruited me? I know it wasn't for guidance in international relations."

"If that's your way of saying Vorik is a spy, I know."

Tibby raised her eyebrows. "You've expressed doubts. Repeatedly. But the tale of the faction..."

"I did want to believe that, I'll admit. He's saved my life numerous times, so..." Syla shrugged.

"And he's handsome. Especially when he smiles. And eats blackberry desserts."

"I don't care about *that*." Eager to change the subject, Syla pointed at the book. "Is there anything in there that might be helpful?"

"Probably not, but I'm reminding myself of the hypotheses we currently have about how artifacts that were left for humans by the gods work. The problem with studying them has always been that it's rarely permitted to disassemble such invaluable tools, but that needs to be done to figure out how things work. Still, a few mishaps throughout history, not with the shielders but with other artifacts, have given us some knowledge."

"There's a reason the monarchs never allowed the shielders to be disassembled for study."

"I know. Being without one has already proven disastrous. We are fortunate that the sun, moon, and earth gods cared enough to build such devices for us. They could have shrugged at the storm god's antics and left us to fend for ourselves."

"I suppose we're lucky so many centuries have passed without something awful happening before." Wishing awfulness had waited another lifetime before striking, Syla looked out the back window again. Thus far, she hadn't seen anyone on the road behind them, but she couldn't shake the feeling that someone would come after them. As she'd been thinking earlier, she felt not like a royal heir but a criminal waiting for the authorities to catch up with her.

"I admit," Tibby said quietly, her gaze back toward her book though she didn't seem to be reading now, "I understand why you thought of me for this mission—I'm not sure how many engineers who were living in the city survived the attack—but I feel that I'm in over my head."

"I'm in over my head too, but you can do this." Syla felt strange encouraging her aunt when she was the younger and less experienced woman, but she did her best to smile and convey confidence. "We both can. We *have* to." Her smile faltered as she quietly added, "There's nobody else left to."

"No," Tibby murmured, her eyes glistening behind her spectacles. She removed them and wiped her eyes and blew her nose.

Syla shifted to the other bench to sit beside her. Witnessing her aunt's tears made her own emerge.

Since the attack, she'd been so busy that she'd denied herself time to mourn, though she'd felt on the ragged edge of collapse all along. Now, in this quieter moment, she and Tibby slumped against each other, tears falling, smudging the lenses of their spectacles. Syla struggled to keep utter despair from creeping in. Her aunt was right. This was so very, very hard.

She'd thought her years in the temple had taught her to deal with death and loss, but it was different when it was one's own family. Even if she'd never been as close to her siblings as they had been to each other, losing so many of them at once… and Mother too. It was too much. Far too much.

Why had the gods let the stormers assassinate her entire family? It wasn't fair.

While they cried, the carriage trundled on. Syla was glad for Fel looking over them. Maybe he was often surly, but he was indomitable and dependable too.

After a time, Syla wiped her face and returned to the opposite bench so she could more easily check the road behind them. Mourning was a luxury, and she didn't know if it was one they could afford right now.

Tibby sighed, closed her book, and leaned forward, her elbows on her knees. Lowering her voice—as if there was anyone out here to overhear—she said, "I did arrange sea transportation for the shielder, assuming we can find a way to get it to the coast."

"Oh?" Syla brightened with hope. "Through your engineer friend?"

"Yes. Sherrik."

"Will fermentation equipment be involved?"

"No, but since he worked around the ports as a marine engineer, he has a number of acquaintances. He was confident he could get a ship for us. I did have to confide in him about our plan, but we can trust him. I didn't think we could trust the temple leaders."

"No. I didn't tell them exactly what we plan, but they guessed it anyway. They're not on our side."

"That's what I worried about," Tibby said. "Even if you're the rightful ruler of the Kingdom now, I doubt you'll be able to wave your hand, especially here, and get what you need. Even back home, I'm not certain. As I'm sure you've figured out, there are people who might prefer that *you* disappear along with all your siblings, thus opening up opportunities for someone else to claim the throne."

"If we can't get a shielder over to Castle Island, there won't be a throne to claim." Syla hadn't checked on that room in the castle and had no idea if the royal throne, which was rarely used in this modern era, had survived or if it was buried under rubble.

"I agree, but you'll need to watch your back. As soon as we're able to return, you should set about gathering trusted troops who will support you—and protect you from those who won't. One surly retiree isn't going to be sufficient."

Syla smiled through the carriage wall in Fel's direction. "He's not always surly. Just when something hurts."

That was admittedly *most* of the time. Poor guy. He deserved retirement.

Tibby issued a skeptical grunt, then fished in a new pack that she'd borrowed from someone at the temple.

"Sherrik gave me this." Tibby held up a cylindrical rod with a pointed tip and a fuse.

Some kind of firework? Syla had seen similar devices around the Summer Solstice Celebration when they were lit off from the castle towers for all in the surrounding city to enjoy. When they *had* been lit off. Would she be able to restore order—and safety—to the Kingdom by the following summer so that the tradition could continue?

Her aunt's words of people trying to get rid of her made her shoulders slump with weariness. Unless one counted the various souls she'd healed in her life and who were grateful—whether magically induced or not—Syla hadn't spent much time trying to win allies or create powerful relationships in the capital. As her parents' fifth child, she'd never guessed there would be a need.

"To signal someone?" Syla asked.

"Yes. Sherrik is going to attempt to get a transport vessel and some guard ships and have them waiting in one of the calmer coves along the north shore. He did mention that it would cost money, and we'd need to be able to pay the captains when we reach Castle Island."

"I'll sell my collection of medical antiques if need be," Syla said before remembering that they were under rubble, likely destroyed along with Moon Watch Temple. Maybe something would be salvageable.

"You'll have the right to draw upon the kingdom coffers."

"Oh." Syla knew vaguely where the vault in the castle was and that it took a moon-mark to access it, but she had no idea about the amount of funds within. Her mother and the royal accountant had handled payroll and everything else financial related to running a kingdom. With all the rebuilding that needed to be done, Syla doubted there would be a lot extra, but for this… "I'll find a way to pay."

They had to.

"That's what I told him." Tibby nodded. "We'll have to get the shielder close enough to shore so that it can be loaded on a ship."

"We'll figure out something. A travois made from driftwood and kelp, if nothing else."

"We'll—*you'll*—have to figure out Captain Vorik as well. I *hope* the enforcers already caught him and dealt with him, but I fear he'll show up again."

Syla couldn't push aside her aunt's concern. She well remembered the look they'd shared before Vorik had gone over the edge and the promise he'd made, that he would return. To *have* her, he'd said, but that wasn't all he had in mind.

"He's determined," Tibby added, "and you're..."

"My extreme beauty and allure are drawing him. I know."

Tibby snorted.

"It would have been more flattering if you had nodded in agreement."

"Sorry. Engineers are practical and realistic."

"Don't worry. I have a plan if he shows up again." Syla delved into her pack and pulled out one of the big candles.

"You'll beat him on the head with that? Or club him in his cock?" Her eyes lit with enthusiasm at the notions.

"You've a violent streak, my aunt."

"Practical," Tibby repeated.

Since she didn't seem to recognize the significance of the candles, Syla opened her mouth to explain, but that feeling of being followed whispered over her again, and she looked out the window.

For the first time, someone else was visible on the road behind them. What looked like an armored carriage, accompanied by numerous horses with riders, was heading in the same direction as they.

"A coincidence?" Syla murmured but worried it wasn't.

The rain and distance made it hard to make out details, but she thought that might be the same armored carriage that had been sent to collect Vorik. Would it now be used to collect *her*? To keep her from reaching the shielder?

She doubted anyone on the island, even Lord Ravoran, knew where exactly it was, but, like her aunt, they might have an idea. Most of the shielders were underground, where nobody would easily stumble across their chambers, but numerous people had probably guessed their approximate whereabouts over the years.

"We've got a carriage coming up from behind," Fel called from the driver's seat.

"Can you go faster?" Syla asked.

The carriage lurched sideways, caught in a rut.

"No," Fel stated.

The horses *did* pull it out, but they soon came to a stop.

"The road ahead is washed out by the rain," Fel said. "It's going to be hard to go farther, but we're in the foothills of this big craggy volcano anyway. I doubt the road goes on much farther."

Tibby put away her book, and Syla opened the door. Rain pelted her shoulders, and water gushed past around the horses' hooves.

Washed out was an understatement. A river flowed down from the heights of the volcano, and crossing it would be treacherous, whether in the carriage or on foot or horseback. The road did continue on the other side of the rushing water, but reaching it would be a challenge.

"I think we can get across on foot," Fel said, then eyed Syla and Tibby. "It'll involve getting wet and fighting the current."

"Nothing we haven't done before," Tibby said. "*Recently*."

Not to mention the downpour was already soaking them. The only boon was that it was summer, so it wasn't a chilling rain.

Syla looked back to check on the other carriage, but they'd gone around a bend, and a lumpy black lava-rock formation blocked the view. She climbed onto a wet boulder, water pooling in the divots on top, and crouched behind a pine tree to hide herself in case anyone from the other party was watching.

At first, she couldn't see the armored carriage, but then it trundled into view, coming out from behind a more distant rock pile. Behind it, a half dozen men in gray uniforms with black piping rode on horses, axes and bows balanced across their laps. They'd come expecting a challenge. To have to fight.

"That's enough people to force us to return." Syla grimaced. "If they catch up with us."

And they weren't far behind. Fel was their only combatant, and would he even fight the enforcers? Like he, those men were presumably loyal to the crown. They were his allies. If she'd been crowned as her mother's successor, the men might have obeyed her, but nothing was official yet, and as a mere princess... she doubted they would leave if she told them to.

"This way." Fel pointed upstream to a spot where rocks protruding from the wash might make the crossing easier.

Grim-faced, Tibby appeared ready to follow him.

Syla scrambled down from the boulder but held up a hand.

"We don't have much time," Fel said.

"Aunt Tibby." Syla faced her. "Back at the farm, you were able to get some of my memories from my mind."

"With my magic, yes." Tibby lifted her hand, showing the moon-mark on the back. "You could learn to do that too."

Fel eyed her hand—*both* of their hands—like the marks meant they were dangerous vipers, not to be trusted.

"Could you do it now?" Syla asked. "To get the location of the Harvest Island shielder from me?"

Would that work? It had been so many years since her father had taken Syla and her siblings to visit it, making sure they could find it in the future if need be. In quizzes she and her siblings had endured after that, she'd also had to point out the location on a map. But as far as actually finding a route up the volcano to its chamber today...

"I could try," Tibby said, "but why? You're coming with us."

"Absolutely, you are," Fel said sternly.

Syla smiled, relieved he still wanted to keep an eye on her after all the trouble being her bodyguard had caused him. "Those enforcers will be after me. They shouldn't care about you two."

Tibby lifted her marked hand, as if to say they *would* care about her.

"We don't even know if the temple leaders passed on that you're kin and marked," Syla said. "I'm *certain* the enforcers are mostly here for me. If you two go ahead, I'll pretend to be stuck here when they catch up. I can buy time for you to find the shielder."

Tibby hesitated, then nodded. "Logical."

Syla stepped forward so they could share a link through their marks again.

Fel scowled. "I'll stay with you, Your Highness. You're my charge, and I'm duty-bound to protect you."

"My aunt will need you to protect her. *And* figure out how to get the shielder from its resting place to the sea where the ship can reach it." Syla worried about the logistics of that, but if anyone could figure out how to tote such a load with only two people, an engineer could.

"*She* is not my charge," Fel said. "She doesn't even like me."

"Try being less surly when you're together, and maybe that'll change." Syla nodded for her aunt to initiate the link.

Fel scowled at her. With surliness.

"I'll stay with you and fight these men off," Fel said, "and then we'll all continue on together."

Syla kept herself from pointing out that he hadn't managed to defeat one rider, so taking on a squadron of a dozen enforcers wouldn't be a good idea. That wasn't a fair comparison since that rider was far from a normal human. Still, the odds were against Fel. *Very* against him.

Meeting his eyes, Syla said, "Sergeant, I need you to go with Tibby and help her get the shielder home. That's what the *Kingdom* needs. I'll be fine. Nobody's going to kill me." She tried to sound confident about that. She *thought* that was true, that people would want to find ways to use her rather than get rid of her, but how certain was she?

She wasn't. Once they captured her, and she was confident Tibby and Fel had been granted enough time to disappear and find the shielder, Syla would try to escape.

Fel clenched his jaw at the notion but said, "I don't have any choice, do I?"

"Are you still feeling bound?" Syla smiled sadly, not delighted to use his compulsion to make him obey her, but... she *did* need him to obey her, so maybe it had all been for the best.

"To do as you wish, yes."

"Good. Protect Tibby."

Magic was already trickling from Tibby's hand, flowing into Syla, and, as before, she sensed her aunt's presence in her mind. At first, Syla pictured the map her father had used to test her memory of the location. She envisioned the volcano and a spot on the west side far from the road. Then she thought about the route they'd taken to it when she'd been a girl, of picking a path through jumbled black rocks dotted with seagull nests and a few stunted trees growing here and there in places where dirt had settled over the centuries since the last eruption.

Still scowling, Fel climbed onto the boulder, taking the spot Syla had used. He knelt, hidden behind the pine, and looked at the road.

"They're not far," he whispered down. "You've only got a minute or two, especially if you don't want them to see us."

Tibby held up a finger, her forehead bunched with concentration. Thunder rumbled, the rain continuing, running down their spectacles and dripping from their jaws. Syla again focused on the map and thought of her memories of the trek.

"I think I have... as much as you can give." Tibby frowned as she released Syla's hand.

Did that mean it wouldn't be enough?

"Your moon-mark might guide you a bit when you're close," Syla offered.

"Let us hope." Tibby followed Fel upstream, toward the rocks protruding from the wash. Slick from the water, they looked as treacherous as the current, and Syla hoped they would make it across.

Meanwhile, she climbed into the driver's seat and picked up a riding crop so that when the men came upon her, they would believe she'd been trying but failing to urge the horses across. They were stamping their hooves, shaking rain off their coats, and looking uneasily skyward each time thunder rumbled, so it ought to be a convincing scene.

It didn't take long for the first of the men to arrive. The horse-back riders had gone around the armored carriage to take the lead and reached the wash first.

"Is that her?" one called.

"Halt, Your Highness!" another shouted, as if Syla were on the verge of convincing the horses to cross.

Fel and Tibby were still in her view, navigating across the wash upstream. She didn't think the men could see them through the boulders, but they would if they drew even with her.

To buy them more time, Syla jumped down and ran off the road in the opposite direction. The men were gray blurs in her peripheral vision, so she heard more than sensed them turning their horses, harnesses jangling, to follow her. When she glanced back, she spotted one lifting a crossbow, but another man batted it aside.

"Just capture her," he snarled.

Off the road, the ground was rocky and uneven, and Syla's foot caught. She banged her knee on a boulder and almost fell down. Body weary from the battering she'd taken the last few days, she was tempted to stop and let them swoop down upon her, but Fel and Tibby would never find the shielder if they were pursued by the soldiers. Syla needed to keep those men from noticing them.

Clambering over a boulder and down a slope, with the wash roaring right beside her, Syla ran. In the rough terrain, the men had to dismount and follow her on foot. That gave her a few more seconds than she might otherwise have had, but the enforcers were taller and faster than she and soon caught up.

One man wrapped an arm around her waist and hoisted her off her feet with a grunt. She wasn't the lightest of princesses, not like svelte Venia had been, and he staggered. She squirmed about to keep them distracted a little longer.

His grip tightened, and another man arrived, grabbing her by the legs.

"I'm on a mission for the Kingdom," Syla yelled. "I must politely insist that you *release* me."

In the awkward position, it was hard to be polite, but she refrained from calling them thugs, brutes, or troglodytes. They were, after all, men who'd sworn an oath to the crown and who *should* be loyal to her, if only because she was her parents' child. But if she pissed them off, they might forget that.

"We've orders, Your Highness," one said calmly as they toted her back to the road. "We need to take you back with us. It's for your own protection."

No, it was so she couldn't take the shielder.

When they reached the road, the enforcers set her upright beside the armored carriage. It had arrived, its driver gazing across the wash and around the rocky slope as he stopped his horses.

"The temple people said she had a bodyguard," the man said.

Syla wiped her spectacles, using the gesture to hide her glance up the wash. Fel and Tibby had disappeared.

"I lost him," she said when several faces turned toward her.

Wet and bedraggled with water running from short hair plastered to their heads and down their shaven faces, the enforcers looked like they would prefer to leave rather than hunting for Fel, but their expressions were skeptical.

"You *lost* him? On the road from the temple to here?"

"The rider got him." Syla placed a fist over her heart and looked skyward in a sign of grieving. "The *dragon* rider."

"Captain Vorik? Shit. I knew he was still around."

Several men looked about, hands on their weapons as they surveyed the slope much more carefully than when they'd believed they were only looking for Fel.

"He probably has orders to steal or destroy the shielder, and she was going to lead him right to it." The man didn't spit with disgust, but his expression conveyed the feeling nonetheless.

Syla's cheeks warmed, even though she'd had no intention of doing that. She'd been trying to get *rid* of Vorik.

But not doing a good job of it, she admitted to herself.

"Why didn't he kidnap you again?" another enforcer asked. "Especially if he got your bodyguard?"

"He was questioning me, but then he saw your carriage coming in the distance."

The man swore. "That means he's close. He was *just* here."

Syla nodded, almost wishing Vorik *were* there. Even without his dragon, he had the power to drive these men off or at least keep them busy so she could find the shielder. Except, she reminded herself, he wasn't an ally. For the sake of her mission, she ought to wish that he'd fallen from that cliff and been swept out to sea.

Thunder rumbled again.

"Let's take her back." One man opened the door in the armored carriage for her. "That's most important. If riders are skulking around out here... Well, we'll warn the lieutenant, and he can decide if men need to be sent back out to hunt for them." In a mutter, he added, "Hopefully after the rain stops."

Another soldier waved toward the gray sky. "The gods aren't happy with the riders, and they're taking it out on us."

"The gods forsook us long ago."

Syla let the enforcers guide her into the carriage, noting the thick metal walls and the bars on the window in the door. Even though escaping from the rain had some appeal, she wasn't pleased by the situation. Especially when the door shut, and a *thunk* sounded. The lock turning.

She had been demoted from princess to prisoner.

28

Syla squeezed water out of her robe, leaving a puddle on the floor and the hard bench of the armored carriage as it trundled back the way it had come. Outside, the rain had lessened, but the sky remained gray. Ominous. Even though the air wasn't cold, the metal box had a chill to it that made Syla wish for a towel and a change of clothing.

Her enforcer escort had collected the horses and carriage that she, Fel, and Tibby had driven from the temple. If those two couldn't find the shielder and signal Tibby's engineering ally to come with a ship, they would have a long walk back to civilization.

At least the enforcers hadn't found them. Syla didn't know if they'd fully believed her story that she'd *lost* Fel, but, perhaps deterred by the rain, they hadn't searched for him.

The lock clicked, and one of the enforcers opened the door. Startled, Syla stared at him. The carriage was in motion, and he rode beside it. He swung off his horse to enter, then closed the door behind him, a sword in a scabbard clunking on the metal bench as he shifted it on his belt, then sat opposite Syla.

"I'm Sergeant Tunnok, Your Highness. Son of Minor Lord Arvon of the Bogberry Tunnoks."

That was one of the original founding families of Harvest Island, Syla recalled, and numerous men and women from that line had been chosen to govern here, but Syla didn't know much about the clan, other than that they owned a lot of orchards and, of course, bogs.

"Good afternoon, Sergeant. Are any of your men in need of healing? I've a knack for it." Syla smiled politely, not wanting them to have a reason to resent her or go along with a plot to *get rid of* her. It also crossed her mind that, if any did need and want healing, it might be an opportunity to magically gain an ally or two. At least temporarily.

Tunnok sat back, studying her, and didn't answer right away.

"Do *you* need healing?" she offered.

"I'd heard that King Blaylok's youngest served in a temple and is a strong healer."

Syla chewed on her lip, wondering what it meant that he referenced her father, who'd passed five years ago, instead of *Queen* Lia, her mother, who'd been ruling since then. Maybe he'd been loyal to the king but hadn't transferred that feeling to the queen? Both of her parents were descended from those original people chosen by the gods to carry the moon-mark and lead the Kingdom, so they'd had equal right to rule, at least according to the divine laws, but people didn't always see things that way.

With both now passed, it probably didn't matter. Syla swallowed and looked out the window, tamping down emotions that welled in her chest. This wasn't a safe place to reveal her feelings.

"That's correct," she said.

"Lord Ravoran thinks you came here to take our shielder." Tunnok waved in the direction of the volcano.

"To make sure it isn't being sabotaged as we speak by riders. We also seek to study it to see if a schematic could be made and taken back to Castle Island to help us repair *our* shielder. It still has some power, you see. I'm hoping it can be fixed."

"You, a healer, know how to make a schematic of a magical item?" Tunnok didn't add *of anything*, but his skepticism implied it.

Syla realized her mistake in bringing that up. If she mentioned her aunt, he might send men back to look for her.

"Sergeant Fel studied and practiced engineering in the military before he was recruited to be a bodyguard to protect my siblings and eventually me in the castle," she said. "I'd hoped *he* could draw a schematic."

"He's not moon-marked."

"No. But he has quite an aptitude for mechanical things." Syla remembered Fel tearing pieces out of her aunt's magical tractor but kept her expression earnest.

"But he's lost, you said. Does that mean he's dead? We didn't see any bodies along the way."

"I didn't see him die. He charged off to confront—to protect me from—Captain Vorik. That's when I took the reins and got away. He told me to, but it was hard to leave him. Do you think he might have escaped?"

The sergeant's expression remained skeptical, and she worried he'd stopped long enough at the temple to get more of the story, such as how she'd claimed Vorik wasn't a prisoner and had spent hours in his room, tending his wounds.

Belatedly, it occurred to her that she had no reason to answer the sergeant's questions. *She* was the one who had the authority to question him and expect answers.

But she'd never been trained to act or *feel* like a leader. After so many years in the temple, where she'd had responsibilities but hadn't been in charge, not wanting anything to do with the bureaucracy, she saw herself as a normal person with some magical healing ability.

"If you'll excuse me, I'm quite tired, Sergeant." Syla leaned against the wall, as if she meant to slump against the cold metal and sleep. "But I'd appreciate if it you'd keep an eye out for my bodyguard. Just in case he survived. And watch out for the rider, too. He's very dangerous."

"Oh, we know."

Tunnok didn't take the hint and leave. Instead, he presumed to shift to *her* bench, sitting scant inches from her, and he looked at her chest. No, at *all* of her, giving her a long perusal.

The thick healer's robe didn't reveal much skin, but since it was so damp, it *did* hug her curves more than it otherwise would have.

Tunnok didn't let his gaze linger inappropriately for too long, instead shifting his focus to her face, but unease swept through Syla at this familiarity. She wasn't such a ravaging beauty that she'd endured many unwelcome advances in her life, but she also wasn't so plain that she'd been completely ignored. In particular, she'd had a few encounters with men who'd grown overly amorous after she'd healed them. Her station had always insulated her somewhat, but now that everything was in upheaval and the queen was dead… did she have that protection?

What was going through this man's mind as he gazed at her through slitted eyes? He had to see her as… vulnerable. And was he wrong?

Syla curled her fingers on her leg, wishing for the first time in her life that she'd studied more than healing, that she'd learned how to use her magic in other areas. Such as self-defense. Until the invasion, she'd rarely had to worry about such things.

"Back in Hazel Harbor," Tunnok said, "after we heard about the dragon attack on Castle Island, there was speculation about what might happen if the entire royal family was slain."

Why did Syla have a feeling he'd been a *part* of that speculation?

"Would another government have to be established?" Tunnok mused. "With different leaders? Of course, the power of the Moonmarks, and their ability to control the remaining shielders, suggests they would have to be involved... or at least kept as close allies, but other old families, such as my own Tunnok line, are well-respected and might have the knack for ruling. Most of the males have served in the enforcers or fleet." He touched his uniformed chest. "Some have even battled dragons and riders at sea. We're considered good stock."

Syla stared at him. Somehow, this wasn't what she'd expected him to bring up.

"Those prepared to step in with the appropriate alliances or perhaps marriages might be able to win favor from the populace and other elites."

"I'd think worrying about repelling the dragons and stormers would be of greater importance at the moment," Syla said, "than figuring out who's going to be the next ruler of the Kingdom."

"That is important, yes, but someone must step forward to lead us to a victory against them, and you..."

"I what?" She scowled at him.

"You may play a role, but a healer as monarch? Who would back that?"

"I am my mother's heir, whether I'm a *healer* or not." Syla had never wanted to be queen, nor did she feel qualified, but it was insulting to have someone who didn't know her at all assume she wasn't capable.

"Of course." Tunnok presumed to pat her hand. Condescendingly.

Perhaps a testament to her strong emotions, her quarter-moon birthmark flared silver. Usually, it only did that when she was drawing heavily upon her power to heal someone.

Tunnok drew back, as if startled. Or stung. But Syla didn't think the magic had done anything to him.

Too bad.

"My mother passed some time ago," Tunnok murmured, watching her hand and not presuming to touch it again, "so my father would be available for a marriage. Were you suitably wed to someone from a well-respected and powerful family, you might find that others would be less likely to oppose your appointment as queen. And my father served as island lord for more than a decade, so he has the experience."

"Sergeant Tunnok, are you proposing to me on behalf of your father?"

"I haven't discussed the possibility with him yet, but he's always done what's best for the family, so I think he would be amenable."

"How old is he?" Syla couldn't believe this stranger was bringing this up, especially with her mother and siblings barely passed. Wasn't it possible some of her kin had been found while she'd been gone? Maybe, even now, one of her siblings was being crowned and getting the capital back into order.

"I believe he turns eighty next year, but he's still of fit mind and reasonably fit body."

Her jaw dropped at the idea of marrying someone fifty years her senior. As far as she knew, her family hadn't even contemplated a wedding, political or otherwise, for her. She'd always told them she was married to the temple, to healing, and to helping people. Not… being a part of someone's political plans.

"He might yet be able to rouse himself to give you an heir, children to rule the Kingdom into the future, but if *he* can't…" Tunnok smiled and draped an arm over the back of the bench, brushing her shoulders. "I would be happy to step in. I trust you'd prefer someone a little younger and fitter."

"I'm not looking to get married to anyone right now, Sergeant, and I'd prefer to ride back alone."

"Are you sure you wouldn't like to get out of those wet clothes and warm up? It's dozens of miles to town, and we..." His eyelids drooped as he considered her. "I've ensured we won't be disturbed."

More than lust, his expression held calculation and a fantasy about some future in which his son would be heir to the throne.

"It's strange, I know, but sitting as a prisoner in a cold metal box doesn't get me excited about being with a man." Syla looked him in the eyes, so he couldn't mistake her rejection. "I am not going to marry your father or have sex with you, Sergeant Tunnok."

The horrible thought that, if he forced the matter, she possibly *could* conceive a child came to mind. Back home, she had access to all the medicinal herbs that one could desire, including contraceptives. But here? Did she have yerathma root in her first-aid kit? She thought she might. That could help if she needed to handle the matter after the fact, but she would prefer *not* to need to worry about that.

Uneasy for multiple reasons, Syla willed the sergeant to leave and for this to go no further. Surely, if she yelled, some of his men would come to check on her, to help her. Or *was* that a surety? He'd said they wouldn't be disturbed. Was that under *any* circumstances?

Had her mother and siblings been alive, Syla would have been positive someone like this wouldn't bother her, someone with a good name and lands that could be taken by the crown, but now... Now, she didn't have her family. And she'd sent away her bodyguard. She couldn't even call out to Wreylith for help, not with the shield up around the island. Of course, the red dragon hadn't implied she would come again if Syla *did* reach out through the figurine.

"We need not have sex right now," Tunnok said, "but I suggest you *do* consider what I've laid out. There may be other offers as time passes and events unfold, but I think you'll find this one better than most. Others will simply want to kill you so that you need not be factored into the equation. As I said, there's already speculation. It won't be that safe for you in Hazel Harbor or even back in your own capital. Not without powerful allies."

"I will keep your warning in mind."

"Good." His gaze drooped to her chest again, then to the tie that held the robe closed. "Before I go, why don't you let me see what exactly you can offer besides your name and your moonmark. So I can tell my father, of course."

"No." Her heart pounded. What would she do if he tried to force the issue?

"My men are loyal to me," Tunnok said softly. It sounded like a threat. "They can protect you from what comes, should you choose to ally with my family, but they won't interfere with the questioning of a prisoner."

"Do you try to get *all* of your prisoners out of their robes for questioning?"

"Only if there's a chance that I might need to service them in bed later." His eyelids drooped. "Or now. Is this your fertile time, perchance?"

Her fingers tightened into a fist. By all the deranged storm god's creations, did he think he was going to impregnate her by *raping* her? That such a child would be a legitimate heir?

"Given the *stress* I've endured lately, including this exceedingly appalling discussion with you, I doubt I'll be fertile all year." Syla stood as much as she could in the carriage, her head brushing the ceiling, and thrust her finger toward the door. "Get out."

Tunnok laughed shortly before his arm snaked out, and he yanked her down into his lap. He was hard through his trousers, and fear blasted into her, fear that he might be able to make his horrible plan come to fruition.

"I'm not going back out into the rain when there's a warm woman inside." Tunnok reached for the flap of her robe.

Syla grabbed his wrist but wasn't strong enough to push him away. Fury blazed within her, and she willed her power into him, sending a tendril of magic shooting toward his groin.

Always before, she'd used her gods-gift to heal injuries, but she knew everything Kingdom healers had learned over the centuries about human anatomy and used her power to squeeze the veins running into his penis to cut off circulation. Thanks to her fear, she must have squeezed more than she'd intended because Tunnok gasped in pain. With a lurch, he pitched her to the floor and rolled to the side, grasping his groin. Afraid he would still be able to lash out at her, Syla reached up and touched his side, then sent more power into him. It curled around his heart, tightening just enough that he would feel it.

Tunnok's eyes grew round as he scrambled away from her to break the link—or try. Her birthmark glowed brightly with the light of the moon, and, for the first time she could remember, a visible silver tendril hung taut in the air from the back of her hand to his chest, linking them. With a tightening of her power around his heart, she might kill him. The realization that she knew exactly how to do that sank in, the clarity startling as it came to her.

"I said *get out*, Sergeant," Syla said, a tremor in her voice.

She was scared, whether for herself or for Tunnok, she didn't know. It had never occurred to her that she could use the same magic that healed people to hurt them. She'd never *wanted* to discover that.

"Sergeant!" a rider called from the road ahead. "There's someone out here. An arrow—"

"Shit, Boszik!"

Hand clutched to his heart, Tunnok lunged for the door.

Syla lowered her own hand, willing her power to release him. Feeding on her emotions, it almost had a mind of its own, and several long seconds passed before the silver tendril disappeared and her moon-mark stopped glowing. Finally, Tunnok was able to open the door and stumble out of the carriage.

It had stopped moving. Outside, horses neighed in terror. Tunnok straightened and looked around, but before he stepped away from the door, someone shouted a warning. It came too late. A white arrow whizzed out of the gloom and lodged in his eye.

With new terror swarming her, Syla lunged to the far side of the carriage, putting her back against the wall and hoping the metal would protect her. The legs of another enforcer flopped into view, someone else downed by an arrow. A *gargoyle-bone* arrow.

"Vorik?" she wondered, but he hadn't managed to keep his bow when he'd fallen into the ocean. Only his sword. It had been in the scabbard strapped to his back.

Shouts outside accompanied the *twang-thwumps* of crossbows firing. Scared equine screeches and snorts drowned out the calls of the men, and Syla expected the horses harnessed to the carriage to take off running. But it didn't move, even when thundering hooves announced at least some horses departing. Maybe arrows had sliced through the harnesses? Or someone had cut them?

"Take cover behind the carriage!" a man yelled.

"She's up there!"

She?

That couldn't be Vorik.

More crossbows fired, but the enemy archer was far deadlier than the enforcers. A crossbow quarrel went astray, hit the door, and ricocheted into the carriage. Syla jumped as it clipped the wall inches from her head.

She might die at the hands of her own people. Not that she was sure these enforcers counted as that. She looked grimly at Tunnok's body. He wasn't moving, and she suspected that had been a mortal wound. Whatever he'd been, it hadn't been an ally, and she struggled to feel remorse for his passing.

She crept toward the door, thinking to close it as some measure of protection. Too bad she didn't have the key. As she pulled it shut, she glimpsed the enemy and paused, gaping. She'd seen that woman before.

It was the rider captain who'd attacked Wreylith, who'd wanted *Syla*.

Silver hair pulled back in a severe braid, she leaped, somersaulted, and attacked the men, some firing at her and some rushing up into the rocky terrain toward her with swords. None of them came close to hitting her. Like other riders, she wore black gloves that hid her hand and whether or not she was tattooed. But within seconds of watching her fight, Syla knew she was like Vorik, bonded to a dragon and flush with its power. And, when the woman's cool gaze skimmed across Syla, her blue eyes lighting with triumph, Syla knew the captain still planned to kill her.

It grew quiet outside the armored carriage, and Syla feared her escorts—no, they'd ultimately been her captors—had all been killed. All by one woman.

One dragon-rider woman who was as strong a fighter as Vorik. As strong and as deadly.

Having no delusions about the captain being part of a friendly faction or here to help her in any way, Syla rooted through her pack, seeking something she could use to defend herself. She'd just learned she could use her power for more than healing, but she doubted that would be enough against the magically-enhanced rider woman.

Syla lifted one of the big green Candles of Serenity but snorted. There was no way this enemy would allow herself to be locked in a space with no ventilation. The carriage would have worked wonderfully for knocking someone out, but it wasn't as if the rider captain would look at Syla and think thoughts similar to those of that ambitious sergeant.

"Maybe I can club her with it."

Syla thought of her aunt's belief that she might do that to Vorik and would have smiled, but she was too worried. She hoped Fel and Tibby were far away, that the rider hadn't chanced upon them first.

After returning the candle to her pack, Syla poked around, rejecting the food and water she'd brought. Her knuckles brushed against the wings of the dragon figurine, and she pulled it out.

The magical glass felt cool in her hand, not warm and inviting. Besides, as she'd been thinking earlier, there wasn't a way for Wreylith to reach her, even if the dragon could be convinced to help.

The door opened with a bang, revealing the rider captain, stone-faced and cold, with a sword pointed toward the interior of the carriage. Toward Syla.

Syla eased the figurine back into the pack, not wanting to draw her enemy's attention to it, lest she take it, but the sharp-eyed captain caught the movement.

"Throw your pack out, and then, you, follow," she ordered.

"What happened to the enforcers, Captain… ah?" Syla asked to buy time to think. She knew perfectly well what had happened to the men.

"I'm Captain Lesva of the Moonhunt Tribe, and what happened to them is the same that's destined to happen to all gardeners who stand in our way and have no use." The woman smiled coolly, without a hint of compassion in her eyes. "You have a use. For the moment."

"Glad to hear it," Syla murmured.

Something about the distaste—and was that *hatred*?—in the captain's eyes made Syla wonder if it wouldn't have been better for her if she *hadn't* had a use. Then, presumably, her death would have been swift.

But she had a mission. She couldn't let herself be killed. At least as long as the rider wanted something, Syla had hope of escaping.

"Throw out the pack," Lesva repeated.

Syla eased to the door and dropped her belongings to the ground. The bow that Lesva had used to kill so many soldiers hung across her back with a quiver, white-feathered arrows sticking out of it. A lot of them. Maybe she'd already yanked those she'd used out of the bodies of the dead.

"Wouldn't want to waste," Syla murmured, climbing out as ordered and keeping her eye on the sword.

She would *try* to use her magic, she decided, but she had to touch someone to establish a link, whether to heal or to hurt. And Lesva didn't look *touchable* at the moment.

"Is there anything you need in that pack to reach the shielder?" Lesva asked.

"I just need to be alive to access it." Syla held up her moon-mark, knowing she wasn't giving anything away. The riders already knew it was required to access and use the shielders. "And I've got food and water and candles."

"Open your pack."

As Syla knelt and did so, Lesva looked up and down the road. Expecting more enforcers to arrive? Or maybe she knew about Fel. But Syla had sent him away. She couldn't hope that he would come to her rescue.

And Vorik? Syla had no idea where he was. Though she believed he had evaded capture, he had no way to know where she was. He might believe she was still at the temple. Even if he knew she'd left, it wasn't as if he could ride his dragon over the protected island to look for her from the sky.

Syla suspected she was on her own for finding a way out of her predicament.

"Those candles are huge," Lesva remarked as Syla pulled items out of her pack to show they were innocuous. *Most* of them were.

"I think it'll be dark in the place where the shielder is stored." Syla couldn't tell if her captor was suspicious of the candles. Did she recognize the faint scent? "I want to be able to take notes and draw schematics."

"You're not going to get to do that." Lesva waved with her sword to indicate Syla could close the pack with all the items inside. "Put that on, and start walking."

Glad Lesva hadn't forced her to cast the candles aside, Syla tied the pack shut and shouldered it, but she was wary, with dread curling through her stomach. "Walking where?"

"To the *place where the shielder is stored*." Lesva echoed back the vague words. "You're taking me there."

"To what end?"

Eyes closing to slits, Lesva said, "I'm going to destroy it and bring its broken shards to General Jhiton. Then he'll see my value and promote me. *I'll* be his most trusted officer, not Captain Vorik."

Syla almost asked if Vorik was *still* the general's most trusted officer or if Lesva knew anything about his supposed affiliation with the Freeborn Faction. After all, she'd attacked Vorik. She must have believed him an enemy at the time? Or... had she? Maybe she'd simply wanted to get him, as a competitor for that general's favor, out of the way at the same time as she tried to capture Syla.

"Together," Lesva added, "we'll destroy *all* of your shielders and claim these lush islands for our people."

Together? She and... the general? Jhiton? Did she imagine being more than an officer for him?

"If you destroy all the shielders," Syla pointed out, "the islands won't be protected from aerial predators. They'll end up as ravaged and dangerous as the rest of the world."

"Not with our dragon allies guarding them. General Jhiton

won't make a foolish mistake. I know he has this all planned out. We *will* be triumphant."

Something about the gleam in Lesva's eyes reminded Syla of Sergeant Tunnok's face when he'd been contemplating his political future and a son ruling the Kingdom. Whatever Lesva wanted, it was probably more than a promotion.

Syla didn't care about the specifics. All that mattered was that she couldn't lead the woman to the shielder. If it came to it, she would have to die before doing that.

29

WITH CAPTAIN LESVA FOLLOWING CLOSE BEHIND, SWORD TIP pointed at the back of her neck, Syla walked toward the volcano.

Hours had passed since they'd left the squadron of enforcers, every man dead, most with arrow holes in their eyes or hearts but some with their throats cut. Lesva had been ruthless. And to have killed so many, she had to be more capable and deadly than Syla had ever imagined a woman could be. That Lesva had the same kind of dragon-gifted magic as Vorik... There was no doubt.

The question was how could Syla get away from someone like that? Could she sneak off while Lesva slept? Did the rider even *need* sleep?

Syla surely did. Her feet were numb from the miles they'd walked, first on the road and then onto a path snaking toward the back side of the volcano where a black field of hardened lava overlooked the sea. Other than a few goats browsing on clumps of vegetation that grew out of crevices, this corner of the island saw little life. There were no witnesses to this trek, to Syla's peril.

For now, she meandered along, avoiding the route she remembered that led to the tunnels—ancient tubes hollowed out by lava flows—and the shielder chamber. She didn't want to lead Lesva to it or risk running across Fel and Tibby. Unless she found a miraculous opportunity to escape, she could only hope to buy time. Time for Fel and Tibby to find and extract the shielder, getting it away before Lesva spotted them, or time for Vorik to find Syla.

Even if Vorik had nothing to do with the Freeborn Faction and he truly was that general's loyal, right-hand man, Syla believed he would save her from Lesva. He had before, after all. Whatever his orders were, they differed from this woman's schemes.

"May we stop to rest?" Syla asked.

It wasn't raining, but the darkening sky promised that night would bring more precipitation. If Syla could find a cave and convince Lesva that they should shelter there for a few hours, maybe she could light one of the candles, and it would knock out her captor.

Lesva answered with a prompt, "No," and poked the sword tip into the back of Syla's neck.

Worse, she stepped forward and grabbed Syla's shoulder painfully.

"You *are* leading me to the shielder, right?" Lesva asked, her lips near Syla's ear. The words were spoken softly—dangerously—and were barely audible above the roar of the sea and the wind whistling across the black lava fields.

"You've given me little choice."

Lesva's grip tightened, nails digging in like a dragon's talons. "You will take me there, or I will kill you, cut off your hand to use the mark, and find it myself."

Syla licked her dry lips and looked toward the sky, willing Vorik to find them. One more time, she needed his help.

"The magic doesn't work that way. As a student of history, I can point out times when it's been tried by enemies of the Kingdom, enemies who failed. I have to be alive for the power to live." Syla waved her moon-mark, a little tempted to grip Lesva's hand and attempt to use her magic as she had with the sergeant, as a weapon instead of to heal.

But that sword prodded painfully into the back of her neck, and it had drawn blood more than once, whenever Syla's pace had grown too slow. Syla feared Lesva would drive it into her at the least sign of resistance.

She glanced around, again hoping to spot Vorik. And that he would spring onto Lesva and kill her.

As if her captor could read her rebellious thoughts, Lesva drove a boot into the back of Syla's knee.

Startled, Syla couldn't keep from losing her balance. Her legs crumpled, and her spectacles almost flew off. She clasped a hand to her face but dared not do more, not with the blade against her neck.

"Who do you keep looking for?" Lesva demanded, the wind kicking up and whipping her braid about. "The bodyguard and librarian that you were flying with? Did they survive?"

Librarian? Is that what she'd assumed Aunt Tibby was?

Syla licked her lips again. She didn't want to answer any of her captor's questions, but if her goal was to buy time, a conversation would do it.

"They didn't survive, no," Syla said. "I'm lucky that I did. Falling into the sea way out there was treacherous."

"Tell me about it. Especially when you're injured."

If Lesva had been seriously injured, it didn't show. She'd had no trouble dispatching all those trained enforcers. Maybe some of those dragon powers allowed faster than usual healing. Vorik, after all, had leaped out a window, onto a roof, and climbed down a cliff, despite his grievous wounds. And his wounds hadn't distracted him in the least when he'd been... thanking her.

Despite her precarious position, Syla's cheeks flushed at the memory. She couldn't keep from glancing around the black fields again.

"Is it Vorik you're looking for?" For the first time, Lesva sounded more amused than angry. "I'm *positive* he survived that fall and swim."

Syla didn't look back at her, instead scouring the landscape in the deepening gloom for a cave. They'd been walking around the base of the volcano, but they might be more likely to find one on higher ground. The entrance to the shielder chamber was up there, though, so Syla hesitated to search in that direction. Ahead, in an area reminiscent of that on which the temple perched, a cliff dropped away a hundred feet into the sea. Syla hadn't walked close to the edge, not wanting Lesva to be tempted to shove her over, but such an area might hold caves. Lovely caves for resting by candlelight.

"Do you think he'll leap to your defense again?" Lesva's tone shifted from amused to mocking. "He fought me once, after all. He must be willing to do so again, no? Has he won your trust with his actions yet?"

"I think that's the way." Syla pointed, not wanting to speak about Vorik with this woman. "There's a cave that leads into an ancient lava tube. That's what I've been looking for."

Lesva eyed her. The captain's face was a blur in Syla's uncorrected peripheral vision. As Vorik had observed, her spectacles couldn't help with that. The world was simply an indistinct blur when Syla couldn't look straight at it. And with Lesva's taloned fingers still digging into her shoulder, she wasn't inclined to meet the woman's mocking gaze.

"Show me." Lesva sounded suspicious.

If only the captain were dumber. But she'd survived a lot, and Syla dared not underestimate her.

Syla walked toward the cliff. Even before they neared the edge, her heartbeat kicked up, thumping rapidly in her ears. With an enemy walking right behind her, how not? Lesva wouldn't hesitate to kill her if she decided she didn't need a moon-marked guide.

The wind also kicked up, scouring the lava rock and tugging at the healer's robe. By now, it had dried, and the hem kept flapping about Syla's knees. It was a contrast to the tight-fitting riding leathers that Lesva wore, clothes that accented her lean and powerful form.

Syla couldn't bring herself to approach the cliff too closely, though caves would more likely be found in its vertical face. The thought of crawling down the treacherous rock held no appeal. Even as a little girl, before she'd needed spectacles, she hadn't been the most agile of climbers. She recalled being startled by a squirrel and falling out of a tree and into an apple cart one summer. Venia had witnessed the clumsiness and teased her relentlessly for weeks.

A pang of sorrow stabbed at her heart at the memory.

"If you're thinking of ending your life instead of betraying your people," Lesva said, no doubt noticing her long look at the cliff, "I'm afraid I can't allow that. Not until you show me to the shielder."

"A pity," Syla said, though she had far too much to do to commit suicide. The Kingdom needed her.

Determined, Syla looked left and right along the top of the cliff. Just visible in the gloom lay a jumble of rocks perched about twenty feet back from the edge. Getting there wouldn't be too treacherous, and a dark spot in the center looked like a hole or maybe the cave that Syla hoped for. It probably didn't lead to a lava tube, but maybe she could come up with a reason to linger inside. Searching for a hidden entrance, perhaps. By candlelight.

While Syla had paused to look around, Lesva had gazed over the precipice. Jagged rocks protruded from the churning white sea far below. Should Syla fall over—or be *pushed* over—she had no doubt that she would die upon those rocks. She briefly entertained the notion of trying to push *Lesva* over, but she could never match the woman physically. Besides, Lesva probably had the peripheral vision of a hawk. No. Of a *dragon*. She wouldn't be caught by surprise.

"That looks familiar." Syla pointed at the rock jumble.

One of Lesva's eyebrows twitched, but she waved with the sword for Syla to lead the way.

Yes, that was a cave in the rock jumble, one that slanted downward, under the lava field, and went deeper than Syla had expected. Maybe it *did* connect to the warren of tubes within the volcano. For the sake of her candles, it would be better if it were a small and enclosed space.

Before stepping into the cave, Syla couldn't keep from looking around one more time, hoping to see...

"He's not coming for you," Lesva snapped, poking her with the sword. Her earlier amusement had vanished. "Though I'm sure he'll be flattered that you're pining for him."

Jaw clenched, Syla couldn't keep from slanting a dark glower over her shoulder before stepping into the cave.

Lesva snorted. "You know he was only helping you because General Jhiton ordered it, right? Seduce the princess. Learn what she knows."

"I gathered it was something like that." Syla wasn't surprised, but hearing it stung.

She lifted both hands to grope her way into the dark cave. It smelled of fish and seaweed. Birds or other animals must have brought their meals up here from time to time.

"He's known for his allure to women," Lesva added, following her closely, as if Syla might sprint off and escape.

If only she could. There was nothing hawk- or dragon-like about her vision, and in the gloom, she stumbled over the uneven floor of the cave.

Fortunately, there wasn't far to go. After sloping down, the cave widened, the floor flattening into something akin to a room, but it didn't continue on from there. They were out of the wind, and there wasn't much ventilation. Maybe...

Syla turned slowly. Lesva was outlined against the dim light coming from the entrance. Lean and hard, her sword in one hand, she gazed coolly back at Syla.

"This might be the spot," Syla said. "I remember there being a sigil on the wall, but I was here on a much brighter day."

One lie after another. They made her nervous, especially since Lesva was so good at seemingly reading her mind.

"Light those candles," Lesva said.

Syla licked her lips. "All right."

She knelt, tugged the pack off, and reached for the flap. But she froze as the sharp gargoyle-bone blade came to rest under her chin, forcing her to look up at Lesva. In the dark, she couldn't see the woman's face, but she suspected the captain saw every detail of hers, including the fear in her eyes.

"I think you're lying to me," Lesva stated, "and hope that if you dawdle long enough, Vorik will come for you."

"I'd be foolish to lie to someone as dangerous as you."

"That's the truth, but I think you're a fool. You were *especially* a fool if you ever thought Captain Vorik would go against his brother's wishes, betray his people, and help a pudgy, blind gardener female."

Indignation heated Syla's cheeks—she wasn't pudgy or *blind*, damn it—and she hated that she wasn't in a position to respond, that the cool bone blade could cut her throat with the barest of wrist flicks.

"Do you want me to light the candles or not?" Syla tried not to show her fear.

"Go ahead. Let's see if this *sigil* is here."

Hating that her hands shook, Syla dug out the candles and set them near the stone walls, far enough apart that their scents would spread more easily. More quickly. Unfortunately, the sedative always took time to impact her patients, even in a small surgical room in the temple. How long would the scent need to induce sleep on someone in a *cave*? She had no idea.

Using a dragonspark match, Syla lit the candles. Moving slowly, she stood, gripped her chin and pretended to survey the wall. She knew there wouldn't be a sigil, and she tried to watch Lesva out of the corner of her eye instead of examining the back of the cave.

"There's nothing there," Lesva stated coolly.

"I could have sworn..." Syla murmured, as if confused by the lack of markings.

"You're wasting my time." Lesva strode toward her, radiating irritation. "The general thinks the moon-marked have the ability to resist torture, but *I* believe that's a myth. You're going to tell me exactly how to find the shielder."

Syla backed up, grasping for another way to buy time. The first hint of eucalyptus and more pungent dragonquell wafted into the air, but it would take so long before it affected Lesva, if it did at all. Who knew what immunity her dragon-gifted magic gave her?

Lesva sheathed her sword and drew a wickedly curved bone knife. Eyes gleaming with determination and the fervor of her mission, she lunged.

Syla backed into the wall and couldn't retreat farther. She kicked, trying to keep the woman from reaching her, but Lesva used her knee to knock aside the attempt, then gripped the front of Syla's robe, fingers clenching the thick fabric as she pinned Syla against the wall.

For the first time, they were touching.

Syla lifted her hand and grasped the woman's wrist as if she meant to push her away. Lesva braced herself, powerful muscles ensuring she wouldn't budge. But Syla didn't push. Instead, she sent her magic flowing into the rider. As she'd done with the handsy sergeant, she tried to turn her healing power into a weapon, guiding tendrils of it toward Lesva's heart.

But the dragon tattoo on the back of the captain's hand flared blue, and Syla sensed Lesva's own magic coming to her defense. It charged through her body, blocking Syla's tendrils and pushing her power out.

Eyes closing to slits, Lesva leaned in close. "You're more of a threat than my people believe, aren't you?"

"I'm a healer first and foremost. Don't forget you need me to reach the shielder."

"Don't worry." A cold smile stretched Lesva's face. "You'll survive this. But you'll also be begging to tell me everything you know."

Syla wished she had something brave to say. She wished even more that the candles would kick in, that Lesva would pitch over backward and pass out.

She did not. She raised her dagger and rested it against Syla's throat. But it wasn't the blade she used to inflict pain. The power that now defensively patrolled Lesva's body, keeping Syla's attacks out, flowed from the back of her tattoo and into Syla.

The dragon-fueled magic tore through her veins, biting her nerves all along the way, eliciting pain such as Syla had never known. She couldn't keep from throwing her head back, clunking it on the stone wall, and screaming out.

At first, Lesva only hurt her, using her power as a torture implement. Then she lessened the force slightly and said, "Tell me where the shielder is."

Panting, the agony still present, Syla shook her head. She tried to push back with her own magic, but Lesva was too strong.

"Tell me," the woman repeated, unmoved by Syla's pain. "Telling me is the only way this will stop."

When she did not, the pain intensified again, and Syla could only scream.

30

As twilight descended, Vorik crouched on a rock ledge. Boulders at his back kept his silhouette from being visible by those he watched. Oblivious to his presence, Syla's allies, Fel and Tibby, climbed a scree-covered slope toward a gap in the rocks.

Was that a cave entrance? Anticipation thrummed within Vorik as they headed straight toward it.

While searching for Syla, he had chanced across the bodyguard and the aunt. He'd expected her to show up, as well. He'd *wanted* her to show up. Not only because he had a perhaps misguided notion of continuing the sexual encounter they'd begun in the temple but for the sake of his mission. Wasn't she the one who knew the location of the shielders? Had she given Fel and Tibby a map? They hadn't yet pulled anything out to look at, but, with the aunt in the lead, they climbed without hesitation.

Vorik had contemplated leaping into their path and questioning them, but it would be better if they unwittingly led him to the shielder. And past the protections that would guard it. Then he could confront them.

But where was Syla?

As the gloom deepened, Vorik gazed around the rocky slopes and broken top of a volcano that had erupted intermittently over the centuries. He could also hear the roar of the sea and knew they were close to the cliff-filled northwestern shoreline. Once, the island had reputedly extended much farther in that direction, with the volcano that had formed it closer to the middle, but time and rising seas had sunk what had been lower land.

With dozens of square miles around the volcano, Syla could be anywhere out there, but why would she have parted from her allies? To run off and lead someone else astray while they went for the shielder? Could another rider be out here? Sent to capture her and get the location of the shielder?

Vorik recalled that Captain Lesva had been after Syla—and had also fallen into the waters around the island—and he shifted uneasily on his perch. As powerful as he, Lesva might well have made it to shore.

Lost in his thoughts and scouring the terrain, longing to spot Syla, Vorik almost missed the pair entering the cave. He returned his focus to them as they disappeared inside and waited to make sure they wouldn't come back out. When a lantern flared to life, then dimmed as they carried it deeper into the cave, he knew they were descending into the earth.

He hopped down from his perch and jogged toward the cave.

We may be close to finding the shielder, he spoke telepathically to Agrevlari.

Good. I grow weary of sitting out here on this perch. The fishing is not that wondrous.

I wish you could fly over here and look for Syla while I follow these two. Vorik shared an image of Fel and Tibby with the dragon.

She is not with them?

No. I'm worried... She may be in danger. The next image he shared was of Lesva. *I have a hunch.*

Her danger will matter little if you're able to obtain or destroy this island's shielder without her. Then I and other dragons will be able to hunt the delicious elioks.

I see where your priorities are.

Dragons have not held any secrets from their human riders about what they want from this alliance.

Oh, I know. But Syla does matter. She... Vorik sought a way to explain without admitting that he cared... more than he was supposed to.

You still seek to mate with her.

Well, yes, but that's not why *she matters.*

Not *only* why, anyway.

As the daughter of the deceased monarch, she should know where the shielders are located on all *the islands,* Vorik continued. *Remember, that's what General Jhiton wants. And I'm sure you and your dragon kin would also enjoy the prey on those other islands.*

Oh, yes. A great many soft and succulent animals that are extinct in other parts of the world may be found in the Kingdom. Some were gone long before my time, and I yet crave them, longing to experience their fine flesh on my tongue.

You're making me hungry, Agrevlari. Vorik crept into the cave, not lighting a lantern for himself. Since he'd fled with nothing but his sword, trousers, and boots—not even his shirt—he didn't have that option, but with his dragon-magic-enhanced vision, he could see in all but the darkest of environments. Reminded of the keenness of dragon vision, he added, *Can you use your magic and fine eyes to try to spot Syla from out there while I follow these two?*

Certainly. It would be much easier if I could fly over that area, but I will let you know if I detect anything from this distant perch.

Thanks. You're a good dragon.

One deserving of many elioks.

Clearly.

Vorik padded silently around jumbled boulders, the cave floor angling downward, then turning into a rockfall that sloped to a lower level. At that point, the passageway appeared to end at a stone wall with no side tunnels one might take. But Fel, Tibby, and their light had disappeared.

Vorik, sensing a hint of magic, patted around the area, certain they'd gone through a hidden entrance.

Yes, his hand swept through air that only *looked* like rock. He stepped into a lava tube more than twice his height. It was largely straight, and, right away, he spotted the backs of Fel and Tibby about thirty yards ahead. He pressed himself against a lumpy section of the side of the lava tube, willing himself to blend in in case they sensed a threat and looked back.

And Fel did. More than once. But he was a mundane human, lacking enhanced night vision, and he gave no sign that he spotted Vorik. He and the aunt continued on.

Slight magic emanated from the stone behind Vorik's back, left by the gods to protect this area, perhaps, in case the volcano erupted again. Letting his fingers trail along it, he followed the others.

After perhaps a quarter of a mile, the ancient lava tube appeared to dead-end at another rockfall. But the wall to the left of it was unnaturally smooth, as if someone had carved it with tools.

"In Syla's mind, I saw a rune glowing here." Tibby pointed to the smooth section.

"Maybe it only glows for the royal family," Fel said.

"It should glow for me too." Tibby waved the back of her hand at the wall.

Nothing happened.

Vorik crept closer. Was this the spot? Might the shielder lie right behind that rock wall in a hidden chamber like the one under the castle?

Your suspicion was correct, Agrevlari spoke into his mind, the telepathic voice muffled. By the rock? Or perhaps the magic protecting this place.

What? Vorik stopped his advance.

Captain Lesva has captured the princess and is, judging by the screams drifting all the way to sea to reach my ears, torturing her.

Dread slammed down like a lead weight in Vorik's belly.

Lesva had wanted to capture and torture Syla all along. Damn it, he'd failed her by not finding her earlier.

Fury replaced his dread, and his hand tightened around the hilt of his sword. Storm god curse the captain, this wasn't what Jhiton had ordered. He'd specifically told Lesva *not* to go after Syla.

And Syla didn't deserve this. She was innocent. A healer. She *helped* people. She wasn't a soldier or an enemy of any kind, other than that she'd been born in the Kingdom instead of into one of the tribes.

The sounds of humans aren't easy for a dragon to understand, Agrevlari added, *but I believe she is experiencing great pain.*

Vorik clenched his jaw, torn between wanting to sprint out and locate Syla and knowing the pair ahead was close to finding a way into the shielder chamber. With a few swift thrusts from his magical sword, he might be able to destroy the artifact, but he couldn't gain access without a moon-mark. He had to wait for Tibby to figure out how to get inside.

In the meantime, Syla was in pain. Pain she didn't deserve. Vorik closed his eyes but didn't wrestle with the decision for long. He had to help her.

I'll come back for the shielder, he told Agrevlari, spinning and running back toward the tunnel entrance. *Guide me to Syla.*

What will you do? Lesva is your fellow officer.

Kill her, Vorik thought, furious that Lesva was disobeying orders—that she was *hurting* Syla. But Agrevlari also followed the ways and mandates of the Sixteen Talons. Indeed, Jhiton's dragon was *his* superior officer. Not wanting to risk his intentions being reported back, Vorik said, *Stop her. There's no need for torture when I now know the way to the shielder.*

Excellent. I believe Wreylith might not wish her dead. Because she carries the krendala.

Yeah, your sexy red dragon is my primary concern here too. As Vorik climbed the rockfall upward, he glanced back, worried he was going too quickly and making noise as stones shifted underneath him.

Yes, Fel was peering in his direction. He must have heard or instinctually sensed a threat.

There was nothing to be done. Tibby hadn't found a way in yet.

Vorik would help Syla, and then he would come back. He wasn't abandoning his mission. This was logical.

Even if it wasn't... he decided he didn't care.

31

Never in Syla's life had she known such pain. Captain Lesva's dragon magic ripped through her veins, biting into every nerve, as if every horrible creature the storm god had ever made was tearing through her body. Over and over, Syla tried to summon her own magic to defend herself, but the rider's power was too great. She screamed until she was hoarse, choosing to do that rather than spitting the words that wanted to burble forth, the answers to Lesva's questions. At least her magic helped her in that arena. She didn't know how much longer she could last, but she hadn't yet spoken of Fel and Tibby—or the locations of the shielders.

Lesva, her cold face inches from Syla's, watched her writhe in pain. There was no hint of sympathy in the rider's eyes. Only cold calculation laced with irritation, irritation that Syla hadn't yet spewed forth her secrets.

To either side of them, wax melted as the Candles of Serenity continued to burn. The scent of eucalyptus and dragonquell hung in the air but not as thickly as Syla was accustomed to. This wasn't an enclosed room. Since the cave had an exit, the salty sea air swept in with the tides, keeping the odor from pooling deeply.

Or so she thought. In the middle of one of Syla's screams, Lesva yawned.

It was the first sign that she might feel the sedative power of the candles. And did the pain scouring Syla's nerves lessen slightly?

Outside, thunder rumbled. Lightning flashed in the dark clouds over the sea. Lesva yawned again.

Too disheartened at failing and too flustered to concentrate, it had been some time since Syla had attempted to use her magic to push away Lesva's, but she gathered her flagging strength to try again. Maybe this time...

Lesva shook her head, as if to push away the fatigue. She also looked at one of the candles. The look turned into a suspicious squint.

Had she figured out the scent was affecting her?

With the captain's attention shifted, the pain lessened a little more. Afraid Lesva was on the verge of kicking over the candles to put them out, Syla called to her magic, willing it to drive out the enemy power and heal the damage Lesva had done.

This time, perhaps thanks to fatigue creeping into the captain, Syla had more success. Like a broom cleaning detritus from a hall, her power swept the dragon magic out, pushing it back toward Lesva, toward the glowing dragon tattoo from which everything originated.

Scowling, Lesva faced her. Syla sensed the woman summoning her power again, intending to fight back. But then her head twisted toward the cave entrance.

Had she heard something beyond the roar of the sea? Syla used the distraction to thrust the rest of the rider's foul magic out of her body.

Instead of fighting her, Lesva released her and stalked toward the entrance.

Without the support of her enemy pinning her, Syla's legs gave way, muscles rubbery from all she'd endured. She collapsed to her hands and knees and gulped in air, as if she'd half-drowned. Her entire body shook in the aftermath of the experience, of minutes —or had it been *hours*?—of enduring the pain.

Syla almost collapsed completely, flopping onto her side, but movement at the cave entrance drew her eye. Not only did Lesva stand there, her sword in hand, but another person had arrived, a dark figure outlined against the stormy night sky.

Shadows hid his face, but Syla knew who it was, even before lightning flashed behind him, the white light limning his body.

Vorik.

"You're not taking my prisoner, Captain." Lesva crouched and raised her sword, prepared to fight.

Though Syla was relieved to see Vorik, she also worried for him. Lesva looked like his enemy, not his ally. If she killed him, with only a Kingdom woman for a witness, would Lesva have found a way to achieve the promotion she wanted? By eliminating their general's right-hand man?

That close to the entrance, she was probably far from the candles' influence and wouldn't be slowed in a fight. Had Vorik and Lesva been normal human beings, Syla would have assumed a man would have the advantage in a physical confrontation, but she'd experienced for herself how strong Lesva was, how dangerous and deadly the dragon magic made her.

"You're torturing her for no reason." Vorik's voice was icier than Syla had ever heard it.

Though he also carried his sword, he looked past his colleague to Syla. More concerned for her than for the battle at hand?

Syla waved to indicate she was all right, even if she wasn't. She didn't want to be a distraction.

"Oh, there's a reason," Lesva said. "I will find and destroy the shielder. Without lowering myself to some smarmy seduction scheme. You are a noble *warrior*, Vorik. It's beneath you."

"*I* am following our general's orders." Vorik glanced at Syla again.

Wishing she weren't hearing this? The revelation of everything?

Since she'd already figured it out, it hardly mattered.

"You are the one who's gone rogue and is going against his wishes," Vorik added.

Thunder boomed, punctuating the sentence. It wasn't raining on the island, not yet, but a storm raged scant miles off the coast.

"He won't care how the mission is accomplished once the islands are laid bare for our people and our dragon allies. You know that."

"You are disobeying his orders," Vorik said. "He *will* care about that."

"Not if he doesn't find out." Sword still raised, Lesva took a step closer to him, like a cat creeping up on its prey before pouncing.

Not looking concerned—or anything like prey—Vorik watched her approach without moving. "I've already found the shielder. Your disobedience and tormenting of an innocent woman is for naught."

He'd *found* it? *How*?

Using the stone wall for support, Syla pushed herself into a sitting position.

"Innocent? She's a *gardener*. A gardener princess from the very family who has for generations denied stormers an opportunity to return to their homeland. My mother tried, and she was killed when her identity was found out. Because we won't bow down and grovel before their throne and embrace their stupid laws, they hate us. And they resent us for our alliance with the dragons. They've *always* resented us." Lesva prowled closer to Vorik.

Unfortunately, every step took her farther from the candles' scent. She wasn't yawning now.

"Syla is a healer." Vorik didn't sound moved by his colleague's rant. Thank the gods.

"A *healer* wouldn't be so good at keeping her mouth shut when someone's interrogating her. I don't know what she is, but she was *trained* to keep her secrets, the secrets that make these lands inaccessible to our people. She's an enemy, and I'm certain she'd happily see you or any other stormer dead. You can't possibly know if she's *innocent*. She could have killed our kind many times. Or denied them healing when they washed up on gardener shores."

"I'm certain she has never killed nor denied anyone healing. I doubt she's even looked crossly at one of our people. She healed *me*." Vorik brushed the sutures in his side. "When she knew she shouldn't have."

Though her muscles remained weak and wobbly, Syla clawed her way to her feet. Since she was at the core of this conversation, she wanted to stand, not lie crumpled like a hapless victim.

"Is that why you're defending her? She used her healing magic on you, and you're bound?" Lesva's words rang with realization, as if she'd found the explanation she sought.

"She didn't use her magic on me. Only thread and bandages."

"Then it's that you like her soft body and big boobs and want to sink your cock into her."

"Lesva, do not do this. Walk away. Your dragon is waiting for you beyond the barrier."

"Why you'd prefer a weak, useless gardener princess to a powerful warrior woman who can make you scream—who *has* made you scream—I can't imagine, but I suppose I'm not surprised. Men will screw anything." Lesva stepped closer. "I thought you were too noble, too *honorable*, to be a spy and seduce a woman, but maybe your brother's mission got you excited. Maybe—"

She didn't finish the sentence. Instead, she sprang at Vorik, slashing at him with her sword.

He wasn't surprised and flicked his own blade to meet her powerful blow, parrying it without obvious effort. When he backed up, Syla sensed it was only so they would have more room to maneuver, so they would be out in the open and not constrained by the cave walls.

Too bad. She looked wistfully at her candles, wishing she could have thought of a way to lure them both back here for long enough to sedate them. Especially since Vorik had said he'd found the shielder. She needed to slip away and discover if that was true. What if he'd chanced upon Fel and Tibby? And killed them after they'd found their way into the shielder chamber?

That awful thought propelled Syla along the wall toward the entrance.

Outside, clangs rang out over the roar of the sea and rumble of thunder as Vorik and Lesva fought, the magical gargoyle-bone blades sounding more like steel than natural material. In the dark, on the rough footing of the lava rock, they leaped in and out, parrying and thrusting, as if they could see perfectly well and had the flattest battleground imaginable.

They were as evenly matched as Syla had feared, and their deadly dance mesmerized her, making her pause to watch. Vorik, she thought, was a little stronger, a little faster, but he didn't, she sensed, want to kill Lesva. If they had, as Lesva had implied, slept together, maybe he had feelings for her. It didn't seem to go both ways. If Lesva felt anything for Vorik, she didn't show it. She snarled and grunted as she attacked, determined to defeat him. To *kill* him.

Syla continued toward the cave entrance, a stiff wind blowing briny air against her face as she drew closer. It was hard to ignore the battle as the combatants fought back and forth, their speed amazing as they danced and darted, using all the ground between the cave and the cliff.

She almost wished it were daylight so she could see them better, but she needed to tear her gaze away and make use of her opportunity. She had to find Fel and Tibby and fulfill her duty.

After exiting, she crept away from the cave and the battle, but the wind made it difficult. It whipped at her robe and weary, battered body. She willed power into her veins to carry healing magic to her beleaguered nerves and sweep away the lingering pain from Lesva's torment.

When she glanced back, she caught Vorik looking her way as he deflected a rain of blows from Lesva. Even though Syla couldn't see his features in the dark, she sensed determination in him, and he turned to the offensive.

He must have decided that he had to finish the fight before Syla could escape. He, too, was prioritizing his mission.

When he fully committed, Vorik turned the tide quickly, putting Lesva on her heels. Though she managed to parry all the blows that whistled toward her head, she had to give ground. Her back was to the cliff, to the hundred-foot drop, and with every step of retreat, she drew closer and closer to the edge.

Syla couldn't keep from stopping to stare. Would Vorik drive her over? Despite their past? Despite his feelings for her?

When she was only a foot away from the edge, Lesva glanced back. Aware of how close she was to falling—to being *pushed* off—she dug in, holding her ground. Her movements had been precise before, exuding controlled power, but they now grew frenzied. Desperate.

Lightning flashed, revealing her face, her mouth open as she panted. Sweat gleamed on her forehead.

Vorik didn't relent. The light revealed the cold anger on his own face. He was pissed at Lesva. Pissed about the torture?

Though the thought touched her, Syla made herself continue

away from the battle. As soon as one of them was victorious, she would once again be in danger. The *shielder* would be in danger.

"Vorik!" Lesva's shout sounded more like a plea.

Syla couldn't keep from pausing and looking back again. She was in time to see Vorik knock Lesva's blade out of her hand and sweep the tip of his own weapon to her throat.

They paused in that tableau. Syla didn't know if Vorik would finish Lesva off. Her gaze darted about as she attempted to read his face. She didn't seem to know either.

Thunder boomed right above them, and lightning streaked toward the cliff. It struck something on the rock face, and a great *crack* sounded. Abruptly, the edge of the cliff gave way with Lesva and Vorik on it.

Syla gaped as rocks crumbled, and they both fell from view. Vorik twisted as he plummeted, trying to lunge in the air to find purchase.

Wind whipped at Syla's robe again, and she stared at the black sky. Had that lightning strike been natural? Or… were the gods still about, not as departed from the world as mankind believed?

Movement at the crumbled section of the cliff drew her gaze back to earth. Vorik, his sword still in hand, climbed over the edge and stood. He turned to look down at the churning sea. Had Lesva fallen all the way down? Did her body lie mangled upon rocks?

Whatever had happened, Vorik must not have been worried about her returning because he turned away from the cliff. Sword lowering, rain spattering his bare muscled chest, he looked at Syla.

She'd moved thirty or forty yards during the battle, but she could feel the power emanating from him even across that distance. Lightning flashed again, showing his heated eyes boring into her, and a tremble went through her. She hadn't gotten nearly far enough away to escape him. If she ran, with a few long strides, he could catch her.

And, in her heart, Syla didn't want to run. She was drawn to the powerful dragon rider, the man who'd defeated the horrible woman who'd been torturing her. Even if Vorik was an enemy, and she had no doubt that he was, she wanted to embrace him and thank him for coming for her.

Before she'd made a conscious decision to do so, she found herself walking back toward him. Yes, *drawn* was the right word. As he watched her, sword still in hand but lowered, his eyes intense, she remembered the night before, thrashing as he brought her more exquisite pleasure than she'd ever known.

She had to be careful. She needed to find the shielder and finish her mission, not throw herself upon Vorik. She would only thank him.

He waited for her to come to him, as if certain she would. And he wasn't wrong.

Only when she was a few feet away did he step forward and meet her, wrapping his strong arms around her, pulling her against him.

"I'm sorry," he whispered as she said, "Thank you."

He kissed the side of her neck as she gripped his shoulders, ensuring he wouldn't release her.

"I'm sorry you had to endure that," Vorik said. "I've been looking for you since I escaped the enforcers at the temple."

"My route here was… circuitous."

To say the least. Her body melted against his, feeling safe, even if she wasn't. Being in his arms was amazing, and she wanted so badly for him to be… not an enemy. Someone she could trust.

The fact that he wasn't brought tears to her eyes, and she removed her spectacles. All through Lesva's torture, she hadn't wept, but now… now her emotions got the best of her. She was on the verge of sobbing. She didn't want to, but so much had happened. So much horribleness. She needed a release.

Vorik drew back enough to see her face and brushed his thumb over her wet cheeks. "Are you in pain?"

Syla shook her head and drew a breath, trying to steady herself, resolving not to collapse in front of him. "Not... now that you're here." What a smitten thing to say, but she couldn't retract it. "Not now that she's stopped, I mean. She's gone." Syla glanced toward the cliff, the edge a blur with her spectacles off. "She *is* gone, right?"

"She won't trouble us again tonight."

She stared at him. Did that mean Lesva *hadn't* died? That he'd seen her injured and swimming out toward her dragon? If so, that woman had a hundred lives.

Vorik lifted Syla and carried her to the mouth of the cave. He sat with his back to the stone wall, pulled her down into his lap, and wrapped his arms around her.

"Cry, if you wish," he murmured into her ear. "I'll watch the sky for you."

The gentle words broke down Syla's resolve, and she buried her face in Vorik's shoulder and wept.

32

Vorik was not, he told himself, aroused by the woman in his lap, the warmth of her body, the appealing weight of her arms around him, the feel of her face buried against the side of his neck, her lingering tears dampening his skin. She'd stopped crying, but after being tortured, horrible pain inflicted on her, she didn't need him lusting after her. As he held her, doing his best to make her feel safe, he gazed toward the roof of the cave and concentrated on *not* allowing his body to act inappropriately, especially since she wouldn't miss it, not when she was sitting on him.

It didn't help that his feelings for her intensified every time they met. He'd been horrified to hear Syla's screams, wanting to slay Lesva the instant he'd arrived, but he'd also been impressed that she'd withstood that, keeping her secrets despite the pain. That must have irritated Lesva to distraction, but it only made Vorik more certain that Syla wasn't *soft*, as Lesva had insultingly said.

He'd even arrived in time to sense... he wasn't entirely sure what he'd sensed, but Syla had been using her power to fight off Lesva's power. That wasn't a talent he'd expected from someone specialized in healing magic. Somehow, Syla had not only endured all that Lesva had inflicted upon her, but she'd managed the wherewithal and stamina to fight back. She was incredible.

The thought made him wrap his arms more tightly about her, turning his face enough to nuzzle her ear and inhale her scent. Neither of them had bathed, except in the sea, but it was intoxicating nonetheless. *She* was intoxicating. He wanted so badly to do as he'd promised when they'd last parted. To *have* her.

But now wasn't the time. Unfortunately, he didn't think there would be a time later either. After he destroyed or helped destroy the shielder, she wouldn't want anything to do with him.

Syla drew her face back from his neck—from his touch.

Again, Vorik tried to quell his horny thoughts, certain that she felt him and knew what he wanted. What his *body* wanted. His mind knew his body couldn't act on its desires.

"This wouldn't be wise," Syla whispered, her gaze remaining on the side of his neck instead of toward his face. She licked her lips, as if, despite the words, she wanted to kiss him instead of pulling away. "Not when our missions... We are on different missions."

Vorik didn't insult her by bringing up the faction, not after Lesva had confirmed all of Syla's suspicions about him. Now, she knew the details of General Jhiton's orders and why Vorik had been helping her.

Compelled to honesty, he rubbed her back and snorted softly. "This is actually rather in line with mine."

Syla shifted her gaze from his neck to his face.

He smiled sadly and stroked her cheek. "I suppose if you didn't divulge any secrets for Lesva, you won't confide them to me in the throes of passion."

She didn't pull away from his touch. If anything, she leaned into it, her eyelids lowering, as if she longed for it. For *him*.

"Kingdom secrets," she said, "aren't generally what I spout when I'm passionate and excited."

"In the temple, you cried my name."

"That shouldn't be a secret to you."

"No, I've been aware of my name almost my entire life." Vorik smiled again. "I liked hearing you use it."

She brushed her fingers along his jaw. "I would have liked it better if it had been the name of a lowly peon who'd genuinely defected from the stormer military."

His desire flared at her simple touch, and his voice turned husky when he said, "In this moment, a part of me wishes that was what I was."

He caught himself leaning closer, tempted by her touch, her inviting lips, but she wouldn't want—

No, she leaned in as well, and she kissed him, her lips as warm and appealing as the rest of her body. His arms tightened around her as he kissed her back. His lips stroked hers, his tongue tasting her. The memory of having his mouth between her *other* lips sent a flush of heat to his groin, and he sought to deepen their kiss as his hand strayed to the knot tying her robe shut.

But she leaned back, pulling her mouth from his, though she didn't try to slide out of his lap. Her delicious weight remained against his hard length, and he longed to keep her close, but she couldn't truly want this. Not after what she'd endured.

Magical torture, as he well knew, was painful. It didn't have to leave permanent damage to the body, not the way a blade or other implements did, but it *could* damage the mind. It often traumatized a person.

Vorik sensed, however, that it was more what Syla had learned —or had verified—that was the problem.

"Did you accept your orders eagerly? Excited by the idea of..." Syla lifted her hand from his shoulder to wave at herself.

"No," Vorik said.

Syla raised her eyebrows. With skepticism?

"I've enjoyed the company of women." Vorik kept himself from saying *many* women, certain that wouldn't impress her, and none of the others mattered now anyway. *This* was the woman he longed to be with tonight. "And the general, knowing that, decided on this scheme. Lesva was right, however, in one thing. You may not believe it after all this, but I do strive to be honorable with my enemies, to face them openly and fairly, without artifice."

"I... believe it."

"But I don't... I can't disobey orders. General Jhiton is not only my commanding officer, but he's my older brother and the man who raised me after our father died. I probably wouldn't have survived without his guidance and protection. There are no shields to protect my people, and our lives aren't easy."

"I gathered from your delight at blackberries growing wild by the lighthouse."

"They were so good." Vorik closed his eyes, distracted by the memory. Wouldn't a few of those be delightful right now? If they had a bowl full, they could feed them to each other, she dropping one into his mouth, and he one into hers. He would watch as she chewed slowly, then slipped her tongue out of her mouth to lick the berry juice from her lips. "That dessert you made with them was *wonderful*."

"I'll make you ten more if you leave our shielder alone."

He laughed softly, though he felt bleak, wishing... Oh, he didn't know what he wished. That they weren't at odds with each other. If she'd been a simple gardener woman, he might have talked her into returning to his home with him, in abandoning her quest. But she was the only surviving heir to the Garden Kingdom throne. She wouldn't set aside her duty for him, just as he couldn't set aside his duty for her.

"Twenty?" she offered with a sad smile.

"If only I could say yes. What a bounty that would be. And I trust you wouldn't even poison them."

"You probably *shouldn't* trust me, you know."

"I know." Vorik offered his dashing smile, though he didn't know how much she could see in the poor lighting without her spectacles. They lay to the side, carefully placed by the stone wall.

"You're amazing, Vorik," Syla whispered, her eyes locked on his face. "I wish you were really my ally. I could use an ally right now. Badly."

Yes, she could. After all she'd endured, she deserved someone standing at her side, driving off her enemies. Vorik regretted that he couldn't be that for her.

What he needed to do was shift her aside and jog up the slope of the volcano to find the aunt and the bodyguard—and the shielder. He had to fulfill his mission. He had to destroy that artifact.

Instead, he nestled Syla closer, reveling in the feel of her soft bottom against his hard body. He longed to kiss her again, to do *more* than kiss her.

Once more, she touched his jaw, her fingernails rasping against the two days' beard growth there. The light touch sent a fresh flush of heat and arousal through him. Too bad she'd pulled back from his kiss, that she didn't want to have sex with someone who couldn't be an ally.

Or did she? She leaned in and ran her tongue along his lower lip.

He froze, his cock hardening, his entire body growing taut with the desire to pull her robe off and deliver on the promise he'd given her before leaping out the tower window. Was she... Did she want...?

Maybe the shielder could wait. Rain had started, and it spattered them when the wind gusted toward the cave mouth. The weather was dreadful. Surely, even if Fel and Tibby had found the artifact, they would wait until morning to try to move it.

"I've never been with someone like you," Syla whispered, then sucked on his lip as one of her hands found his chest, fingers curling, her nails grazing his bare skin, her thumb brushing across his nipple.

He growled at the jolt of hot pleasure that rushed through him and reached for the knot on her robe again. Her touch was too much. Enemies or not, he needed her. He would have her, and she would scream his name and enjoy every steamy second of their joining. Then… then he would complete his mission.

But her hand moved to catch his. He growled again. Why was she teasing him if she didn't want him?

She shifted off his lap, and he almost surged after her, wanting to grab her and pin her to the wall, to push her robe up and thrust—

No. He clenched his fists and closed his eyes. He was honorable, damn it. Whether this mission was or not. He wouldn't take a woman who didn't want—

"Come with me," Syla whispered.

Vorik opened his eyes. What?

She stood next to him and tilted her head toward the back of the cave where two candles glowed invitingly and the ground was dry. When he met her gaze, her eyes burned with desire. She nodded, then turned, picking her way toward the back of the cave. Her hips swayed, and when she bent to maneuver around a rock, her butt pressing against the material of her robe, he almost groaned at the intensity of his need. She looked over her shoulder with her eyes still full of her desire. Her desire and an invitation.

Vorik rose to his feet, realizing her own passion was as great as his. She knew this was a bad idea, but she wanted him so much that she didn't care.

He strode toward her. Yes, the shielder could wait until morning. He wanted this. He wanted *her*.

33

SYLA'S HEART POUNDED AS SHE REACHED THE DRY AREA AT THE BACK of the cave, a spot squarely between the two candles. She turned to face Vorik, to make sure he didn't think anything odd of her inviting him into the interior and away from the rain, though, as they'd kissed, it had crossed her mind to straddle him so that he could plunge into her and satisfy her need right there.

Never would she have thought she could feel such an attraction to a man she *knew* was working against her, who was using her for his own means. For his odious *general's* means.

But Vorik genuinely wanted her. She knew that. And he would probably feel bad about leaving her after sex to go destroy her people's only means of defending themselves from dragons.

Of course, her plan was to *not* let him do that.

Halfway into the cave, Vorik paused. His fiery gaze was locked upon her, his desire radiating off him, but his nostrils twitched. He'd caught the scent of the candles.

Lesva hadn't grown suspicious of the scent until she'd yawned, but what if Vorik had encountered the sedative before? Or what if he simply found it odd that she'd grabbed such strongly scented candles to bring along?

Keeping her gaze on him—it wasn't hard as that bare chest of his made her eyes want to linger and explore—she shifted her hands to the knot at the flap of her robe, the knot he'd wanted to untie.

Right away, he noticed her movement, and his attention swung back to her. His eyes flared with such interest that she felt sexier than she ever had. But she was nervous and fumbled at the knot, her fingers flustered.

Not moving, Vorik watched. Why did the image of a predator waiting to spring come to mind? He wanted to leap upon her, to ravage her. And she wanted to be ravaged. Especially beside these candles with their heady scent.

Finally, she got the knot free, but she was slow to open the flaps and show her naked and vulnerable body to him. Lesva's words about her softness and *big boobs* flared in her mind, and she felt self-conscious. A part of her wondered why Vorik, who could have any woman, was even aroused by her.

But she made herself push the robe off her shoulders, telling herself he *was* aroused. She'd felt that sitting in his lap, and, by the light of the candles, she could see the bulge against his trousers, so swollen it was a wonder he didn't tear through the leather.

And when her robe fell to the ground and he growled and strode forward, she knew she'd read him right. He wanted her.

And he was upon her so fast, pushing her back against the stone wall and kissing her, that it startled her. But her body knew what to do. Maybe he *was* a predator and she the prey, but she'd never been so excited to be in that position in her life.

His hungry kisses aroused her, his tongue sweeping into her mouth, demanding that she open for him. And she did. Eagerly. She barely felt the hard roughness of the cold rock behind her. All she was aware of was his heat, his power. *Him.*

While they kissed, Syla gripped his shoulders, letting her hands stroke and knead his corded muscles. His own hands explored her body, roaming and cupping, as if her full curves excited him. His desire for her aroused her almost as much as his lips and his hands, and she pressed herself against him, molding her body to his.

As he kissed her, hands stroking her expertly, her core heated, slick with need. She caught herself rubbing against him, longing to have him out of those trousers so there would be nothing between them.

"Take them off," he whispered between kisses, as if he'd read her thoughts. More likely, he read her pushing into him, wanting to feel him more fully. His fingers brushed through her hair, his touch on her scalp sending another flood of heat through her. "Take them off *now*," he ordered with a needy growl.

The words made her tingle with excitement, the desire to obey, and she scraped her hands down his chest toward his waistband.

"I want you to touch me," he added, more softly, as if apologizing for his insistent command.

She kissed him as she unfastened the clasp of his trousers. She wanted to touch him too.

"I've wanted your hand around my cock since you rode on my dragon with me," he added, the admission coming between kisses as his mouth left hers to nip and lick at her throat.

Her nipples tightened with pleasure as his lips drew nearer, and she almost forgot her mission with his trousers. But she got the clasp unfastened. Before she could shift the trousers off his hips, his cock freed itself, as if it had a mind and desires of its own. Thick and hard, it thrust itself into her hand, and Vorik growled with lust and maybe triumph.

"I've wanted you too," she whispered.

"Since the dragon ride?" He moved against her hand while he stroked her breast, not forgetting to attend her.

She found having him in her grip arousing all by itself. Never before had a man's penis interested her overmuch, certainly not drawing her to stare and consider it magnificent, but this was different. *He* was different. The taut musculature of his body and the magical power that he emanated drew her like nothing ever had before.

"Since you thanked me in the temple," she whispered, though that wasn't the truth. That dragon ride had interested her far more than she should have let it.

"I think you're lying to me, Princess."

"It's... what we're supposed to do, isn't it?"

As the inane words tumbled out, she kept looking at him, her hand around him, stroking him. Eyes half-closed, he rocked in response to her ministrations. To have the power to affect someone who was himself so powerful was a wonder.

She caught herself lowering to her knees and touching her cheek to his erection, then daring to slide her tongue along his thick length.

Vorik groaned and thrust toward her, such eagerness and desire in his voice that it excited her further. Her needy core throbbed, making her long to climb him and let him thrust into her, but she didn't give in, not yet. She reminded herself that she wanted their time together to last, though she couldn't quite remember why. She was too distracted by him, by his naked pleasure at her touch.

She slid her mouth around his tip, drawing him into her. He groaned again, thigh muscles quivering as he fought the urge to plunge deeply into her, to risk hurting her.

Enjoying his taste and his scent, as intoxicating as the candles, she curled her fingers around his ass and took him deeper. He gripped the back of her head, fingers rubbing and scraping through her hair as he barely resisted pulling her hard against him. Instead, his ministrations inflamed her, and she took him eagerly, again struggling against the urge to maneuver to have him between her legs. She was so hot and ready for him.

Maybe he knew that because he caught her under the arms, lifting her to press her against the cave wall, to pin her like a captive. He kissed her hard as one of his hands swept past her breast, raising fire as his fingers trailed lower, then slid into her.

She gasped, bucking at the intense sensation, and clenched around him.

"You're as ready as I am, Princess," he whispered, his eyes satisfied as he rubbed her. "*Syla*."

Her name on his lips aroused her even more. They were enemies, but he cared enough to use it, to respect her with it.

She moaned, almost painfully aroused, his touches blasting her with pleasure. She couldn't find words to respond, only nodding and wanting him to continue.

He'd taken over control, stroking her molten core as he kept her against the wall, kissing her with need that matched hers, pausing only to add, "Since the dragon."

He watched her, waiting for a response as his fingers brought her to such exquisite heights that she almost cried out his name, begging for him to take her fully. Never had she needed anyone—*anything*—so badly.

"Since the dragon," she panted, writhing against him, gripping his shoulder with one hand and finding his hard length with the other. "Take me, Vorik."

"Oh, I will." With satisfaction and lust turning his eyes fiery, Vorik lifted her leg to hook over his hip and drove into her.

He roared, letting her know the intense satisfaction as he gave in to what he'd wanted since their first ride. As he filled her, she yelled his name to the storm, to whatever gods watched. Fingers digging into his shoulders, she was as eager as he for the next thrust, accepting all of him as he plunged deep. Panting and kissing, they fenced with their mouths as they rocked together, each deep plunge more satisfying than the last, each bringing them closer to the ultimate ecstasy.

With the sea smashing against the rocks outside and thunder rumbling, they cried out for each other. Again and again, they came together, sweat gleaming on their bodies, their pants and groans of need filling the air. Growing more and more desperate for a climax, Syla felt more frenzied and out of control than she'd ever been in her life. And she felt more alive.

Thunder crashed one more time, and her pleasure exploded like solstice fireworks. She clung to him, thrusting her breasts toward him, as waves of intense satisfaction swept over her.

His eyes fastened on her chest, on the trembling pleasure of her aftermath, and with a final great plunge, Vorik came. With his roar as he poured himself into her, she believed that he'd wanted her as badly as he'd claimed. For as long as he'd claimed. And when he lowered to the ground, taking her with him and cuddling her close, she believed he regretted that they were on different sides.

Syla wished this were purely about enjoyment, but as he kissed her and stroked her gently, she couldn't help but glance at the candles. They'd burned halfway down, and their scent filled the back of the cave, but nothing during their sex had suggested Vorik felt any sluggishness. She almost laughed at the thought. He'd been *anything* but that. Images of powerful predators came to mind again. Of dragons.

She kissed him and trailed her fingers down his taut abdomen, wondering how she might keep him occupied for another hour or however long it would take for the candles to kick in. *If* they kicked in. Earlier, she'd worried if his dragon-bond would keep him from being affected. But Lesva had been starting to yawn. Maybe it would simply take longer to work on someone with such magic?

Vorik nuzzled her gently, shifting her in his arms so that they were snuggled with her back to his chest, cupped to him. She would have loved to spend the night like that with him but expected him to remember his mission any time and leap to his feet and run out. How could she keep him here?

He surprised her by shifting her hair aside, kissing the back of her neck, and taking one of her breasts in his hand. Her body responded instantly, nipple tightening in anticipation, as if there might be more.

"You were magnificent," he murmured, his thumb brushing her sensitive skin. "And deserve more than I gave."

"What you gave was, uhm..." The most intense pleasure she'd ever received. "Good."

"Good." He snorted softly, then kissed her neck again. "After the days you've had, I wish I could give you pleasure that would last you the rest of your life."

Did his voice sound slightly muzzy? Sleepy?

His fingers traced her breast, almost lazy in their movement though they stimulated her, and her nerves perked, wondering if there might be more tonight.

"I wish I could give you a berry cobbler every day for the rest of your life," she said. "We make them out of apples, cherries, and peaches, too, you know."

"I love apples," he murmured, eyes closed.

His fingers slid lower, brushing between her legs, but they merely came to rest there. That was a little disappointing, but Syla reminded herself that she wanted him to fall asleep. To fall into a deep unconscious state that would last for hours.

"And the drink your people make from them," he added. "Cider?"

"We make all kinds of drinks, alcoholic and not. Juice, cider, brandy, applejack, and one of my relatives does an apple liqueur that he mixes with syrup to pour over ice cream."

"What is... ice cream?" Eyes still closed, Vorik yawned and rested his stubbled jaw against her bare shoulder.

"It's made from cow's milk and cream, sugar from beets, and various flavorings like strawberries and blueberries." What a thing to discuss during a seduction, or in the aftermath of a seduction. Were enemy agents supposed to be interested in fruits and desserts?

"You get hunks of rock ice from the ice man, put them around a special mixing barrel, then whip together the ingredients inside, and the ice chills the mixture. Then you either have to eat it all right away, while it's frozen, or store it in an icehouse. When we were kids, it was always a special treat to have ice cream in the summer."

Vorik's breathing was even.

Syla watched his face, trying to tell if he'd nodded off.

"I think you'd like ice cream, Vorik," she murmured.

He didn't react to the comment, and she carefully—and with reluctance—removed his hand from her thigh and eased out of his embrace. His eyes remained closed, his breathing even.

The candles burned cheerfully, each with about one-third of its length remaining. They ought to continue to exude their sedative scent for a couple more hours, maybe longer. She *hoped* longer. Once Vorik woke up, he would realize what she'd done, that she'd thanked him for coming to help her by seducing *him*.

It had been for the good of the Kingdom, she told herself, and hoped he wouldn't hate her later. At the least, she thought he might not *blame* her, but she didn't know. The thought of him deciding she was a true enemy, one to be targeted and captured instead of protected, saddened her deeply, but she had no choice.

Careful to be quiet, even though she knew his slumber was deeper than normal sleep, Syla hurried to put on her robe, shoes, spectacles, and grab her pack and head out into the night.

34

THE RAIN STOPPED AND DAWN CREPT OVER THE LAVA-ROCK TERRAIN as Syla navigated higher on the slope of the volcano, the pack she'd dragged all over the island heavy on her shoulders. There wasn't a trail, and she kept stubbing her toes and banging her knees. Though Lesva's magical torment hadn't been as debilitating as physical torture would have been, she could feel the aftereffects bogging down her movements. Making her slower and wearier than she wanted.

Aware of the minutes passing—the candles burning ever lower as Vorik slept—she sighed in vast relief when she spotted the cave she'd visited years before, the one that led to the shielder.

She hurried toward it, hoping Fel and Tibby were safe within and had gained access to the artifact chamber. But she couldn't help but worry that they were dead, that Vorik might have found them before he'd come to her. It hadn't sounded like he'd yet located the shielder, so she hoped that wasn't the case. But everything might have been a lie. The artifact might already have been destroyed.

No. Syla glanced upward. Though she couldn't sense the

magic of the barrier unless she was right next to it, the lack of dragons in the sky suggested that it remained up.

She scrambled through the tunnel, down an old rockslide, and into a lava tube. At the end, a door within a stone wall was swung inward, and silver light flowed out. She sensed magic in that direction as well, mingling with the illumination.

That had to be from the shielder, its protective door opened by Tibby's moon-mark.

Syla ran, needing to verify that she was correct and that her allies were both alive.

When she peeked through the wide doorway, the glowing orb and the intricate mounting surrounding it were the first things she saw. Then she noticed her aunt among a scattering of old parchment scrolls—where had those come from? Tibby was using a wrench-like tool to unfasten the orb from the mounting system while Fel stood guard behind her. He spun toward the doorway and lifted his mace but lowered it again.

"Your Highness!" Such an expression of genuine delight came across his face that it warmed Syla's heart.

"Sergeant Fel." She smiled, relieved to see them alive and well. "Aunt Tibby. I'm glad you're both all right. I worried... Well, that Captain Lesva captured me, and I've been worried she, uhm, they might have gotten to you before finding me."

"The horrible woman who tried to kill us with her dragon?" Tibby asked.

"Her dragon, her troops' dragons, her sword... All in all, she's had it out for me."

"I dare say so. You... escaped?" Tibby knelt back and looked her up and down.

"I..." Syla thought about mentioning how she'd learned to use her power for something besides healing, but being able to threaten to stop a man's heart was nothing to be proud of. Besides, there wasn't time to explain everything. In the end, her power hadn't been what stopped Lesva anyway. "Vorik found me and knocked her off a cliff."

Technically, lightning had destroyed that section of the cliff, but he'd been the one to drive Lesva back to the edge.

Fel groaned instead of cheering and looked toward the lava tube. "Is he with you?"

He hefted his mace again and bared his teeth.

"No. I left him unconscious in a cave near that cliff, breathing in the vapors of two Candles of Serenity."

Tibby's forehead furrowed, but during the various surgeries Fel had endured over the years, he must have learned about the candles because he looked enlightened rather than puzzled.

"Good idea," he said. "Smart of you to bring some from the temple."

"Thank you." Syla hoped he wouldn't think to ask how she'd managed to convince Vorik to loiter in the back of a cave long enough for the vapors to affect him.

"But why is that rider *unconscious*? Why didn't you cut his throat while he was out?" Fel made a slashing motion across his own throat.

"I didn't have a knife."

True, but they both knew she wouldn't have done it anyway.

Fel looked at her in exasperation.

"You could have rolled his body off the cliff." Tibby knelt forward, returning to her task.

"He's heavy, and I'm not that strong."

She scowled. "*I* would have found a way."

"That's because you're a clever engineer and know how to build a travois out of kelp and driftwood."

Tibby lifted her chin. "Yes. And we may need another travois to haul this across the rocks and to the cove." She glanced at Fel. "You said it's a couple of miles from here?"

"The spot where I fired the flare? Yes. There's a cliff there, too, but in that spot, it's only twenty or thirty feet down to the water. Assuming your friend is watching and shows up with a ship, we ought to be able to lower the shielder down to it."

"Do you need help? We'll have to do that all quickly." Syla waved to the great artifact, wondering if the three of them together would be able to lift it out of the cave and carry it two miles. Her aunt might need to build *more* than a travois. "We'll only have a few hours before the candles burn out, and Vorik wakes up. And... I think he knows where this place is."

"I thought I sensed someone watching us last night." Fel shook his head.

"Whether he knows where we are or not, he can hunt us down," Tibby said. "He'll *especially* be able to hunt us down once the barrier drops, and his dragon can help him."

"Yes." Syla shrugged.

She'd known she was only buying them a few hours. Hopefully, it would be enough. It *had* to be enough. The idea of doing all this and losing the shielder in the end and leaving both islands unprotected... It would be as bad a betrayal as the one her sister had inadvertently made.

"I don't suppose you would like to tell me where Vorik is." Fel drew a dagger sheathed on his belt and held it up, turning the blade as if Syla had wanted to examine it. "I keep my weapons very keen. He wouldn't feel a thing."

"No."

"It's for the good of the Kingdom."

"No." Syla waved at the shielder again. "We'll just have to do this quickly."

"Your niece is stubborn," Fel told Tibby.

"That runs in the family, yes." Tibby pushed one of the scrolls toward Syla. "Here. The schematics I was hoping to find were here. As well as magical tools. There must have been a kit left with every shielder, but some ancestor of ours probably moved them into a special spot in the castle and forgot about them. Look at the schematics, and grab a tool from that kit over there. The shielder wouldn't let Fel touch it while its activated, but you should be able to help. Apparently, the artifacts trust that we—" Tibby waved her moon-marked hand, "—aren't a threat and will do the right thing."

The significant look that Tibby gave to Syla suggested that *she* was less certain they were doing the right thing.

Unfortunately, Syla wasn't certain either, but she knelt to help. They didn't have much time.

The great and powerful, created-by-the-gods-themselves orb that was the shielder... rolled.

Syla almost laughed as, after having heaved and levered the artifact out of the lava tube and the cave above, they were able to push the heavy sphere across the ground. At first, she worried about scratches or even breaking it, but Tibby, who was alternating pushing and waving her newly-discovered scrolls and tools, assured her that it was very sturdy. Had the rider who'd infiltrated the chamber under the castle not had a magical gargoyle-bone blade, he likely wouldn't have been able to cut into the shielder there and destroy its parts.

Despite its rollability, the orb still weighed more than two hundred pounds, and there was nothing like a road or even a path on this side of the volcano. Pushing it along wasn't easy, but it *was* doable. If slow. Syla couldn't help but glance at the sun creeping higher in the sky as they navigated toward a cove Fel had visited earlier.

"Maybe you should run ahead and see if a ship has arrived," Syla suggested to him, feeling the weight of time.

Any minute, those candles would burn out, and Vorik would wake soon after. Few trees grew out of the rocky landscape, so there was little to no cover. A man might have found a spot to crouch down and hide, but the orb was taller than any of them, and, even though its silver glow had ceased when they'd removed it from the mountain, it gleamed, its sides iridescent and strikingly beautiful in the morning sun.

"Are *you two* going to push this thing without me?" Fel grunted, straining to shove the orb past a rock, bags under his eyes promising he needed sleep. They all did. "*She* can't even push for more than a minute without stopping to push her spectacles up or look at a scroll."

"I'm not stopping *that* often," Tibby said with a shove of her own, "and it's not my fault that my nose is sweating, which causes my spectacles to slip. I lost my strap for keeping them in place."

"And the scrolls?" Fel asked.

The orb scraped past the rock and rolled more freely for a few steps.

"They contain information and the schematics for the shielders, for devices made by the *gods*." Tibby touched one of the scrolls tucked into a rope she'd tied around her waist like a belt. Her trousers had been torn at some point and were half falling off. Everyone in their little group was bedraggled and in need of sartorial care as well as medical treatment. "While we do all this shoving, I'm thinking, wondering if the schematics might be used to repair the shielder in the capital. With this one to look at, as well, maybe it'll be possible, and we can return protection to both islands."

Fel's grunt suggested he didn't accept that as a suitable excuse for not pushing.

Beside him, Syla threw her weight against the orb as assiduously as he. Perhaps more than the others, she was well aware of how close they were to disaster. If they didn't get this onto a ship soon...

Except that wouldn't be the end of it. Even if a sturdy cargo vessel waited for them, they would still have to sail for hours to reach the harbor on Castle Island. The memory of the dragons flying over the sea between the islands and attacking them came to mind. Even if they avoided Vorik, how, by the eyes of the moon, would they get past loitering dragons?

"Trouble coming." Tibby, who'd been adjusting her spectacles again, pointed to the north.

A powerful blue dragon was flying in their direction.

Syla swore. "How far are we from the cove?"

"Another mile," Fel said.

The dragon, its great wings flapping hard, was flying fast. They would never reach the cove before the creature arrived.

"We have to hide this." Syla looked around bleakly.

Other than a stunted tree no taller than she, there was nowhere to hide anything, certainly not an orb eight feet in diameter. Thanks to its dormancy, it didn't exude magical energy, the way it had when she first walked into the chamber, but with that beautiful iridescent exterior, the dragon wouldn't miss seeing it. Nobody within three miles would.

"Where?" Fel kept pushing, but he looked at the oncoming dragon.

Good question.

Syla removed her robe and tossed it over the top of the orb. She ran around it, tugging the material to hide as much as she could, but, as large as the loose healer's robe was, it only covered the top of the big orb.

Fel stared at her making adjustments as if she were daft. The dragon flew closer.

"Maybe if we lean casually on it, as if it's an interesting rock formation," Syla suggested and did so, resting her shoulder on the orb. She crossed her arms over her breasts, feeling foolish for standing naked in her shoes.

A dragon probably didn't think anything of human clothing,

but what about its rider? She imagined Lesva staring condescendingly down at her.

"Lean casually," Fel grumbled, then stepped out in front of the orb with his mace in hand and glowered defiantly at the dragon.

"You're a brute," Tibby told him. "Weapons can't solve all problems. They can't even solve *most* problems."

"You're still angry because I beat up your nefarious tractor, aren't you?" Fel asked without taking his gaze from the dragon.

Blue scales gleaming strikingly in the sun, it had reached the shoreline and kept flying in their direction. It didn't have a rider, but that didn't mean it wasn't allied with the stormers. Even if it was a wild dragon, like Wreylith, it would probably pluck up the orb and maybe even destroy it. All the dragons wanted access to these islands, the same as the stormers.

"I'm perturbed about that, yes." Tibby joined Syla in casual leaning, trying to use her body to cover up another portion of the orb.

The dragon looked down at them, slitted yellow eyes cold and intense. A chill went through Syla as she feared defeat had already found them.

But the dragon didn't slow down as it flew over them. After that look—that dismissive look?—its gaze returned to its route ahead. Further, the dragon shared a telepathic vision, that of a furry gray animal the size of a horse but with an elephant's trunk that snuffled at mushrooms on the forest floor. That was an eliok, wasn't it? In the vision, the dragon was swooping down between the trees to obtain the creature.

A gleeful thought accompanied the imagery: *Delicious prey!*

"Did you hear that?" Tibby wondered.

"Yes." Syla looked toward the sea. "But I don't think the message was for us."

The dragon might have been calling to others of its kind, inviting them to join the hunt.

"If that one sensed the barrier is down, others will too, and they'll be here soon." Fel hung his mace on his belt and pulled down the robe, handing it to Syla. "We need to get out of here before one working with the stormers shows up and knows the significance of this giant orb."

They returned to pushing, Fel alternately grunting and directing them. He pointed toward the cove they were angling for, the lava-rock field sloping downward around it. They would have to be careful not to let the orb start rolling of its own accord. A vision of trying to pluck it out of the ocean came to Syla's mind.

"I forgot to ask earlier," Fel said, glancing at Syla and scanning the area around the cove, "what happened to the enforcers? Are they still out here? Do we have to worry about them jumping out at us?"

"Oh. Yes." Tibby blinked and looked at Syla. "How did you get away from them?"

The urgency of their mission must have made them forget the circumstances under which they'd parted ways. Neither had asked how she'd come to be with Vorik.

"I'll explain later." Syla grimaced, spotting another dragon on the horizon. "But they're not a threat, no. Not that particular group anyway."

Grim, she remembered the ambitious sergeant and all the other men that Captain Lesva had slain. It worried her that Vorik had implied his colleague had survived that fall and that she might return to be a problem for Syla. She had enough problems to worry about.

"All right." Fel pointed. "That's where I lit the flare."

"I'll check." Tibby ran ahead, reaching the cove first.

As Syla and Fel pushed, sweat dribbling down her spine, she kept an eye on the new dragon. It was green, but she didn't think it was Agrevlari. Still, Vorik's dragon had to be around somewhere. And once Vorik woke up and communicated with him, they would reunite and come after the shielder. It was his mission. He had to.

"They're here!" Tibby blurted with relief, waving at someone in the cove below.

Thanks to gravity, the orb rolled more easily the last hundred yards. Fel ran around it, shoving his back against it to stop it a few feet from the edge of a cliff. It was, as he'd said, not as high as the others they'd encountered on the island, but Syla still wouldn't want to fall off it.

She dragged her sleeve over her sweaty forehead and joined her aunt on a precipice overlooking the cove. Tibby gripped her shoulder and pointed downward.

There were not one but five ships down there. The largest wasn't the cargo vessel that Syla had imagined, with a hold that might have contained the shielder and hidden it from view, but a whaling ship with harpoon launchers on each end. The four smaller craft accompanying it were armored guard ships, their rails lined with cannons. Such vessels usually accompanied cargo ships on journeys between the islands. They would have holds, but they would be filled with ammunition.

"A whaling ship isn't what I imagined," Tibby said, "but that we got anything at all is a wonder. I'm going to give Sherrik a kiss when I see him next."

"Will you be able to keep from looking at your scroll long enough to manage that?" Fel asked.

"By employing suitable self-restraint, yes." Tibby gestured to a gray-haired man who came out of the wheelhouse of the whaling ship and waved to her.

"Is that your engineering friend?" Syla asked.

"No. I doubt Sherrik came along. I presume that's the captain of the whaling ship, the one we'll have to pay for transporting us." Tibby pointed for the man to bring the vessel closer to the cliff. "I don't see anything like a crane for lifting. We may have to push the orb over the edge and into the water. It should be sturdy enough to survive that, though the thought of treating it so makes me ill. I fear we don't have time for a more elaborate solution."

"I agree." Syla spotted a gray dragon joining the green one flying over the sea. And did they have riders? Her vision was too blurry at that distance to be certain, but she feared so. "But it can't go on the big ship."

"What?" Tibby looked at her.

Syla pointed at the whaling vessel. "That's going to have to be the decoy ship." She shifted her finger to one of the guard vessels. "*That's* going to take the shielder home in its hold."

"The hold will be full of cannonballs and powder," Fel said.

"They can move the ammunition out or over to make room. The shielder can't sit out on the deck where every dragon and rider in the sky can see it."

"I don't think—"

"This is our only chance," Syla said firmly. "You and I will go on the decoy ship and try to lure all the stormer dragons after us while Aunt Tibby and the shielder go the long way around Castle Island and slip into the harbor, hopefully unnoticed by our enemies. She'll get it installed and restore protection to our homeland. And we... We'll keep the dragons busy so they don't think to check out that ship."

Fel looked at her. "That's a suicide mission."

"I know. I'm sure you're again regretting that you feel urges to obey my wishes." Syla thought about telling Fel to go with her aunt again, but Vorik would be suspicious if her bodyguard wasn't by her side. Besides, they would need every fighter who was capable of defending the whaling ship. They had to survive long enough for the real transport vessel to escape.

Fel waved away the comment with a chopping motion. "*I'll* go on that ship if it's to face off against dragons. You should stick with your aunt. Get yourself and the shielder back home."

"I can't," Syla said. "Vorik will be looking for me. If I'm not on the whaling ship, he'll know it's a decoy."

"He's not out there among those men." Fel pointed toward the horizon, his less myopic eyes identifying for certain that the dragons carried riders.

"Not yet, but he will be. He's their commander."

"*Vorik.*" Fel spat the name like a curse. "You should have let me cut his throat last night."

"I know," Syla said sadly but couldn't regret the choice.

35

Are you going to snore the whole day away, Vorik? Agrevlari's telepathic voice floated into his sleep-heavy mind.

Vorik groped for the wherewithal to respond—and to open his eyes. A deep, foggy blanket enshrouded him, and he struggled to wake up.

Are you unaware that the barrier around this island has dropped? Agrevlari added. *I assumed you had been responsible until I found you slumbering in this cave.*

Mouth and nostrils oddly dry—no, *parched*—Vorik finally managed to open his eyes. He patted around, remembering that Syla had been with him. Yes, *with* him. In every sense of the word. The memory made him smile, recalling that they'd had wondrous sex, and then he'd dozed off fantasizing about apple desserts she'd mentioned. But his smile vanished when he realized she wasn't there. He lay naked in the back of the cave. Alone.

You've been out for hours, Agrevlari said from somewhere nearby. Was he perched right on top of the cave? *And unresponsive to my attempts to wake you, though it was only in the last hour that the barrier created by the shielder disappeared and I was able to fly close to you. I considered going to hunt on the island, as I've already seen a couple of my kind arrowing in to take advantage of the now-exposed succulent prey, but there are enemies about, and I figured I should protect you. You are most welcome, by the way.*

Thank you. Vorik sat up, trying to figure out what had happened.

His trousers, boots, and sword remained where he'd dropped them, but all trace of Syla was gone. All trace except...

His gaze fell on one of the candles that had been burning when she'd enticed him into the back of the cave. The wicks had been fully consumed, only tiny amounts of wax remaining.

He grabbed a nub and lifted it to his nose. That scent they'd emitted. He remembered it well, though he'd thought little of it the night before. Many candles smelled, after all. His own people often put citronella oil in theirs to keep away mosquitoes carrying disease. But this... Something told him this was different. He never slept so heavily. Like the rest of his people, he never relaxed fully and was always on the edge of awareness, alert to the many dangers that lurked in the world. Had his slumber been normal, he would have heard Syla dressing and leaving.

"She drugged me," Vorik said, his emotions a jumble.

He felt more chagrined that he'd fallen for it than that she'd done it. He didn't blame her for that. They were enemies, after all, and he'd been lying to her and trying to trick her all along. Because of his orders. His mission.

Reminded of that mission, Vorik lurched to his feet and grabbed his trousers. Only now did the ramifications of Agrevlari's words sink in.

"The barrier is down?" He sensed the dragon right above him.

It is indeed.

"That means she got the shielder and deactivated it. She must right now be toting it toward the harbor so it can be taken on a ship to their island." Vorik paused, one foot in a boot. "But do they have a carriage? Or did they walk all the way from the temple on foot?"

When he'd come across Fel and Tibby, he hadn't seen any signs of horses or a means of transporting a large artifact.

You walked to this locale on foot.

"Yeah, but I didn't plan to carry a huge artifact back across the island with me." All he'd meant to do was *destroy* the thing. "Those things must weigh hundreds of pounds."

A small load for one of my kind.

"I'm positive Syla doesn't intend to give it to a *dragon*."

No, her plan was to take it back to Castle Island. She needed to find a ship.

After dressing, Vorik jogged for the entrance.

"If they're trekking all the way to the harbor, we can easily catch them." Outside, he turned, looking above the cave toward the green dragon perched on the rocks, using a talon to pick something out of his fangs. The remains of his breakfast? Maybe Agrevlari hadn't been as assiduous about standing guard as he'd implied. "*Especially* if I'm riding you."

A dragon most certainly makes a journey easier.

"Especially one with clean teeth."

It's important to care for your gums, lest you get fang rot.

"I've heard that." Vorik climbed the rocks and onto Agrevlari's back. He patted the dragon, relieved to be reunited with him. "Did you see if Lesva made it?"

She was grievously injured during your battle, but she managed to swim beyond the barrier, and Verikloth plucked her up.

"I see." Vorik didn't want Lesva dead, but he also winced at the thought of having to speak with and work with her after their duel.

They said they were returning to headquarters and would report everything—emphasis on everything*—to General Jhiton.*

Vorik winced again. Since Lesva had been disobeying orders,

he hadn't been wrong to stop her, but... if he didn't find and destroy the shielder before Syla activated it on Castle Island, Jhiton wouldn't be pleased with him. Lesva might succeed in casting blame on him for his... soft attitude toward Syla.

And would she be wrong?

"Let's go, my friend." Vorik patted Agrevlari again. "We need to find the shielder."

Agrevlari bunched his muscles, prepared to spring into the air, but he paused, his snout pointing out to sea. *Wreylith has returned to the area.*

"She may have sensed that the barrier is down and come to hunt here."

Perhaps she missed my wit and has returned to allow me to court her.

"I doubt it."

Your skepticism wounds me. Can you not support me in my mating endeavors, as I have supported you?

"I didn't realize you were supporting me."

Neither time when you fornicated with the princess did I interfere or comment on the techniques used in the seduction or accomplishment of the mission. I believed you would perform better if I did not intrude upon your concentration.

"Yes, I appreciate the lack of commentary, but we weren't fornicating. At least not the first time." Trying to urge the dragon to stay on task, Vorik pointed toward the slope of the volcano, in the direction he'd last seen Fel and Tibby.

Stimulation of a sex orifice was involved.

Vorik rolled his eyes, but Agrevlari was springing into the air, so he didn't complain, other than to say, "I didn't know you could see so much from way out on the rock."

A single dragon eyeball rolled back toward him as Agrevlari flew up the slope. *Through my link with you, I see much.*

"I'm sure Syla would be flattered to learn she had an audience.

Come, my friend. Let us find the shielder and complete our mission. *Then* I'll support you in your courting endeavors."

Excellent.

Agrevlari flew faster.

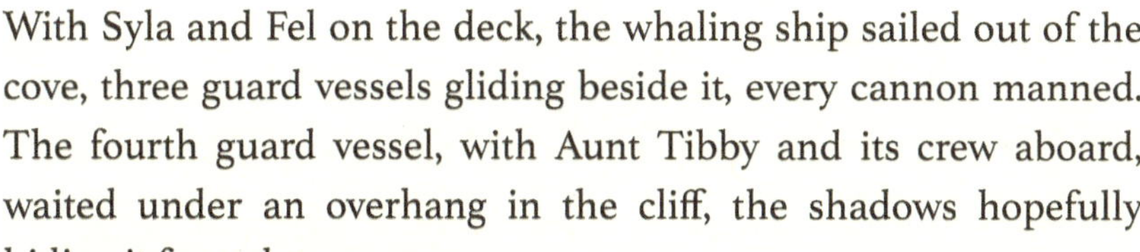

With Syla and Fel on the deck, the whaling ship sailed out of the cove, three guard vessels gliding beside it, every cannon manned. The fourth guard vessel, with Aunt Tibby and its crew aboard, waited under an overhang in the cliff, the shadows hopefully hiding it from dragon eyes.

While they'd prepared, another of the great creatures had flown over the area, but no rider had sat astride its back. It, like the first, had headed inland. It hadn't even glanced down at the cove, which was fortunate, since the orb had been bobbing in the water then, halfway to being loaded onto the guard ship.

They'd been lucky that the dragons with the riders remained a couple of miles out to sea, almost as if the barrier remained in place, keeping them back. By now, they had to be aware it was down, so Syla didn't know why they hadn't approached. Were they waiting for more allies to arrive? Or for Vorik to join them and take command? Had he woken up? By now, the candles must have burned out.

A fake orb, which was nothing more than crates of provisions and cannonballs that the crew had hurried to unload from the cargo hold of one of the guard ships, was tied under a canvas tarp near the harpoon launchers at the back of the deck. With the help of a few crewmen, Syla and Fel had done their best to pad and shift the crates so that the pile appeared rounded, like the orb.

Of the riders and dragons out there, it was likely that only Vorik had seen the other shielder and knew what one looked like.

Syla hoped that even he didn't realize that the orb could be removed from its mounting and only it would be transported.

Once the whaling ship sailed out of the cove, the dragons were more visible. They flew back and forth, doing the aerial equivalent of pacing. It appeared that they, or perhaps their riders, were discussing something. Or, as she'd been thinking, waiting on someone.

Her hand strayed to a pocket in her robe, to the figurine she'd managed to retain through all the chaos of the last few days. Unfortunately, she doubted Wreylith was around. Even if she was, why would the red dragon come to help Syla? Unless she had endured another run-in with a basilisk, she had no reason to do so. Still, Syla mulled over ideas in her mind, seeking something she could offer Wreylith to entice her to assist her one more time.

The captain of the whaling vessel, a fit man in his fifties, left the wheelhouse and joined her on deck. He eyed her, the canvas-covered pile, then her again. Something that looked like a piece of cane or a thick stalk stuck out of the corner of his mouth, and he chewed on it while he did the eyeing.

"Thank you for taking us onboard, Captain..." Syla realized she didn't know his name since Aunt Tibby and her engineer friend had arranged all this. Had they warned him that he might die on this voyage? That they *all* might?

"Radmarik." He surprised her by bowing to her. From the way he'd been eyeing her—and what he'd caught of her plan—he'd looked like he wanted to punch her. Or maybe strangle her. "My wife promises me I'm honored to serve you."

"Your, ah, wife?" Syla looked at Fel, who stood a few feet away, as if he might know what to make of the comment.

But he was staring bleak-faced at the dragons while flexing and loosening his grip on his mace. He didn't return her look.

"Well, she's more of a girlfriend, I suppose you might say, but we've a mutual intent to be married if the laws ever allow."

"Why wouldn't they?"

"She's not from *around* here." His big wave seemed to encompass the entire island. Or… the Kingdom as a whole? "If you catch my meaning."

"Is she a stormer?" Syla asked quietly in case the crew didn't know or wouldn't approve.

"Something like that." Radmarik smiled, shifted the cane to the other side of his mouth, and gazed contemplatively at the dragons. "I figured this would be dangerous when I agreed to it, but I didn't quite realize… I might not see her again."

Syla didn't know how to answer that even though she'd just been thinking something similar.

"We had good sex yesterday anyway before I sailed off. Real good. It always is." Radmarik smiled again. "She's quite athletic, as you might imagine."

Syla's mouth drooped open. This was not the direction she'd expected this conversation to go.

He eyed her again. "I suppose it's not appropriate to discuss such things with princesses."

"It's… not a subject that comes up often within my earshot."

"Because of your royalness? Or because you're a healer, and the people around you are too ailed to have sex on their minds?"

"Some of both, I suppose. If I may ask, Captain, how much did Aunt Tibby's engineer friend—Sherrik, right?—say I would pay you when we reach Castle Island?"

"Funny thing about that. Sherrik went from captain to captain, trying to hire a cargo ship or, in the end, any ship with a willing crew, able to take on a mission for the good of the Kingdom. But he was rather elusive about what the mission was. Finally, he started telling people it was to help Princess Syla Moonmark save the Kingdom from dragons."

"And that moved you?"

"Nope. It didn't move any of the captains he was trying to finagle with promise of payment later from the royal coffers."

Syla raised her eyebrows. Since the captain was here, *something* had finagled him.

"I thought one or two might have been willing to sign on as it's always good to curry favor with the royals, however young and far removed from the throne they are." Radmarik spat out a piece of cane that he'd chewed off.

"I'm not that young. I've been a healer for almost ten years." She couldn't deny that she'd always been removed from the day-to-day running of the Kingdom though.

"Good to curry favor with healers too. You never know when —" He made a stabbing and twisting motion with his cane.

"Quite." Syla eyed the macerated end, then returned to watching the dragons.

Maybe they hadn't yet attacked because they were waiting for the ships to clear the cliffs and be easier targets. But she couldn't imagine dragons having any trouble navigating among rock formations.

"My wife was the one who suggested I help you. Sugar cane?" Radmarik offered her the unappealing stick, the macerated end wet with his spittle.

"No, thank you."

"My wife brings me some when she comes through. It's gathered from the Lagobar Swamps where gargoyles are more prolific than squirrels. It's a training ground for young stormer warriors, especially those who hope to earn the interest of a dragon and become a rider. The sugar cane is a prize, and you've usually got to battle a few fang bats, swamp vipers, and the gargoyles themselves to acquire them. Fortunately, my wife doesn't mind a challenge." Radmarik grinned. "She endures being mated to me, after all. I can't imagine that's easy, but maybe I'm sexier than you'd think at first glance. When I attempted to woo her, she tolerated it. It only took me fifty or sixty encounters to convince her of the appeal of my bunk."

With her gaze on the dragons, Syla only half-listened to the story as she raised a hand to decline the offering. "It looks like a stick."

"Yup, that's right. Real fibrous but sweet. It's one of the few treats that grow wild out there in the inhospitable climes of the world beyond the shields."

She glanced at it, thinking of Vorik's love for fruit and cobbler. Berries growing untended had seemed so amazing to him. Maybe the—what was it?—sugar cane was the best the wilds of the rest of the world could offer.

"So your wife *is* a stormer." Syla wondered why such a person had recommended helping her. If anything, the wife should have wanted her to fail.

"An outcast, yes. She used to be a rider and bonded to a dragon." Radmarik lowered his voice. "She's one of the leaders of the Freeborn Faction now."

Syla rocked back. It wasn't that she hadn't believed that the faction existed, but after Vorik had tried so many times to claim to be allied with it, she'd stopped thinking it would come into play at any point in her journey—or her life.

"Does she... do they... want to see the Kingdom continue?" Syla asked. "With its shielders left intact?"

"From what I gather, the faction doesn't have any love for you or the current—or is it former?—regime, but they do believe it would be best if the islands remained as protected sanctuaries from dragons and other deadly predators. The rest of the world is a harsh place. What they're fighting for is for *all* humans to have access to the islands. My wife did suggest that, if you live, you might be more amenable to negotiations in favor of the faction than your predecessors were. Presumably, as a healer, you've a gentle soul." Radmarik raised his eyebrows. Asking if that was true?

The memory of Sergeant Tunnok clutching his heart sprang to Syla's mind, and she felt like she'd betrayed her profession. But that had been an extenuating circumstance, surely. Dealing with Captain Lesva too. She *was* a healer, and would help any human, Kingdom subject or stormer tribe member, as long as the person wasn't trying to kill her. Or destroy all that she loved.

Realizing Radmarik was watching her intently, as if her answer mattered, Syla nodded. She was more worried about surviving the day than planning her next steps, but, recalling Tunnok's ambition, she knew the future would be challenging if she meant to make a claim to the throne. She had no idea if she should even try, but, with all her kin gone, who else had more right? And cared more about the Kingdom? Whatever she chose to do, she could use allies for the road ahead. More than her aunt and aged bodyguard.

"I would be open to negotiations," Syla said. "The sun, moon, and earth gods intended that *all* humans be protected from the mad storm god's creations. And I believe, even if the ancestors of today's stormers left the Kingdom for various reasons, their descendants should have the opportunity to return."

"Good. Good." Radmarik returned the cane to his mouth. "I'll do my best to see that you make it back to your castle, though it would have been better if you'd popped up with that big ball in the middle of the night, when all those dragons weren't about." He waved toward the horizon, then back toward the island.

"I'm afraid they would have sensed it as soon as the barrier dropped, no matter what time of day it was." Syla looked back since the captain was squinting as well as pointing in that direction.

A familiar green dragon was flying from the shoreline toward them. Her gut clenched.

That was Agrevlari with Vorik on his back.

The green dragon beat his powerful wings, easily going against the wind to fly quickly toward them. And Vorik...

Syla licked her lips, nervous. As great a warrior as he was, he might be able to dodge the cannons and sink the ship without the help of any of his allies.

As they drew nearer, his gaze scoured the deck of the ship and lingered on the tarp-covered pile before shifting to her.

With her poor vision, she struggled to see his expression, to tell if he was angry. If he felt she'd betrayed him.

"How are your eyes, Captain?" she asked quietly.

"Very good, Princess."

"Does that rider look furious and vengeful? Or... just determined?"

Radmarik lowered his sugar cane. "I'd say determined, but I've encountered him before. That's his expression before he attacks a fleet of ships and leaves them destroyed."

"I take it Captain Vorik isn't a part of the Freeborn Faction."

Radmarik laughed. "No, Princess. He's General Jhiton's most loyal and trusted officer."

"That's what I thought."

Syla slipped her hand into her pocket, wrapping her fingers around the figurine, though she hadn't yet thought of something she could offer to entice Wreylith to help. Nor could she determine if the dragon remained anywhere near Harvest Island.

Even if Syla could somehow convince her to come to their aid, it wouldn't be enough. Six dragons with riders were flying about over the sea now. Seven if one included Agrevlari.

The green dragon carried Vorik closer, wings extending and tilting for a dive. To swoop down and get what they believed was the shielder? Or to get *her*?

Jaw set, Vorik's eyes were on Syla.

"Better take cover, Princess." Radmarik pointed toward the

wheelhouse, then stalked off and yelled, "Ready all the cannons and harpoon launchers!"

With his keen ears, Vorik doubtless heard the order, but he didn't appear worried. Agrevlari started his dive, and Vorik drew his sword.

Fear slammed into Syla as she worried her lover from the night before meant to slay her for tricking him.

But Vorik's head snapped up, and he looked into the distance. Agrevlari aborted his dive. Another huge black dragon had appeared, its dark scales swallowing rather than reflecting the sunlight, and was heading toward the group flying about out there. Dressed in black and carrying multiple swords, its rider was as dark and ominous as the dragon.

Radmarik cursed. "That's General Jhiton."

36

CAPTAIN VORIK, GENERAL JHITON SPOKE TELEPATHICALLY INTO Vorik's mind.

Few riders, even those bonded and gifted with dragon magic, could use their power to send their words to other humans, but Vorik had long known that his brother could, and that he could hear responses as well.

Yes, General?

Feeling the need to swiftly redeem himself, Vorik had been about to dive down, combat Syla's bodyguard and any crewmen who attacked him, and have Agrevlari pluck up what he assumed was the shielder tied down beneath a tarp. He'd hoped to handle it by himself, not needing to call in any of the other dragons and riders in the area, dragons and riders, he now realized, who must have been waiting for the general's arrival before taking action.

Captain Lesva arrived injured at headquarters this morning with an interesting report.

Was it of how she disobeyed your orders, attempted not once but twice to thwart my mission, and do what she wished? Vorik wanted to continue down to the whaling ship and have Agrevlari snatch up the shielder, but his dragon must have received an order or comment from Jhiton's powerful Ozlemar to hold up because Agrevlari banked and didn't continue his descent.

From the deck of the ship, someone fired a cannon. It boomed, the deadly projectile sailing toward Agrevlari's belly. He twisted, not only avoiding it, but catching it with his talons as if someone had tossed him a ball in a children's game.

That was not her report. Fortunately, Jhiton sounded more dry than irritated. *There was discussion of your penis and it ruling your actions.*

Hardly that, Vorik replied, attempting to convey a telepathic scoff, but he shifted uneasily on Agrevlari's back. He would never admit it to his brother, but his penis *had* been too involved in his actions lately. Especially the night before. He should have realized the significance of those candles—and that Syla, his surprisingly wily Syla, wouldn't mindlessly have sex with him while waiting for him to finish his plot against her people. *I was merely following my orders. It was, I trust you remember, your wish that my penis be involved in the action for this mission.*

Even drier, Jhiton said, *I believe I just said for you to win the princess's trust.*

Come now, brother. You knew what you intended. You specifically brought up my record with women—and the appeal of my devastating smile.

I believe those were your words, but, yes, I suspected you would sleep with her. That is not important. The shielders are. Captain Lesva did not believe you would find the one on this island, but the barrier is down, and wild dragons are already inland hunting prey. You succeeded, my brother. Is the shielder destroyed? Or simply removed?

Vorik blew out a slow breath of relief as Agrevlari circled, remaining in the area but staying out of range of the cannons on the various ships. Just because he'd caught one didn't mean he could easily handle a barrage from many sources at once. More than one dragon had fallen under such combined power.

Princess Syla removed it, Vorik replied, *intending to take it to her island to replace the one that was destroyed. It is as you predicted all along.*

Excellent. Is it now being carried on that whaling vessel? That is what Lieutenant Taglamor believes. That they are hoping to keep us away long enough to reach the harbor on Castle Island.

I think so too. Syla and her bodyguard are aboard. Vorik thought about mentioning that he hadn't seen the aunt, but she wasn't a combatant and would likely be belowdecks. For that matter, *Syla* should be belowdecks where harm wouldn't as easily reach her. But he smiled slightly, not surprised that she wasn't.

It is not that wise of a plan, Jhiton observed. *Did they not know we are patrolling the waters between the islands? Since their island isn't currently protected, they must expect to have many hours exposed to dragons.*

The surrounding guard ships have a lot of cannons and crewmen manning them. They must believe—or at least hope*—that they can keep us away long enough. And perhaps they believe that, if they get in trouble, they can activate the shielder from their harbor. Or even from that ship.* Vorik blinked. He hadn't considered that earlier, that a barrier might be established on the sea as well as on land. Was that possible?

Jhiton looked sharply at him. *That would make sense. If they believe they can activate it at any time, they may even want to separate our forces. If they established a barrier in the middle of a battle, they might trap some dragons inside of it.*

Is that going to make you hesitate to attack and try to reach it? Vorik didn't want to fire upon Syla's ship and watch it go up in flames with her aboard, but if his brother ordered it... what choice did he have?

We will *attack it, and we will destroy the second shielder. Our dragon allies crave to hunt the elioks and other prey on that island, and I've promised them that after we do this, they may. We will, however, not commit all our forces at once, and I will watch for sign that the princess intends to lift that tarp and use her moon-mark to activate the shielder. We will be careful.*

All right, Vorik said, but he bit his lip, contemplating ways to keep Syla alive.

Judging by the determined look on Jhiton's face, he intended to sink that ship. Probably *all* of the ships.

Vorik would have to get Syla off before that happened. She would never forgive him for helping destroy a second of her people's shielders, but... it didn't matter. What mattered was that she survived. If she hated him forever afterward, so be it.

Syla felt like a coward for crouching in the protected wheelhouse while men fired cannons and harpoon launchers at the approaching dragons and Fel stood like a rock before the fake shielder with a crossbow pointed skyward. But she had no weapons, no way to attack dragons. Even if she could now use her power for more than she'd previously believed, she would have to touch an enemy to affect him or her. That was the way her healing magic worked.

"I'm not inviting any of them down for touching." She thought of Vorik, but he was among those preparing to attack, his Agrevlari flying side by side with the ferocious black dragon.

They hadn't yet joined the others in diving low to spit flames and fire arrows at the ships, but she had no doubt they would. With his brother here—his commanding officer—Vorik wouldn't show Syla any mercy.

As cannons boomed from the guard ships, and a flaming harpoon shot from the bow of the whaling vessel, she pulled the figurine out of her pocket again. Asking Wreylith to come help wouldn't be fruitful, but she had to try anyway.

When she curled her fingers around the red glass, it was warm to her touch, and an image of the red dragon flying through the bright blue sky came immediately to her. Did that mean Wreylith was close?

Yes, through the link, Syla saw the red dragon flying over the sea toward Harvest Island's cliff-filled northern shore.

For a silly moment, she thought Wreylith had sensed her peril and was coming to help, but the dragon's route would take her past the battle, miles to the east. Of course. She had to have heard the barrier around the island was down and that she could hunt prey. The elioks. Maybe those other wild dragons had even told her.

Syla grimaced at the thought of poor Harvest Island being inundated with dragons, but, if they primarily wanted to hunt, maybe they would leave the towns and croplands alone. The elioks were in the forested wilds to the southwest, an area only lightly populated by humans, mostly nomadic hunters and foragers.

You're welcome, Syla thought, attempting to send the words through the link that existed between Wreylith and the figurine.

Puny human, you dare interrupt me during this important time! came Wreylith's booming response.

A blue dragon dove low over the whaling ship, talons angling for the canvas-covered decoy as its rider fired arrows at the crew. Syla held her breath, forgetting to reply. All it would take was one dragon lifting that tarp, and the riders would realize the trick, that the shielder was on another ship.

From the deck, numerous archers loosed arrows upon the dragon and its rider, and a swift-thinking gunman swiveled a cannon on a rotating mount to fire at the dragon. The weapon boomed, its projectile shooting straight for the aerial assailant.

The dragon spun in the air, defying gravity as it dodged the cannonball. Though it succeeded, the maneuver altered the dragon's route. Its talons clipped the railing of the ship instead of wrapping around the decoy. Its wings splashed water before the creature gained altitude again, unhurt. No doubt, it would fly up, bank, and dive again. Or another would. Thus far, none of the cannonballs had struck the agile dragons.

I thought you were dead, Wreylith added when Syla didn't respond.

No, not yet. My death may be imminent though. Before these dragons kill me, I wanted to let you know that I've removed the shielder from Harvest Island. You and your kind may hunt the elioks.

You!

Yes, I.

Why would you remove the barrier that keeps dragons from these islands?

Castle Island is more populous, so we need the shielder over there. We do plan to repair ours and replace the one on this island, so I suggest you hunt your fill soon.

Wreylith didn't answer. Was she even now hunting?

Crouched in the doorway of the wheelhouse, fingers clenched around the jamb, Syla spotted the black dragon circling high above. Was the general watching and commanding his troops from afar, or would he be the next to try for the decoy?

Agrevlari left the black dragon's side and dove for the ships.

Vorik glanced down at Syla, but Agrevlari angled for one of the guard ships. Dare she believe he was choosing another target because he didn't want to hurt her? To sink *her* ship?

I will inform the others that the abeyance may be brief, Wreylith said.

Do you know where to find elioks? Syla asked, inspiration finally coming to her.

Vorik raised his sword, and Agrevlari dodged cannonballs as he plummeted toward the crew.

I could tell you, Syla added. *Thanks to my herbalism knowledge—and being aware that the foragers who sell to my vendors compete with the elioks—I know where they spend most of their time.*

A dragon may find prey without a human! Wreylith boomed in indignation.

Are you sure? You're not familiar with our islands, right? Elioks are never out in the open. Flying over their territory won't allow you to see them.

Their appealing scent will guide me!

Or I could tell you where they live. Then you could swoop down and catch many before the barrier returns. Syla expected Wreylith to tell her that the plan to repair the shielder would come to naught and the islands would be laid bare to dragons for all eternity. It wasn't a bad bet.

What Wreylith asked was, *Is your death truly imminent? Must I make this decision immediately?*

Through the figurine, Syla sensed that the red dragon had reached land and was flying past the volcano, joining a couple other dragons—the ones Syla had seen soaring overhead earlier—in the area.

Cries of alarm came from the guard ship as Agrevlari blasted it with fire. Crew members jumped overboard to escape the inferno. Vorik threw something that exploded when it struck one of the cannons—and a keg of powder near it. Flames roared into the air, mingling with the dragon fire, and soon the ship was engulfed.

Agrevlari flew away, unscathed. Vorik's face was grim and determined, giving no sign that he or his general would demand or accept surrender.

My death is very imminent. Syla tried not to sound desperate, but if she couldn't make a deal with Wreylith soon, the stormers would not only sink all the ships, but they would learn about the decoy and soon find the other ship. They would destroy the shielder, kill Aunt Tibby, and be one step closer to the utter destruction of the entire Kingdom. *You saw when you brought me here that stormers and their dragons are determined to kill me.*

Their pet *dragons,* Wreylith said with scorn. Sounding somewhat less insulted, she added, *It is not honorable to kill a healer.*

I agree wholeheartedly. Torturing one isn't wonderful either. Syla doubted the dragon would be sympathetic, but she shared her memory of Lesva's interrogation.

They target you because you have magic? The moon-mark?

Yes, Syla admitted, though she hated to remind any of the dragons that she had the power to activate the shielders that kept them away from their beloved prey.

And are descended from Queen Erasbella.

Yes, Syla replied promptly, though she hadn't yet figured out why her great-great grandmother mattered to the dragon. *I may be one of the last of her living descendants. If you could help me before our line is forever ended, I would be grateful. And I wouldn't call to you for assistance again. I'll even give you the figurine so you can cast it into the sea or do what you wish to ensure you're not disturbed again.*

The dragon snorted into her mind. *You would not. A dragon is too powerful an ally. You cannot resist touching that figurine and calling to me.*

You do have allure.

Certainly.

Another dragon dove toward the whaling ship, straight toward the decoy. Syla was surprised that none had yet bathed the vessel in flames. Maybe they believed the shielder would have some magical defense? Or that it would explode under dragon fire and harm not only the crew but nearby attackers?

Once more, Syla looked up at the black dragon. Agrevlari had joined it again, and the two dragons circled, their riders looking... not at the decoy but back toward land.

Syla's heart lurched. Was it possible they'd realized this was a decoy? Could they have somehow sensed that the shielder was on another ship, one that might now be leaving that cove?

The elioks live in the forests of Edor along the rainy coast to the southwest, Syla told Wreylith, in part because she doubted, as she'd briefly hoped, that she would succeed in trading the information for help. *They love the tart redfall berries that grow as a ground cover beneath the great cedars, and they also adore the squat yellow merikland fungi that are used in healing tinctures.*

Excellent. It would be difficult for a dragon to spot prey that hides under great cedars.

You'll have to dive between the trees to reach them.

An appealing challenge.

On his black dragon, the general pointed downward, toward the whaling vessel.

Agrevlari and three other dragons obeyed what must have been an order to attack. This time, Vorik wouldn't choose another target. Commanded by his brother, he couldn't.

"Stand your ground," Captain Radmarik yelled and ran to man one of the harpoon launchers himself.

He dipped the projectile into a bucket of pitch, lit the end on fire, and blasted it at one of the dragons arrowing toward the ship, wings pressed to its side so that it gained speed.

Another dragon sped toward the decoy. And Agrevlari... Syla gulped. Was he heading straight toward her?

She didn't want to retreat, but she had no way to defend herself against dragon talons. Tucking the figurine into her pocket, she backed into the wheelhouse. The wooden walls and ceiling would not protect her from a dragon determined to reach her.

She looked around for a weapon, anything she could use to defend herself. She spotted a stick with a metal hook on the end, the kind of thing one used to light lanterns from a distance. Almost laughing at the ludicrousness, she snatched it up.

Booms thundered outside. The deck pitched sideways as something—a dragon?—struck the hull, and the ship rocked as if it were in the greatest of storms.

Flames grew visible through the doorway of the wheelhouse. Syla spotted Fel leaping to swing his mace at the blue dragon. This time, it had landed on the decoy, talons curling into the canvas. Its maw turned toward him, fire roiling in his throat.

"Look out!" Syla cried and stepped in that direction.

Before she reached the doorway, a thump and crunch came from right above her. The memory of being in her room when a dragon—Wreylith—ripped the roof off came to her. Then, exactly that happened. Great fangs crunching through wood, a dragon tore the roof off the wheelhouse.

Agrevlari perched above her, shards of wood tumbling from his fangs.

Syla hefted the metal hook, though it would do nothing to harm the powerful dragon. Vorik leaned into view from his back and opened his mouth to speak, but his gaze jerked to something in the air instead.

Wreylith! Agrevlari cried.

The red dragon slammed into him like the wrath of the gods. Screeches that almost shattered Syla's eardrums erupted as the huge creatures tumbled away, Wreylith's talons slashing, raking deep into Agrevlari's scales. The dragons disappeared from her view, a tremendous splash sounded, and the ship rocked in the waves.

Syla grabbed the wheel and hung on. Lesser splashes continued, and more screeches assailed her ears.

With smoke hazing the blue sky above the de-roofed wheelhouse, Syla couldn't see if any more dragons were coming. Spatters also darkened the lenses of her spectacles. Water? No. Blood. Agrevlari's?

As soon as the rocking lessened, Syla wiped off her lenses and rushed to the doorway, reminded that Fel had been in danger. The entire *crew* had been.

Outside, the smoke was so dense that it took her a moment to spot Fel. He was alive, still fighting with his back to the decoy. Talon holes had been torn into the tarp, but it remained in place, tied over the pile of crates. Thank the departed gods, no dragon had attempted to set it on fire yet.

The one who'd tried was... Syla peered about, attempting to locate the blue dragon and figure out what was happening. There. He was... swimming? No, he must have been knocked into the water. One of his wings appeared broken.

As she stepped farther out onto the deck, looking for Agrevlari, a great red dragon appeared over the railing, rising out of the water like a jumping whale. Wings flapping and spattering water droplets, Wreylith snaked her long neck toward Syla.

Fear froze her, fear and confusion. For a moment, Syla thought the dragon was angry and would end her life. But, as she had before, Wreylith wrapped her maw around Syla and flung her into the air.

Cursing in alarm, Syla flailed awkwardly while flattening one hand to her face to keep her spectacles on. The hook flew out of her other hand as she groped for something to grab. The dragon's back. She had to land on the dragon's back.

But Wreylith was already zipping after a nearby foe, and Syla saw only a streak of red—her tail. She reached out, catching it in a bear hug, and wrapped her legs around it. She smashed her face against the scales to keep her spectacles from flying away and hung on with every muscle. Terrified.

Fire danced in the air all around her. Someone attacking Wreylith? No, a gray dragon was spewing flames at a blue dragon with a rider. Was that the gray that Syla had seen flying overhead earlier?

Wreylith's tail swished as she flew about, her jaws snapping at enemies and driving others away from the whaling ship. As she was whipped left and right, Syla struggled to figure out what was going on. It took her a moment to realize that Wreylith had not only come to help, but she'd brought allies. The other wild dragons that Syla had seen—and even more?

She craned her neck to look up and spotted Agrevlari with Vorik still on his back, flying over a smoldering wreck that was all that remained of one of the guard ships. Though blood leaked from numerous gouges in his flanks, the green dragon did not angle back toward Wreylith. Instead, he flew toward one of the other wild dragons.

That male desires to mate with me and will not attack me, Wreylith stated as she flew around the whaling ship, snapping at a scaled enemy that lingered in the area, its rider firing at the crew. *Many of the domesticated dragons seek to rut with a free wild dragon of my stature.*

Syla knew little about the bonded dragons but suspected Agrevlari would be highly offended at being called *domesticated.* Or a *pet.* That was what she'd said earlier.

At the moment, Syla did not care. She dared lift her head a little higher, hoping the stormers would give up. But there were more dragons with riders than wild dragons, and Vorik and Agrevlari were succeeding in driving the one they'd targeted away.

I've not had much experience with porting humans about, Wreylith said, *but I've observed that they usually choose to ride on the back, not the tail.*

The tail is easier to hang on to. Syla's stomach tried to exit through her throat when Wreylith barrel-rolled to the left to avoid a cannonball—damn it, those men were firing at the *wrong* dragon. *Especially when you do that.*

Before, you used your magic to aid in clinging to my back.

I remember. I just—

A dark shadow crossed through Syla's vision before she could finish the thought—or consider how she might use her magic to maneuver from the tail to Wreylith's back. The huge black dragon blotted out the sun as it flew toward the whaling ship.

No, not the ship.

It was plummeting toward Wreylith, talons outstretched, maw parted and sharp fangs gleaming in the sunlight.

I don't think that one wants to mate with you, Syla thought.

No, he's old and grumpy and doesn't even remember how to rut. Hold on.

Syla did, squinting her eyes shut and hoping Wreylith could handle the big dragon. But, before the black reached them, a green blur swept in from the side. It—was that Agrevlari?—crashed into the black dragon, knocking it from its route. Both dragons tumbled past, missing Wreylith by only feet.

Flames blazed, and thunderous angry roars came from the dragons as they twisted in the air. The black appeared to be trying to get away, but the green, like a rabid dog, bit him and clung to his flank.

Still hugging herself to Wreylith's tail, Syla gaped as she spotted Vorik and Jhiton... hanging on to their dragons, both their faces stamped with shock.

"Call off your dragon, Captain!" Jhiton yelled as his mount twisted again to bite the green.

Agrevlari was smaller, but he didn't give up, instead slashing with his talons even as he lost a chunk of scale and flesh to the deadly bite of the black.

"I can't!" Vorik called back. "He's in love with the wild dragon!"

Jhiton swore.

Wreylith emitted a clucking noise that Syla hadn't heard before. Was that how dragons... laughed? She sounded *smug*.

After flapping away from the battling males, Wreylith landed on the half-destroyed wheelhouse of the whaling ship. Two of the beleaguered cannon men started to aim toward her but,

Captain Radmarik, his cane still in the side of his mouth, called them off.

"You don't fire at the dragon the princess is riding, men."

Since Syla was still hanging on to Wreylith's tail, it was debatable if she was *riding* anything, but, politely, nobody pointed out the dubiousness of her position. The weary crewmen slumped, relieved that Wreylith wasn't attacking. Fel, face bloody but his mace still in his hand, looked toward the sky.

The black dragon was now chasing Agrevlari, heading out over the ocean and away from the ships. From his rapid wingbeats, the black was pissed. Vorik and his general remained astride their dragons, but neither appeared to be in control of their mounts. They were too far away for Syla to see well, but the general's back was stiff. He was irked.

And Vorik?

He turned to look back at Syla and saluted before their dragons flew out of view.

The tail shifted, and Syla tightened her grip, but Wreylith was lowering her to the deck. Syla let go, thankful to have solid wood under her feet. She was about to thank the dragon for helping, but Wreylith opened her fang-filled maw and roared.

With their general departing, only a couple of the dragons with riders had remained in the area. Whatever that roar meant, it was enough to make them fly off. Only the wild dragons remained, appearing unconcerned about Wreylith's commentary. One even plunged into the water for a swim.

A hand came to rest on Syla's shoulder. Fel.

"Are you all right?" he asked.

"I think so." Syla pulled out the dragon figurine and held it up to the sunlight, Wreylith's great form behind it. It was amazing how similar they looked. "She may be starting to like me."

Wreylith's eyes locked onto the figurine. She roared again, then whipped her neck down so quickly that it startled Syla into dropping the little artifact. Before it could clatter to the deck, Wreylith caught it in her great maw, then sprang off the wheelhouse and flew away from the ship. The wild dragons took off after her, heading to Harvest Island, no doubt to hunt the elioks.

"*Like* may be an optimistic word," Syla said.

"She could have lit us all on fire before leaving," Fel pointed out.

"True."

Syla was sad that she was losing her link to Wreylith, but, once all the dragons had disappeared from the sky, and the whaling ship was on course for Castle Island, she admitted that things were looking up. Hopefully, Aunt Tibby was safely underway in her own ship, with none of the stormers aware that it carried the shielder.

Syla dreaded returning home to all the clean-up, funerals, and political maneuvering she would have to deal with, but if they could get the shielder working to protect her home... that would be something. She would endure the rest. There was no other choice.

EPILOGUE

"What is your bodyguard doing?" Aunt Tibby lowered her magical tool and frowned toward the doorway of the stone chamber under the castle.

Sergeant Fel had one leg stuck out behind him as he faced the wall and leaned his weight against it.

"Calf stretches, I think." Syla was holding a scroll open for her aunt while she tinkered. Earlier, she'd had the distressing duty of directing the removal of her sister's body, so this was an appealingly simple task.

Tibby had already replaced the broken shielder with the new one, which thrummed happily, silver light bathing their faces. Now, at Syla's urging, she was trying to figure out if the other one could be repaired. It was even more damaged than when she'd last seen it. The stormer that Vorik had *pretended* to run through had probably bashed it a few more times before leaving. He and the enemy that Fel had killed were gone when Syla, Tibby, and Fel had arrived in the chamber.

At least a protective barrier was once again around Castle Island, keeping dragons and other winged predators away. The populace could now rebuild and prepare refugee camps for those who came over from unprotected Harvest Island. Syla had already sent a ship with a message for Lord Ravoran, inviting him to direct people here until they could find a better solution. She'd promised to do her best to return a working shielder as soon as possible, but she didn't know if that would be possible. And, if Wreylith's enthusiasm for elioks was anything to go by, the island had to be swarming with dragons by now. Hopefully, they were too busy hunting in the forests to harass people.

"Well, they're distracting," Tibby said.

Ignoring her, though he could surely hear the words, Fel switched legs and continued his stretches.

Syla had offered to tend his fresh wounds and suggested daily servings of bone broth to help rebuild his ligaments and tendons, but he'd only given her a baleful look as he'd rubbed his hip and *not* invited her to heal anything.

"He's not making any noise." Syla held the scroll closer when Tibby waved her finger. "Are you distracted by his movement? Or is it his taut physique?"

That comment made Fel *and* Tibby give her baleful looks.

"Princesses aren't supposed to notice such things," Tibby said.

"What about engineers?"

"He destroyed one of my tractors."

"So... you're not going to admire his physique?"

"Absolutely not."

Fel sighed, glared over at them, checked the hallway to make sure no enemies were creeping up, then started stretching his hamstrings.

With the door closed, a moon-mark required to open it, Syla didn't expect anyone to intrude. That was, after all, why she was down here, holding a scroll for her aunt, instead of up in the castle.

The chaos when they'd sailed into the harbor had been

exhausting to look at before they'd even stepped on land. From what she'd eventually gathered, after managing to find troops available to carry the shielder to shore and up to the castle, everyone had assumed Syla was as dead as the rest of her family. It hadn't occurred to her to send a message back to the military leaders or anyone else at any point after she'd been plucked out of her bedroom by Wreylith. Admittedly, she'd been busy, but it might have been wise. There had been, in her absence, a quick funeral, which had included her as well as her mother and siblings.

In the following days, numerous known and long-lost relatives had been putting themselves forward as candidates to become the heir to the Kingdom. A few merchants had suggested replacing the monarchy with an oligarchy, assigning themselves prominent positions. The military had attempted to instate martial law and had forbidden people from leaving their homes. Promptly disobeying, families fearing for their lives had fled into the hills. For good or ill, frequent attacks from dragons, wyverns, cloud strikers, and even a gargoyle that had flown up from the south, had kept anyone from making serious headway into creating a new regime.

Syla did think that Colonel Mosworth had shown some relief when she'd appeared. A few of her mother's bureaucrats who'd been struggling to hold the castle together had as well. Their expressions had suggested less that they loved and cared about Syla and more that they were eager for someone to foist the mess on.

Now that the barrier was back up, Syla would have to figure out how to take and hold power, at least until all the shielders were restored and the Kingdom was safe from stormers and non-human enemies. After that... let someone else more capable rule if they wanted. It was not something she'd ever craved, and the memory of Sergeant Tunnok's ambition made her weary.

"I don't know if this is going to be possible." Tibby had been looking back and forth from the innards of the original shielder to the scroll, and it had been some time since she'd touched anything with her tool. "Not unless the gods themselves return to help."

"It's possible to repair it." Syla nodded at her. "I'm sure of it. And you're the perfect person to make it happen. Feel free to recruit others to help you. I'll pay them from the coffers."

"Have you figured out where the coffers are yet?"

"Somewhere... safe. And cofferly."

"We're in trouble," Tibby told Fel.

He turned from the wall and surprised Syla by shaking his head. "No. She'll find a way."

"To fix the shielder?" Tibby asked. "Or find the coffers and keep the Kingdom from falling apart?"

"All of that, I think. She befriended a *dragon*."

"Befriend is an even stronger word than *like* and probably does not apply to my tempestuous relationship with Wreylith," Syla said, "who we may never see again."

"You'll find a way." Fel pointed at the hallway. "But you'd best not disappear for too long. You need to be seen by the people and start solidifying relationships with your allies. More allies than your bodyguard and your aunt."

Syla didn't disagree, but unless one counted her colleagues that had survived the destruction of Moon Watch Temple, she didn't *have* any other allies. She wished she could claim Vorik and Wreylith, but one was an enemy who'd tried to use her and the other a mercurial wild dragon. It would be safer if neither showed up in her life again.

"Any suggestions on how to do that?" Syla sighed, set the scroll aside, and joined Fel, trusting that her aunt could study the schematics without her.

"One." Fel eyed her as she used her moon-mark to open the

hidden door. "Many, *many* soldiers are in the castle infirmary as well as the temples around the capital that weren't destroyed."

Syla winced. That was something else she needed to do, recruit and appoint people to help the overwhelmed healers of the city. Right now, there weren't enough people caring for the wounded.

"I'll make time to visit as many of them as I can." Syla wondered if Fel had comrades among the badly injured.

"Especially the officers." He gave her a significant look as they walked into the tunnel and toward the intersection that would lead them up into the castle.

Maybe it was a testament to her weariness that she didn't catch his meaning. "Everyone, I should think."

"*Especially* the officers. Use your magic, and bind them to you. Whether they want it or not."

They'd reached the intersection where a lantern burned in a sconce, and she stopped to stare at him. "You of all people can't possibly be recommending that. I mean, if they wish my magical healing and understand what feelings it might inspire, I'm always willing to use all the power I have on the injured, but—"

"You're going to need loyal officers. Given your predicament, you can't be particular about how you earn their loyalty."

"I..." Syla couldn't believe he was recommending this. He who had groused numerous times on their mission about feeling *bound* to obey her.

"General Dolok—the colonel's superior—has numerous broken bones and burns that have kept him in the infirmary since this started. I suggest visiting him first."

"So he'll resent me as he does my bidding?"

"He might resent you less than you'd think." Fel headed up the passageway toward the stairs, only limping a little after his various stretches.

"Do *you* resent me less than I'd think?"

Less than he'd indicated when he'd gone off to protect Aunt Tibby instead of her?

"Less than I should," he called back, then waved for her to follow.

She did.

Fel hadn't left her side, other than for biological necessities, since they'd stepped off the whaling ship. By now, his retirement date had to be close, but he hadn't mentioned it lately. Maybe he realized she needed him. The *Kingdom* needed him.

"Which way to the general?" Syla asked when they reached the courtyard.

Little rubble had been removed in the days since they'd last walked these grounds. The bodies, at least, had been cleared, a great funeral pyre burned in addition to the one dedicated for the royal family. It bothered Syla that she hadn't been present to say goodbye to all those she'd lost. When there was time, she vowed, she would hold a private ceremony. She needed that closure. She needed much more than that, but, unfortunately, the world wouldn't grant it.

"I'll take you," Fel said but stopped in the middle of the courtyard to look up.

Remembering the wyvern attack, Syla followed his gaze, her heart starting to pound before she detected a threat.

When she did spot something, it was so far overhead that she wasn't sure what it was. A red... dot? She removed her spectacles and wiped them before looking again. Fel was eyeing her, as if she should already know what that was.

"A dragon?" she guessed.

Since the barrier was back in place, they could only fly high above the island.

"*Your* dragon," Fel said.

"Wreylith? She's hardly that. She took back her figurine."

"She could have roasted the entire ship," he reminded her.

"Clearly, it was her adoration for me that kept her from giving in to that impulse."

"It was... something." Fel's eyebrow twitched. "Maybe you bound her with your healing."

"I don't think so. There's some kind of link between her and that figurine, but..." Syla shrugged. "She took it back."

Once more, Fel looked upward, something catching his eye. "Look out."

He gripped Syla's arm and pulled her back a step. Something hit the flagstones and bounced higher than their heads before striking down, bouncing up again, then finally settling with a clatter. Syla stared.

"That thing is a lot sturdier than it looks." Fel waved to the red glass—no, it most certainly wasn't *glass*—dragon figurine.

The elioks were magnificent! Wreylith boomed into Syla's mind, but she kept flying, not staying for a chat.

Syla picked up the figurine. Did its return mean that Wreylith would answer and, maybe even help, if Syla called to her again?

"Are you *sure* you didn't bind her?" Fel asked dryly.

"That's not possible with a dragon."

"If you say so. Either way... let's go see General Dolok."

Syla followed him. She didn't know about the methodology he suggested, but Fel was correct. If she intended to return order to the Kingdom and save its people from stormers and dragons, she needed allies.

In a hurry to hunt, Agrevlari only flew Vorik *partway* up the volcano before banking sharply and tilting his back to suggest his rider depart. Though it would have only taken the dragon another twenty seconds to reach the top, where General Jhiton was waiting, Vorik didn't complain as he hopped off. He wasn't in a hurry for this private meeting, the first since his dragon had ignobly attacked Jhiton's dragon, spoiling the attack on the whaling vessel and their plans to acquire the shielder. Of course, their plans had been derailed before then, as soon as Wreylith had shown up with her unexpected allies, but his people might yet have pulled out a victory if not for Agrevlari attacking Ozlemar to protect the female for whom he pined.

Are you sure you should be hunting in the same area as Wreylith and her allies? Vorik asked as Agrevlari flew toward the forested southwest corner of the island. *We did just engage in battle with them.*

Dragons do not hold grudges. Besides, she should be quite pleased with me.

Ozlemar isn't pleased with you.

Ozlemar is an ancient, grumpy broken horn of a dragon with a walrus tusk permanently lodged in his anal sphincter.

He's one of your commanding officers, you know.

Wingleader Saleetha is my direct superior.

Ozlemar is her *superior.*

Our ranks negate nothing I said. Agrevlari tilted his wings insouciantly, then disappeared from view as he descended toward the forest.

As he climbed, Vorik spotted the black dragon they'd been speaking of sunning himself on a ledge, his dark scales like shadows that absorbed the surrounding brightness. One of his yellow eyes opened to watch Vorik. Ozlemar's expression was baleful, and was that a growl that reached Vorik's ears over the distant roar of the sea?

Vorik gave Ozlemar a wide berth, suspecting that more than eagerness for hunting had kept Agrevlari from flying close.

"Dragons," Vorik murmured.

Jhiton glanced down at his approach.

Though he wanted to drag his feet, certain his brother felt irritated—if not vengeful—after that disgraceful end to the battle, Vorik made himself jog up so he wouldn't be late. He didn't need to give the general any more reasons to be vexed with him this week.

When he arrived, Jhiton stood on the rim of the crater that marked the apex of the volcano, its peak having blown off long ago. His twin swords were sheathed at his hips, and the wind ruffled his short black hair as he gazed into the distance. His hands were clasped behind his back, one fist curled around something.

Not a dagger that he would thrust into Vorik's chest. Whatever it was, the hidden item was too small for that.

When Jhiton did not speak right away, Vorik stood at his side, joining him in gazing out over the landscape and the ocean beyond. From the elevated perch, they could see the entire island, though it spanned thirty miles at its widest, and the far ends were indistinct, even to a rider's keen vision. He had, however, no trouble making out the lush croplands that started up beyond the foothills of the volcano, thousands and thousands of acres of cultivated orchards and farms with harvest season underway. There would be plenty of time before winter to gather, preserve, and store food.

Maybe that was what Jhiton was thinking about when he slanted a long look at Vorik. It wasn't that decipherable, but it wasn't obviously hostile. That was a relief.

"Sorry about the mishap with Agrevlari," Vorik said. "I should have anticipated something like that as soon as Wreylith showed up. I've known about that infatuation for a while."

"When you ally with creatures as mercurial as dragons, you must expect that occasional chaos will be thrown into your battle plans."

"Yes," Vorik said.

Jhiton, who'd been openly irked *as* that kerfuffle was happening, must have had time to cool off. He even appeared... content? A slight smile curved his lips as he held out his hand. Several hazelnuts lay on his palm, not yet shelled.

"With the shielder gone, Harvest Island will soon be ours." Yes, that *was* a content expression on Jhiton's face.

"This is what you wanted from the beginning?"

It probably should have occurred to Vorik sooner. Castle Island had crops, too, but it wasn't as devoted to farming as this place, and the gardeners would defend their capital and more populated island assiduously. Maybe that was why Jhiton had never spoken of occupying it after they'd invaded.

"It's not *all* I want, but if it is all we can acquire and hold for the long-term... it alone could change the lives of our people."

"The gardeners will try to get it back."

"I'm aware. That is why we must maneuver and fight for more. Since this is wedged between their other islands, it would be vulnerable to attack from all sides, and, as they have just learned themselves, it is always more challenging to defend what one has than fly in for raids and then disappear. Eventually, we'll need to secure the islands around this one." His eyes narrowed to slits. "If not take over the entire Kingdom. Only then could we ensure that our people are fed not only this winter but for all winters going forward."

"Ah." It saddened Vorik to imagine attacking the Kingdom subjects further. No, he admitted with a snort; it saddened him to imagine attacking *Syla* or causing her further grief. She'd already endured so much. He hated to add to her misery.

But passion burned now in Jhiton's eyes as he gazed toward the sea and plotted. Vorik didn't try to dissuade his brother from his path, not when his own performance on this mission had been far from stellar. Jhiton might feel content now, having achieved his first goal, but he wouldn't forget that Agrevlari had attacked his dragon in front of a lot of witnesses, not only stormers but all the gardeners on those ships. That had been embarrassing for both of them. Going forward, Vorik would have to work harder than ever and follow every order precisely to ensure the general didn't lose faith in him.

"What hold does the princess have over Wreylith?" Jhiton asked.

The question surprised Vorik, since he'd been thinking of other things, but he should have anticipated it. "She has a krendala for the red dragon."

Jhiton's expression grew stern. He couldn't have appreciated being blindsided by the arrival of the wild dragon—*dragons.* "You didn't think to mention that in the excruciatingly brief report you gave to Lieutenant Wise?"

Vorik winced, realizing he should have sent far more details back, including that Syla had secured Wreylith's help previously. But he hadn't expected that to happen again. After all, Wreylith had dumped Syla in the ocean outside of the Harvest Island barrier without, as far as he'd noticed, offering to wait or provide further assistance.

"I should have," Vorik said.

"Yes."

"How did she get it? How did a wild dragon become linked through a krendala to start with? And when did it happen?"

"I don't know."

"Will Wreylith assist her further?"

"I don't know that either."

"You will learn that information. It will be important for our future plans." Jhiton thumbed the hazelnuts in his hand as he gazed toward the south. Though they were too far away to be visible, other Garden Kingdom islands lay in that direction. Jhiton might have chosen Harvest Island for a starting point, but it wasn't the end of his ambitions.

"Oddly," Vorik said, "Princess Syla didn't invite me to visit her at the castle."

"We will find a way to ensure you see her again."

Since they would still be enemies, and Vorik would have to attempt to cajole, wheedle, or *seduce* information out of Syla—all acts that she would see as a betrayal—he shouldn't have looked forward to the possibility. But the words immediately made his body hum in anticipation as his mind conjured memories of their joining—and musings of how *future* joinings might go.

"I don't object to that," was all he said.

Jhiton gave him a knowing look. "I assumed."

THE END

AFTERWORD

Thank you for picking up the first adventure in my Fire and Fang series. I hope you enjoyed meeting Syla and Vorik (and the dragons). If you have time to leave a review for *Sky Shielder* or can share the word with your fellow readers, I would appreciate it!

If you'd like to continue on with the story, the second novel, *Red Dragon,* will be out in December of 2025.

For a free bonus novella featuring Queen Erasbella and Wreylith (a background story but a bit of a romance and adventure in its own right!), please sign up for my newsletter:

https://lindsayburoker.com/book-news/

I also send out monthly emails about sales, free books, and new releases.

Want to follow me on social media for very important updates on dogs and dragons with book and introvert memes sprinkled in? Here are those links:

- https://www.facebook.com/LindsayBuroker/
- https://x.com/GoblinWriter
- https://www.instagram.com/lindsay_buroker/

www.ingramcontent.com/pod-product-compliance
Lightning Source LLC
LaVergne TN
LVHW050916080826
845145LV00001B/105